TOWARDS A DARK HORIZON

It is the 1930s and having survived the Great Depression, the Neill family must now face up to the hardships of war. The legacy Ann has inherited from her kindly employer has been a godsend, but just as the lives of Ann and Lily Neill and their father Johnny look set to improve, the threat of war with Germany looms and they seem headed for a dark horizon. Coping with the trials and tribulations of working-class life in their close-knit Dundee community, no one can escape the conflict or what fate has in store.

TOWARDS A DARK HORIZON

TOWARDS A DARK HORIZON

by

Maureen Reynolds

Magna Large Print Books
Long Preston, North Yorkshire,
BD23 4ND, England.

British Library Cataloguing in Publication Data.

Reynolds, Maureen
    Towards a dark horizon.

A catalogue record of this book is
available from the British Library

ISBN 978-0-7505-2989-1

First published in Great Britain 2008
by Black & White Publishing Ltd.

Copyright © Maureen Reynolds 2008

Cover illustration Courtesy of P.W.A. International

Published in Large Print 2009 by arrangement with
Black & White Publishing Ltd.

Magna Large Print is an imprint of Library Magna Books Ltd.

Printed and bound in Great Britain by
T.J. (International) Ltd., Cornwall, PL28 8RW

I dedicate this book to my grandchildren –
Stephanie, Bernadette, Natalie, Samantha,
Gordon, Andrew and James

1

King George V and Dad Ryan were dead.

The early morning papers carried the sad news of the royal demise – 'At 11.55 p.m. on the 20th of January, King George V died peacefully.' There was no mention of Dad Ryan.

I was busy in the newspaper shop early that morning when my cousin Danny rushed in.

'Ann, my nephew Patty came to tell us that Grandad Ryan died last night. He got up from his bed just before midnight, complained about a pain in his chest then died right in front of Granny.'

I was shocked and I looked at him with sympathy. I knew he was so fond of his late father's family who all lived in Lochee.

I showed him the newspaper headline. 'He must have died about the same time as the King.' I was struck by the coincidence. After a lifetime of poverty and obscurity, Dad Ryan had departed his earthly life in royal company.

Danny's pale face had dark circles under his eyes and I saw them glisten with unshed tears. In the dim gloom of that winter morning, the only bright spot was his auburn hair which stood out like a fiery halo around his head.

He wiped a hand over his eyes. 'I've got to get to work at Lipton's but I'm going over to Lochee tonight. Will you come with me Ann?'

I thought about his mother – my Aunt Hattie. 'What about your mum? Will she be going?'

He gave a deep sigh. 'Well you know how she feels about the Ryan clan. I don't think she's visited them in years. I've no idea why there is this feud because they are all so tight-lipped about it but I'm sure she'll not want to visit them.' He gave me a pleading look. 'I would really like you to come. Maddie won't manage because she's on duty at the infirmary.'

I wondered if Maddie knew about Danny's grandad.

As if reading my thoughts, he said, 'I went round to the porter's lodge before coming here and I left her a message.'

I knew Maddie would be upset at not being with her fiancé at this sad time. The Ryan family were all so pleased to hear of his engagement to her and she would feel that her place was by his side but being a humble student nurse meant she had so little free time from her nursing duties.

I made up my mind. 'I'll come then Danny but I don't want to be in the way. There will be loads of people there. You know what it's like – all the neighbours as well as the family. Will Ma Ryan cope with us all?'

He nodded. 'You know what she's like – she's almost indestructible.'

Then he was gone. I knew Dad had already left for his work at the fruit and vegetable warehouse in Dock Street so this sad news would have to wait until early evening.

As was normal, Lily, my sister, was staying with our grandparents in their flat in the Overgate. A sudden thought struck me. Had Danny told them? But there was nothing I could do till I finished work in the early afternoon.

I still couldn't believe my good luck at getting this job as vacancies were as scarce as gold dust in these poverty-stricken and jobless times. I had been unemployed for almost a year after the sudden and tragic death of my late employer, the dear Mrs Barrie, who hired me as a housemaid in her large house in Broughty Ferry and who had been so good to me – even remembering me in her will with a legacy of six hundred pounds and all her leatherbound books. In spite of my legacy I still needed to work and help keep Lily as I wanted to preserve my nest egg for her upbringing. Since Mum's death just after her birth, I pledged to dedicate my life to my sister.

The shop, filling up with the early-morning workers made me forget Danny's sad news for a short time. The shop's owner, Miss Boyd, or Connie to her friends, deftly handed out papers, cigarettes and sweets. Connie was woman with a soft angelic look. I put her age around sixty but I could have been wrong by a margin of ten years on either side. She had inherited the shop from her late father so it must have been a long-established business. She had the reputation as being a bit of a dragon but, after working with the awful housekeeper Miss Hood at the Ferry, everyone else seemed like sweet-natured angels.

As I stacked the papers in bundles for the paperboy, my thoughts returned to Danny's family. The Ryans all lived within spitting distance of each other. His aunts, Kit, Lizzie and Belle, were all trying to live on a pittance because their husbands hadn't worked in donkey's years – just like thousands of other families in these hard times who had little or no work. Then there was the matriarch of the family, Ma Ryan – an indomitable figure reputed to have the second sight. I knew she would take this latest death in her stride just as she had done with all the other sadnesses in her life. She had lost six children in infancy and her one remaining son Pat, Danny's father, had died in a tragic accident not long after being invalided out of the Great War with a bad foot injury, the result of shrapnel from an exploding shell.

At teatime I told Dad the news. He remarked with his own wry sense of humour, 'Well, Hattie will be pleased that her father-in-law died in such good company as the King. You wait and see, Ann, it'll be her main topic of conversation.' He put on a falsetto voice. '"Oh, yes, my father-in-law died at the same time as King George V."' He gave a lopsided grin. 'As if anyone cares about such trivialities. If you give me a minute, I'll come with you both to Lochee.'

I put my coat on. 'We'd better get a move on to the Overgate because I promised Danny I would meet him there. He wasn't sure if Hattie would go with him.' I turned to Dad. 'What is the true story about the feud between Hattie and the Ryan family?'

Dad shook his head. 'God only knows but it's lasted since Pat's funeral. She did visit them for a few weeks after his death but, for some reason, she got the impression they didn't like her so she just stopped going. I know Hattie can be a pain in the backside with her snobby, hoity-toity nature but, on the other hand, the Ryans didn't treat her well either.'

I was amazed. I always thought of them as a family with lots of warmth and affection for one another and they were all devoted to Danny.

We made our way down the steep slope of the Hilltown. The street was quiet. A few brave souls had disregarded the cold sleety showers and had gathered in dark doorways. The topic of conversation was the King's death. 'Aye, the young Prince of Wales is now on the throne and him not married yet.'

A muffled voice answered. 'Well he'll have to find himself a wife now because we can't have a king without a queen.'

Personally, I couldn't see why not but I had another death on my mind.

When we arrived at my grandparents' house at the Overgate, it was packed with people. My grandparents, Hattie, Danny and Lily were surrounded by neighbours, all offering their condolences. Alice and her daughter Rosie, my Granny's next-door neighbours, were there and I then noticed to my dismay that Granny's sister Bella was sitting in the midst of the throng.

Dad groaned out loud – Bella wasn't his favourite person. I thought she must have heard his reaction but she gave no sign as she patted her knee with an impatient hand and looked at us.

'Come over here, Ann, and talk to a lonely old woman who's not feeling very good.'

Dad rolled his eyes in disgust and made straight for Rosie who beamed and went red with pleasure at the sight of him – a look that hadn't gone un-noticed by Bella. She snorted. 'When is your father going to propose to that woman? After all, your poor mother has been dead now for nearly five years.'

This remark, so typical of Bella, stopped me in my tracks. It may have been nearly five years as she said but Mum's death a few hours after Lily's birth was still a raw spot with me – a long and painful memory. There was a lump in my throat and I almost burst into tears but Danny appeared at my side.

He whispered as he led me away, 'Never heed Bella – she's aye putting her foot in her mouth.'

Hattie was standing beside Granny. She had a furious look on her face. Fate had been kind to Hattie. Apart from a few lines around her eyes, her skin was still smooth while her short hair was glossy and black – a very handsome woman. Still, at that moment, she looked annoyed. Her eyes were dark with fury and, although her lips were moving, no sound reached our ears. In fact, we were almost touching her before we heard the whispered words, 'I'm telling you, Mum, I'm not going to Lochee – not for all the tea in China.'

Granny was shocked. 'You must pay your respects to them Hattie. After all, he was your father-in-law and, if Pat was still alive, then he would be with the family at this sad time so I think you should be in Pat's place.'

Hattie snarled, 'Well, I'm not going and that's final.' Then, realising that Danny had overheard, her tone softened. 'You don't want me to come to

14

Lochee with you, do you? You've got Ann for company and they won't miss me.' She gave him a pleading look but he wasn't pleased.

'Well, I can't make you go, Mum, but I think, out of respect to Dad, you should be there.'

Like a fish in some dried-out pool, Hattie opened her mouth then quickly closed it again. She had no answer – no escape. Even so, she gave in with bad grace. 'Oh, all right,' she snapped, her dark-brown eyes glittering with ill humour. 'Let's go and meet up with the Ryan clan.'

Dad joined us and we made our way towards the door. Then Bella called out in a petulant tone, 'Tell them all at Lochee I'm asking for them but don't mention that I might be the next one to go – especially the way I feel tonight.'

With this dire warning ringing in our ears, we made our way to the tram stop. The evening had turned much colder but the rain had stopped. A bitter wind wrapped itself around our legs and we were grateful when the tramcar, looking like a golden oasis in the darkness, ambled along the steel tracks towards us. It was packed with passengers but we all managed to get a seat.

Hattie was squashed in beside an old woman. Fat and shabbily dressed with thin strands of grey hair escaping from a checked woollen headsquare, she was the exact opposite of my smartly dressed aunt.

Although I couldn't see Dad's face, I knew he would be chuckling over Hattie's predicament – especially as the old woman kept looking at her and trying to strike up a conversation.

Danny and I had managed to get seats together

but I was worried about him. He looked so unhappy.

'I just wish Maddie could be here instead of me,' I told him. 'Have you heard from her yet?'

He shook his head. 'I'll probably hear from her tomorrow.' Then he turned to face me, anguish written all over his face. 'I just wish Mum would get on with the Ryan family, Ann.'

I remembered Dad's words. 'Well, maybe it's not all her fault Danny. Maybe something happened years and years ago that caused this feud. Maybe you'll never know the reason.'

Meanwhile a few passengers were having a noisy discussion on the merits of the new King Edward. 'Well, let's hope the new king can get us back into work,' said one thin-looking man with a lean hungry expression and a jacket that was three times too big for him. He had either bought it second-hand or else he had lost a great deal of weight.

His slightly plumper companion piped up, 'I mind fine when he was the Prince of Wales and he visited the unemployed miners in the Rhondda Valley in Wales. He was really sympathetic to their plight so let's hope he puts a ruddy big fire under the fat arses of this government and gets us back to work.'

My head began to ache with the noise and the stuffy cigarette smoke so I was thankful when we reached our stop and we stepped out on to the wet pavement.

Hattie brushed her coat with her immaculate leather-gloved hands, almost as if brushing away her close contact with the old woman.

We made our way along the wet street which was poorly lit with gas lamps, the grimy glass barely letting any glow escape.

Dad whispered to me that the woman beside Hattie had chatted non-stop for most of the journey but, because he was seated in front of her, Hattie's expression was hidden from his view – much to his annoyance. 'She really needs taking down a peg or two,' he said.

It was a family joke, this snobbishness, no doubt made worse by her jobs with 'the gentry', as Bella succinctly put it, first of all with her late employer in Glamis Road and latterly with Maddie's parents, the Pringle family, who lived in a big house in Perth Road. Her job there was to look after Joy who had been born on the same day as Lily.

Atholl Street – or Tipperary as it was better known – was quiet. Even the nearby pub was almost empty but it was a Tuesday and there was little money in Tipperary on weekdays. In fact, there was precious little money on any day.

The streetlights with their grubby cracked glass windows and broken gas mantles tried to cast their light over the pavements, leaving the crumbling tenements in a dark, shadowy and sinister-looking mass.

'Where are we going, Danny?' asked Hattie in a querulous voice. 'Are we meeting at Ma's house or one of the daughters' houses?'

'Patty said to meet up in Kit's place. It's over there.'

'I know where it is, thank you very much,' said Hattie sotto voce.

17

When we reached the outside staircase, it was in total darkness.

'Oh, great,' she growled.

Danny ran ahead. 'I'll go up and get Kit to open the door and you'll be able to see where you're going.' He raced up the stair like a young deer.

Hattie was in no mood for such tactics. Her voice was bitter with sarcasm. 'No doubt, when Kit opens her door, we'll all be overwhelmed by the light. Better shade your eyes, Ann.'

We remained silent. When she was in one of her moods, we knew there was nothing we could say that hadn't been said a hundred times before.

As it was, Kit's house was too far along the lobby to be of any great help in shedding light on the worn stairs but Danny soon reappeared. He had a tiny torch and he shone it in front of his mother's ascending feet and up she went like some queen climbing an unknown flight of steps.

I had a sudden mental image of Queen Mary. Was she also climbing stairs in her huge palace? Of course, unlike the grotty old torch which was Hattie's lot, her passage would be brightly lit by many grand lamps.

Kit's tiny kitchen was full of people – far more than had been in the Overgate. When Hattie entered, the chatter died away.

A cheery fire burned in the grate. This was in sharp contrast to my previous visits and I wondered at what cost Kit had managed to put on this display of warmth.

An empty chair was placed right beside this blaze, next to the bulky frame of Ma Ryan. It was

18

obviously intended for Hattie.

Ma Ryan was inscrutable, like some fleshy, wrinkled Buddha. If she had been crying over the sudden demise of her husband, then it wasn't evident.

On the opposite side of the small room, Kit stood with her two sisters, Lizzie and Belle. They were all pale faced with red-rimmed eyes. Kit was thin and weary looking. Her dress was faded and worn, no doubt from too many washes, and it hung from her thin shoulders. Even her auburn hair seemed more subdued now and thin grey wisps were visible.

Her sisters were twins and neither had her colouring or her looks. Their square gaunt-looking faces were topped by short grey hair and, although they were only a couple of years older than Kit, they looked older and more matronly. I had seen photographs of them as young women and they hadn't aged as well as Kit but, like hers, their dresses had seen better days. And just like Kit's husband, their men had also been out of work for many years. Obviously all these years of having to make do on little money and not enough to eat some days had left its toll on them all.

Still, Kit had put on the best spread she could afford – from the warm glow of the fire on this chilly January night to the plate of meat paste sandwiches and the small tin of biscuits on the well scrubbed wooden table.

A large teapot sat on the gas cooker and Kathleen, Kit's daughter, was doing the rounds and filling up all the cups. Kathleen had the same radiant red hair as Danny. Her fine boned face had a creamy pallor that contrasted well with the brilliant hair. She was dressed in an ancient-looking jumper and a cheap black skirt but at fifteen she was as slender as a willow and had a flawless radiance that hinted at future beauty. Tonight, however, her eyes were also red rimmed and I knew she was very close to her late departed grandad.

Hattie sat beside Ma who turned towards her daughter-in-law and took her hand. Hattie, tongue-tied for once, managed to stammer out a few phrases of sympathy. Ma's face was like a blank page, her emotions firmly under control.

I looked over to where Danny stood with Dad. Danny was visibly upset and Kit had a thin arm around his shoulders. He was very fond of the Ryan family, more so because his father had died when he was a baby. He had never known him but the family had made up for that. He was their 'laddie' as Ma kept calling him.

Although my subconscious had registered it, it wasn't until that moment that I realised there were no children in the room and, more importantly, apart from Dad and Danny, there were no men.

Then, as if in answer to my unspoken thoughts, the door to the tiny back bedroom opened and Kit's husband George emerged. George was a tall man of six feet one inch – a trait that wasn't shared by the majority of Irishmen in the neighbourhood who were nearly all of medium height. They were all thin hungry men who had been out of work so long that they had forgotten what a wage packet looked like. For years, their lives had revolved around the dole office, the parish relief committee or, if they were lucky, a couple of pints of beer on a Saturday night.

George was a lovely man. He was so easy-going that his nickname was 'the Gentle Giant'. Still, that didn't stop him getting into a fight with any bully who tried to push weaker people aside. Many a time he had stepped into the middle of some brawl if he thought someone was getting a rough deal and many a punch he'd got for his troubles. He now stood in the doorway with a glass of stout in his huge fist. He seemed confused by all the women until his eye landed on Dad and Danny.

He marched over. 'We're in the bedroom with the coffin,' he said in a whisper that echoed around the room.

Hattie went white but sensibly remained silent.

He whispered again. 'Come on through and say a last cheerio to your grandad, Danny.'

Danny seemed uncertain but he didn't look at his mother.

Then, making up his mind, he said, 'I can't stay long, George.'

His uncle beamed. 'That's fine, lad – just a quick cheerio.'

Danny had taken one step towards the room when into the kitchen strode Martin Murphy, a neighbour. Small and beefy and very belligerent, his glass was empty which seemed to annoy him greatly and, when he spoke, he sounded like a disgruntled Jack Russell terrier – snappy and loud. 'Och, it's yourself, Danny. Now, you'll be joining us for yer grandaddy's wake. We sit up all

21

night and pay our respects to the dead so to speak.'

I looked at Hattie. She had half risen from the chair and, for a brief moment, I thought she was going to haul Danny from the room and the clutches of Martin Murphy. Her attitude didn't surprise me but, to my astonishment, I noticed the effect Martin's words had on Kit and Ma. Kit stepped forward and almost collided with Kathleen and the teapot. Meanwhile Ma's face dropped its blank look and she looked concerned.

'Kit, don't let Danny stay for the wake,' she turned to Hattie. 'Take him home, lass, as it's not a thing for a young laddie.'

She glared at Martin but her words fell on deaf ears. He puffed out his beefy chest and glared back at her. 'Don't be daft, Ma. What harm can it do? Surely if seventeen-year-auld Sammy Malloy is there then so should Danny pay his respects.' He turned to Dad. 'You come in as well, Johnny.'

Now it was my turn to be worried. Both Dad and Danny had their jobs to go to in the morning and the last thing I wanted was for them both to be up all night drinking.

Life had been hard enough for us after Mum's death. Dad had taken this so badly that he drowned his sorrow in drink. He had taken his unhappiness to the pub. Fortunately, Maddie's parents had found him a job in her uncle's warehouse and he had stopped drinking – apart from an occasional pint of beer on a Saturday night.

By now, George realised the big mistake he had made and he tried to usher Martin back into the bedroom. Martin let out a roar of annoyance that brought other neighbours, the Malloys, senior and junior, into the kitchen. They had obviously drunk too much beer and they were both on the verge of aggression. Mick Malloy, the father, thrust his unshaven face within an inch of Kit's furious expression. 'Will you stop your whinging, woman, and let the laddie mourn his Grandaddy?'

Then, before Kit or Hattie could stop them, they swept the two men into the bedroom. A sheepish-looking and worried George followed them while young Sammy gave Kathleen a long leering gaze.

Before the door closed, I had a sneak view of the bedroom's dark interior. The black shape of the coffin, highlighted by glowing candles, was surrounded by the shadowy shapes of the mourners. Cigarette smoke wafted out of this hell-like scene, along with the pungent smell of beer, and then the door was firmly closed in the faces of the outraged women.

'That Mick Malloy and his son are just toerags and idiots,' said Kit to a furious-looking Hattie who was trying desperately to keep her social smile in place.

If I hadn't been worried myself, I would have laughed at her comical expression but it was no laughing matter. 'Dad has his work tomorrow and so has Danny.' My voice was tight with worry. 'If they don't turn up, they'll lose them, Kit.'

Ma Ryan called out from her chair, 'Don't you worry, lass. They'll not be staying for long – even if I have to haul them out myself.'

On that note of promise, we swallowed our tea and finished off a meat paste sandwich. Then we

23

said our goodbyes.

Before we left, Ma asked Hattie, 'Will we see you at the funeral on Thursday? The service will be held here at ten o'clock and the interment at Balgay cemetery afterwards.'

I saw that Hattie was having great difficulty in keeping her voice under control. The last thing she would want was to lose her dignity in this shabby little room. Even so, her answer surprised me. I was waiting for a polite refusal but she said very quietly, 'Yes, Ma, I'll be there.'

A flicker of emotion leapt into Ma's eyes. 'Thanks for coming, Hattie. It's been great to see you again.'

Hattie thanked Kit and her sisters for the tea and then we headed towards the dark stair again. Our passage was helped slightly by the light of the torch, which Hattie promised she'd get Danny to return. That is if he was ever allowed back after tonight, I thought.

I was tensed up and waiting for the explosion. I wasn't disappointed. Halfway down the street, Hattie stopped suddenly and stamped her feet in anger. 'Imagine letting a young lad go to a wake. A wake, I ask you! Sitting up all night with a dead body.' Her voice held a hysterical note of fury. 'I've never heard anything so barbaric in my entire life.' She snorted with derision. 'Of course, it's just an excuse for a good-old booze-up. The women in that family haven't a decent dress between them but their men can still find money for beer.'

Thankfully, the tramcar arrived at that moment and put a temporary stop to her tirade. Even so, she was like a coiled spring all the way home and

24

it was a wonder her gloves weren't torn to shreds by the way she twisted them. It was like sitting next to a smouldering volcano and an erratic one at that. I had no idea when it would erupt.

The eruption came in the kitchen at the Overgate. Granny almost fell backwards under the onslaught. Hattie's voice had even risen a decibel or two and Granny had to tell her to be quiet. 'For heaven's sake, keep your voice down. I don't want Dad or Lily to wake up.' She nodded over to the bed in the corner of the room where Grandad lay snoring. On the Richter scale it would have registered a three.

There was no sign of my sister but I knew she would be in the tiny room that was just off the lobby – the room that resembled a cupboard and had been mine in my younger days.

Hattie was in full flow although she did lower her voice, a lowering that emphasised her words and they emerged from her mouth like machine gun bullets – sharp, fierce and hurtful.

She repeated her earlier tirade then started on the Ryan family. 'What a bunch of bloody morons they are – letting Danny go to a morbid thing like that and him having to get up for his work tomorrow.' She then whirled on me. 'And what about your father? If he misses a day then he'll get his books and his marching orders.'

I opened my mouth but Hattie hadn't finished. 'Bosses nowadays don't have time for outdated and moronic customs like wakes.'

I opened my mouth again but this time Granny butted in. 'Well, Danny isn't a laddie any more, Hattie. He's almost a grown man and as for

25

Ann's dad...'

Her silence unnerved me. 'Please don't let Dad go back to his drinking,' I said in a mental prayer.

'Well, as for Johnny,' said Granny, 'he's also a grown man and able to take responsibility for his actions.'

I got the impression this wasn't what she meant to say but her better judgement had prevailed. We all knew that, since Mum's death in 1931 after giving birth to Lily, he had walked a tightrope kind of existence – drinking heavily and getting into the wrong sort of relationships. It was still common knowledge that Marlene Davidson, one of his ex-girlfriends was still telling everyone who would listen, 'Yon Johnny Neill is a rotten beggar.' She was still bemoaning the fact that he hadn't married her – in spite of her looking after him so well when he lodged with her.

Then there was Rosie from next door. She worshipped him but even she couldn't get him to pop the question. She visited the house every spare minute she had and she had even given up her work with the Salvation Army, which had been a big thing in her life, but to no avail.

Hattie's voice brought me back from my reverie. 'All I'm saying is this – it's a disgrace and the funeral will be an even bigger booze-up.'

'Still, you said you would go,' I said.

Hattie glared at me. 'What else could I say with them all looking at me like I was some kind of freak?'

Granny was annoyed. 'I wish you would stop all this moaning about wakes and funerals. After all, this sitting up all night with a dead body is just a

26

custom and it's probably a tradition with the Ryans.'

Hattie wasn't giving up her anger without a fight. She snapped, 'Well, thank goodness Danny has been kept away from all these so-called traditions and customs. Another thing – I know Pat wouldn't have wanted anything to do with this because he was too good and much too sensible.'

'That's the truth,' said Granny, 'but don't forget that the only perfect husbands in the world are the ones who are dead.' She glanced fondly at Grandad whose Richter scale had now dropped to zero.

I felt I had to say something. 'I don't think you can blame Ma Ryan or Kit and her sisters for this. I noticed Ma jumped out of her chair and told Kit not to let Danny go. No, in my opinion, it is those awful Malloys' and Martin Murphy's fault.'

Sammy Malloy's face swam into my mind. I hadn't liked the leering look he gave Kathleen and I hoped the little sod didn't have any ambitions in her direction.

Hattie rubbed her eyes. She looked so weary that I almost felt sorry for her until I remembered that Danny was grown up and in full control of his own life. He was engaged to be married to Maddie and they had already planned the wedding. It would take place after Maddie's final exams at the end of her nursing training. No, Hattie had to realise she couldn't rule his life forever.

Granny made tea – strong and sweet for me and her, weak and sugarless for Hattie. Living like a lady in the Pringle house had given her a taste for tea with lemon but lemons were the last thing Granny would keep in her cupboard.

Hattie conceded I was right. 'Yes, I did notice that Ma Ryan and Kit did their best but it was useless against those awful men. Those Malloys and that Murphy man can smell drink from a mile off.'

She turned to me, now all sweetness and light. 'Will you come to the funeral with me, Ann? I feel I need another woman from my own family to back me up. After all, I haven't seen the Ryan family for a while.'

Granny told me later that she almost told Hattie that she hadn't visited the Ryans since Pat's funeral in 1917 but she decided to remain quiet.

I had to give this request some thought. I started work at seven in the morning in time for the early morning trade and I finished at one o'clock. Sometimes, if needed, I did an evening shift from four till six o'clock but I got every Sunday off.

'I'll speak to Miss Boyd in the morning, Hattie. Maybe if I offer to work some extra hours she'll let me off.'

On that uncertain note, she stood up and smoothed her leather gloves over her white hands. Hands that were still pretty in spite of her age and not red and raw like Granny's or the Ryan women's – or, for that matter, like my own. She was growing old gracefully it would seem.

She was almost out the door when Granny called after her. 'You'll be thinking I'm terrible but I forgot to ask what Dad Ryan died with?'

She looked annoyed but then she quickly put

on a sorry face.

'Oh, it was his heart I think. Ma did say that he was quite ill with bronchitis a few weeks ago but she thought he was feeling better. According to Danny, he's always been bothered with his chest and his lungs. Coughing and spluttering but would he give up his cigarettes? Not him. Puffing away on his "Wild Woodbines" every day. He even called them "Coffin Nails" and that's what they've become – nails in his coffm.'

The room became quiet after she departed and we sipped our tea in hushed harmony.

I was forever grateful to my grandparents for looking after Lily while I worked. Our routine hardly ever varied. After work, I would pick Lily up from the Overgate and we would have our tea when Dad got in from his work. Then, in the evening, I would return to the Overgate with her. One problem loomed on the horizon. She would be starting the school after the summer holidays and I wasn't sure how we would manage then.

As if reading my thoughts, Granny said, 'Maybe Miss Boyd can give you different hours when Lily goes to the school. Something will turn up, Ann. It aye does.'

I smiled at her. Dear Granny – forever the eternal optimist.

'Do you want to stay here tonight?'

I shook my head. 'No. I've got Dad's pieces to make yet, for his work in the morning.'

In spite of the rain, the Overgate was still busy with people. From a distant church steeple a clock chimed nine o'clock and a cold penetrating wind swirled around my legs. Like some mini typhoon, it whirled into doorways and the narrow closes, catching discarded litter and sweeping it into miniature mountains of debris. People hurried by, their bodies shivering in thin coats and jackets and their heads bent against the weather. It was clear they weren't out for a nocturnal stroll as they hurried towards tiny shops that were still open or, in the case of the men, emerged from one of the many bars that lined the street.

On reaching home I climbed the stairs realising for the first time how weary I was. Because of the urgent summons to Lochee, I hadn't lit the fire and the flat was cold. There was no sense in lighting it now so I put a match to the gas jets of the oven and left the door ajar. The room soon became cosy and I was grateful for its warmth as I still had some chores to finish as well as having to make Dad's sandwiches for his dinner break at work.

I also wanted to write to Greg. I had known him for over a year now after Maddie arranged for me to visit him while he was a patient in her ward. I remembered how against the idea I had been at the time but it had turned into a wonderful friendship. I smiled at the memory. Although his parents lived near Trinafour in Perthshire, where his father was a shepherd, Greg was a librarian in the public library in Dundee.

For the umpteenth time over the last few weeks, I wished that I could speak to him but he had been sent to Glasgow on a temporary transfer. A few weeks ago, he had given up his lodgings in Victoria Road on the advice of his boss at work and the future didn't look very rosy from my point of view.

I got out my notepad and began to write down all my news, including the death at Lochee. I wrote, 'He died at the same time as the King.' After I wrote it I wasn't sure why I thought this dubious claim to fame was somehow important.

I tried hard not to think about all the good-looking girls Greg would constantly be coming across – wonderfully smart and vivacious girls with nothing on their minds except clothes and having fun. Still, this wouldn't do, I thought – this feeling of self-pity – so I ended my letter cheerfully.

In spite of thinking about Greg, my mind kept returning to Lochee. I had the strangest feeling that something was wrong, but I couldn't put my finger on it. Even as I addressed my letter to his new lodgings in Renfrew Street, I still couldn't shake off this niggly feeling and it lasted until I went to bed.

I thought back to Ma Ryan's and Kit's reaction when Mick Malloy pulled Danny into the back room. Had they looked frightened? I thought they had but surely I was wrong. After all, it was just a custom amongst the Irish community – this sitting up all night with the deceased. A shiver of fear made me tremble and I hugged my hot-water bottle. 'Don't let Dad drink too much,' I prayed out loud as I snuggled down beneath the blankets.

I don't know what time Dad came home as he had the alarm clock in his room but I do know it was in the still, quiet hours of the morning. I heard him moving around quietly before he headed to his bedroom.

31

Thank goodness he's home, I thought. Then I fell asleep into a deep place, still feeling afraid of some unknown thing.

Something was definitely wrong. I saw it in Dad's eyes as he ate his breakfast. Gulping down strong sweet tea before dashing off to the warehouse. He had that evasive look I well remembered from the old days when he was hiding something from me.

My sleep had been full of horrible dreams and I didn't feel rested. Because of this sluggishness I was now struggling to get to my work. Dad sat hunched at the table while I washed my face using water from the cold-water tap at the sink.

I still had the strong feeling of impending doom. 'Dad, how did the wake go last night?' I caught the startled expression on his face as I lowered the towel from my eyes but he replaced this look with a charming smile – a smile which didn't quite reach his troubled eyes, I noticed.

'Och, it was fine but we didn't stay long. We both left about four o'clock.' He glanced at the clock. 'Heavens, is that the time? I'd better dash or I'll be late for work.' On that note he rushed out of the room and I heard his tacketty boots clattering down the stone stairs.

Of course, by now, I was well and truly worried but I didn't have time to think about it. Miss Boyd would now be surrounded by piles of newspapers and in dire need of my help. I turned out the gas lamp and headed out the door, determined to tackle Dad in the evening. Something had happened last night and I wanted to know what it was.

Connie Boyd's shop was situated a few yards from our close which was ideal for me. It was a tiny shop made even smaller by the large amount of stock she kept. She had a small lending library in the back of the shop. A cupboard-sized space with wooden shelves that were filled with books she had collected over the years – mostly crime novels, romantic stories and Wild West cowboy sagas. She also carried a small selection of classics like *Treasure Island* and *Jane Eyre*. The books were in reasonable condition but some of the covers had seen better days. They weren't in the same league as my legacy of books from the late Mrs Barrie which were being kept by the Pringle family until I had space to keep them myself.

One of my duties was to inspect a book when a customer returned it. To make sure any turned down pages were placed back or else to remove the bookmarks which ranged from the disgusting to the comical.

Miss Boyd still retold the story of one find almost twenty years earlier when a compromising letter was returned with a book. The lady had almost certainly hidden it from her husband and had forgotten about it. Although Connie knew who she was, nothing was ever said and the woman never appeared in the shop again.

I loved my job. There was a magical mixture of smells from the newspapers, snuff, cigarettes and the aroma of boiled sweets. The paperboy was already in the shop when I darted in – a thin gangly-looking lad of thirteen with a thin white pinched face and red-raw knees. He didn't quite fall over with the weight of his bag but it was touch-and-go some mornings when he staggered out with this heavy satchel over his shoulder. I felt sorry for him. He lived with his widowed mother and his paper-round pittance helped her eke out the measly wage she earned by washing stairs.

Connie called out after him, 'You'll soon be needing long trousers, Davie.'

He muttered something about saving up for them. Poor soul, I thought.

The shop soon filled up with customers – a lucky few on their way to work and the unlucky jobless majority just popping in for a paper or some other essential.

I heard laughter and I turned around. It was Edith, Amy and Sylvia. Three young friends on their way to the spinning sheds at Hillside Jute Mills further down the Hilltown. I liked them. Barely fifteen years old, they were full of life and laughter in spite of their long hard day in the mill.

'Hurry up and serve us, Ann, or we'll be late again. We don't want to get quartered again as this will be our second time this week,' said Sylvia, laughing. 'At this rate, we'll not have any wages to pick up. Give me five Woodbines and two ounces of clove balls for Edith. She doesn't smoke like Amy and me and it'll be the death of her. Everybody knows that smoking is good for you.' She gave Edith a pitying look. 'I mean you're not grown-up unless you smoke.'

Edith was unabashed – she just liked her sweeties. I could hear their laughter as they ran off down the hill and I smiled at their pure pleasure in life.

I was kept busy until dinner-time but, during

one quiet spell, my thoughts returned to my earlier uneasiness.

'Half an ounce of Kendal Brown snuff, Ann.'

I blinked at old Mrs Halliday who was standing waiting patiently at the counter. 'Eh was a weaver in my young days and you needed snuff to clear out your nasal passages.'

I smiled to myself as I weighed out the snuff on the tiny scales. It was a story she told me every time she came into the shop. It was the same with her choice of book from the lending library.

'Now, let's see what you've got for me this time.' She put on a pair of tiny, wire-framed spectacles and scanned the shelves. 'Now, let's see.'

After a few minutes she pulled a volume from the shelf. 'Right then, Ann, I'll have another detective story. I just love a good murder mystery. It makes you appreciate the fact that you're still alive and kicking.'

For a brief moment, I recalled how dear Mrs Barrie had also loved a good murder mystery in spite of owning a super library of leather-bound books.

I was writing Mrs Halliday's name in the ledger when the doorbell gave a loud metallic ping and Maddie burst in, almost taking the door off its hinges. Her face was red with the cold and she had tears in her eyes.

Mrs Halliday didn't seem to notice as she went out but I had the most awful feeling of foreboding that had nothing to do with Dad Ryan's death.

'Oh, Ann, I got Danny's letter about his grandad and I'm so sorry to hear it.' She stopped and wiped her eyes. 'I went down to Upton's shop this morning because I have a few hours off and Danny told me the engagement was off.' Tears were now rolling down her cheeks. 'He says it's better we don't get married. What happened at Lochee last night? He won't tell me.'

I gasped so loud that Connie popped her head around the door of the back shop – a tiny space only big enough to house a chair and a gas ring. When she saw Maddie, she nodded and ducked back again behind the door to finish her cup of tea.

Maddie grasped my arm in her agitation. 'I'm telling you that Danny has broken our engagement, Ann.'

Although alarmed by this news and her manner, I tried to keep calm. 'You must have misunderstood him, Maddie. Danny is besotted by you and he would never hurt you like this.'

Her large blue eyes were still wet with tears. 'But it's true. I have three hours off today and I went to Lipton's shop to see if Danny would meet me at his dinner break but he looked so different somehow when he walked me to the door. Then he told me that he was releasing me from the engagement and he wouldn't see me again.' She wiped her wet cheeks with a small sodden handkerchief. 'I tried to speak to him but he says his mind is made up and that's that. What does he mean, Ann?'

She turned her tearful face away when a customer came in. The woman's mournful expression matched my own worried mood. 'Terrible news about the King is it no'?'

I nodded bleakly. This had been the main topic of conversation since his death.

'I'll have a single cigarette, Ann.'

I handed over the cigarette from the box of fifty which lay under the counter. Connie had loads of customers like this one who were too hard up to buy five cigarettes so she kept them supplied with whatever amount they could afford – sometimes that was just a single purchase like this one.

I turned back to Maddie. She seemed to think I could work miracles with Danny but I was as much in the dark as she was. I told her this but I added, 'Dad was in a strange mood this morning. Perhaps they've both had too much to drink last night.' Although I was saying the words, I wasn't believing them. I knew Dad could maybe cast aside a lady-love but not Danny.

Maddie pulled on her gloves. 'I've got to get back to the infirmary, Ann, and I've no more time off this week except for a few hours on Sunday afternoon.'

'Look, Maddie,' I said, with more conviction than I felt, 'I'll try and see Danny tonight and get this horrible mess sorted out – one way or another.'

As she reached the door, she turned. 'It wouldn't be Minnie who's caused this ending, Ann, would it?'

I was shocked. Minnie was an old school friend of Danny and it was true that he had taken her to the pictures over a period of a few weeks but that had been a few years ago. Minnie was now married to one of Lipton's assistant managers and she now had a little boy.

37

Maddie saw my shocked expression. 'Well, her husband is still living in Clydebank and she's back in Dundee. According to Bella, the rumour is that they've separated.'

Blast Bella, I thought, with her meddling gossip and her easy way with passing on any juicy titbit. I had also heard this rumour but I didn't think for one moment that Minehaha, as I called Minnie because of her resemblance to an Indian maiden, was behind this mystery.

I didn't have a plan in mind that afternoon as I set off for Granny's house except I didn't want her to hear of this change of heart on Danny's part. I knew she would be just as shocked as I was and just as much in the dark.

As it turned out, it was a wasted journey because Lily wanted to stay. She had been invited to have her tea in her friend's house and I didn't have the heart to disappoint her.

I made my way homeward and I was caught in a heavy sleety shower that left my coat and shoes sodden. I planned to tackle Dad when he came home but the problem was Connie. She needed me in the shop for an extra hour at teatime so I had no choice but to leave him a note saying the meal would be a little later than usual.

After a hectic hour at the shop, I made my way wearily homeward. My note was still propped up on the mantelpiece. Dad had obviously seen it because he had added a small pencilled message. 'I'll get my tea at Rosie's. See you later.'

I was mad. Although he often ate his tea with Rosie and her mother Alice, I was desperate to tackle him tonight. Damn. It was almost as if he

38

was dodging me. Without taking my coat off I headed for the Westport and Danny.

Hattie answered the door. She looked totally surprised because I hardly ever visited her at home. 'Ann, is there something wrong?' She sounded worried.

I tried to keep a cheery expression in spite of all this worry. I smiled. 'No, Hattie, I just wanted to see Danny. Is he here?'

She shook her head. 'No, I expect he's at Lochee but come in.'

I didn't really want to socialise at that moment but I moved towards her tiny living room which was immaculate – but then it always was. The furniture was well chosen and good quality. There was a lovely smell of lavender and beeswax polish.

When she saw me sniffing, she pointed to the large bowl on the sideboard which was filled with dried flower heads. 'Mrs Pringle always gathers her flowers in the summer and dries them. I gathered all the lavender heads and they make a lovely perfume for the house.' She sniffed the bowl with her eyes closed. 'It brings back all the summer smells in winter.'

Not for the first time was I struck by her genteel, refined nature. She was so different from the rest of the family.

'I'll make some tea,' she said as she headed towards the small cupboard area which was barely large enough to hold the gas cooker and a tiny sink with a well-scrubbed draining board.

I sat down in a lovely squashy chair by the side of the brightly burning fire. The wireless was on but she switched it off when she appeared with the tea tray which held two dainty china cups and saucers and a small plate with biscuits. I couldn't help but compare it to Kit's house with its bare basics and tiny fire.

'I didn't really want Danny to go to Lochee tonight but I suppose it is his grandad who's died and not some obscure member of that family.' She put down her cup and compressed her lips into a disapproving frown. 'Mind you, I expect they act like that with any death in their family. I mean look at that awful business last night. I ask you, Ann, it's almost inhuman to sit up all night with a dead body.'

I stopped her because I had heard all this tirade before. 'Hattie, did Danny say anything about last night?'

She almost choked on her biscuit. 'Say anything?'

'Yes. Did he say anything about the wake?'

She gave this a moment's thought. 'No, although I was glad when he came in about four o'clock. I was still awake and feeling worried about that stupid custom but he went off to work this morning and I went to my work at the Pringles' house as usual. When I got back he wasn't here so I just assumed he had gone to Lochee.'

I tried to look nonchalant. 'When does he normally get back from Lochee?'

By now she was suspicious. 'Look, Ann, what's this all about?'

I knew I couldn't mention anything to her – at least not until I had spoken to Danny – but I also didn't want to lie to her. If she knew the real reason for my visit, then she would have a fit of

40

hysterics. She was so pleased when the engagement was announced because she thought Maddie was a real catch for her Danny. Now, if she even guessed the engagement was off well, it didn't bear thinking about.

'Oh, it's just a message from Maddie,' I said innocently. 'She came into the shop this morning and asked me to pass on something to him.' It was almost true I told myself.

Her face cleared. 'Oh, I see. Well, just tell me the message and I'll pass it on.'

Oh my God, I thought. I stuttered a bit. 'It's just ... it's just that she's sorry about Dad Ryan and she won't be able to get off for the funeral. That's all,' I lied.

'Well, I'll pass it on and you'll see him tomorrow at the funeral.' She made a wry face. 'Actually I wish I didn't have to go but I suppose it's expected of me. I hate funerals as they are so depressing.' She refilled my cup and offered another biscuit.

There was nothing I could do but eat up then try to make my escape as soon as possible.

As I stepped into the street, the cold sleety showers had died away and it was a bright frosty night with a star-studded sky. Still, I didn't have time to admire the sky's glory because my mind was in a turmoil. Danny's behaviour was so out of character that it left me stunned and I couldn't see a way forward. All Maddie's dreams looked dead but I still couldn't believe it. It had to be a silly misunderstanding but where were the main players in this drama? Both missing.

For a brief moment, I thought of going to Lochee. As I passed the tramcar waiting to pick up its motley quota of passengers, its windows glowed in the frosty darkness. I walked away from this temptation, determined to tackle Dad as soon as I got home but, to my dismay and alarm, he was already in his bed – an unheard-of state of affairs in our house because he normally retired to his small back room around eleven o'clock or sometimes even midnight. For him to be in his bed by ten o'clock was a first.

I knew then there was something serious going on but, apart from marching into his room and shaking it out of him, there was nothing I could do. Tomorrow, I promised, tomorrow neither Dad nor Danny would escape. After the funeral I was going to get to the bottom of this mystery. I fell asleep with this plan in mind – a plan that was made all the more resolute by the sight of his furtive look as he dashed out through the door after a meagre breakfast.

I had arranged with Connie to have time off for the burial at Balgay cemetery but not for the Mass in Kit's house. I was feeling ill and tired and my sleep had been filled with distorted dreams. I shivered in the cold morning air.

The customers were also shivering, their breath escaping in long streamers of white vapour as they came through the door.

'There's snow in the air,' was the favourite saying that morning and I hoped it wasn't true.

The snow started falling about nine o'clock and the streets were soon covered with a fine white powder. Small children were rolling in this with excited whoops of glee. What a day for a funeral, I thought, wondering if the weather would be as wintry for the King's funeral.

The scene at Balgay was depressing. The snow fell from a grey leaden sky and it was so cold that I soon lost all feeling in my fingers and toes. I looked over to where Danny was standing beside his aunts and uncles. He moved slightly and I saw Ma Ryan. She was dressed in a thick, old-fashioned-looking coat and she wore a pair of stout black boots that had seen better days but were still sturdy.

Hattie stood beside her. Looking smart in a fur-collared black coat and really fashionable suede bootees. These two stood out because, unlike the rest of family with their red-rimmed eyes, Ma looked composed while Hattie looked impassive. Danny's face was a chalky-white blur but his red hair was as bright as ever.

It was a large funeral with most of the men from the community turning out to mourn an old neighbour. They stood in their ill-fitting jackets and coats, holding their cloth caps in careworn hands. Their heads were bowed, either in silent prayer or in an effort to escape the relentless snowflakes.

I wondered if Dad had managed to get a few hours off from his work and I peered into the crowd. He was standing with Maddie's Dad, Mr Pringle, and I was so pleased he had managed to come. As for Mr Pringle, I knew the Ryan family would appreciate his appearance. I knew Dad would make his escape as soon as the graveside service was over – not like the majority of men here who were unemployed and for whom this day was like hundreds of others in their lives.

43

Unlike Dad, they didn't have a job to go back to. Once again, I said a silent thank you to Mr Pringle for all his help in finding this job for him at his brother's warehouse.

Balgay cemetery was now a familiar place to me as Lily and I would come here regularly to put flowers on Mum's grave – a resting place that had now been made more personal by the addition of a small granite headstone, which had been my first purchase with my legacy from the dear Mrs Barrie.

As the priest's voice carried over the heads of the mourners, my mind went back to my days at the Ferry. How happy I had been in the company of Mrs Barrie but the horrible Miss Hood had made my life such a misery. I wondered if she was still in hospital – or the asylum as most folk referred to it.

In my mind, I also went over the speech I was going to deliver to Danny, rehearsing every word. I intended to tackle him as soon as we reached Kit's house.

Now the service was over and we made our melancholy way back to Lochee. The men all refused the offer of hospitality. 'You'll have enough to feed without us,' was the general tone.

Once again, Kit had put on the best spread the family could afford under their straightened circumstances. A large fire burned in the grate, tended by young Kathleen who kept adding coal to it in between serving the tea.

We all huddled around its warmth and the hot tea was a blessing, helping to erase the chill from our bones. I sat beside Hattie but Danny was huddled in the far corner with Kit's husband.

I went over. 'Hullo, Danny, I think you're dodging me.' It was said teasingly but he gave me such a haunted look that my heart grew cold with worry. Something was far wrong and, at that moment, I didn't think there was much help I could give him or Maddie. This anguish, whatever it was, went deep and it showed. His eyes, normally so bright, were now blank and if he hadn't been standing, I would have sworn he was dead.

'Danny, I'll walk back home with you or we can get a tramcar.' I went to put my arm through his but he shrank back like some trapped animal. He didn't answer or even look at me.

I gave George an anxious glance but he shrugged. 'Leave him to himself for a wee while, lass.'

Anger rose in me. If there was one thing I wasn't going to do it was to leave him alone like this. This was Danny – my cousin and friend since childhood. He had helped me through the tragic death of my mother and all the traumatic times with Miss Hood at the Ferry so there was no way I was going to abandon him now. Whatever the cause, it had all happened after his grandad's death but George wasn't going to tell me so I went over to Kit.

'I'm worried about Danny,' I said bluntly. 'What's wrong with him?'

Kit tried to look surprised but failed. 'Oh I don't think there's anything the matter with him. He's just missing his grandad.'

I was adamant. 'No, Kit, there's something far wrong and it all started the night we were here –

45

the night of the wake. And another thing, I think the men know about it but they're keeping it quiet. Dad is dodging me and so is Danny.'

She looked at my white face then said quietly, 'I'll speak to Ma about it.'

We looked towards the fire where Ma and Hattie were sitting. Hattie looked uncomfortable but Ma had a queer expression on her face and she was gazing at Danny.

I went over to her but, before I could speak, she held up her hand. 'Danny has to work things out for himself.'

Hattie looked at her in dismay then at me. The chatter in the room died away and I had a terrible feeling of the calm before a violent storm.

Then Hattie spoke. Not in her normal cultured tone but in a strident voice. 'Why is everyone harping on about Danny? There's nothing wrong with him but you're going on and on about him.'

Everyone looked at her. Her cheeks had twin spots of colour and she was trying to put on her gloves as if she was leaving. She looked over to her son but he stared back. His face was drained of any colour.

Then his face twisted with grief. 'My father was a murderer, Mum, and you never told me,' he shouted. 'A murderer!'

Hattie looked at him in amazement and sat down so hard on the chair that its legs squeaked in protest. In fact, had she been a plumper woman, the chair would have broken.

2

The room went deathly quiet. The only sound came from the fire as the wet coal made little hissing noises – like a nest of snakes, I thought, which was absurd but I couldn't help but think it.

I stood frozen by the wall, unable to take my eyes away from Danny's white face. After a second or two which seemed like hours, a noise erupted in the small room. It sounded like a wail. Hattie gave a loud cry and tears streamed down her cheeks. Another absurd thought entered my mind. I had never seen her cry before or even lose her demeanour. Now I was witnessing both.

Ma Ryan put a plump arm around her shoulders which was another first in my eyes while Kit moved over to Danny's side. His eyes were glassy with unshed tears but his initial defiance had deserted him and he looked drained of all emotion.

Kit said, 'Danny, what are you saying? Your dad wasn't a murderer. Who told you that?'

At first, I didn't think he would answer her. His face had a closed look which I had never seen before.

Kit put her thin arm around him. 'Who was it, Danny? Tell your Auntie Kit.'

Danny gazed at her for a full minute and I suddenly realised I was holding my breath.

'It was Mick Malloy.'

Kit glared at her husband who took a step backwards under this icy stare. She led him over to Ma's side. Her arm still around his shoulders.

'Tell me what he said.'

Hattie began to protest but Ma held up her hand.

'No, Hattie, I think we should hear what Danny has to say then maybe we'll get it sorted out once and for all. I think I know what he's about to tell us.'

I looked at her in amazement. Surely this wasn't her famous sixth sense at work.

Danny kept his voice low but he held his head high. 'Mick Malloy told me that my Dad shot a soldier in his regiment during the war and that he committed suicide afterwards because he was a murderer.'

Hattie was outraged. 'He did no such thing and I won't sit here and listen to all these lies!'

Ma Ryan cut her short and she turned to Danny. Her normally impassive face now creased with anxiety. 'It's true Danny about your dad shooting one of his mates in his battalion...'

Hattie shouted angrily, 'That's not true!'

Ma gave her a puzzled frown. 'He must have told you about it, Hattie. I mean we all knew.' She glanced at Kit and her sisters and they nodded sadly. 'You see, Danny, your dad was made to do a dreadful thing – to shoot this deserter – but it was an order from an officer. Seemingly this young lad ran away from the trenches – not because he was a coward but more likely because he was suffering from shellshock.' Her voice became harsh with anger. 'But those officers in charge thought they knew better and they picked out three men for the firing squad and the poor soldier was shot at dawn.'

Danny turned an anguished face to his granny. 'He could have refused. He didn't have to do it.'

'But you see, Danny, your dad didn't shoot the lad. He told us that the three men aimed away from the soldier but that the officer then shot him with his own revolver. Still, this was small consolation to Pat. He was a good Catholic and, to his mind, this was a crime against an innocent man and, in God's eyes, he was just as guilty as if he killed the lad himself.'

Hattie cried out, 'But he was sent home because he lost part of his foot. He told me he'd stepped on a mine.'

Ma looked ill. 'We didn't know that this was all you knew, Hattie. Obviously he didn't want to worry you about the true reason for his discharge.' She stopped and looked at Kit, as if unsure about going on with the story.

Kit knelt in front of Hattie. 'He shot himself in the foot with his own rifle because of the soldier's death. It was preying on his mind. When he came home we all assumed you knew this. Then the years went by and you never mentioned it. Ma always had a strange feeling about you. She was never sure how much you knew but us women...' She gestured to Belle and Lizzie who looked sheepish. 'Well, we thought you were ashamed of Pat.'

Ma said, 'I often got the feeling you didn't know the whole story, Hattie, but, when you stopped visiting us after the funeral, I wasn't sure.'

49

Suddenly everything fell into place. Was this the reason for the Ryan family's apathy towards Hattie? Did they think she was so ashamed of her own husband and his family and didn't care enough to come to them for comfort and sympathetic support?

Ma looked tired and Kit continued with the story. 'One thing is certain Danny – your dad didn't commit suicide. He was deeply in love with your mum and they both loved you. He was here that last day and he got into company with a few of his mates – Mick Malloy and Martin Murphy to name but two. He didn't drink much as a rule but he was depressed that day, thinking about the poor lad whose parents would just have been told he had been killed in action. When he left the pub, he came back here and Ma gave him a good talking to – told him to forget the whole sorry incident, if only for the sake of his wife and baby. He promised he would.'

She glanced at her mother and Ma nodded sadly. 'If he had intended taking his own life Danny then I would have felt it in my bones and, although I'm not saying I wasn't deeply worried about him, I know he didn't plan on killing himself.' She looked at Danny's white face. 'It was a tragic accident son. His foot was really very sore that day and he was limping badly.' She was near to tears as she relived that terrible time. 'We think he stumbled as he crossed the road on his way home and he fell in front of the tramcar.'

Kit took Hattie's hand while Belle and Lizzie stood beside her. It was a tight protective circle and I wondered if Danny's father had made the right decision in not telling his wife – all these years and she could have had this warm support.

When Kit spoke she sounded angry. 'I'm just so sorry that it's all come out now because of that stupid man, Mick Malloy. It should have remained in the past where it belonged.'

Deep sobs shook Hattie's slim body and Danny moved quickly over to her. I also went over and it was as if my body was being worked by strings as I still felt no emotion in the face of all this drama. Still, I knew it would hit me soon.

Then George appeared at Hattie's side and he gave her a hug. For such a large man he was extremely gentle and, because he wasn't used to speaking a lot, he was a bit hesitant. 'We all thought Pat had told you, Hattie, but, as Ma says, he maybe wanted to spare you all the terrible details. Believe me, it's been a heavy burden all these years. Kit and I often thought of mentioning it but Ma said it would all come out in good time – when you were ready.'

Ma nodded wearily. 'That's right. After Pat died I knew it was a terrible accident and that it was God's will but he was really looking much better on that last day. I just knew that, after my telling him off, he planned to forget it and get on with his life with his wife and wee laddie.' Her face became bitter. 'The folk I hold responsible for this tragedy are the head bummers – the generals and officers who should never have been allowed to put soldiers in that position and as for shooting a young laddie for seemingly deserting his post ... well, it's plain and simple murder.'

George said, 'But they were the murderers,

Danny, Hattie – not your dad.'

During all these revelations of happenings in the far-distant past, I had remained numb and speechless with the horror of it all. Had my own father seen these atrocities or worse still, had he been put in the same situation? One thing was sure – too much had been covered up. Was it better to know at the time or was it worse if it came out later, courtesy of people like Mick Malloy?

George turned to me. 'Get the coats, Ann. Kit and I will take you all home.'

Hattie was devastated. Her dark shadowed eyes contrasted with her pale face and she looked as if she had aged a good ten years.

I took Danny's hand. 'Come on, it's time to go home.'

To be honest, I can't remember much about the homeward journey except for the silence. On the tramcar, I sat with Danny while Kit held on to Hattie's hand. George was in the rear – a solid stalwart. As the tramcar drew near our stop, Hattie suddenly didn't want to go to her own house. 'We'll go to the Overgate,' she said to Danny, her eyes still brimming with tears.

A few of the passengers recognised Kit and George but, if they were curious, they kept silent – no doubt thinking that this quiet grief was a leftover from Dad Ryan's funeral.

Granny's eyes were like saucers when we all walked in. Even Lily stopped looking at her book and they both gazed at us with puzzled frowns, Lily obviously imitating her granny. There was no sign of Grandad and I assumed he had gone out for his tobacco.

Hattie immediately ran towards her mother, crying loudly. Meanwhile, Danny remained between Kit and George and he stood there, white faced with shock.

'For goodness' sake, Hattie, what's the matter?' Granny was worried because her voice was sharper than normal – a sure sign she was out of her depth. 'What's the matter?' she repeated, looking at Kit and George.

George said, 'They've had a bit of a shock, Nan. I think we could do with a cup of sweet tea.'

Granny still didn't move so I went over to the sink and filled the kettle. To be honest I was glad to be busy – grateful for anything that would keep my mind away from Danny's ravaged face. I wanted so much to help him like he had helped me over the years – to be a strong and staunch ally to him – but I was ashamed to admit that I didn't know what to do or say. I felt so helpless.

Then I noticed that Lily was still gazing wide-eyed at this dramatic scene and I suddenly realised I didn't want her to hear this terrible story. I went over and picked up her book.

'Let's go through to Alice's house where you can look at your book in peace.'

She trustingly took my hand and gave me a toothy smile. My heart jumped with emotion as I left her with the next-door neighbour. It would now seem that Danny and I both had our own tragedies. My mum dying a few hours after Lily's birth and now Danny's father with his wartime horrors.

Thankfully, by the time I returned, George had told Granny the whole story. She looked stunned and the room was silent.

Someone had placed a crochet blanket around Hattie's shoulders but she was still shivering and her hands trembled in her lap.

'I can't believe this,' said Granny. She looked at Kit who nodded tearfully. 'You're telling me that Hattie and Danny knew nothing about this?'

George looked unhappy. 'I don't think more than a handful of folk know about it, Nan. In fact if Pat hadn't confided that day to me and Mick Malloy, then nobody would have known a thing about it.' His voice trembled as if he was on the verge of tears. 'I advised him to tell Ma. You see I thought Hattie had been put in the picture. Well, he told Ma the whole story and Kit and her sisters were in the house that day and everyone was so distressed and unable to take it in. Ma told him firmly to forget the terrible incident for the sake of himself and his family.' He looked firmly at Hattie and Danny. 'One thing is clear – he was coming home with the intention of putting the past behind him and that I do know. Then there was this awful accident.'

Kit spoke softly, 'We are all sorry for the way we've treated you, Hattie, but we thought you were so ashamed of Pat that you couldn't bear to even see his family. We almost mentioned it at Pat's funeral but Ma wasn't sure if it was the right time. In fact, she's had this feeling for years and she said the story had to come from you but, as the years went by, we became more disappointed that you shut us out of your life – almost as if we reminded you too much of Pat and maybe you wanted to forget the entire Ryan family.'

Fresh tears ran down Hattie's cheeks. 'We've been at cross purposes all these years, Kit. Of course I didn't shut you out but I felt so alienated at the funeral that I thought the same thing – now that Pat was dead, you didn't want to know me.'

Granny refilled our cups and said, 'It looks like you were all wrapped up in separate worlds of grief and distress at that time and all these mis-understandings arose.'

I left the four of them huddled together at the fireside and I went and sat beside Danny. He had been almost silent since we arrived at the house and I was worried about his chalky-white face. His eyes were dull with grief and pain and it seemed as if only his hair retained any life and vibrant vitality. I had never seen him like this before – it was almost as if he were dead but still breathing.

'I think the truth should aye come out at the beginning or else remain forever buried, Danny.' I tried not to sound bitter about the Malloy reve-lations.

He remained silent. His head bent.

'I've had Maddie in the shop, Danny,' I said quietly, not wanting anyone to hear me. 'You've got to see her and explain everything. She's heartbroken – especially when she doesn't have a clue what the matter is.'

He stayed silent and didn't look at me.

'Look, Danny, write her a note and arrange to meet her on Sunday.' I felt I was hitting my head against a brick wall. 'If you give me the note, I'll deliver it.'

He shook his head.

I was getting annoyed with him but I didn't

want to show it. I didn't want to raise my voice and let the others hear my pleas.

Then suddenly the door flew open and Bella breezed in. Putting on her 'coffin face' as Granny called it. She noticed Kit and George but sat down beside Danny, breathing noisily. 'Those stairs get steeper every time I climb them.' She looked around for sympathy but it wasn't forthcoming.

She looked at Danny. 'I'm really sorry to hear about your grandad but he was getting on and we don't live forever.' We were all shocked. This was typical sympathy from Bella. The Neill family had been used to it all our lives but it was the last straw for Danny.

He leapt to his feet. 'Thanks for the sympathy, Bella, but Ann and I are just leaving.'

We left her gasping with indignation and I could well imagine her outraged comments about the manners of the younger generation. She glared at me as Danny went over to say goodbye to the group at the fire. Still, I was in no mood to worry about her feelings.

As we walked along the still-busy street, I tackled him again. 'You'll have to see Maddie and explain things to her.'

He turned an anguished face to me and we stopped. 'How can I, Ann? What will she think of my dad, tell me that? What about her parents? Do you honestly think they'll want me for a son-in-law when they hear this?'

I was shocked by his intensity. And his un-characteristic stupidity. 'Of course they will, Danny, and so will Maddie. She loves you and she won't give a toss for what happened all those

56

years ago. I mean she'll be upset and sad for you. Nobody wants you to forget your dad but it was all so long ago. Maddie wants you and not some old memory – no matter how tragic it was.'

He shook his head. 'No, I can't tell Maddie or her parents. She'll soon find someone else and forget about me.'

I knew then that his mind was made up. He had a stubborn streak and there was nothing I could do – at least not on this cold snowy afternoon. Suddenly I felt so weary. This sad incident had happened so long ago but, like some sin, it was still casting a long shadow. Blast that idiot Mick Malloy, I thought.

We finally reached the imposing entrance to Lipton's shop and he said goodbye.

I gave it one last shot. 'Danny, before you go, will you promise me that you'll see Maddie on Sunday? You owe her that much and, whatever you choose to tell her, at least it'll be to her face.'

He didn't answer and I spoke louder. 'Danny?'

Although he looked unhappy about it, he nodded.

'Promise me?'

He nodded again then darted into the shop like a scalded cat.

I retraced my steps back to the house. Danny and I had left without saying a proper goodbye but, when I reached the close, I found I couldn't face Hattie, Kit or George – not to mention Bella – so I set off for the Hilltown and my work.

Connie was sitting in her little back shop when I arrived. On hearing the bell, she popped her head out. 'Och, it's you, Ann. I'm having a cup of tea because it's so quiet. Mind you, Thursday is aye the same. No money to spend.'

I had to smile in spite of all the worry. No money on a Thursday and precious little on other days, I thought.

'I know you did say you would work this wee bit extra to make up for your time off this morning,' said Connie, lighting a cigarette and blowing a long stream of blue smoke into the shop. 'But, as you can see, Ann, there's no customers around. Just you get off home and you can maybe do a bit extra another time.

In one way, I was grateful to get home but, in another perverse way, I would have liked some company that afternoon to take my mind away from the traumatic morning.

By the time Dad arrived home from the warehouse, I was shaking like a leaf. I had spent the entire afternoon going over and over the story. I could well understand the agonies that Danny was going through and, to make it worse, I couldn't help him – or Maddie.

Dad's face still had its wary look. Although he hadn't gone back to Kit's house after the interment and didn't know the story was out, he did know something. I was sure of that.

'What time did you leave Kit's house?' he asked.

I didn't answer his question. Instead I said, 'Dad, did you know about Pat Ryan's terrible time in the war?'

His face went white and he gave me another wary look.

'It's all right,' I told him. 'Danny blurted it out

58

during the funeral tea. Of course it was bedlam. Hattie has been in tears ever since and Danny is going...' I stopped. I didn't want to mention Maddie. If the engagement was truly off, then the news had to come from them. I didn't want to be the bearer of bad news.

'What is Danny going to do?' He sounded suspicious.

'Nothing. Tell me, did you know about this?'

He sat down in front of the fire. The meal was simmering on the stove but we both ignored it. He passed a grimy hand over his eyes and for a moment I thought he was crying but when he spoke, his eyes were dry. 'I didn't know about it until the night of the wake. Mick Malloy got so drunk and started speaking about the days before the war – how happy they had all been as young pals before it started. He then went on about the horrors of it. The mud and the trenches, the smell of death that was always in the air ... well, some of us tried to shut him up but he seemed hell-bent on reliving the terrible times. Then, when he mentioned Pat ... well, it was a huge surprise to me and a terrible shock for Danny. He went really white and I thought he would faint but he just sat so quiet and never said another word. George tried hard to minimise it but the damage was done and the deed was out.'

I was puzzled. 'Why was it never mentioned at the time, Dad?'

Suddenly he was angry. 'The only thing that remains is that all this death and destruction was for nothing – a few feet of land. Oh, no, Ann, none of us old soldiers talk about those days and

59

do you know why?'

I shook my head numbly.

'Well, I'll tell you why – because most of the sights were too terrible to remember. Thousands of men gassed and blinded with mustard gas. Then there was the mud. Acres and acres of it – stretching as far as the eye could see. Mud and barbed wire and dead bodies – that was our daily view. At the battles of Neuve Chapelle and Loos, there were so many dead soldiers that just about every house in Dundee got a telegram, telling them that their husband or son or brother had been killed. Pat's involvement with the firing squad was a terrible, terrible thing for him but the real culprits were in the comfy cosy offices of the War Office. They directed the officers to shoot deserters which, in our minds, was barbaric but it was a barbaric time. Pat's horror was just one horror amongst thousands of others.'

I wished again that Mick Malloy had stayed silent. What good did raking up the past ever do?

'I don't want to sound callous, Ann, but I'm starving,' he said as he went over to the sink to wash his hands.

I knew he was far from being cold-hearted. He just wanted to get on with living and leave all the unhappy memories where they belonged – in the past.

'For what it's worth,' he said, sitting at the table, 'I had nightmares for years after. In fact, I still do from time to time. I'm back in that sea of mud and filth and noise. I'll tell you this – I'm grateful to wake up in my bed in the morning. Joe feels the same. We survived the horrors while lots of our mates perished and, believe me, for years after we both felt so guilty about it.'

Joe was one of Dad's oldest friends. They say that every dark cloud has a silver lining and this was mine. Dad had never opened his heart to me like this before and I was grateful for the chance to know him better.

I had one favour to ask him. 'Dad, will you tell this story to Danny just like you've told it to me? I think it will help him understand what his dad went through – just like a thousand others.'

He shook his head. 'I don't think anything will help Danny at this moment. He has his own life to lead and his own problems to sort out.'

'Please, Dad.'

He reached over for another slice of bread to mop up the remains of his stew. 'I don't know. If I thought anything I said to him would help him, then I would do it but not just now. Leave it for a few days because anything I say to him now won't penetrate his grief.'

I had no option but to agree. Anyway, I had to go and pick up Lily – something I wasn't looking forward to. It had nothing to do with my sister but everything to do with the house in the Overgate – perhaps Hattie, Kit and George were still there.

Much to my surprise, the house was deserted when I arrived. Rosie appeared from next door with Lily. She had been eating beans on toast and had a bright orange ring around her mouth.

'Your granny and grandad are at Hattie's house, Ann. They had to call the doctor because Hattie was ill.' Her plump face was sympathetic. 'I think the stress of the funeral was too much for her.'

I wondered how much she knew. 'What about Danny?'

'I've no idea – I expect he'll be with his mother.'

Good – she doesn't know the story, I thought.

'I think your granny is planning on staying with Hattie tonight, Ann – at least that's what she said.'

'Thanks for looking after Lily. I'll take her home then head for the Westport.'

Rosie shook her head and her large bun of hair at the nape of her neck almost came loose. 'We can look after Lily till you get back from Hattie's house. It's no bother.' She gazed at Lily with affection. 'Isn't that right, my wee pet?'

Lily grinned. 'I haven't finished my beans yet and Rosie has got me a cream cake so it'll take hours to eat it all, Ann.'

I smiled at them. 'I'll be about an hour.'

As I made my way to the Westport I thought about Rosie – darling Rosie, she was totally devoted to Dad. In spite of this devotion, he hadn't asked her to marry him yet. It was my dearest wish and, although no one could ever replace Mum, Rosie came a good second best.

As it turned out, I was away for a good two hours. Danny and Grandad sat in the pristine living room while Granny was in the bedroom with Hattie. Grandad looked as if he was dying for a puff of his pipe but he wouldn't want to smoke in this lovely room. Danny looked even more ill than when I left him and I was concerned. By the look on his face he didn't want company – maybe he preferred to mourn alone.

I went into the tiny back bedroom and was

immediately taken aback by its elegance. The bed had a satin bedcover with a matching squashy-looking quilt. In the corner was a kidney-shaped dressing table with a frill made from the same ice-blue satin. At any other time, I would have remarked on its beauty but not tonight.

Hattie lay motionless in her bed and was fast asleep. Granny sat on a small padded chair by the side of the bed. She looked tired but she gazed at me gratefully. 'Och, you've come, Ann. Thank goodness because we don't know what to do about Danny. He won't talk to us and this is not like him to be this way.'

My heart sank. 'He won't talk to me either, Granny.'

She shook her head sadly. 'It's a terrible business. We had to call the doctor out for Hattie because she went hysterical after you left. What Bella thinks about it all, goodness knows. You know what an old gossip she is.'

'How is Hattie?'

'Well, the doctor gave her something to make her sleep but there was seemingly a terrible scene when Danny came in from his work. She begged him not to tell Maddie or the Pringles anything about his father.'

My heart sank even further. 'That's stupid. I told Danny to tell them everything. This won't make any difference to his engagement to Maddie or to her parents.' Although I was saying the words, I knew now there was no hope of him telling Maddie or indeed anyone about his late father. What a mess.

Granny shook her head. 'Well, you know Hat-

63

tie. She'll do anything to keep up her pretence of being a lady. She can't help it.'

I was suddenly worried for my grandparents. They both looked so weary. 'Granny, if you both want to go home, I'll stay here for a wee while – in case Hattie wakes up.'

She looked relieved. 'We'll keep Lily overnight, Ann.'

She went through to collect Grandad. I could hear the quiet voices as they said their goodbyes to Danny.

After a few minutes, I also joined him. Hattie was sleeping peacefully and I knew I would hear her if she became distressed again. However, Danny was another matter. He sat by the fire, gazing solemnly into the flames. He didn't turn his head when I came into the room. My heart was like a stone when I looked at him. I didn't know what to say to him and I was totally surprised by this. We had been so close to one another all our lives and we could almost read each other's minds but not this time. It was as if he had shut me and all his family out of his life and his thoughts. I put a hand on his arm.

Like a sleepwalker, he looked at me with dull, lifeless eyes and I was shocked by his expression. 'Danny, please talk to me. You've had a terrible shock but don't let it ruin your life.'

Suddenly, as if a veil was lifted from his face, his expression changed to normal – the old Danny I knew and loved. 'Ann, don't worry about Mum or me. We'll be fine but we just need time – that's all.'

'Oh, Danny, take all the time you need. I'll stay

here tonight in case your mum needs me.'

'No, Ann, just you get away home. I'll be here and Granny is coming back tomorrow so everything is fine.'

His voice was firm so I had no option but to go home. He obviously wanted to be alone. At the front door, I almost told him what Dad had said about the horrors of the Great War but I didn't. Perhaps, I thought, he had heard enough about that terrible era. I did, however, remind him to go and see Maddie on the Sunday and, although he agreed, I could see his heart wasn't in it.

I hardly slept over the next two nights and I was secretly dreading Sunday morning. There had been no more word from either Maddie or Danny. Where and when they were meeting was also a secret but I hoped they would still be together after it.

As it turned out, my Sunday leisure was dictated by Lily. She danced through to the kitchen and said she wanted to go to Broughty Ferry to see Jean Peters.

'Please, please, Ann, can we go?'

I had little choice in the face of such eagerness so we set off for the bus. I was actually quite relieved to get away from the house and my worries for a few hours.

Jean and I had met up on a few occasions since my departure from Whitegate Lodge but most of these meetings had been in the Broughty Ferry in a small teashop on the High Street. She still lived with her husband in Long Lane and I knew that her inheritance from Mrs Barrie had made their lives comfortable – something we had in common.

The street was almost deserted when we got off the bus and I was once again reminded how quiet this place was compared to Dundee – except maybe during the summer months when people were attracted to the beach and the water. Today, in spite of some watery sunshine, the wind blew cold and straight from the North Sea.

Lily was full of excitement as we stood on her doorstep. She was as fond of Jean as I was. She was a good friend to me and had been my ally against Miss Hood in my days at Whitegate Lodge.

Jean opened the door, her hands covered in flour. 'Well, I never! I was just thinking about you, Lily.' Pleasure was written all over her face. Being childless herself she always spoiled any child in her company.

Lily hopped from one foot to another, desperate to be asked in but remembering her manners which I had warned her to do earlier.

Jean knew this and she teased Lily by making her stand outside.

Doing a good imitation of Granny, Lily put her hands on her hips and said, 'Can I come in, please?'

Jean roared with laughter and I was suddenly grateful for this joyous sound. It had been days since I had heard anyone laugh or even seen someone smile. We had been all wrapped up in Danny's private gloom. She ushered us into her small living room. The flames from the blazing fire were reflected in the old-fashioned but highly polished furniture.

Lily went to help with the tea. Jean called out from the tiny scullery. 'You know where the biscuit barrel is, my wee pet.'

Lily set the table with such a serious look that I almost burst out laughing. As I didn't want to hurt her feelings I managed to control this urge.

There was no sign of Mr Peters. 'He's out,' said Jean. 'Gone to do a job for one of our neighbours.' She put the teapot down beside the fire. 'He's more or less retired now but he still likes to keep his hand in and do the odd job now and again. My legacy from Mrs Barrie has made our lives more comfortable.'

She placed a large plate of floury scones in front of Lily. 'Well, wee lass, eat up.'

Lily needed no second bidding and she proclaimed after scoffing her third scone and jam, 'I aye feel hungry when I'm at the Ferry. Granny says it's the sea air.' She sounded so comical that we both burst out laughing.

She was certainly growing up fast these days and, thankfully, she was healthy and sturdy. I thought of Maddie's sister Joy and the differences in their appearance. Although both born on the same day, when they were together, Lily towered over the fragile-looking Joy.

After tea Jean suggested a walk to the beach. Lily had her coat on in a flash and we set out. The watery sun had disappeared and was replaced with a cold greyness. The sea and sky seemed to merge on the horizon and the beach was deserted. The sand, left shiny wet by the receding tide, stretched before us in a pristine panorama and was unmarked by any human feet. Abandoned by the receding seawater, a brown strip of seaweed lay like a tidemark of lost, drowned souls.

Thankfully I couldn't see Whitegate Lodge from this vantage point. As if reading my mind, Jean said, 'I never go near the house now that Mrs Barrie's dead.'

Tears came into my eyes when I recalled my late employer. It had been in the month of January when I started work as a housemaid at Whitegate Lodge and it had been my first sight of Miss Hood. I wondered if all my troubles were destined to happen in January.

Jean squeezed my arm. 'Is everything going well for you now, Ann?'

I thought of Maddie and Danny and, although I didn't mean to mention them, it all came out. However, I kept quiet about Pat's wartime experience. I knew Danny wouldn't want his father's name bandied about or for the whole sorry story to become public knowledge. I just told Jean that he was upset after Dad Ryan's death.

Jean listened quietly as we watched Lily run over the expanse of wet sand. She said softly, 'Well, Ann, I hope they manage to sort it all out but you mustn't let it worry you. They have to make their own decisions and mistakes.'

'But Danny was aye there for me, Jean,' I protested. 'You mind how much he helped me when Lily was a baby.'

'That's what I mean, Ann – you were just a bairn yourself then and you had your baby sister to look after and support but that was a good few years ago and you are both older now. He must make up his own mind, either rightly or wrongly, and Maddie must do the same.'

She was right of course. I looked at her, my eyes

glassy with tears.

She continued, 'You've carried enough on your young shoulders, Ann – your sister and your dad plus the sad death of your mum. Maybe it's become a way of life for you to take on all your family's burdens.'

I looked at Lily. She was trying to outrun a seagull. Her face registering dismay as it flew into the air with a noisy squawk.

'I would advise you to let go and just enjoy yourself,' said Jean. 'Your sister is growing up, your father may marry Rosie, Danny may or may not marry Maddie but these things are out of your control, lass. Take Jean's advice and let go.'

I still said nothing as I watched Lily run over the sand with the sheer exuberance of being alive.

She went on, 'What about Greg? No doubt you'll want to settle down one day with him.' Her eyes twinkled. 'Then you'll know what real worries are like when you're an old married woman.'

'Greg is still in Glasgow and anyway we are just friends. I could never leave Lily and go off into the far blue yonder. You know that, Jean.'

She shook her head sadly. 'What a pity! At your age, you should be out enjoying yourself and not worrying over everybody – especially not Danny or Maddie. Now promise me, Ann.'

'I promise,' I said but I didn't believe I could keep such a promise.

Lily ran up to us. Her shoes plastered with wet sand and her cheeks red with the chafing wind. Her eyes were full of laughter.

'Och, me, would you look at yourself?' said

Jean, throwing up her hands in mock horror. 'Let's get back for our tea.'

Lily led the way with an excitement that made me wonder if my sister's life revolved around food.

As we walked back I asked Jean about Miss Hood.

'As far as I know, she's still in the mental hospital but, of course, I haven't been to visit her.' She stopped and looked at me keenly. 'Now promise me you'll not go back and see her – after all, she did try and kill you.'

I shook my head. 'No, Jean, I'll not go back. It's just that I feel so sorry for her but I know I'm being stupid.' I didn't add that I still had nightmares about the housekeeper. Although I sympathised with her sorry life, I still recalled the heavy candlestick in her hand and the noise it had made when it missed my head and hit the wooden banister at Whitegate Lodge. 'No, Jean, don't worry – I won't see her again.'

'Mrs Barrie left us both our legacies so we could have some comfort in our lives so please do what she would have wanted you to do and that's to enjoy yourself.'

Dear, dear Mrs Barrie, I thought, as tears came into my eyes.

After a lovely tea, we said our goodbyes to Jean and my heart felt lighter. Her advice was sound and I fully intended to stop worrying about Danny but, back home in the Hilltown, all my good intentions flew out the window.

Maddie was waiting for me in the house. Dad and Rosie sat beside her but the atmosphere was heavy. As if conversation had been difficult. On seeing me, Dad and Rosie both jumped up. It was as if they were both being worked by identical strings.

They took Lily's hand. 'Let's go and see Granny,' they said, almost in unison.

Lily looked delighted. She was certainly having a busy Sunday.

When they disappeared through the door, Maddie burst into tears. 'Danny has called off the engagement but he won't tell me why. Do you know?'

I took her hands in mine. 'No, Maddie, I can't help you. It has to come from Danny.'

She looked at me with bewilderment. 'Then you do know why?'

'No, Maddie. All I can say is that he's taken Dad Ryan's death very badly but just give him time on his own.' I felt terrible. On the one hand, I wanted to tell her the whole sorry story because she had a right to know but, on the other, I knew I couldn't betray Danny. He would never forgive me and I couldn't live with that.

Maddie wiped her eyes. 'I offered to give him back the ring but he didn't want it.'

For some reason this cheered me up. 'Well, then, Maddie, the engagement is not really broken, is it? Cheer up – it'll all work out. Believe me.'

'Do you think so, Ann?'

How could I tell her I wasn't a hundred per cent or even ten per cent sure? But I couldn't let her leave without a bit of hope.

We walked back to the infirmary together and I left her at the porter's window. As she walked away down the long corridor, she turned and waved – a golden vision in the drab painted corridor.

I was suddenly so angry. 'Blast you, Danny Ryan!' I said aloud. 'You're going to lose her to somebody else and it's your own fault.'

The porter stuck his head out of the window. 'Did you say something, Miss?'

Still angry, I said, 'No, I'm just talking to a brick wall.'

My heart wasn't in my job next morning when Amy, Edith and Sylvia came tumbling in. They were roaring with laughter and my mood immediately picked up and even Connie was amused.

'What's causing all this hilarity?' I asked them as I weighed out Edith's sweeties and gave the other two their cigarettes.

Sylvia piped up. 'We're just drawing lots to see who'll write to the dishy King Edward and offer him her hand in marriage.' They collapsed into peals of laughter.

Connie said, 'Oh, he'll have somebody in his sights if I know men. They aye do, the cunning beggars.'

The girls set off for work and, once again, I could hear their laughter as they hurried off down the hill.

Amidst the pomp and ceremony of a state funeral that contrasted starkly with Dad Ryan's, King George V, ruler of Great Britain and the Empire, was laid to rest the following day. It did cross my mind that maybe the royal household also had skeletons in their closet but I quickly dismissed the idea. It had been a long week.

3

The German army was on the march again. Dad's friend Joe arrived at the house, waving a newspaper. 'German troops march into the Rhineland in defiance of the treaties of Versailles and Locarno.'

Dad had just finished his meal and was sitting with a cup of tea beside the fire. He looked at his old friend. 'Aye, I've seen it, Joe, but I don't think they'll start anything this time – not after the carnage of the last war.'

Joe wasn't so sure. He said gloomily, 'I disagree with you, Johnny, and what makes it worse is that nobody seems to be able to stop them. You mark my words – if they get off with this, then it'll be the turn of some other country next year. You know what this lot are capable of.'

I left them talking about this possible new war. As far as I was concerned, I was too busy worrying about the uneasy peace that had settled on us since January.

I took Lily's hand and we set off for the Overgate. When we arrived, it was clear that Granny hadn't heard about this new aggression from Germany as she was too busy with Bella.

'I'm telling you, Bella, that there's nothing wrong with Hattie or Danny.'

Bella was having none of this whitewash – or 'twaddle' as she called it. 'Well, tell me this then,

Nan. Why have they broken off their engagement? I mean one minute they're both hunky-dory and then the next they're not speaking.'

Granny made a dismissive noise.

Bella went on. 'Aye and there's Hattie – she's going around with a face like thunder, looking like she's lost a half a crown and found a tanner.'

Granny knew she couldn't escape from this cross-examination. 'Danny and Maddie have decided to wait a wee while before they get married and Hattie is not pleased with it.' Her voice was firm. 'And, as far as I'm concerned, the matter's closed.'

Bella didn't look convinced and I didn't blame her. As far as excuses went, it was pretty flimsy but this was the story that Hattie had invented.

'It's nobody's business but ours,' was her general statement after she had recovered from that terribly traumatic night when the doctor was called out.

It was then decided, after her return to work, that, if anyone asked, this was the answer to give. In fact, we couldn't do much else when faced with Hattie's firm refusal to let the Pringles know the truth. Both Granny and I had tried to reason with her but to no avail.

'What will the Pringles think?' she had said at the time.

'I would just tell them the truth, Hattie, but, if you don't want to do that, then at least tell Maddie and she can decide if she wants them to know. Then take things from there.' Granny had tried to be tactful but it had all fallen on deaf ears so that was the story we all stuck to.

Thankfully, as far as Hattie was concerned, Maddie had said very little except to say the engagement was off for the time being. So we all settled into this uneasy calm. I didn't see much of Danny and even less of Maddie and, in a way, I was grateful because I didn't know what to say to them. I was also grateful to be kept busy at the shop and looking after Lily and the house.

Joe became a regular visitor. 'I'm telling you, Johnny, that this Hitler guy is a dangerous wee dictator.' He also kept referring to the last war and telling Dad about a possible new one as if Dad could do anything to stop it – as if he could wave some magic wand.

During these visits, I normally left the two men to their cigarettes and blethers. Connie had said I could visit her at her house if I ever wanted to get away from Joe's doom and gloom. She knew him well. Her house was in Stirling Street, in a nice block of tenement houses. It was much more posh than ours but it wasn't better kept. The square-shaped living room held so much furniture that reaching the fireside was like tackling an obstacle course.

'This is the way my father left it and I don't have the heart to throw out his things,' Connie said.

Actually, I liked it because it resembled the furniture shop on the Hilltown with its mixture of everything.

One night in the early summer, Connie said, 'Although it's a secret in the British newspapers, I've heard through the trade that the King is seeing a married woman. Her name is Wallis

Simpson and she's American.'

I was agog with excitement. 'How did you find out?'

'Well, it's in the American papers but it might just be a rumour. If she does get a divorce and marry him then this will be her third marriage.' Connie looked sad. 'Lucky for her I say and here I am – I can't even get *one* man.'

I wanted to ask her a favour. 'You know that Lily is going to the school this summer, Connie?' She nodded.

'Well, I wondered if I could maybe change my hours so that I can take her to the school in the morning and pick her up in the afternoon?'

'Aye, that's no problem, Ann. If you start at six thirty, work till eight, then come back at nine and work till your usual time, will that help?'

I thought it was great and I said so. That would give me time to pick Lily up from the Overgate and get her to the school gate in time for her classes and the afternoons were nearly always free anyway. Thank goodness that was settled, I thought. Granny was right when she said it would all work out. If Danny and Maddie's lives were sailing on choppy seas well at least mine seemed to be on an even course.

Then the two letters arrived on the same day – a lovely hot day in August. The first one came from Greg, which wasn't unexpected, and the other one came from Mrs Pringle. Greg's said he was coming to Dundee on the Sunday and he asked if I could meet him while Mrs Pringle invited me to her house on the Saturday.

'Bring Lily with you, Ann, as she'll be good

company for Joy,' she wrote.

On the Saturday afternoon we both set off for the Perth Road. Lily seemed strangely quiet and not like herself while I felt wary at the thought of Maddie's mother and I wondered who else would be there, dreading the thought of Hattie and Maddie in the house also. Then I felt guilty by these thoughts – some friend I was turning out to be.

With its smooth green lawns surrounded by banks of colourful flowers, the garden at Perth Road was a delight. The flowers' perfume lay heavy on the warm sunny breeze. The garden sloped down towards the river and, although it was sheltered by a long green hedge, it was possible to see the Tay's silver sheen through the greenery.

Mr Pringle was weeding. Dressed in an old short-sleeved shirt and a battered straw hat, he looked the picture of a country gardener – except that this garden lay not far from a busy road and the noisy bustle of the city. He waved.

Mrs Pringle was sitting by the open French window. She called out, 'Come in, both of you, and have something to drink.'

We went into her lounge. On my last visit, about a year ago, her settees and chairs had been covered with lovely rose-patterned covers but today they were covered in plain cream linen. It made the room seem cool and uncluttered.

I thought of Connie's house with its collection of possessions. If I owned a house like this, would I go for this quiet look because it was so elegant or would I choose the cosy clutter?

Joy was sitting on the rose-coloured carpet with

a pile of books. She gazed at us when we entered and she rose to her feet when she saw Lily. Normally Lily would have gone over to her and the books but not today. She clung to my skirt with her chubby hand.

Mrs Pringle said, 'Do you want to go to Joy's room and play with her toys, Lily?'

To my amazement she shook her head.

Mrs Pringle glanced at me but I could only shrug my shoulders.

'Do you both want to go outside and help in the garden?'

Lily didn't answer and she hid her face against my skirt. This was so unlike her.

I bent down. 'Lily, go and play with Joy. After all that's why we're here.'

She gave me such a strange look but, after a moment's hesitation, she let Joy lead her upstairs towards the bedroom.

'I've no idea why she's like this, Mrs Pringle,' I said.

She smiled and handed me a lovely china cup and saucer. It held a fragrant-smelling tea.

'It's Earl Grey tea,' she explained. 'Hattie and I just love it.'

I memorised the name. Earl Grey. Granny would want to know everything about this unexpected visit.

Mrs Pringle stirred her tea for a long time, as if getting up the courage to ask me the one question I dreaded. I sat in silence and let the perfume from the fragrant roses that framed the window waft towards me. It was so peaceful sitting in this lovely room but I knew what was coming.

She put her cup down without tasting it. 'Ann, I have to be honest with you when I say that Mr Pringle and I don't understand about Maddie and Danny breaking off their engagement.' She looked me straight in the eye. 'Do you know why?'

I didn't know what to say. There was no way I could tell her the truth but, on the other hand, Maddie's parents had been so good to us. She had got me my job with Mrs Barrie at Whitegate Lodge and Mr Pringle's brother had given Dad the job at his warehouse. I didn't want to lie to her but what could I say? I looked around to see if Hattie was in the house.

As if guessing this, Mrs Pringle said, 'Hattie is off today, Ann. That's why I asked you to come. I've asked her and she says she doesn't know. She says that Maddie wants to wait till her final exams are over before committing herself.'

'What does Maddie say?'

'That's the point – she hasn't said anything. She just told us that the engagement is off for the time being and that's all.' She looked so concerned that I suddenly wished I could tell her the whole story and the truth. Blast Hattie for being such a snob or Danny for being an idiot. I had hoped that Danny, once he had got over his initial shock, would perhaps see sense but now his mother had made it much worse by getting him to promise to say nothing.

Mrs Pringle asked, 'Well, Ann?'

'The only thing I know, Mrs Pringle, is that Danny was so upset after Dad Ryan's death that it's put him a bit wrong. His dad died when he was a baby and the Ryans have aye been his family. Ma and Dad were more like his parents...' I stopped. What was I saying? If Hattie heard this she would be mad. 'Well, not like his parents but more like...' I shook my head. 'I don't know what I'm saying, Mrs Pringle.'

She looked at me, a shrewd expression on her face. 'I do know what you're saying, Ann. I think you do know what caused this break-up but you're a very loyal girl and now I've put you on the spot. I'm so very sorry.'

I was mortified. 'It's me that should be sorry, Mrs Pringle. I just hope that, given time, things will work out for them both.'

She raised her cup. 'Then let's drink to that, Ann.'

I don't remember much about the homeward journey. On all my previous visits to Maddie's house, I was always so entranced by all the lovely things that I relayed them to Granny as soon as I got home. Today, however, after my visit, I was oblivious to the warm sun and the flowery perfumes from the gardens and it was as if I walked home with my own personal black cloud over my head. I was also worried about Lily. Was she sickening for something? I hoped not as she would soon be going to school.

Dad and Rosie were both in the house when we got back.

'What did Mrs Pringle want to see you about, Ann?' he asked.

Rosie didn't know the full story so I didn't want to mention it in front of her.

I smiled. 'Och, she just wanted Lily to come

over and see Joy.'

Rosie took Lily's hand. 'You'll be staying with us tomorrow when Ann goes to see Greg.'

Lily snatched her hand away and burst into a flood of tears. 'No, no, no. I want to go with Ann. I don't want to stay here.' She threw herself down on the chair and fresh tears erupted.

We all looked at one another in amazement.

I went over to her. 'I'm just meeting Greg for a wee while, Lily, and then I'll be home to see you.'

She flung her arms around my neck. 'I want to come as well. I want to come.'

I looked at Rosie who seemed stunned. She was so good to Lily and now she couldn't understand this outburst. And neither could I.

Dad decided to be firm with her. 'Now look here, Lily, your sister is due a day out on her own and that is that.'

Lily began to cry again and I couldn't bear the sight of her pathetic sobbing. Her cotton frock was wet with teardrops and her face was red with crying. I picked her up and sat her on my knee. 'All right, Lily, you can come with me to the train station.'

Dad looked as if he wanted to say something but instead he put on his jacket and he and Rosie left.

After they had gone, I spoke to Lily. 'Now, Lily, what's brought this on? You've stayed with Rosie before and never had this carry-on. What's the matter?'

'I don't want you to leave me, Ann. I want to go with you.'

I looked at her crumpled face. 'Don't be stupid,

81

Lily, I'll never leave you. You can come and meet Greg tomorrow and you can even decide where we'll go for the day.'

This cheered her up. We decided to have fish and chips for tea and we made a quick trip to the chip shop at the top of the Wellgate. By the time we got back and laid the table she seemed to be back to normal.

The next day was as hot as the Saturday. Lily, dressed in her summer frock and sandals, was ready long before I was. I hadn't seen Greg for a couple of months and I wanted to look my best.

For some reason Lily was agitated. 'Hurry up or we'll miss the train, Ann.'

I didn't own a large wardrobe of clothes but I chose the best of what I had – a full-skirted cotton dress and white sandals. I brushed my short dark hair until it gleamed then I joined Lily at the door. She was hopping from foot to foot.

'Right then, Lily, off we go.' I knew we were far too early for Greg's train but I didn't want to upset my sister. For the life of me, I couldn't understand her strange behaviour.

The interior of Dundee West Station was cool and dim after the bright sunshine outside. We bought two platform tickets and sat on one of the benches. We had an hour to wait but Lily seemed quite happy. The station was full of people either waiting for a train or disembarking from one. The noise was incredible as the smoky steam engines chugged to and fro.

Lily was fascinated by all this activity. Another thing that entranced her was the chocolate machine and I let her put some money in it with a dire warning – 'Don't get chocolate over your clean frock.'

She promised to stay chocolate free and I thought of Greg. What would I tell him if he asked about Danny and Maddie? I would have to stick to the story I had told Mrs Pringle and I hated all this subterfuge. Still, I had no choice.

A disembodied voice crackled from the loud-speaker, announcing the arrival of the Glasgow train. Then a mighty engine appeared, pulling a string of carriages. Doors were flung open and a multitude of people stepped off. I craned my neck to try and see Greg but the milling masses made this impossible. I held on to Lily's hand in case I lost her.

'I can't see Greg,' she cried.

Neither could I. We waited until the platform cleared but there was no sign of him. My mind went numb. What had happened to him?

Lily was upset. 'He's not coming, is he, Ann?'

'Of course he is. He wrote me a letter telling me to meet him at the station.' I was confused but tried to keep calm for her sake.

Another train came and went. The platform filled up with people then went quiet again. I stood undecided for a moment then said, 'Come on, Lily, it looks like Greg's not coming.'

Her small face crumpled but I bent down. 'Maybe I've got the wrong date. Maybe it's next week I've to meet him.'

She looked alarmed. 'Can I come with you next week, Ann?'

I nodded, too upset to speak. I knew I hadn't made a mistake with the date.

The sunshine was glaringly bright when we stepped out of the station. I was mentally making up some sort of story to tell Dad and Rosie when, to my amazement, I saw Greg standing on the pavement by the station entrance.

He saw me and looked astonished. 'I've been waiting here for you, Ann. Were you in the station?'

I nodded, happiness flooding back. 'We bought two platform tickets, Greg. I thought Lily would like to see the trains.'

He seemed to see Lily for the first time. His face fell. 'Lily, have you come to meet me off the train?'

Lily jumped up and down. 'No, Greg, I'm coming with you and Ann said I could choose where we're going.'

Greg looked at me and I thought he didn't seem pleased by this arrangement. He said, 'I see, Lily. Did you not want to go with your dad and Rosie?'

Lily looked as if she would burst into tears again and I gave him a warning glance.

He smiled at her. 'I just wondered, Lily. It's wonderful that you've come to see me and we'll have a great day.'

Her face lit up and I said, 'Well, Lily, where do you want to go?'

There was no hesitation. 'On the Fifie – I want to go on the Fifie.'

I looked at Greg warily and he smiled. 'Well, then, it's the Fifie for us.'

We stood in a long queue at the office in Union Street for our tickets to cross the River Tay to Newport on the ferry. Craig Pier was packed with people all taking advantage of the lovely weather. We watched the procession of vans and motorcycles drive over the metal ramp then it was the turn of the passengers to board.

Greg had said very little during this wait and I knew he found Lily's presence a bit disconcerting. He had obviously thought we would be alone on our day together. When we climbed to the upper deck, I thought Lily would be entranced by the water and would want to watch it through the rails but she stuck to my side like glue.

'How are Glasgow and your job, Greg?'

He smiled. 'I like it and the library is a great place to work but I miss you, Ann.'

I felt myself blushing and said nothing.

He went on. 'I may be there for a while yet but it isn't permanent – maybe a year or two.'

My heart sank. Not permanent? How temporary did Greg think two years were? It seemed like a lifetime to me and I said so. He took my hand and didn't say anything else until the ferry docked at Newport.

With Lily still jammed by my side, we made our way up the narrow street to the green grassy slopes that seemed to be everyone's destination. I had made some sandwiches for a picnic plus there was a small bottle of lemonade for Lily. We sat on the coarse spiky grass and ate them in silence.

The river was beautiful in the sparkling sunshine. The city lay on the far bank in a grey smoky haze. This sprawling city was teeming with life but it all looked so peaceful from this vantage point – which was more than could be said for the large family who sat on the grass beside us. The tired-looking mother tried to keep the squabbling youngsters apart while the baby wailed loudly. The husband, looking like he had no part in this family, lay on his side, fast asleep. Every once in a while, he would open his eyes and yell at the children. 'I'm telling you to shut up or I'll throw the lot of you in the water.' I wondered if this was what marriage was all about.

Greg stood up. 'Let's go for a walk,' he suggested.

I rose stiffly to my feet and brushed the grass from my dress. We set off up the street and I had the feeling the day wasn't going well.

A small cafe lay at the top of the hill and Greg ushered us in. It was busy but the customers spoke quietly. Not like the large unruly family on the grass. I was grateful for a seat as it had been uncomfortable sitting on the hard grassy slope.

Greg took some money from his pocket and gave it to Lily. 'You go over to the counter and get whatever you like, Lily, and we'll have tea.' He turned to me. 'Is that all right, Ann?'

I nodded. Tea ... poison ... what did it matter? I was just getting over the trauma of Danny and Maddie and now something was far wrong with Lily.

There was a queue at the counter and she politely waited for her turn. I felt guilty about not wanting to take her with me. What a dreadful person I was.

Greg took my hand and I tried to explain. 'I had to bring her because she's really upset about something. I did want us to be on our own.'

'So did I, Ann, because I want to ask you something I...' He stopped when Lily appeared with her ice cream and the shop's owner carrying the tea on a tray.

Lily handed Greg his change but he let her keep it. This made her face brighten but she ate her ice cream with a solemn look on her face.

I wanted to ask him what he wanted to ask me but he didn't mention it again.

He looked at his watch. 'I have to catch the six-thirty train, Ann.'

As I didn't own a watch, I asked him, 'What time is it now?'

'Half past four.'

'Well, we'd better get the next boat back, Greg.'

We finished our tea and set off back down the hill to the pier. The ferry was just docking. We boarded it and made the return journey with Lily wedged in between us.

Greg opened his mouth to say something but decided against it. My heart was heavy. What was he going to tell me?

When we reached Craig Pier, he said, 'Let's have our tea in a restaurant.'

Lily was delighted. 'Oh, that's great, Greg! I've aye wanted my tea in a restaurant.'

I smiled at her delight. As it turned out, there weren't many restaurants open because it was a Sunday so we ended up in a fish and chip shop, in the sitting-in room. The wooden chairs were a bit cramped together but the meal was lovely and fresh. I hadn't realised just how hungry I was but the sea air had given me an appetite. Lily was the same although I did notice that Greg didn't eat all his meal. Had he lost his appetite because of the day's events?

After the meal Lily made signs that she needed the toilet but she didn't want Greg to know. I noticed the sign on the faraway door and I pointed this out to her. She didn't want to go on her own but I whispered to her, 'You'll be going to the school in a couple of weeks so you'd better get used to going on your own.'

She made a great show of not wanting to go but nature took over and she ran towards the door.

I decided to take the bull by the horns. 'What did you want to say to me when we were inter-rupted, Greg?'

He put down his knife and fork and looked at me. 'I was just going...' Suddenly Lily was back at the table. He laughed out loud and it was good to hear him sound so joyous. 'That must have been the quickest wee-wee on record, Lily.'

She looked embarrassed but she did smile at him.

We then set off for the station. When we got there, the three of us went on to the platform to await his train.

Greg spotted the chocolate machine. 'Go and get a bar of chocolate to take home, Lily.'

What a gourmet day out she was having, I thought.

He turned quickly to me. 'I was going to ask you to marry me, Ann, and come to live in Glasgow. It'll only be for a couple of years then we'll be back in Dundee.'

I was taken aback but delighted with his pro-posal. Then I remembered Lily. 'I can't go off and leave Lily on her own, Greg – much as I would like to be married to you. You do understand?'

He nodded. 'I know. Today has shown me that she does need you.'

I had tears in my eyes. 'I've got to stay with her till she's old enough to fend for herself.'

'I did think your dad would have married Rosie by this time.' Greg seemed perplexed by this omission on Dad's part.

'I mean, if you were working here, then it would work but I can't leave – at least not yet.'

He squeezed my hand. 'I understand, Ann, but I'm going to ask you again at some other time and I hope you'll say yes.'

My heart soared at this. I thought my refusal was the last I would see of him. 'Oh, Greg, I hope you do and that I can say yes. Does that mean we'll still be writing to each other?'

'Oh, I hope so. This is just a hiccup and we'll be together in the future – I just know it.'

Before I could answer, Lily was back and Greg's train was being announced. He waved from the window as the train departed into the distance and I waved back until my arm was sore and he was merely a distant blur in the golden sunshine.

Lily and I set off for home. I wasn't going to tell a soul about my proposal. It was my secret. I also wondered if Dad would ever ask Rosie to marry him – I knew it would be the answer to her prayers.

A couple of weeks later, Lily went to the school. On that first morning, I collected her at the Overgate and delivered her in front of the gate of Rosebank School. She was still in her clinging frame of mind and I hadn't been able to get to the bottom of it.

She clung to me at the gate. 'I don't want to go, Ann.'

I knelt down beside her. 'Of course you want to go, Lily. You've talked about nothing else for months.'

'But I don't want to go now.'

'Look, Lily, I'll be here at four o'clock to meet you when you come out.'

She gazed at me with dark solemn eyes. 'Promise me and cross your heart.'

I promised her. She reluctantly stepped towards the gate where another little girl was also hesitating.

Her mother urged her, 'On you go, Janie. Look here's another wee lassie. Take her hand and you can both go in together.'

Lily looked dubious but the woman placed Janie's hand in hers. The woman looked at me. 'I'm sure your mother doesn't mind, do you?'

She thought I was Lily's mother.

'No, I don't mind.' I gave Lily an encouraging wave. 'I'll see you at four o'clock.'

The two girls looked backwards for most of their journey across the playground but soon they were whisked away into the school.

The woman sighed deeply. 'Well, that's one down and five more to follow.'

I looked at her with amazement. 'Five more children under five?'

'Aye, two sets of twins and I'm expecting again.'

I went home, shattered by this news. I thought I was hard done by but there were lots of women who had no lives except having children and living on the poverty line.

I was back at the gate before the school got out. I was afraid to be late in case Lily got upset again. Something was bothering her and I hadn't been able to find out the reason. Because of this, I tried to keep our routine the same every day to make her feel secure. There was no sign of Janie's mother and I wondered if this would upset her. I also wondered whether we should take Janie home if her mother didn't come to the gate to meet her.

Within minutes, a small crowd had gathered at the gate and the children emerged into the warm sunshine. I saw Lily with Janie and both girls looked apprehensive. I called out and Lily ran over with her friend at her side. I was on the point of asking Janie if she wanted to walk home with us when a thin, scrawny-looking man, about five foot three inches tall and dressed in a grubby cardigan and baggy trousers, appeared. He called out to Janie and she began to run towards him. I almost pulled her back until she said, 'Hullo, Daddy. The school was great fun and I've made a new pal. Her name is Lily and here she is.'

We were duly introduced to him and I felt uncomfortable because I was a good three inches taller than him. Still, this didn't seem to bother him and he grinned at me. Showing a row of brown teeth. I kept thinking of his wife and all her twins and thought that fathers certainly came in all shapes and sizes.

Lily was in a good mood and she chattered all the way home about her first day at school. 'We got to play with Plasticine and we got our dinner in a big room.'

'What did you get for your dinner?'

'Mince and tatties and rice pudding.'

'My word, Lily, you had a better dinner than me – I had a cheese piece.'

'We're going to do our sums tomorrow and get our reading books and I think the dinner will be even better.'

I breathed an inward sigh of relief. Lily's first day at school seemed to have been a great success. Maybe now her strange behaviour would pass. Then, when we were almost at the house, she gripped my hand. 'You'll be at the school tomorrow, Ann? You'll take me there and be at the gate when it's finished?'

'Of course I'll be there, Lily. When have I ever told you a lie?'

She smiled and seemed happy with my response. Perhaps, I thought, this insecurity was all part of growing up. Had I been the same at her age? I couldn't remember.

Joe arrived at the house that evening. He was now nicknamed Cassandra because of his dire prophecies – his doom-laden statements about Hitler and Mussolini. Then there was the Spanish Civil War which he said was a forerunner of another world war.

His words fell on my deaf ears because I was more interested in the great royal romance. Connie seemed to have lots of information about it although the newspapers didn't print much. Working in the paper shop kept me up to date with all the world events and Connie always remarked every morning, 'Now what is the big story on the planet this morning?' She would scan the headlines before remarking on some event like the Olympic Games. 'I see Jesse Owens has won loads of gold medals at the Olympic games in Berlin. I hear that Hitler wasn't keen to give him his medals. He's got a bee in his bonnet about folk not being pure and Aryan. He's banned Jews from taking up public office jobs. Aye, it's the Jews today but it'll be somebody else's turn tomorrow.'

I was shocked by her statement and I was growing tired of Joe's incessant talk about the world situation. Still, it was the big romance that had captured all our imaginations – so much so that even the Jarrow hunger march almost went ignored in the tiny shop. Then, one day, the headlines were full of the so-called secret love between the new King and Wallis Simpson.

Connie remarked dryly, 'Aye, it'll be a wedding soon because she's just got her divorce.'

I thought it was all so romantic and I missed Maddie so much during this time. We could have spent hours discussing it.

We were now into December and I was dreading the winter months. Lily had settled in her school all right but it was hard going. With all the running back and forth between the Overgate and our house, I felt I was never off the road. It was fine in good weather but I didn't relish having to take her out in all the bad weather. She was a healthy little girl but I always worried about her.

On the eleventh of December, Connie was almost beside herself with excitement. I was barely in the shop that morning when she said, 'Ann, we'll have to listen to the wireless tonight because the King is going to make a speech. I think he's going to tell us about his engagement to Wallis Simpson.'

I knew there had been loads of speculation about a royal crisis but this was something new.

'Now mind and put on your wireless,' she reminded me when I was finished my work.

It was raining hard when I ran home and my feet got wet. I had so much to do in the house but putting the fire on was my first task. As soon as it was ablaze I sat down to warm my feet and, although I didn't feel tired, the warmth from the flames must have put me to sleep. I woke up at four o'clock in a panic. Lily would be standing at the gate, wondering where I was. I dashed out without putting on my stockings and I ran all the way to Tulloch Crescent and the school.

The street was deserted and all the parents had gone. There was no sign of Lily. My heart was in my mouth and I felt sick. Where was she? I ran into the empty playground but the janitor told me that everyone had gone home, that he hadn't seen a little girl on her own.

I ran back up the house but there was still no sign of her. Then I remembered Janie. Had she gone home with her? I knew she lived in Dallfield Walk but I didn't know the number of her house.

I ran back down the road. The janitor was still in the playground and he gave me an open-mouthed look as I charged past. There was a tiny shop at the top of Dallfield Walk. A tall, thin man in a grey overall came through from the back shop and it was at this point that I realised I didn't even know Janie's surname. Whenever Lily spoke about her friend, it was always 'Janie did this' or 'Janie said that.' The man was waiting patiently at the counter.

For a moment, I almost turned and walked out but panic took over. 'I'm looking for a family that lives in this street. I don't know their surname but they have a wee lassie called Janie and two sets of twins. Do you know them?'

The man smiled. 'I'm sure the entire world knows them, lass – especially with all those bairns which I'm sure is some kind of record in the bairns' stakes.'

I didn't have time to chat so I was a bit abrupt. 'Can you tell me where they stay, please?'

If he had noticed my sharpness, he made no mention. He said, 'It's right at the bottom of the street – the very last close.'

I thanked him and ran off down the steep slope. Then I remembered how stupid I had been. I still didn't know their surname and judging by the number of doors on each landing, quite a few families lived in this close. I knocked at the first door.

An old woman peered out, suspicion written all over her face. 'Aye, what do you want?'

I explained my mission and she pointed up the stairs. 'It's the Baxter family you want.' She then shut the door quickly in my face. I felt like a cat burglar who hadn't been successful.

I ran up the stair and knocked on another door. There was no name-plate but I could hear children squabbling. Mrs Baxter came to the door. I hadn't seen her at the school gate for some time and the reason soon became clear. She was enormous, her thin smock barely covering her swollen belly. She didn't recognise me at first until I explained who I was.

'Did Lily come home with Janie, Mrs Baxter?'

She looked puzzled. 'No, she didn't. My man picked Janie up but he didn't mention your wee lassie.'

She still thought I was Lily's mother but I didn't have time to explain. 'It's just that I was late and, when I got to the gate, Lily was gone.' I was almost in tears.

'Och, you poor lassie,' she said. 'Come away inside and we'll ask Janie if she saw her.'

The room was tiny and it was clear there wasn't enough room for all its occupants but everything was clean and reasonably tidy. I could see through an open door to the back room and it seemed to consist of beds and cots.

Janie was reading a comic by the side of the fire.

'This is Lily's mother and she can't find her. Did you see where she went after the school, Janie?'

Janie shook her head. 'No, Mum.'

My heart sank. 'Where could she be?'

Then Janie said, 'I heard her say she was going to her Granny's house because she couldn't see her sister at the gate.'

Mrs Baxter was puzzled again. 'Her sister?'

'Aye, I'm not her mother, Mrs Baxter – I'm her sister.'

I was filled with dread. Surely Lily didn't go all the way to the Overgate on her own? She would have to cross the busy Victoria Road plus the other crossings at the foot of the Wellgate and Reform Street.

I thanked them and ran out. I knew Lily could manage to find her way to the Overgate because we walked there every day but I was afraid because she was on her own for the first time in her life. What had made her do a stupid thing like that?

There was a short cut I often used in the early days and I set off down Irvine Place and out into Ward Road then skirted around the High School before darting down a narrow lane that led on to the Overgate. By the time I reached the house my heart was pounding and I was sweating. I rushed in, fully expecting to see Lily with Granny. I was disappointed and I almost cried when I saw Bella sitting with a cup of tea in her hand.

Before I could speak, she snapped, 'About time you showed up. Having your auld granny trailing up the road with that sister of yours.' She was obviously annoyed at having her tea interrupted.

'So Granny has gone to the Hilltown with Lily?'

Bella grunted with annoyance. 'I've just told you that. Your granny wasn't expecting her to burst in like that, crying and wailing. In my opinion it's a skelp on the erse that bairn needs and not all this attention lavished on her. I mean, here I am, an auld woman and does anybody bother about me? No they don't.'

I was so angry but I didn't have time to argue with her. 'If Granny comes back then tell her I was here and I'm on my way back home.'

I ran all the way home, not taking any short cuts this time. If they were headed this way, then I would meet them. But, to my relief, they weren't on the street and I found them both in the house. Lily sat at the table, her face puffy and streaked with tears. She was eating her tea and Granny was putting the fire on. I realised it had gone out because, in my haste, I had forgotten to bank it up with coal.

Lily didn't look at me when I walked over. 'Where did you go? Did you go straight to the Overgate, Lily?' Worry made my words come out harshly and she burst into another flood of tears and large wet teardrops were falling into her plate of sausages.

Granny and I both gave her a hug. I said, 'I'm not getting on to you, Lily, but I was worried about you. What made you run off to the Overgate?'

'You didn't come for me and I was left on my own,' she sobbed. 'So I just went to see my granny.'

I wiped her face. 'Now listen, Lily, I was just a wee bit late but you're not to run off like this ever again. Is that clear?'

She nodded, her face a picture of despair.

'Well, then, eat up your tea and we'll both go back with Granny.'

I went over to the fire which was now blazing merrily. Granny handed me a cup of tea but gave me a warning look that said, 'Not now.' I sat down gratefully on the fireside chair.

As usual, Granny was a tower of strength. She put Dad's dinner on the stove, wrote him a brief note to say we were all at her house and then we departed for the Overgate once again.

'You can have your tea with Grandad and me, Ann.'

I was exhausted and I realised I hadn't eaten since my sandwich at dinnertime. When we arrived back at the house I was glad to see that Bella had departed.

'Away you go upstairs and play with your pal – she's expecting you,' Granny said to Lily.

After she left the room, I turned to her. 'There's something far wrong with Lily. She never used to be so clingy as this, Granny.'

She agreed. 'I think she's had a fright of some kind. Leave it with me, Ann, and I'll try and sort it out.'

Granny, Grandad and I sat down to our meal. I was starving and tired and, to my dismay, I noticed the rain battering against the window. I would get another soaking on my way home.

Granny wanted me to stay. 'You can make up the 'shaky doon' on the floor, Ann. It's not that comfy but it'll do for one night.'

Much as I hated the thought of going out in the cold rain, I declined the invitation. As I headed homewards, I made a mental promise never to be late at the school gate again. Whatever was bothering Lily seemed to hinge on her security but I couldn't think what had brought about this deep worry of being abandoned. Dad wasn't at home when I arrived so I finished off my chores and went straight to bed.

The next morning Connie was agog at the abdication speech. 'Did you listen to it, Ann?'

I felt stricken. What with all the trouble with Lily, it had gone clean out of my mind. 'No, Connie, I forgot about it.'

She looked at me as if I had taken leave of my

99

senses. 'Forgot about it? How could you forget about it?'

'It's a long story, Connie, and I don't have time to tell you about it but tell me what he said.'

Connie looked dewy-eyed. 'Och, Ann, he told the world that he couldn't be king without the support of the woman he loves. It was so romantic that I was nearly in tears.'

'It must have made Wallis Simpson feel loved and wanted to hear a man tell millions of folk that he's given up a kingdom and an empire for love,' I said.

Then the three girls from Hillside mills arrived. Sylvia was also dewy-eyed. 'Did you hear the King last night, Ann?'

Before I could answer, Connie butted in. 'No, she didn't. She was busy.'

Edith was astonished. 'Busy? You mean too busy to listen to the speech?'

I was getting a bit fed up by this now but I was also angry with myself for missing it. I had followed the story so avidly when it had finally burst on to the newspapers' front pages.

Amy said, 'Just give us our usual, Ann.' She turned to her companions. 'Well, that lets us off the hook. He'll not need a wife now that he's in love with Wallis Simpson. Just imagine – this will be her third marriage. Some women have all the luck!'

Connie said cheerfully, 'That's what I said to Ann.'

'Aye,' said Sylvia, 'here's us lot – five women and not a bloke between us.'

They all laughed as Connie shouted after them,

'How do you know that I've not got a bloke tucked away someplace? I've had my moments I can tell you young things.'

'Was that at the beginning of the century, Connie?' said a voice floating in through the open door.

The entire morning was filled with gossip about the King's speech. Everyone who came into the shop had heard it and it appeared that I was the only person in the country to have missed it.

During a rare quiet moment that morning, I thought what a strange year it had been. It began with one king's death and ended with another king's abdication. And the year wasn't quite over yet. I wondered what other dramas might lie in store.

Imagine a king giving up his throne, his country and his empire for the sake of the woman he loved. Who, without her support, couldn't carry on with the heavy responsibility of duty. Would Greg give up his job in Glasgow for me? And another thought; would Dad give up everything for a woman he loved?

Then I realised I was too tired to care.

4

It was eight o'clock on Hogmanay and Dad was out. After finishing his tea, he got himself togged up for the night's festivities and had disappeared with Joe and a few other cronies.

Lily and I were in the throes of the New Year clean. This was a ritual that Granny and my late mum always tackled before the midnight chimes – the thorough cleaning of the house. Lily had the polish and duster while I was on my knees scrubbing the kitchen linoleum. Lily seemed quite happy but she was still clingy and we hadn't been able to get to the bottom of it although Granny had tried hard enough.

I had just risen to my feet when someone knocked on the door. Lily rushed to open it and I almost collapsed in astonishment when I saw Maddie on the doorstep.

I ran forward. 'Och, Maddie, it's great to see you...' I stopped.

She wasn't alone. I saw a tall young man at her back. The light from the stair lamp was dim but I knew it wasn't Danny. Then I noticed they were both dressed to the nines while I resembled Cinderella. Not quite sackcloth and ashes but not far from it.

'Come in, Maddie. How are you?'

They both stepped into the kitchen which, thankfully, was clean and smelling fresh. The light in the kitchen was also better and I saw the extent of their finery. Maddie was dressed in a lovely blue satin evening gown which hugged her slim figure. She was as lovely as ever and once more I mentally scolded Danny for letting her go. The young man looked ill at ease in his dark suit and highly polished shoes while I was conscious of my old frock and dingy-looking apron. And I knew my hands were perfumed with carbolic soap. Still, I could hardly vanish into the bedroom and get changed.

Maddie and her companion sat down and she introduced him. 'Ann, this is Colin Matthews. He's come to work in Dad's office and he's taking me to the New Year Ball in the Queen's Hotel.'

I smiled at him and he shyly smiled back. I liked him but the question was, did Maddie also like him? Well, I thought, it's Danny's own fault.

I jumped up. 'Would you both like some tea or a wee sherry?' I had bought a bottle of sherry and one of whisky in case any of the neighbours came first-footing. But that wouldn't be tonight because Lily and I were planning on bringing the New Year in with our grandparents.

Colin didn't say anything but Maddie said no. They had only a few minutes to spare before setting off for the hotel.

'I just wanted to see you both again as it's been such a long time since we've spoken.'

I was almost crying but had to hold back the tears. 'Och, Maddie, it's great to see you again because I've missed you.'

She nodded and I saw that she was almost in tears herself. 'Ann, I have a whole Saturday off at

104

the end of January. I'll come here and we'll take Lily to our teashop in town and we'll have a good old blether as well. What do you say?'

'That would be great, Maddie, and I look forward to it.'

Meanwhile, Lily was sitting there, her eyes like saucers with excitement. She couldn't take her eyes away from Maddie's frock.

'I love your frock, Maddie. Has Joy got one like it?'

Maddie smiled. 'Well, Lily, not quite the same but she has one the same colour.'

Lily looked wistful and I knew she was dying to touch the shiny fabric because she was sitting on her hands, which was a sure sign she wanted to feel something. This was a habit I had taught her when she was young. 'You can't touch everything you see so, if you're tempted, then just sit on your hands.'

Maddie stood up. 'We'd better get going, Ann and Lily. Have a lovely New Year and I'll see you on the last Saturday of January.'

Colin also stood up and I had a sudden thought. 'How did you get here, Maddie? Surely you didn't come along the wet streets in that bonny frock?'

She laughed and I was suddenly reminded of our very first meeting in 1931. That had also been on Hogmanay.

'No. Colin is driving Dad's car. We've left it outside.'

'What? At the bottom of the close?'

She nodded. Lily was through the door in a flash and by the time we emerged she was standing on the wet pavement. The car, an Austin, was parked on the steep slope under a gas lamp. People passing by were turning to stare at it. Curiosity was stamped over their faces and their eyes almost popped when the couple emerged in their grand clothes. I don't think the Hilltown had ever seen anyone so grand looking.

'The neighbours will be thinking you're royalty, Maddie. They'll be saying, "Was that Wallis Simpson and the King in your house last night?"'

She roared with laughter. 'Surely not.'

'No I'm just joking – you're far better looking than Wallis,' I said truthfully.

'Wasn't it a lovely romantic story, Ann?' she said, looking wistful.

'Aye, it was and I was just thinking how great it would be if we could have got together to discuss it, Maddie.'

Her smile disappeared and she took my hand. 'I know. Now you will meet me at the end of the month?'

'Of course I will. Now away you both go and enjoy yourselves at the dance.'

I watched as they both got into the car and with a quick wave they were gone. Meanwhile Lily was still jumping up and down with excitement.

'Can I have a braw frock like that when I grow up, Ann?'

I smiled at her childish delight. 'Of course you can but let's get out of this awful wet night.'

For some reason I didn't immediately follow her up the stairs but remained standing on the pavement, watching the rear lights of the car as it disappeared down the hill. I glanced across the road and got another surprise. Standing in the darkness across from me was Danny. Although his face was in the shadows I noticed his bright red hair. I called to him but he didn't come over. I called again, 'Danny, is that you?'

There was no reply. Right, I thought, I'm going over and I'm going to pull him out of his hiding place. As I set off across the street, a crowd of men emerged from the pub opposite. They were either full of beer or high spirits or maybe both because they strung out in a long snake-like line, singing and dancing. I stood back to let them pass and, by the time I reached the other side, there was no sign of Danny.

I was angry and frustrated with him. Then a thought struck me. Had he seen Maddie with another man? It all depended on how long he had been in those shadows. Damn, damn, damn him, I thought. Then I realised I was standing in the wet drizzle with no coat on and my dress was soaked. I ran back towards the house. Lily was putting her polish and duster away and I was aware of a fainter, more expensive perfume – obviously Maddie's.

Lily didn't mention Danny so, thankfully, she hadn't seen him. In fact, if I hadn't lingered to see the car go away, then I wouldn't have seen him either. Had he been on his way to see us or merely passing? Was he on his way to see another girl and that was the reason he had ignored my call? I was getting in a tizzy over this and I still had the wet frock clinging to my body.

'Let's get ready to go to the Overgate, Lily,' I said, pulling the wet garment over my head.

I had bought Lily a lovely woollen dress to wear for tonight but it wasn't in the same class as Maddie's blue satin one. As she put it on, she sighed. 'I really like this frock, Ann, but it's no' like yon bonny blue frock that Maddie was wearing.'

'I know, Lily, but a blue satin frock wouldn't keep you warm, would it? I mean it's fine for a dance but you couldn't wear it to the school.'

'No I suppose not.'

Although I had my nest egg, I was wary about using money from it too often. Lily had a good many years ahead of her and I would need every penny of it to keep her clothed and shod. My dress was quite old but it was still in good condition. It was a deep chocolate-brown colour and very plain. I looked like Cinderella compared to Maddie in her beautiful creation but it was good to see her again. Did her young companion think we were uncouth people? Then I remembered his shy smile and I thought not.

I couldn't get Danny out of my mind. What was he doing skulking across the road and then fleeing like some dispossessed refugee when approached? I also hoped Dad wouldn't drink too much tonight. He had certainly started early enough but I also hoped he would be with Rosie.

Lily arrived in the bedroom. She was ready to go and she even had her coat buttoned up to her neck. As we were leaving she said, 'Why is Maddie with somebody else and not with Danny?'

Why indeed. 'She's just going to a dance with Colin. You heard her – he works with her dad in his office.'

'Does Danny not mind?'

'Well, Maddie and Danny have agreed to wait until her exams are over before they make any plans, Lily.' I hoped this would satisfy her and keep her quiet on this thorny subject.

'Does that mean I'll not be a flower girl at the wedding?'

'Och, I don't know, Lily. Better wait till you're asked.' If I sounded harsh, she didn't say but she didn't mention the matter again and we set off towards Granny's house.

People had started to congregate around the City Square and all the barrows were in place. They had a huge selection of fancy hats, hooters and calendars piled high on each barrow. There was also a large amount of dressed herrings – poor wee fish dressed in crêpe paper coverings similar to frilly dresses.

Lily's eyes were like saucers. 'Can I buy something, Ann? Please?'

'What do you want?'

She inspected the entire contents of every barrow before making up her mind. As I waited, I recalled the one and only time I had brought in the New Year in the Square. It had been the Hogmanay after Mum's death and I had been with Maddie and Danny. How long ago it seemed.

Lily had decided on her purchase. 'Can I have a hat, please?' She chose a garish-yellow hat with a motto pinned to its brim.

'Take a calendar for Granny and something for Grandad.'

She chose a calendar with a cute-looking Scottie dog and a dressed herring.

When we reached the house I was dismayed to see Bella sitting with Granny. There was no sign of Grandad.

I had made up my mind to keep quiet about Maddie's visit, at least for the time being, and the sight of the gossip-loving Bella reinforced this – but I hadn't reckoned on Lily.

The minute our coats were off, she launched into the story of the evening dress. 'Och, Granny, you should have seen it – it was lovely. I'm getting one like it when I grow up.' She looked at me. 'Ann says so.'

Before I could answer, Bella butted in. 'So she's shown her face at last, has she? Snobby wee besom turning our Danny down like that.' She looked at Lily. 'What else happened?'

Being a child, Lily was full of the event. She gladly chattered on. 'She was with a man called Colin who works in her dad's office and they're going to a ball in the Queen's Hotel. They came in a car and we went down the stair to say cheerio to them because they didn't want to be late for the ball.' She finally stopped and beamed at us.

'You're quite the wee parrot, aren't you?' said Bella, snapping at her, which annoyed me because she had asked for the details from her.

Lily went quiet and went to sit in the corner by the fire with her book. I was mad at Bella for taking all the pleasure of Maddie's visit away from Lily. What right did this crabbit old woman have to chastise a child? Because of my anger I was frightened to say anything in case I went too far. Instead I asked Granny, 'Where's Grandad?'

She was setting the table with a plate of shortbread and sultana cake. Getting ready for the crowd of first-footers who would come streaming through the door after midnight.

'He's gone to the pub down the road with some of his cronies. He hardly goes to the pub these days because he doesn't like the cigarette smoke. It makes him cough for days after.'

I was glad he was out with his old pals and I just wished that Granny could also have a break but Bella never once offered to do anything. It was the same on all her visits. She commandeered the best chair then did nothing but complain and criticise.

I noticed the house had been cleaned in preparation for the New Year and I thought Granny looked tired. Still, it was difficult to tell with her. We had all relied on her strength over the years and I hoped she wasn't doing too much.

Lily was still sitting very quietly. I went over and noticed she was silently crying. I knelt down and put my arms around her. This made her sobs vocal.

Granny came over and asked, 'What's the matter, my wee pet? What's wrong with you?'

She continued to cry but said nothing.

I said, 'Tell us what's wrong, Lily. We can't help you if you don't say a word, can we?'

Before she could answer, Bella snapped, 'For heaven's sake, stop fussing over her. It's aye the same – "Lily what's wrong?" or "Lily what's the matter?" Just let her cry if she wants to. That's my advice.'

I spoke without thinking and I was angry. 'Well, Bella, we don't need your advice. It's Granny and me who are bringing up Lily and I don't see you helping very much.'

Bella seemed outraged by my tirade. To tell the truth, I hadn't meant to be so harsh with my words. Bella glared at me and said huffily, 'Well, it'll be a different matter when you're married to your young man – who'll look after her then, tell me that?'

Lily burst into a fresh bout of tears and clung to me.

I was annoyed by Bella's outburst but she was well known in the family for coming out with the wrong thing at the wrong time.

Before I could answer, she snapped, 'I just told your sister that she'll have to go into a home when you get married. You can't expect your granny to work her fingers to the bone for the two of you.' She sat back in her chair, well pleased with herself.

I looked at Granny and we both realised at that moment the reason for Lily's insecurity. It was this stupid woman's remarks.

Granny's face was white and I knew she was beside herself with anger. She marched straight up to Bella. 'How dare you speak like that to a wee lassie? Especially when it's none of your ruddy business. You've aye had a selfish streak Bella and, if the world is not revolving around you, you don't like it.'

Bella stood up. 'I'm not putting up with this. I'm leaving.' But she stood still as if hoping Granny would persuade her to stay.

Instead, Granny said, 'Right, Bella, I'll get your coat.'

As Granny went into the lobby, I comforted Lily. 'Now listen to me. Bella had no right to tell you all that nonsense, Lily. I'm not getting married to Greg – at least not just yet – and I'll aye be here for you. Do you understand that?' She nodded and I continued, 'I'll be here until you're grown up and then it'll be your turn to leave me.'

Her grip tightened around my neck and she put her wet face against mine. 'Och, Ann, I'll never leave you – never!'

I said, 'Well, then, that's settled – we'll never leave one another.'

She gave me a watery smile.

Meanwhile Bella was still on her high horse. She was either waiting for her coat or an apology. Granny appeared with the coat. She stomped out of the house in high dudgeon, vowing never to darken the door again.

After her departure, the room became quiet. Granny went over to the table and returned with a plate of shortbread and cake. She then brought over the bottle of sherry and two small glasses. 'Speak about families at war. Now I know where Hattie gets her nature from.' She looked at Lily. 'Go and get your bottle of cordial, wee lass.'

Lily ran to the cupboard and came back with her blackcurrant cordial and a tumbler. Granny filled the sherry glasses and passed the plate around. 'Let's bring in the New Year early, Lily. I feel I need this sherry to calm me down. What a year it's been! Nothing but trouble but let's hope next year is better.'

We raised our glasses to that. I planned to tell

her about my sighting of Danny but that could wait. So we sat in companionable silence and sipped our drinks. Lily's face was still tearstained and she looked so solemn. I gave her a huge wink and she burst into peals of laughter.

'Away and wash your face, Lily,' said Granny. 'We don't want you looking like that when the bells ring, do we?'

Lily went over to the sink by the window.

'And another thing, we want to hear you laugh more and you've not to listen to folk like Bella ever again.'

'Granny's right, Lily, and, if I'm ever a wee bit late at the school gate, you've to stay where you are or go home with Janie if you're asked.'

She nodded happily. All her little dark clouds now vanished. I just wished she had told me earlier about her worries.

A sudden noise erupted from the street. There was the sound of people's voices and the rasping sound from hundreds of hooters. It was midnight.

'Happy New Year to you both,' said Granny. 'We're now into 1937.'

There was a knock on the door. Granny smoothed her hair and removed her apron. She then went to welcome her first-foot.

To her utter amazement it was Bella.

'I've come to say sorry for what I said. I didn't mean it, Nan.'

Granny hugged her. 'Come away in, you daft beggar.'

Bella looked contrite when she came into the room.

Granny said, 'Bella has come to say sorry to us

114

and I think we should accept her apologies. What do you say, Lily?'

Lily was confused by being in this sudden spotlight. She glanced at me but Bella said, 'I should never have said what I said and I'm sorry.'

It was then that I suddenly saw her for what she was – a sad, lonely old woman and, although I was still annoyed by all the worry she had put Lily through, her apology had to be a first in that we could ever recall. There was hope for her yet.

I spoke for both of us. 'Thank you, Bella, we both accept your apology but it's not to happen again. I'm not planning on leaving – either now or in the future – and Lily knows this.'

Bella fell into her chair and Granny offered her some shortbread and a sherry. Then a loud knock on the door startled us.

'Oh my God!' said Granny. 'What a racket!'

It was Dad and Grandad with a crowd of their pals. I noticed Joe amongst them and I hoped he wouldn't go on about Germany. He made a beeline for Bella. Birds of a feather, I thought, but they both seemed to enjoy each other's company. Bella could rabbit on about her bad health while Joe gave his dire prophecies of another war.

I then noticed that Dad wasn't with Rosie and my heart fell. I had hoped he would take her out this Hogmanay and I even harboured notions that he might propose to her at this time. After all, it was a favourite time for marriages and announcements of betrothals.

Rosie and her mother Alice soon put in an appearance from next door and, although Dad spoke to them both, he didn't leave the company of his friends.

Rosie moved over to my side and my heart sank even further when I saw how she was dressed. I knew my wardrobe was hardly Coco Chanel but Rosie didn't seem to have the knack of wearing anything that matched. She looked like an over-stuffed sofa. Her shapeless green dress was covered by an equally shapeless brown cardigan. She wore thick lisle stockings and her shoes could only be described as sturdy and sensible. Her hair was tied back in a large bun at the nape of her neck and, as usual, strands kept escaping from the thick net. The sad thing was that she was quite a good-looking woman but not when she looked like this. She gave me such a lovely smile and I felt so sad.

Dad was very fond of her as she was such a lovely person. But Connie, who really knew men, always said it was the outer wrapping that men went for – no matter how shrewish or sharp was the core.

Rosie had been talking and I realised with a feeling of guilt that I hadn't been listening. She gave me a prod. 'What do think, Ann?'

I stared at her. What was she talking about?

'Ann, do you think your Dad likes me?'

'Of course he does, Rosie. Why are you asking?'

She blushed a deep shade of red. Although she was in her forties, it gave her a girlish, naive look and I suddenly felt so sorry for her. If I could have given Dad a sharp kick at that moment, then I would have gladly done it.

She lowered her voice although it was hardly necessary with all the loud merriment in the room. 'If I tell you something, Ann, will you keep it to yourself?'

For a brief wild moment I thought Dad had already proposed to her. I nodded eagerly.

'Well, I've just been thinking that I'm not going to wait any longer on your Dad asking me to marry him.'

She stopped and bit her lip while my mind was in a turmoil. Was Rosie telling me she had found someone else?

She glanced around the room as if umpteen pairs of ears were listening. When she was satisfied they weren't, she went on, 'It's like this. We're now at the end of another year and there's been no approach from him so I thought I would take the bull by the horns and ask *him* to marry *me*. I'll do the proposing.'

I was so astonished that I almost burst out laughing but her face was deadly serious.

'I work with this pal of mine in the mill and she was telling me that, one Hogmanay, she asked her bloke to marry her because she was fed up waiting for him to make the first move.'

'And did he marry her, Rosie?'

Her face lit up. 'Aye, that's the best part. Seemingly he was too shy to ask her and he was glad she had taken the initiative. She told me that's what I should do.'

I was very dubious. I glanced over to where Dad was standing with his pals and they were roaring with laughter. Apart from his initial greeting to Rosie, he hadn't bothered with her company all night. Quite honestly, he didn't seem to be pining away with love for her or, for that matter, too shy

117

to proclaim it.

The last thing I wanted was for her to get hurt. She was too nice a person for that. I wondered if Dad would accept her proposal. I couldn't see it. Although this was what the entire family wanted to see, I always thought, if he did marry her it would be because of friendship and affection. Was he totally and madly in love with her? Sadly the answer was no.

She was gazing at me with her clear brown eyes while trying to tuck the unruly hair back into place. 'Well, what do you think, Ann?'

What did I think? What did I know about men? Precious little which made me the last person to advise her. I wished that Connie could be here. She was a fount of knowledge when it came to people. Although never getting married herself, she had seen so many human emotions over her long years in the shop that she was an expert – at least in my opinion.

Rosie was waiting eagerly for my answer. 'I can't tell you what to do because I don't know what's in Dad's mind.' That was the truth.

'He must have given you a clue, Ann. Does he mention me a lot in the house. I mean we meet up most nights and we get on well enough. Surely he's said something to you?'

'He's never mentioned marriage to me Rosie.' Her face fell.

I didn't want to hurt her so I hurried on quickly. 'But that's not to say that he doesn't think about it himself.'

Her mind was made up. 'Right, then, that's what I'll do. I'll catch him later when he's on his own.'

Blast it, I thought. I couldn't let her make such a big mistake. Dad might accept but on the other hand he could turn her down with his own brand of humour. Knowing him, he might take her proposal with a laugh and not treat it in a serious way.

I didn't know what to do.

She smoothed her wrinkled frock and squared her shoulders.

Oh, no, she was going to tackle him now. I grabbed her arm. 'Rosie, you did ask for my advice, didn't you?'

She nodded, her eyes wary.

'Well, I think you should wait a bit longer before asking him. It may have worked with your pal but I don't think it'll work with Dad. Honestly, I think you should think it over again and bide your time – at least till next Hogmanay – and, if he hasn't asked you by then, well go ahead with your plan.'

She looked as if she was about to cry. 'Next Hogmanay, Ann. That's another year away.'

'Well, you did ask me, Rosie, and that's what I advise. For all you know, he'll maybe ask you to marry him soon. Maybe he's got something up his sleeve that we don't know about. I mean he could maybe be on the point of making a romantic proposal like the ex-King.'

Poor Rosie – her eyes were wet with unshed tears and her romantic notion of being another Wallis Simpson was dashed.

'Right, then, Ann, I'll do what you say and I just hope he'll not be long in asking me. Otherwise, I'm asking him and I don't promise to wait till next Hogmanay.'

It was the best I could hope for and, to my relief, she was no longer on the point of asking him now. Then, suddenly, I had doubts. Had I done the right thing? Maybe Dad was shy of making that first move and maybe he would have welcomed Rosie taking the initiative.

A crowd of people had just entered the room and I noticed a couple of women from the next close. Dad gave them both a kiss that looked so passionate that I was embarrassed for both myself and Rosie. Then they all laughed and I realised I hadn't been wrong in warning her away – at least for the time being.

Why did he have to be such a flirt? What he really needed in his life was a woman who would be just like him and do the same thing back – not sweet and adoring cow-eyed Rosie.

Rosie drifted off towards the crowd that surrounded Dad while I went to put Lily to her bed. She was in her element, going around the room and wishing everyone a happy New Year. Granny saw me take her towards her tiny room in the lobby and she came to give me a hand. The room, although minuscule, was functional and just big enough for her bed. It was also reasonably quiet. The noise from the kitchen seemed like the faraway sound of the sea.

Lily was exhausted. She had wanted to stay up but she was asleep in minutes.

I said to Granny, 'I don't see Hattie. Is she not coming?'

Granny shook her head. 'No, she has to work at the Pringles' house tomorrow. You know how

120

they aye have a crowd of their relations on New Year's Day?'

I nodded. How well I remembered an earlier time when Maddie was annoyed at having to play the piano to entertain them instead of coming to Lochee with Danny and me.

'Danny is not here either,' I said sadly.

'I know. I really thought we would get a visit from him as he never misses a Hogmanay at the Overgate but, to tell the truth, Ann, I've hardly set eyes on him this year.'

I told her of my earlier sighting of him. 'I hope he didn't see Maddie with Colin. I'm not sure how long he was standing across the road.'

Granny patted my hand. 'Well, we can't do any more to help him, Ann, so don't worry about it.'

But I was worried – especially when he hadn't turned up here. He always first-footed his grandparents and I couldn't remember a time when he hadn't. Was he visiting the Ryan family?

Granny was talking about Bella. 'Maybe I should have sent her packing when she came to the door but I didn't have the heart. She is my sister, after all, and we go back a long time together.'

I agreed with her but added, 'I'm not having her putting wrong ideas in Lily's head. As you know, we've had a terrible time with her and we didn't know what was wrong.'

'I'll make sure she behaves herself in the future, Ann.' She sat by the side of the bed with a strange faraway look in her eyes. When she spoke it was in a whisper. 'I'm going to tell you something that not a lot of folk know. She wasn't always like this. In fact, she was the life and soul of any party

121

and she was such a bonny lassie. Then she lost her fiancé in an accident.'

I gasped. 'I didn't know this.'

'No, she doesn't like to speak about it. He was a sailor and he was drowned on one of his voyages.'

Suddenly I felt so sorry for Bella. Miss Hood from the Ferry had also lost out on love and so had Bella. What a great shame for them both! They had both dealt with their loss in different ways. Miss Hood with her mental illness that had turned her violent and Bella who was a true hypochondriac with all the imagined worries on her shoulders.

I went to get my coat. The kitchen was still noisy with laughter and singing. Dad was in fine form but I noticed Rosie wasn't with him. I saw her sitting with Bella and they were having a great conversation by the look of it. I just hoped Rosie wasn't asking for the same advice she had sought from me. Knowing Bella, her answer would be different from mine.

Now I knew the story of her lost love I felt a deep sympathy for her and all my past annoyance of her evaporated. I went over and took her podgy hand. 'Happy New Year, Bella.' I bent over and kissed the dry skin on her cheek.

She looked astonished but her tired eyes lit up. 'The same to you and Lily.'

I thought there were tears in her eyes but I wasn't sure. I left her sitting with Rosie and I went through the door. I didn't go over to Dad because it would mean pushing past a load of people and I didn't fancy that because they were all in high spirits.

The town was still abuzz with noise and merriment. As I walked along the dark streets I kept bumping into revellers. Thankfully, they were all in good humour but I dreaded meeting any who were really drunk. As it was, I made my way safely home. When I opened the door, I saw a light and I mentally scolded myself for leaving the gas lamp on.

Then I saw him. He was sitting by the fire and gazing into the flames.

'Danny! What on earth are you sitting here for? Granny is looking for you.'

He turned away from the shadows and I was surprised by his expression. Gone was the haunted look and he seemed to be back to his old self. 'I didn't feel like celebrating, Ann. I'll go over to Lochee as usual but that's different.'

'Why is it different, Danny?'

He gave this a bit of thought. 'Well, I mean it'll be another day and I know the Ryans will not keep wishing me a happy New Year when I know it'll not be.'

I understood what he was saying. I had felt the same many a year – starting off with hopes and dreams, only to find the new year wasn't any better than the old one.

'Anyway, it's lovely to see you, Danny.' I was on the point of asking about the earlier sighting but he beat me to it.

'I didn't come over earlier because I saw Maddie.'

My heart sank. Oh no, I thought. What a disaster.

'I saw her leave with a man. They were fair togged up to the nines, were they not?'

'Maddie was going to a New Year Ball, Danny. Her parents had asked her to take Colin who's just started work in her Dad's office.'

'Colin,' he said softly.

'Aye but it's just a business arrangement, Danny. She's not in love with him.'

He changed the subject. 'I was speaking to your dad tonight and he was telling me about the horrors of the war. He told me to try and forget about my dad and start this year on a new footing.'

So Dad had kept his promise. 'That's wonderful, Danny. I'm so pleased you feel like this after all your trauma.'

'Well, your dad said the whole war was just a catalogue of horrors from start to finish and my dad was just unlucky to have met one horror too many.'

I was delighted by this news. Did it mean the engagement was on again?

As if reading my thoughts he smiled ruefully. 'You know something, Ann? I was going to get in touch with Maddie this week and beg her to forgive me and try to forget the dirty rotten thing I did to her but I see now that she's found somebody else.'

I was shocked. 'No, no, Danny, she hasn't. You've got to believe me.'

'No, it's better this way, Ann. She'll be much happier with somebody from her own class. I've aye wondered what she saw in me to tell the truth.'

I wasn't going to leave it like this. The next day,

the first thing I was going to do was visit Perth Road and tell Maddie this good news.

Danny looked at me. He knew what I was thinking. 'Now, I don't want you to interfere, Ann. I've made up my mind to let Maddie and Colin enjoy their friendship.' He looked sternly at me. 'Now promise me.'

Much against my will, I promised. I asked myself why Maddie had to turn up here tonight – and with another man.

Danny gave me a wave as he headed through the door and I had the terrible feeling that 1937 wasn't going to be a good year for any of us.

With that feeling of foreboding, I went to bed but I certainly didn't sleep.

At about three o'clock in the morning, Dad arrived with his crowd of pals and they didn't leave till daylight.

5

I met Maddie at the end of January. It was a cold wet day of squally showers with brief spells of sunshine – more like April than January I thought. Lily had wanted to come with me but she had a bad cold and Granny made her stay inside. I promised her a new colouring book and crayons on my return so she was pleased by this bribe and settled beside the fire.

Our little tearoom was full of people so we headed for the coffee lounge in Draffen's department store. I hadn't been back there since my first visit with Maddie a few years ago and I couldn't help but notice the difference in our roles. On that occasion she had been the one in charge and I had been out of my depth. Now, although she wasn't out of her depth, it was clear she relied on me to listen to her.

The waitress appeared – a small dumpy-looking woman with frizzy fair hair and round wire-framed glasses. She peered at us. Maddie took ages to make up her mind then I realised her mind was a million miles away.

'I'll have a pot of tea, Miss,' I said, in the hope of bringing Maddie from her daydream. It worked.

'Coffee please,' she said.

I could almost hear the waitress mutter about reading the menu like a book then settle on two words. However, I wasn't here to enjoy the foibles of Draffen's staff. It was a serious time and I didn't know what to say to her. I began with the infirmary. 'What are you doing now, Maddie?'

She shrugged her elegant shoulders as she slipped off the blue woollen coat to reveal a similar coloured dress underneath. It was a colour that suited her fair hair and gave her an angelic appearance.

'I'm still in the wards and I have another eighteen months to go before my final exams, Ann.' She looked unhappy. 'I have to say I get very sad at some of the cases that come in – especially the children.'

I tried to make her smile. 'Are you still getting semolina every day for your dinner? And have you made any more bloomers with the patients' eggs?'

She grinned. 'Yes to both questions.'

My reference to the eggs stemmed from her first six months in the infirmary when she had mixed up the patients' eggs which had been brought in by their visitors. One lover of a soft-boiled egg had been given one that resembled a golf ball and Maddie's mimicry of his outraged expression had me laugh. Once again I thought how long ago it seemed.

She tucked her hands on her lap like a small schoolgirl when the waitress, still muttering softly, placed our order on the table. 'Will you be wanting anything else?' she said.

I laughed. 'Och, just a rich man, a lovely house, bonny bairns and loads of money,' I said.

The waitress shook her head at us like we were

daft and went off towards another table where the occupants looked sane.

'If you marry Greg, you'll certainly not be rich,' said Maddie.

'Och, I'm just joking. Granny always says, "Marry for love and work for siller".'

'Siller?'

'Aye, it means silver – or money.'

She became serious. 'Ann, what am I going to do about Danny?'

Although I knew it was coming my mind was still in a turmoil. I longed to tell her the whole story about Danny's Hogmanay visit but I had made a promise not to interfere and I couldn't go back on that.

'Maddie, it'll just take time – believe me. I know Danny and nobody will ever tell me that he doesn't love you because I'll not believe it. I think something happened at his grandad's funeral that upset him and he's got to get over it.' There, I thought, I haven't told any secrets but maybe this will explain his odd behaviour and strange actions.

'I would wait for ever for him to come to terms with whatever is bothering him but he won't confide in me and then he breaks off the engagement so I don't know what to think. I'm so confused but I've made up my mind.'

I was suddenly afraid. 'What are you going to do, Maddie?'

She opened her small handbag which lay on her lap and she withdrew a small box. 'I'm going to return the ring,' she said simply and quietly.

'Oh, Maddie, don't do that.'

129

She shook her head. 'I have to, Ann. I can't keep it forever. Anyway, Colin keeps asking me out when I have a day off and I think he's really keen on me.'

'Oh, I see.' I didn't have an answer. 'Well, in that case, Maddie, you just have to do what you think is for the best.'

She looked so sad that my heart went out to her. Then, as if her mind was finally made up, she said, 'Right then, I'll send it back to him by registered post today.'

I felt just as sad. 'I'm really sorry it's come to this, Maddie. I really am.'

She smiled. 'I know you are, Ann, and I'm grateful that I still have you as my friend.'

We called the waitress over.

'Are you wanting your bill?'

'Yes, please,' said Maddie politely. Her shoulders shaking from suppressed laughter.

When we were outside she said, 'That waitress was a real tonic for me as I haven't smiled so much in a long time.' She linked her arm in mine. 'Come on, let's have a good look around the shops – just to cheer ourselves up.'

We spent a couple of hours together but not much more was said about Danny and, although I wanted to say so much, my mind was numb and my tongue speechless.

I bought Lily's book and crayons, explaining why she couldn't come.

Maddie apologised for not coming back to the Overgate to see her. 'I've got to get home and visit my parents and Joy. She's at a small private school and doing well. I hope Lily is getting on fine at school.'

I knew it was all small talk and the real reason she didn't want to come to the Overgate was in case she ran into Danny. But I understood and we said our goodbyes at the foot of the street.

A burst of sunshine shone in a golden glow over the wet streets but was almost immediately snuffed out by a dark cloud.

Although we made a promise to meet up again soon I had the sad feeling that it would be a long time before we saw one another again. However, we did promise to write. To keep in touch that way was better than nothing and I planned to keep her up to date with any news of the family.

As Maddie had said on parting, 'We must keep in touch, Ann – whatever happens.'

It had all seemed so final somehow and when she returned Danny's ring it would be the end of an era. But would it be the end of our friendship? The answer was that I just didn't know. I wondered what would Danny do now.

I hurried back to the Overgate to find Lily eagerly waiting for me. Granny raised her eyebrows but I decided to keep silent on our conversation – at least for the time being. I still harboured the hope that Danny would come to his senses and pay me another visit.

As it turned out, I didn't hear from Danny about the ring but Hattie burst in one night when I was at the Overgate.

'What do you think has happened?' she snapped at us.

'Your house has burned down?' said Granny, jokingly.

'Oh, it's much worse than that!' she cried. 'Maddie has returned her engagement ring to Danny. Now the engagement will never be on again.'

I was surprised – not by the ring's return but by the length of time it had taken. I had met Maddie three weeks ago and she was going to post the ring that day, by registered post. Why had it taken so long?

'Did it come by post, Hattie?'

She gave me a suspicious look. 'Do you know anything about this, Ann?' Her voice was stern.

What do I do here? I wondered. Do I tell the truth or do I lie? Suddenly I was totally fed up with all this subterfuge. In my mind, it was so unnecessary. 'Aye, Hattie, I do.'

Granny stared at me while Hattie looked dumfounded.

I explained. 'I met Maddie a few weeks ago and she was going to return the ring then. The only thing I can't understand is why it's taken so long because she was going to post it that day.'

Hattie's face turned bright red.

Granny, knowing her so well, said, 'What are you not telling us, Hattie? I know you're hiding something.'

She tried bluffing. 'I don't know what you mean.'

Granny wasn't having any of this nonsense. 'How did you find out about this if the ring was posted to Danny with his name and address on it?'

Her bravery collapsed. 'It wasn't posted. It was delivered by hand to Lipton's shop.'

132

I was stunned. Surely Maddie didn't confront Danny and hand over the ring? She had mentioned registered post to me so why had she changed her mind?

Now that Hattie's bravado was gone, she seemed quite willing to spill the beans. 'It was delivered by a company – a private courier firm – and Danny had to sign for it.'

Granny gave her a look. 'Did Danny tell you this himself?'

'No, he didn't but I found the box with the letter in his drawer.'

Granny was shocked. 'Don't tell me that you look through your laddie's things, Hattie? I mean he's a grown man now and he'll not want his mother poking her nose into his private affairs.'

Hattie flared up. Her eyes were blazing. 'I was not poking my nose into his drawer.'

But Granny was adamant. 'Well, how did you manage to find the box and read the letter?'

Hattie was furious now. 'I didn't read the letter but I was surprised to see the box. I'll admit I opened that and saw the ring but that's all. I then saw the brown envelope showing the name of the private courier and the slip showing Danny's signature so I put two and two together. I was quite upset I can tell you.'

She wasn't the only one surprised. What had made Maddie change her mind? She had certainly planned to post it that day. I was sure of that.

'But that still doesn't explain what you were doing in the first place.'

Like all guilty people, Hattie was trying to

profess her innocence. And, like the guilty, she tried too hard by talking too quickly and over-stating every sentence – even repeating herself. Her performance would have been a joy to behold if it hadn't been so sad.

'Well, it was like this...' she chattered on. 'It was like this. I got a present from Mrs Pringle. It was a pack of lavender-scented drawer linings...'

'Lavender-scented what?' asked Granny in amazement.

At any other time, Hattie would have been annoyed at her mother's lack of social skills and how unacquainted she was with gracious living but not today.

'They're scented sheets of paper for putting in your drawers. They make all the contents smell nice. Well, it was like this. I had an extra one over and I thought that Danny might like one so I cleared out his drawer in the tallboy and that's when I discovered the box with the ring.' She gazed firmly at her mother. 'But I did not read any letter. After all, that's private. Anyway, how was I to know that Maddie had returned the ring?'

Granny said, 'He probably didn't want anybody to know about it, Hattie. It's his own business.'

'His own business?' she replied in her cultured voice, her tones so clipped and precise that she could have been giving elocution lessons. 'For heaven's sake, I am his mother. Surely he could have told me?'

Granny looked a bit sorry for her. 'If I was you, Hattie, I would forget about it and make sure he doesn't get to hear of your snooping. He'll tell you in his own good time.'

Hattie was almost crying with disappointment. 'I never thought it would come to this – I thought that, after a few months, he would pull himself together and get back with Maddie. After all, that's what I had to do – put on a brave face and go back to work so why can't he? But can Danny do that? No he can't.'

I had heard enough and I wasn't going to let her run him down. 'Of course you know the reason for that, Hattie, don't you?'

She looked at me as if I had lost my senses.

I continued, 'If you hadn't made him promise not to tell the Pringle family or Maddie, then this whole sorry story would be over and done with. At the time, I advised him to tell them the truth because I don't think they would have given a toss about what happened so long ago. But, no, you made him promise to keep quiet and it's breaking him up. You're to blame, Hattie, not Danny.'

She opened her mouth to speak but no words came out. Meanwhile Granny remained silent.

After a moment or two, she made a sound, her words strangled with fury. 'My fault? My fault, indeed. It wasn't my fault but the fault of that awful Mick Malloy and his band of merry boozers. It was his fault.'

'Aye, in the beginning, Hattie, but not now. If you hadn't been so keen to keep up appearances it would have been over a long time ago. In fact, I just wish that I'd told them the truth – Maddie and her parents. If I hadn't promised Danny not to, then I would have.'

Hattie struggled into her coat.

Granny called after her, 'Now mind what I told you – don't mention what you found.' She turned to me. 'I sometimes think I'm talking to myself with that lassie – she's so pigheaded.'

'I could honestly kick Danny,' I said. 'It's been over a year since they split up and Hattie's yapping on about Maddie returning the ring. What does she think she should do? Pine away with unrequited love, for heaven's sake?'

I told Granny about Colin. 'Maddie wants to be fair to Danny. She doesn't want to go out with another man if she still has her ex-fiancé's ring, does she?'

Granny shook her head. Her eyes were sad. 'There's times when I wish that Dad Ryan was still alive then this wouldn't be out in the air. What a tragedy.'

'Aye, it is, Granny, but it's also a lesson to us all to tell the truth and not have any skeletons in our cupboards.'

She chuckled. 'Och, I don't know about that. I think most families have them – rich or poor, it doesn't matter.'

I looked at her. 'Have we got any in our cupboard?'

'No, I don't think so but I bet the auld Queen Mary is kicking herself for her ignorance of the Wallis Simpson woman. That's a real scandal in the royal cupboards.'

'Well, we now have a new King and it'll soon be his coronation. I wonder if the ex-King will marry Mrs Simpson?'

'Well, he'd better because he gave up his throne for her,' she said caustically.

Would Greg give up his job in Glasgow to marry me? I wondered. That was a thought.

After I left the Overgate, I toyed with the idea of going to see Danny but decided against it. He wouldn't mention the returned ring – I was sure of that. He had hidden it away as if the very sight of it distressed him and now Hattie had unearthed it. Would she keep quiet about it or make a fuss? Anything was possible with her in this mood.

Then, to make matters worse, Greg's letter arrived and it contained disturbing news.

He wrote, 'Danny has asked me to find out some details of accommodation here. He is hoping to get a transfer to Glasgow soon. What on earth is going on?'

What could I tell him? I didn't want to lie to him as well, as I felt my entire life was now one large untruth. Also he knew the story about Maddie and Danny and he knew they wouldn't split up over something trivial.

I wrote back with the truth – or, at least, most of it. I told him the engagement was over and I didn't elaborate. Instead I filled the letter with newsy items which I knew wouldn't fool him but I did say that he could ask Danny why he was leaving if his transfer came through. Then it would be up to him to explain.

I'd planned to see Danny that night but Lily came home from school with some sad news. 'It was twins again and Janie's mummy had the babies but they weren't breathing,' she said with tears in her eyes.

I was upset to learn that this pregnancy had

been another set of twins and, instead of meeting Danny, I decided to visit Mrs Baxter to give her my sympathy. It was dark when I set off for Dallfield Walk and the close wasn't lit when I got there. The door was opened by her husband. Inside, the room was cosy and Mrs Baxter was propped up in the bed in the corner of the room.

She looked white and ill but she perked up a bit when she saw me. 'Och, it's Lily's sister. Come away in and sit beside me.'

The smaller children were obviously all asleep because there was just Janie and an older woman by the small sink at the window.

Mrs Baxter introduced me. 'This is my mum. She's giving me a wee helping hand until I get stronger.'

Mr Baxter said, 'I'll just nip upstairs and see Mac. It'll give you a chance for a blether.' He disappeared through the door.

Janie began to howl which annoyed her granny. 'Will you just bide still till I fine-comb your hair? You know the school likes your hair to be free from nits.'

Oh, the dreaded hair lice, I thought. I was forever washing Lily's hair in Derbac shampoo while the fine bone comb was another torture as far as she was concerned – just as it was for Janie.

There was another howl as the fine-toothed comb caught on a tangle and then it was all over.

I asked Mrs Baxter how she was feeling.

'Call me Agnes,' she said. 'I'm not feeling too bad but it was an awful thing to happen. The bairns weren't premature but they didn't stand a chance with their breathing problems.' She had

138

tears in her eyes and I couldn't imagine a worse thing for a mother – to lose one child was a shame but to lose two was terrible.

Her mother called over, 'Well, Agnes, just make sure you don't have any more. You've got enough to look after and feed so send that man of yours upstairs to bide with Mac.' Although said in a joking manner, I saw that her mother had a serious look on her face.

Agnes lay back on the thin pillows. Although everything was clean, the pillowslips looked threadbare – as did most of the furnishings. The room wasn't any bigger than ours and I suspected that the back bedroom was even smaller. With all the cots and beds I had glimpsed that day, it didn't leave much room for more children.

Agnes gave a wan smile. Her white skin stretched over her cheekbones. 'Aye, I know you're right, Mum, and I don't know why all my pregnancies are twins. But enough is enough and I'm not having any more. I'm not going through that again.'

Her mum wiped her hands on a towel. 'I'm glad to hear it.'

I had brought some biscuits and a few oranges with me and I left them on the table when I left.

'I hope you feel better soon, Agnes,' I said as I opened the door.

She looked at her mother. 'I'm really lucky to have Mum. She comes in every day and gives me a help with the bairns. She lives in the next close so she's aye on hand.' Agnes lay back on her pillow as if these few words had left her exhausted.

As I walked home, I sincerely hoped that she

wouldn't have any more children. I also hoped she would soon be back on her feet again. Some people had such a hard life while others seemed to sail through it – folk like Hattie who was going on and on about a returned engagement ring like it was the end of the world while Agnes had just lost her two babies.

However, as the days slowly turned to spring, Agnes recovered. I got most of my news through Lily. According to her, Janie told her everything, including her granny's words. 'My ma's not having any more bairns because she's got enough with us,' she told Lily proudly.

Then there was the forthcoming coronation which was the main topic of conversation in the shop. Connie said, 'You should see Bernard Street, Ann. It's a wee street off the Hawkhill and they aye do the most wonderful display of decorations to celebrate any occasion.'

We planned to take Lily to see these decorations and, on the tenth of May, a couple of days before the royal event, we made our way to the Hawkhill. Lily was so excited. She chattered on and on about the king and queen and I hoped she realised that it was just the flags she would see and not the actual coronation.

Bernard Street was indeed a delight with its multicoloured bunting stretched from house to house. There were flags everywhere and, although this dark-looking street appeared to get very little sun, the effect of the streams of flags and decorations gave it a colourful festive look. It seemed as if half the population of Dundee was out viewing this spectacle because the area was

140

crammed with people. Children played on the road, where they chased each other with a great deal of noise and shouting, while the adults stood around in groups.

It got so noisy that Connie said, 'I think we'll just wander back to the shop. I've got wee Eric looking after it for a couple of hours.'

Wee Eric was one of Connie's neighbours. A tiny man, barely five feet tall, he was the same age as Connie and they had known one another all their lives. He sat behind the counter and it was impossible to see him behind the pile of newspapers. He stood up when he heard the doorbell. 'I'll get away home now, Connie – now that you're back.' He had a thin squeaky voice which somehow matched his size. He resembled a jovial gnome, all the more so now because his back was slightly hunched.

After he'd gone, Connie remarked, 'Poor soul – he can't stand upright now because of his arthritis.'

I mentioned Agnes Baxter. Connie knew everyone and Agnes was no exception. 'I feel worried about her,' I said. 'You know she lost her twins?'

Connie nodded sadly. 'Aye, I know. The poor wee mites were stillborn and that's an awful thing to happen. The poor wee things.' She hung up her coat on the hook in the back shop. 'But I wouldn't worry about her, Ann. She's got a great man and a great mother. Her man has a pony and cart and he goes around the streets collecting scrap metal and rags. You must have seen him around the streets. He gives the bairns a balloon if they bring him anything.'

I had seen him on the street but I hadn't paid much attention to the man behind the pony.

'Aye, she's got a great man in him. He takes his share of the bairns and her mother does her share so Agnes will be all right.'

'But she has all these twins in her family. She must be run down.'

Connie chuckled. 'Aye, maybe so but she must have known this was going to be her lot when she got married. Twins run in both their families. Agnes was a twin and so was her man. There was sixteen bairns in her family and fourteen in his so big families are in their blood.'

I felt better after this chat. I hadn't been able to get Agnes out of my mind since my visit. I had felt so sorry for her lot in life but I was now relieved to hear that her life wasn't all struggle and doom.

My weekly letter from Greg arrived and it still had news of Danny's hoped for transfer. He wrote, 'Danny hopes to get this transfer and, if he does, then he'll move here at the end of the year.'

My heart sank. If Danny went off to Glasgow, then I knew there would be no hope of him getting back with Maddie. Then I remembered the returned ring. Stop deluding yourself, I told myself mentally – the engagement was well and truly broken so it didn't matter where he went.

I decided to go and see him that evening. Fortunately, he was at home but, when Hattie saw me, she went white. I wondered if she would ever forgive me for my outburst. Still it had to be said – whether she liked it or not.

We decided to go out and Danny put on his

jacket. It had been a lovely sunny day but the wind was bitterly cold. I was well wrapped up in my navy nap coat but this cold wind seemed to penetrate the fabric. Danny looked chilled to the bone and, as we passed a small public house, he pulled me into the tiny snug bar.

I was mortified. There was the time years ago when I had confronted Dad in the Windmill bar on the Hilltown but, apart from that, I had never been in one.

I gave him a stern look but he said, 'Don't look at me like that. I don't come in here to drown my sorrows but it's too cold to be outside and we can't speak in front of Mum because she gets so upset.'

The small bar was empty but a barman soon poked his head through the hatch which served as a counter. Danny ordered a pint of beer for himself and a lemonade for me. We sat beside a dark, deeply scarred table that had a pattern of white rings all over its ravaged surface. There was a stale beer smell and the wooden bench was uncomfortable.

'How are you, Danny?' I tried to sound cheerful but failed miserably.

I told him about the letter from Greg. Fully prepared to defend him if Danny was annoyed at Greg telling me.

But he didn't and, instead, he said quietly, 'Do you remember Minnie MacFarlane's man? Peter got a transfer to Glasgow when they got married and she had her bairn. Well, seemingly Minnie is back living with her mother and Peter wants to come back to Dundee in the hope of a reconciliation with her and the kiddie.'

The penny dropped. 'So you want his job if that happens?'

He nodded. 'It's for the best, Ann. I don't know if Maddie told you about returning the ring?'

I didn't know what to say so I remained silent.

This seemed to unnerve him. 'Aye, she sent it back by a courier firm. It came to the shop.'

'Did that hurt your feelings, Danny? I mean, getting it back like that?'

He nodded. 'At the start it did – when the man arrived. Of course, everybody was agog with nosiness and wondering what was going on but I managed to pass it over – at least I think I did. I mean it's not every man that wants his work-mates to know he got his engagement ring back from a courier.'

'But you feel different now?'

'Aye, I do. The letter from Maddie explained everything – the difficulties of sending it by registered post. It would have to be signed for and Mum would want to know what was in the package. No, Maddie thought this was the most discreet way.'

'And now you're running away?'

He nodded. 'Aye, I am. The funny thing is that I've finally come to terms with what happened to my dad and I know that I've been really stupid. But what's done is done and there's no going back.'

'Of course you can, Danny. You were stupid at the beginning but don't remain stupid. Go and see Maddie and tell her the whole story. Please.' I looked at him pleadingly. 'Please.'

'What about Colin?'

I was exasperated. 'Blast Colin. I mean he's a nice enough lad but Maddie is not in love with him. I've said so a hundred times.'

Before he could answer, the door opened and a gust of icy cold wind swept into the tiny room. Three elderly women stood in the doorway and looked at us with astonishment. We were obviously sitting in their seats and they weren't pleased about it. I looked around and noticed there wasn't any room for them in this snug bar so we stood up.

At the doorway, we were involved in a brief crush as we squeezed through then the women made a dash for their bench. Just in case some other intruders took over their small drinking domain.

The wind felt colder than ever as we said goodbye outside the door. Before darting up the street, Danny said, 'It'll take a while for any transfer to come through so I'll not be leaving tomorrow, Ann. It'll take a wee while.'

I turned away from the wind and called after him, 'I'll see you soon then, Danny?'

His answer was swept away by a vicious gust of wind and I didn't hear his reply. For the thousandth time since Dad Ryan's death, I thought to myself what a mess this was. Still, I had one consolation – life for us as a family seemed to be going from strength to strength. Dad still hadn't asked Rosie to marry him and she was depressed by this but everything else in our garden was rosy.

That was until one lovely warm sunny day in June when Dad arrived home, his face grey and gaunt. He was also distressed and a cold feeling of dread spread over me.

'What's wrong, Dad?'

He didn't reply so I asked him again.

When he spoke, his eyes were glazed with confusion. 'It's just something that happened at work today.'

I was frightened to hear any more but I knew I had to. 'Have you lost your job?' Dad was now working full-time and what a difference it made to him and our finances.

He shook his head.

Thank goodness, I thought. 'Well, what is it?'

He hesitated, unsure how to go on. 'It's... It's...' He stopped and took a deep breath. 'It's Harry the gaffer, Ann – he's disappeared.'

'Disappeared?' I couldn't understand it. Where did people disappear to?

'Aye, he went out for a walk at dinner-time like he aye does and he never came back. There was still no sight of him tonight when we all finished work.'

'Maybe he went home?' I ventured.

Dad shook his head. 'No. The boss, Mr Pringle, went to his house and his wife hasn't seen him since this morning when he left for work.'

'Has anybody looked for him? I mean around all the places where he normally goes?'

'The police were out looking for him but they didn't find a thing.'

I could see he was terribly upset and he didn't even want his tea. Instead he said, 'I've been asked by my boss if I'll pay a visit to his wife. Will you come with me, Ann?'

I was surprised. 'Me? Why do you want me to come with you?'

A deep frown formed between his eyes. 'Well, I don't know what to say to an older woman, Ann, and I thought you might be good at speaking to her.'

'How old is she?'

'I don't really know but she'll be the same age as Harry, I expect – around about seventy.'

'He's seventy and he's still working?' I was surprised.

'Well, he's more than a gaffer, more like a manager, and he's been with the warehouse for years. He gets on very well with Mr Pringle, the boss.' He stopped and the frown reappeared. 'It's funny you should say that but he was thinking of retiring later this year. His legs are playing him up so that's the reason for the short walk every dinner-time.'

I wasn't looking forward to meeting his wife. The poor old soul would be upset and what did one tell a person in this situation? Her husband was missing but where was he? Was he lying injured in some remote spot or, even worse, lying dead?

'Do you want your tea now or later, Dad?'

'I think I'll have it later. It'll not take long to pay the old wife a visit. I was picked to do this but I think one of the older men would have been much better than me. What will I do if she's howling and crying?'

I put a thin cardigan over my working frock. It was a lovely warm evening but I didn't want the woman to think I had dressed up to bring her bad news.

147

'Where does she live, Dad?'

He scrutinised a small piece of paper. 'It's along the Chepington Road somewhere – not the D.E.C.S. bakery end but the other way.'

We set off quickly and we soon reached Chepington Road by going up Provost Road and, at the top, we turned right.

'The Soshie bakery is along that way so we have to head this way,' Dad said as he glanced at the scrap of paper again.

We walked for what seemed miles until we almost reached the Forfar Road. We had long since passed the rows of tenement buildings and we were now in a posh part of the town with its semi-detached houses and lovely gardens.

'Are you sure you've got the right address, Dad? You wouldn't think your gaffer had a lovely house out here.'

He looked puzzled. 'No, this is the right address. Mr Pringle gave it to me himself. As I said, he came out earlier but he thought one of the men should also come and I was picked.' Dad didn't seem happy about his assignment.

We walked for another hundred yards and the house stood in front of us – a sturdy-looking stone villa with a red-tiled roof and a beautiful garden. The number on the front gate was the same as on Dad's scrap of paper but we still didn't believe it.

'Just ring the bell, Dad,' I said, getting fed up with standing on the pavement like an idiot.

After a moment's hesitation, he did.

The door was opened by a fat, frumpy-looking woman whose plump face was made even plumper by her tear-stained cheeks and red eyes.

Dad said politely, 'Mrs Connors?'

He turned to me and I went up the path towards a well-painted door in a lovely shade of blue. I noticed that the window frames were also painted in this shade and they gave the house a fresh look.

Dad turned back to the woman. 'Mrs Connors?'

We were both right. She was an old woman and I had no idea what to say to her. Perhaps Dad could do all the talking.

The woman shook her head and a few chins wobbled but, when she spoke, her voice was soft and cultured. 'No, I'm not Mrs Connors,' she said and then she added, 'Can I help you?'

Dad explained his mission but said, 'If you think it's inconvenient, then we'll just go away.' This was said hopefully.

She seemed doubtful for a moment then she stood aside to let us into a large hall with a wooden parquet floor. This was buffed to a highly polished shine and it was almost possible to see your reflection in its surface. There was a most marvellous scent of roses and I noticed a large bowl of flowers on a small table by the stairs.

What a beautiful house, I thought – maybe not quite as grand as the Pringles' house but it wasn't far off it.

The fat woman showed us into a large room where the rays from the setting sun were playing against one wall. I was determined not to miss a thing because Granny liked to hear about such houses – all the lovely details. The carpet was a creamy colour as were the two large sofas and three chairs. Tall golden lamps stood on highly polished tables and there were at least another three bowls of roses.

There was a woman sitting on one of the sofas and she stood up when we entered.

The fat woman explained, 'This is Harry's wife – Margot.' She turned to the woman and said, 'This is one of Harry's workmates, Margot.' She bustled out of the room saying, 'I'll go and make some tea.'

Margot didn't seem happy but when she saw Dad she held out her hand. 'How nice of you to come Mr...'

'Johnny Neill and this is my lassie Ann.'

She gave him a wan smile but hardly acknowledged me. I studied her in detail, again for Granny's benefit. She was tall and slender and dressed in a summer frock of yellow crêpe de Chine, its rich folds moulded against her body and swayed with her every movement. She had large blue eyes and dark curly hair that was cut at shoulder length. Her bare shapely legs and trim ankles were thrust into a pair of high heeled white sandals and her toenails were painted a deep blood red. It was difficult to put an age to her. She could have been anything between thirty and sixty but, whatever her age, it hung well on her – just like the yellow frock which had a costly look.

The fat woman came back with the tea tray and I caught an angry glance in Mrs Connor's eyes before she covered it up with a charming smile.

'I haven't introduced you to my sister-in-law. This is Harry's sister, Mrs Olivia McQueen.'

Mrs McQueen gave us a tearful look. 'This is a terrible thing. Do the police have any more word on Harry?'

Dad looked embarrassed. 'I don't know, Mrs McQueen. It was Mr Pringle who suggested this visit to Harry's wife just to say how very sorry we all are about his disappearance.'

The sun had now moved around and its rays were centred behind Margot Connor's head. I was struck by the ludicrous thought that it was a blessing the sun didn't shine directly on her face because I thought she wasn't as young as I had first thought.

Mrs McQueen was desperate to find out why her brother had suddenly disappeared. 'Was he anxious about anything, Margot?'

Again that covert angry glance was quickly covered up. Margot shrugged her slim shoulders. 'Of course not, Olivia. He went to the warehouse this morning just like any other day. I think he's lying ill somewhere.'

Mrs McQueen cried out, 'Don't say that! I can't bear it.'

Dad, who was sitting on he edge of his chair, said, 'Don't worry about that Mrs Connors because the police have done a thorough search. We wondered if he was maybe away on some sort of business but forgot to tell Mr Pringle. He'll be home soon just you wait and see.'

'That's what it'll be, Olivia,' said Margot. 'He'll be home as if nothing was wrong – wait and see.'

Olivia said she was going to stay the night with Margot but Margot had other ideas. She picked up the small suitcase and handed it to her sister-in-law.

'Now you get away home, Olivia. I'll be all right here.'

Olivia began to protest but Margot was adamant. 'No, no, Olivia. It was good of you to come when I called you but you have your husband to look after and he's more important than I am.' Although said in a charming manner, it was still a brush-off and I wondered if Mrs McQueen had noticed it. If she had she didn't show it.

After her departure, Dad said, 'We'd better be on our way as well, Mrs Connors. I do hope that Harry shows up soon. I'm really fond of him because he's aye been good to me.'

Margot looked at Dad. 'Please stay for a drink. What would you like? Whisky, brandy, sherry, gin?'

How nice, I thought, to have a house like a well-stocked pub.

'Nothing to drink thanks but another cup of tea would be grand.'

She stood up and again I marvelled at her graceful moves. After a few moments, she came in with a silver tray and a silver tea service on it. She picked up the other tray and, as she took it towards the kitchen, she said, 'Olivia is very well meaning but she always uses the old china teapot. Just like they do in their own house.'

Her elegant hands poured out tea into delicate china cups and she indicated the silver milk jug and sugar bowl with miniature silver tongs.

Then later, after we made our departure, I couldn't help but remark on the gracious house. 'He must get a big pay with his job, Dad, to afford that lovely house and things like silver teapots and bowls of flowers.'

He didn't answer. I repeated my statement and he looked at me with a perplexed frown. 'What on earth has happened to Harry?' he said. 'I mean he's left that grand house and a lovely-looking wife behind. Why would he do that?'

I didn't reply because, to be truthful, there was no answer to that question. An elderly man who seemed to have everything to live for had just disappeared somewhere between the warehouse and goodness knows where. It was a real mystery.

6

Rosie was in a rage. I didn't think I had ever seen her so angry or distressed before. She burst into Granny's kitchen on a hot August evening. Her face was bright beetroot red and I saw the beads of sweat on her brow and upper lip. Her hair, untidy at the best of times, was now in total disarray. Most of it had escaped from the large bun and now hung in straggly tresses on her shoulders.

She stormed, 'Where's that father of yours?'

Granny and I were surprised by her furious tone as she was normally so soft spoken.

I replied, 'I've no idea, Rosie. We thought he was with you.'

She glared at me. 'And so did I. He was to be here for his tea and my mum has kept it hot for over two hours and now it's spoiled.'

Granny was annoyed. 'Och, he's not to take a loan of you, Rosie. Give him his marching orders.'

This sympathy was the last thing she needed and she burst into tears, all her defiance gone.

Granny nodded to me. 'Go and make a cup of tea, Ann.' And then she turned to Rosie. 'Come and sit down and calm yourself. Although I'm his mother, I swear that laddie of mine is more work than a dozen men put together.'

Perversely, Rosie wasn't going to hear a bad word against him. 'Och, he's not that bad, Nan.

It's just that he's not turning up when he says he's coming and he says he's sorry but he forgot about the arrangement. For heaven's sake, he's been coming to see me since Lily's...' She stopped and looked embarrassed. She was going to say since Mum's death.

As I looked at her, my mind kept returning to the cool yellow image of Margot Connors. Poor Rosie. She was wearing a thick woollen frock in a peculiar shade of grey which was neither dark nor light. Over this and buttoned right up to her neck was a chocolate-coloured hand-knitted cardigan. It was as if she wanted to spite the hot weather.

Thankfully, she had calmed down now and I was grateful for that because, to tell the truth, I had a good idea where Dad was and I wasn't the least bit pleased about it.

It was now the middle of August and there had been no sign yet of Harry Connors. When he had first gone missing at the beginning of June there had been a few so-called sightings of him but they had come to nothing and the trail had fizzled out. I kept asking Dad every night about him but, after all this time, we all thought he must be dead.

In fact, a few weeks ago, Dad had said, 'I think Margot – I mean Mrs Connors – knows this but she's bearing up well.'

I bet she is, I thought cynically, remembering her cool image which was in marked contrast to her sister-in-law's distress.

'How is Harry's sister, Dad?' I had asked one evening.

He was silent for a moment. Then he said, 'Well, I haven't seen her since yon first night but Mrs Connors says she's so dramatic.'

'Dramatic?'

'Aye, you know – making a mountain out of a molehill. She's aye going on about Harry being dead and we don't know this for sure and it's upsetting Mrs Connors.' Dad sounded really annoyed at Olivia.

Although I didn't say anything at the time, in my opinion Olivia was grieving for her missing brother while the cool, yellow-clad wife didn't seem to be bothering. Still, maybe I was being mean and cruel. People varied in their methods of grief. Perhaps Margot was all chewed up inside but putting a brave face on things.

Rosie stood up to go and I realised I hadn't heard a word she said because of my thoughts of another woman. Surely Dad wasn't flirting with his missing workmate's wife. I also got to my feet. 'I'll go and bring Lily in as it's time for her bed.'

Rosie stopped me at the door. 'I should have asked him to marry me on Hogmanay, Ann, but you stopped me.'

So I was the culprit now. I tried to be tactful but she was in no mood to be pacified and, to be honest, I didn't blame her. What Dad did with his own time was his business but he shouldn't be mucking Rosie around like this.

I said, 'You remember the man who went missing, Rosie?'

She nodded.

'Well, Dad has to keep in touch with his wife. He's got no option because it was his boss who

157

asked him and maybe he's got bogged down with listening to her worries and problems.'

'Aye, he did tell me about the old woman and that she needs his company but that doesn't excuse his behaviour tonight. He should have told me he wasn't coming.'

'I'll speak to him about it when I see him, Rosie, but maybe he'll turn up here full of apologies before that.'

But he didn't.

I found Lily playing with her friends in the backcourt. It wasn't much of a playground but it did have four washing poles with a threadbare rope tied around them. The small space was alive with children but, when Lily saw me, she shouted out, 'We're playing at Reelifoh, Ann.' As she called to me, the children were srambling around the poles.

'It's time for your bed,' I pointed out and her face fell.

'Just another wee while, Ann. I'm not tired.'

Maybe she wasn't but I was and so was Granny. Still, the evening was lovely and the fresh air was good for her. Her face was red with the effort of the game and her dark hair swung out behind her.

'Right then,' I conceded, 'just another half hour then up the stairs.'

Granny had now been joined by Grandad and his pipe smoke filled the room but, thankfully, the open window kept it to a minimum.

When he saw me, he said, 'Leave the bairn playing, Ann. I'll go down later and bring her up when it's time for her bed.'

Granny was sitting by the open window, a look of annoyance on her face. 'I'll give my Johnny a piece of my mind when I see him – leaving Rosie in the lurch like that. She doesn't deserve to be treated like that so wait till I see the besom.'

I felt the same but I wanted to tell her about the lovely time Lily and I'd had with Connie. I had been on the verge of saying this when Rosie had dramatically interrupted.

'Connie has these scrapbooks, Granny. She keeps cuttings out of the papers and magazines and sticks them in these books. She was showing them to us this afternoon and they go right back to her father's time. It's really great looking at all the photos.'

Granny seemed relieved to be free from Rosie's problems. 'What a grand idea, Ann. I'd like to see them sometime.'

'Well, you'll have to go to her house because the books are very heavy but she would like you to see them. She knows all the history behind all the pictures. There's a bonny photo of the Duke of Windsor and Wallis Simpson's wedding as well as loads of pictures of the coronation.'

Grandad looked over. 'What a load of twaddle – the wedding of that pair. More money than sense if you ask me.'

'Well, we're not asking you so don't butt in,' said Granny. 'Ann and I think it's really romantic.'

Grandad made a noise but continued to smoke his pipe.

Granny sighed. 'You know, it's the same with most men – while we think it's the love story of the century, the men have no time for it. Unromantic beggars that they are.' Still, I noticed she threw Grandad a fond look as she said it.

A silence developed, then it was back to the topic of Rosie – much to my dismay because I was afraid Granny would ask where Dad was and I knew I couldn't lie to her – ever. I didn't mean to be unkind but I asked Granny, 'Do you think Rosie could maybe dress a wee bit more fashionably?'

She looked at me with astonishment. 'More fashionably?'

I stuck to my guns. 'Well, look at her. She dresses like you do, Granny!'

Grandad was annoyed. 'What do you mean by that, Ann? Your Granny looks fine to me.'

'That's what I mean. No offence to Granny but she's years older than Rosie but there's no difference in their frocks.'

Granny seemed thoughtful. After a few moments, she said, 'Ann's right enough, Dad. Rosie's frocks look like hand-me-downs from her mother. Now some men would think this is great because it means they're saving money for the house instead of spending it on fripperies but our Johnny doesn't think like that. With him it's the outer wrapping that counts, not the inner person – much to my regret.'

Encouraged by this, I went on, 'I mean look at Rosie. She's a bonny woman but it's spoiled by her dowdy appearance. I wish somebody would give her a bit of advice about her clothes and hair.'

I knew Rosie was slightly more plump than Margot but not that much. It was the clothes she wore that gave the impression of roundness. She had a lovely skin which was far better than Margot's if I remembered right.

Granny's face fell. 'It'll not be easy telling her because she's aye looked like this. But I'll have a word with Alice and maybe she can persuade her to change a habit of a lifetime.'

On that note I set off for home. Stopping briefly to let Lily know that Grandad was coming for her. The look of delight on her face was priceless. She turned to her friends, saying, 'Oh, good! Grandad will let me stay out all night.' Poor Lily. She had a high opinion of her charms over Grandad but she forgot one thing – Granny.

The evening was still hot. It was a warm sultry heat, almost as if the heat of the day had been trapped by the high buildings and they weren't letting it go. The street was abuzz with children and adults, all taking full advantage of the good weather. They were letting the long golden rays of the sun stroke their thin arms and legs in a vain effort to store up the radiance of summer to tide them over the long dark days of winter.

What was Dad doing now? I wondered. To be quite honest, I didn't really want to know because what I didn't know I couldn't relay back to Rosie. She would have to ask him herself.

Much later that night, he arrived back home. I didn't hear him come in so it must have been very late indeed but that didn't mean he was in the company of Mrs Connors all this time. Perhaps he had paid a visit to Joe but then, if I believed that, I would believe anything.

I asked him the next morning. 'Where were you last night, Dad? Rosie was fair mad at you.'

161

He looked horror-stricken. 'Oh, no! I forgot about her. I was supposed to have my tea with her and her mother.'

'Aye, she said so,' I told him bluntly, still feeling angry with him.

'Was she annoyed?'

I recalled her red face and her manner. I told him the truth.

'I just forgot. I just wish she wouldn't want me to visit her every night. It's just not possible.'

Of course it wasn't – not now that the cool, yellow-dressed Margot was on the scene.

I asked him, 'Is there any news about Harry?'

He looked unhappy as he shook his head. 'I just wish I knew what was in his mind that day and maybe I could have helped him.'

I knew this was the truth because he was fond of Harry. Then something I had ignored last night reared its ugly head.

'Why did you tell Rosie that Harry's wife was an old woman?'

He looked guilty. 'Och, well, Ann, you know what women are like. I didn't want Rosie to feel jealous so I just told her a wee white lie. I don't want her to think I'm enjoying myself with another woman.'

He could have fooled me. 'What are you doing then, Dad, if you're not enjoying yourself in the company of Mrs Connors? I mean you've been to see her just about every night since June.'

He was annoyed. 'No, I haven't – not every night.'

'Well, maybe that's an overstatement but it looks like it. You're ignoring Rosie and it's not fair because she doesn't deserve this. Either tell her the truth about Mrs Connors and give her up completely or stop seeing Mrs Connors.'

He looked at me with dismay. 'That's a terrible thing to tell your father. I'm just seeing a woman through a bad patch. If you can't help someone when they need it, then it's a sorry old world.'

'So you're just helping her come to terms with the disappearance of her husband?'

He was hurt. 'Of course I am. What do you take me for? Harry was one of the best gaffers a man could have and I just wish I knew what had happened to him.'

I suddenly felt sorry for him and I knew I shouldn't have questioned him like this. 'I'm sorry, Dad. It's my fault and I know it's none of my business but Rosie was really upset last night and I felt sorry for her.'

'I'm sorry as well, Ann, but I really forgot about her. Still, I'll go to see her tonight.' He seemed almost cheery as he picked up his piece bag and hurried through the door.

Within a minute he was back. 'Blast it but I forgot – I promised to see Mrs Connors later to cut the grass for her.'

'To cut her grass?' I was mystified.

He explained, 'Well, you saw the size of yon garden she's got. Somebody has to keep it neat.'

'Does she not employ a gardener?'

He shook his head. 'No, seemingly Harry aye did it and I feel I have to keep it shipshape until he turns up.'

'So you think he'll do that, Dad? Turn up I mean.'

163

He looked unhappy. 'Nobody knows what to think any more – even Mr Pringle, my boss. He goes to see Mrs Connors as well but he aye takes his wife along with him for some reason. Margot gets a good laugh at it.'

'Does he look like his brother? Maddie's dad?'

He shook his head. 'Maybe it's because Maddie's dad is a solicitor and that gives him a stuffy look.' He stopped when he saw my face. 'That doesn't matter because Maddie's dad is a great man but he is very precise while his brother is more fun. He likes a good laugh and a joke.'

Mentally I gave full marks to Mrs Pringle for not letting her husband go to see Mrs Connors on his own. For some reason, I couldn't get her cool image out of my mind.

Later that week, I ran into Minnie Fraser and her little boy. The hot spell had continued and it felt as if every day was hotter than the one before. Minnie was still as I remembered her. Her small slim figure and elfish face with its almond-shaped eyes and short dark hair always reminded me of Hiawatha's bride Minnehaha. This was my secret pet name for her.

Her little boy didn't resemble her in the slightest and I thought he must take his looks from his father. Fair haired with blue eyes, he was eating a large ice-cream cone. The ice cream was all over his face and it had even dripped down the front of his shirt and short trousers.

Minnie seemed pleased to see me. 'How is Danny?' she asked. Before I could reply, she said, 'I was really sorry to hear about his broken engagement, Ann.'

I didn't realise it was common knowledge but I should have guessed that bad news always gets around.

'I don't know Maddie very well but I've aye been fond of Danny so it's a rotten shame this has happened.' She sounded genuine.

I asked her, 'Did Danny tell you, Minnie?'

She grinned. 'No, it was Bella. I met her a while ago and she told me.'

Bella – I might have guessed. I thought my outburst would maybe have cured her but it would seem that old habits die hard – especially with her because gossip was like her life's blood.

Minnie continued, 'I don't want to hear chapter and verse, Ann, but I wanted to say how sorry I am about it.'

She glanced down at Peter, her son, as he dropped his ice-cream cone. For a moment, I thought he was about to lick it up from the pavement but she pulled him away and he burst into tears.

I turned to go on my way but she seemed desperate for company. She said, 'I can't stand in the street with the bairn howling like this. Can you come up to the house?'

The schools were back after the summer holiday and I had an hour to spare so I nodded. We went to her mother's house in the Hawkhill with the boy still crying for his lost ice cream.

'I'll get you another one, Peter, so just be quiet. Everybody is looking at you.' This made him cry even louder but, thankfully, we soon reached her close which lay between Hunter Street and Kincardine Street. Like most of the houses in this teeming part of the town, the close was long and dark and her mother lived on the third floor of a dingy-looking tenement.

Climbing the stairs seemed to tire her son out and he almost stopped crying, just giving a heavy sob now and again.

'I hope my mother is out,' she said. 'She did say she was going to the Sosh for her messages.' This was the large Co-operative grocery shop which was a few hundred yards up the street – a shop that catered for the needs of most of the families who lived around its doors.

She ushered me into a small dark kitchen that looked quite bleak. This was because the fire was unlit and the grate resembled a yawning sooty mouth. My own kitchen looked the same and it was clear to see that a bright glowing fire was what made these rooms look cosy.

But, as it turned out, Mrs McFarlane wasn't at the shop. She was on her knees with a tin of polish and a duster and the linoleum had a lovely shine which matched the rest of the immaculately clean room. She took one look at her grandson and stormed. 'For heaven's sake, Minnie, can you not keep your laddie clean? He's aye clarted with something – if it's not mud, then it's ice cream.'

At the mention of the latter, the boy burst into a fresh bout of tears. Mrs McFarlane paid no heed to his howls as she carried him over to the sink and sat him on the wooden coal bunker. Rinsing a cloth in cold water, she vigorously wiped his face which made him howl even more. Meanwhile his granny was having no sympathy with him.

She then inspected his hands and rolled her

eyes at her daughter. 'Will you look at the dirt? He looks like he's been down a coal mine. I'm aye telling you to keep him clean but do you listen? No, you don't.'

By this time I knew Minnie was regretting asking me to the house but, to our relief, her mother picked up her message bag, took Peter's hand and they both departed for the shop. He was still grumbling about his lost ice cream.

The room was quiet after they went and we sat down on the chairs beside the unlit fire. They were covered in a prickly sort of fabric and the chair backs were snowy white linen.

Minnie poured out two glasses of lemonade and we sat in silence for a few moments. As she was a girl I hardly knew, I didn't know what to say but, thankfully, she was eager to talk.

'I don't know what to do, Ann. I can't get a house of my own because they're like gold dust to rent.'

I knew what she meant. We had been in the same boat when we'd given up our house after mum's death but, thankfully, we had managed to get our present flat.

'My man is still in Glasgow and he's living in the house we have there but I was hoping he would put in for another transfer back to the Overgate shop.'

I wondered if she knew about Danny's transfer request.

It became obvious that she did because she went on to say, 'If Peter does come back here, then Danny can move to his job in Glasgow. The only thing is that Peter's quite happy there and it was just me who couldn't make any friends. I know it's my fault because I'm too quiet but I get really lonely with just the bairn for company.'

She looked so unhappy that I couldn't help but ask her, 'So you want to stay here and hope that Peter will also come back?'

She nodded. 'But he'll not come back to stay with my mother. She's so house-proud that it's unbelievable. You saw how she was with the bairn. I'm frightened to get a bit of dirt on him and I'm aye washing him. It's no life for a bairn to live like that.'

'And there's no chance of a house in the near future?'

She shook her head. 'I've tried all the house factors in the town but there's nothing available.'

I didn't know what to say to her. I could hardly tell her that I always associated her not with a house but a wigwam on some Red Indian reservation.

'I've made up my mind tae go back to Glasgow,' she sighed.

At that moment her mother appeared with her bag in one hand and a whimpering Peter in the other.

She sounded exasperated. 'Will you take this grumbling bairn away, Minnie? He's been whinging all the time I've been in the shop.'

Minnie took his hand and turned to me. 'I'll walk down the road with you, Ann.'

We set off and, when we reached the small ice-cream shop, she bought the boy another cone.

She warned him, 'Now make sure you don't make a mess because it annoys your granny.'

She looked at me, her face screwed up in the sun. 'I have to get away from my mother because she's driving me barmy. As I was saying when she came in, it's not that I hate Glasgow – it's a great place – and it is my fault that I'm lonely. I know that.'

I felt sorry for her and for little Peter. I knew her mother was extremely house-proud and bossy because granny told me this when Minnie got married. As Granny had said at the time, 'Her mother will not be pleased with a bairn around the house. I've heard she washes and polishes her floors twice a day.' At the time, I hadn't believed it but it was true. Poor Minnie and Peter had to toe the line in the house or else return to Glasgow where Minnie was unhappy. I made a mental note to keep an eye out for an empty house for her but I also thought that maybe it would be best if she went back to her husband and tried again to settle down.

The sun beat down from a cloudless blue sky and the heat was almost unbearable. I glanced at Peter and, to my dismay, his ice cream had melted and was now dripping down his shirt front.

Minnie cried out, 'I told you to keep clean, Peter, and now look at you!'

'It's not his fault, Minnie. It's the heat and the poor bairn can't eat it quickly enough.'

She sighed loudly. 'I sometimes think I'm getting to be as bad as my mother.'

By now we had reached the Overgate and I suggested they come up to Granny's house to clean him up.

Granny was pleased to see them. 'My, he's

169

getting to be a big laddie, Minnie.'

We cleaned him up as best we could while Granny made some tea. Peter found a box of old comics that had once belonged to Lily and he sat quietly on the floor to look at them.

Minnie relaxed. 'Oh, this is great – being able to sit down without worrying about dropping crumbs on the floor.'

Granny smiled at her. 'Well, you're welcome to come here for a visit any time you like.'

Later on, as she was leaving, Minnie said, 'If I do go back to Glasgow, it'll mean that Danny won't get his transfer – at least not this one. Will he mind?'

'I've no idea, Minnie. I suppose he'll just have to stay where he is and get on with it.'

She smiled. 'Well, as long as he'll not be disappointed.'

As I watched them walk away towards the Hawkhill, I knew her mind was made up.

One thing I was thankful for was the fact I hadn't seen Rosie since her angry exchange that night and I had no idea if Dad was still seeing her. He was still visiting Margot Connors but he had to sort out his own problems as I had enough to cope with.

The hot weather lasted for most of that week with the temperature rising each day. The paper shop was dim and cool and I was thankful for that.

Sylvia, Edith and Amy appeared each morning wearing their pinnies but no coats. Full of life and chatter, they bounded into the shop like young deer.

'The mill is so warm that we're just wearing our peenies over our petticoats,' said Sylvia, buying the usual cigarettes and sweeties.

Connie gazed at her in mock alarm. 'Don't you lassies go showing your legs to the gaffer or else I'll get to hear about it.'

The three girls burst into peals of laughter.

'The gaffer,' said Amy. 'Have you seen him, Connie? He's an old man about fifty. He's forgotten what a woman's legs look like.'

On that cheery note, they all ran off towards their work while Connie shook her head.

'If they think being fifty is old what does that make me?'

I thought of Margot. What was her age? I wondered.

I was waiting for Lily at the school gates when the sky became ominously black. I was also without a coat and I hoped the rain would hold off till we were home. But it didn't. Suddenly a loud crack of thunder sounded overhead and it was followed by large drops of rain. Lily appeared and we raced up the road towards the house. The rain became a torrent and lightning lit up the black clouds. Lily was frightened but I put my arm around her as we raced through the deep puddles of rainwater. By the time we reached home, we were both soaked and we had to strip off our wet clothes. Leaving large wet puddles on the kitchen floor.

As I dried her hair, Lily said, 'I hope it's not like this tonight when we go down to Granny's. I don't like the thunder and lightning.'

I confessed that I didn't like it either. 'I'm sure

the storm will be over by then, Lily.'

But it wasn't. Dad arrived home soaking wet and in a bad mood. Whether because of the soaking or the fact he couldn't visit Margot I wasn't sure.

'Any word about Harry, Dad?'

He shook his head.

We ate our tea and then listened to the wireless. Dad couldn't settle and he was getting on my nerves. He kept walking over to the window to see if the rain had stopped and, when he saw it hadn't, he drummed his fingers against the arm of the fireside chair.

'What's the matter, Daddy?' asked Lily, also noticing his restlessness.

He smiled at her. 'Nothing's the matter, wee pet. It's just that I've got a lot of grass to cut at Mrs Connor's house and this rain is stopping me.'

I looked at him cynically – a trait I was aware of. As I grew older, I had noticed how cynical I had become and I was trying hard not to be.

He saw me and raised his eyebrows, as much as to say, 'What? Don't you believe me?'

It was very hard to believe that he loved grass-cutting so much that he couldn't sit in peace in his own home. No, it was more like it was Margot Connors he was missing and it was then that I realised that Rosie had no chance.

It was nine o'clock before the rain stopped. I quickly got Lily ready and we set off towards the Overgate while Dad made his way towards Margot and the grass. He muttered as he went through the door, 'I don't suppose I'll get it cut tonight but I better go and tell her I'll do it tomorrow.'

As far as I was concerned, he could tell her anything he wanted. I was still annoyed at his treatment of Rosie.

The storm had cleared the air and it was much fresher. The pavements gleamed in a late burst of sunshine and a mini river ran down the gutter, carrying loads of rubbish in its wake.

Lily kept glancing at the sky in case of more thunder but all was calm. Granny thought we weren't coming and Lily told her the whole story of her journey through the storm. She made it sound so dramatic that I wondered if we had both been in the same rainstorm. 'The jagged lightning was just over my head, Granny, and Ann had to cover me up because it was thunder as well. The rain was stotting off the pavement and we got soaked.'

Granny nodded in harmony and the story went on and on. I left them in the middle of it.

The storm caused some flooding in Dock Street and turned the Tay into a seething mass as brown water flowed into the drains and into the river.

At 1.30 p.m. the next day, the river gave up its dead. Harry Connors' body was found.

Dad arrived home early. I was barely in the house with Lily after school when he hurried through the door.

'I'll not be here for my tea,' he said, quickly filling the basin to get shaved. 'Mr Pringle and I have to visit Mrs Connors. Her man's body was washed up today.'

I sat down, numb with shock. 'Oh, no, Dad, what a shame for his wife.'

There were tears in his eyes. 'Aye, it's a damn

173

shame. He was a great guy and really good to me. I'll miss him as well.'

'Was it an accident?'

He shook his head. 'We don't know. There will be an inquiry into it and maybe the truth will come out then.'

Lily sat in silence, her eyes huge and round.

Dad went on, 'I don't know what time I'll be home but I'll get some fish and chips so don't keep anything hot for me, Ann.' On that note, he darted through the door. He was back within a minute. 'Oh, blast it! I've just remembered I was to see Rosie tonight. I was going to tell her that I had the grass to cut and that I couldn't stay for my tea.' He gave me a pleading look. 'Could you tell her about the change in the plan?'

He didn't wait for an answer so I had no option. Still, in the circumstances, I didn't mind. Poor Harry – I didn't know him well but I used to see him when I passed the warehouse door when Dad first started his job there. He seemed an ordinary, pleasant and hard-working man.

I found Rosie in her house. She was standing by the cooker with a spoon in her hand. Something brown bubbled in a pot and she was engrossed in stirring this glutinous mixture. She was wearing her sludge-coloured skirt and a bright floral apron with an enormous pink frill around its edge.

She looked up in alarm when I entered. 'Och, it's you, Ann.' She smiled. 'Where's your Dad?'

'He can't come tonight, Rosie.'

A red flush tinged her cheeks and she looked angry. 'What's wrong with him now?'

I told her the story and she suddenly lost her

sullen expression. Sympathy flooded her face and she sat down. 'Och, what a terrible thing to happen! That poor old woman, Mrs Connors. What will she do now?'

So Dad hadn't enlightened her about Margot's age or her looks. As far as Rosie was concerned she was a poor old widow.

She switched off the gas ring and put a lid on the pot. 'I'll keep this for him because he'll need a meal when he gets back.'

'Dad said he would get fish and chips, Rosie. I'm not keeping his tea for him.'

'I'm sure you're right, Ann, but I'll just keep it in case he wants it.'

It was like talking to a brick wall. Rosie really thought Dad would immediately run to her after his visit to the grieving widow. Maybe it was a blessing that she didn't know the fair Margot.

She came through to Granny's house with me and I repeated the awful story.

Rosie sat with her hands folded on the riotously floral apron and nodded in sympathy. 'It must be awful when your man dies,' she said, 'especially when you're old. It will be a blow to her but your dad will know what to say, Ann. He's really good with words.'

Granny looked at me wordlessly. I had described Mrs Connors and the house in detail to her and we both knew Rosie was living in a fool's paradise.

After she left, Granny said, 'Somebody will have to tell her the truth, Ann. She's under the illusion that your Dad's dealing with a doddery old woman of seventy.'

'But surely, now that her man's body has been

found, Dad will not have to visit her so often. It was just because the man was missing.'

Granny looked doubtful. 'Well, we'll just have to hope so.'

I knew Margot was an attractive woman but she wasn't in the same class as us. She had money and a lovely home. Why would she want Dad's company? I said this to Granny.

'I expect you're right, Ann, but I just hope he doesn't cast Rosie aside for some cheap flirtation like he's done before. I'm not saying this Mrs Connors will be serious about your father but that won't stop her liking him, will it?'

No indeed.

Much later that night he arrived home. He looked weary.

I asked him how Mrs Connors was.

'She's bearing up well although it was a great shock to her. She aye thought he would turn up out of the blue – like he'd lost his memory and wandered away. It seemingly happens to folk quite a lot.' He sighed loudly. 'His sister however was a different kettle of fish. She wouldn't stop wailing.'

He slumped down on the chair and rubbed his eyes.

'Harry's sister seemed really fond of him,' I said.

He sighed again. 'Oh, she was but that doesn't mean she can cast aspersions on Margot.'

Minutes before I had been tired but I now perked up. 'What do you mean?'

'Och, it's just rubbish,' he said. 'She said that Harry wasn't happy living with his wife.'

'And is it true?'

'How should I know? Mr Pringle was also taken aback by her statement. In all the years he's known him, Harry has never said a word about his wife. Mind you, Margot is Harry's second wife. I didn't know that. His first wife died ten years ago and he's been married to Margot for the past six years.'

I was surprised but I should have guessed it – there was the difference in their ages for one thing.

'What did Margot say when her sister-in-law said that?'

'She didn't say much – just shook her head sadly at her. She told Mr Pringle and me later that Olivia had liked the first wife very much but had never taken to Margot. She said that if Harry was unhappy with his marriage then he never said a word to her. As for her, well she loved him very much.'

'When will the funeral take place?'

'Next week sometime, I think. There has to be a post-mortem before he can be buried. We all think it was a bad accident. He was forever walking by the edge of the docks and we think he tripped over something and fell in. It's just so sad and him just a wee while away from retirement.'

He stopped speaking and looked at me. I waited because I knew that look. He was about to say something and he wasn't sure of my reaction. I wasn't wrong.

'I was just thinking, Ann, how are the funds?' He was referring to our small amount of money which I tried to save every week from our wages.

I took the tin down from the mantelpiece and tipped the money into my lap. 'There's three pounds, five shillings and sixpence,' I told him, placing all the coins on the table.

He rubbed the back of his neck – another giveaway sign that he was unsure of how I was going to take something.

Suddenly he blurted out, 'It's just that we've all got to give two bob each for a wreath at the work.'

I breathed a sigh of relief – two bob was all right.

But he wasn't finished. 'Another thing, Ann, I need a new suit. The one I've got is getting really shabby looking.' As if to emphasise the shabbiness he went into his tiny bedroom and brought out the suit.

Although I knew he'd had it for years, long before Mum's death, it was still serviceable. I didn't say so because I had the strong feeling that he had thought this out for weeks. He had never bothered much about sartorial elegance before but, since meeting Margot, it now seemed of prime importance.

'It's because I've been going around with Mr Pringle, Ann. I aye look like a tink compared to him and I would like to look smart at the funeral.'

I suddenly realised how selfish I had been and I handed him the tin with the money. 'Will that be enough for a suit, Dad?'

'Och, aye – I'm not wanting anything from Saville Row. A suit from the Fifty Shilling tailors in the Murraygate will be fine.'

On the Saturday afternoon, he went shopping

and came back with a lovely dark-navy suit which suited his slim figure. He was also carrying a few brown-paper packages from McGill's shop. He saw me looking at them and he explained, his neck getting redder by the minute, 'I paid cash for the suit but I got a shirt, tie and a new pair of shoes on tick from McGill's.' He opened the parcels to show me.

Lily danced around him, saying, 'Oh, you look great, Dad – just like a film star!'

I had to admit I thought the same. Clothes made such a difference as I had experienced with the lovely cashmere coat that the late Mrs Barrie had given me – the one that Miss Hood had destroyed so viciously.

'Aye you look like a real toff, Dad,' I said truthfully.

He smiled and I realised he was still a very handsome man. Did Margot think the same?

He began to speak rapidly. 'I know you don't like getting things on tick, Ann, but I'll pay the two bob every week and I'll cut down on my cigarettes.'

I felt rotten about not offering him money from my legacy but I was trying to leave it untouched except in the direst emergency. Lily still had a lot of growing up to do and that was money for her.

I smiled at him. 'Och, don't worry about it, Dad. I'll manage another couple of bob a week without you cutting back on your fags.'

The funeral was held the following week and Mr Pringle closed the warehouse for the morning to allow all the staff to pay their respects to the late lamented Harry.

Dad arrived back that evening. He looked worn out and his eyes were glassy with unshed tears. 'It was a big funeral, Ann. Harry was well thought of at work and I really liked him a lot.'

'How were Mrs Connors and her sister-in-law?'

'Margot was fine but Harry's sister was just the same as she was when the body was found. Her man tried to keep her quiet afterwards but she started to throw loads of accusations at Margot.' He sounded weary.

'What did she say? Was it the same as last time?'

His face took on an expression of distaste. 'Aye – that and other things. She told Mr Pringle that Margot was aye spending Harry's money and she even hinted that it wasn't an accident.'

I was shocked. 'If it wasn't an accident, then what was it?'

'Well, her man shut her up at that point and took her home. Thank the Lord that the other men didn't hear her. I was with Mr Pringle in Margot's house and that's where the accusations took place. Poor Mr Pringle – he didn't know what to think or say but I said it was just warring women and he agreed with me.'

'Anyway,' I said, 'the fatal accident inquiry into his death will make it clear surely.'

He nodded. 'I hope so.'

I was making the tea when he said, 'Oh, by the way, Margot has asked me to bring my family to see her on Sunday afternoon.'

I stopped peeling the potatoes and turned to stare at him in amazement. 'You mean she wants Lily and me to visit her?'

He nodded. 'And your granny, plus Hattie and

180

Danny if they want to come. I didn't mention your grandad because you know he never goes anywhere where he can't smoke his pipe.'

I was perplexed. 'Why does she want to see us?'

He looked smug. 'She just wants to say a big thank you for all the help I've given her during this terrible time.'

Well that was nice of her, I thought. 'So you'll be asking everybody tonight then Dad because it'll not be long till Sunday?'

He nodded. 'I thought I would come with you to the Overgate when you take Lily there later and I could go over to the Westport and see Hattie and Danny.'

Well that was the plan but, like all well-laid plans, it didn't go quite as smoothly as he thought. First of all, Bella was firmly seated in the best chair when we reached the Overgate. As he said later, with hindsight, he should have waited with the invitation instead of wading straight in with the proposal. Granny was pleased but Bella was over the moon. Dad tried to backtrack but Bella wouldn't listen.

'Och, that's real decent of the woman to invite your family to her house. Is she putting on a meal?'

Dad looked panic-stricken and gave Granny a wordless, appealing look.

Granny turned to Bella. 'I think it's just the immediate family, Bella – Lily and Ann.'

The penny dropped. 'Well, does that mean you're not going, Nan?'

'That's right, Bella. I've not been asked.'

Dad threw her a grateful look. 'It's just Ann,

181

Lily, Hattie and Danny.'

I could almost hear Granny groan inwardly.

Bella was outraged. 'She's asked your sister and her laddie but not your own mother. Well, I think it's a damn disgrace. Och, aye, ask the toffs in the family and not the rest.'

Dad escaped through the door but we had to listen to Bella's moans for ages. Then Rosie appeared and that added fuel to Bella's fire.

Rosie said, 'Did I hear Johnny's voice on the stair?'

Before we could answer, Bella butted in, 'Aye, you did but I expect you'll not be getting asked to the soirée.'

Rosie was puzzled but Bella explained. Rosie looked at me. I shrugged my shoulders and wished that the whole thing had never been mentioned.

I said, 'As far as I know, Rosie, it's just the immediate family that's been invited. It's just a wee thank you for all his help in her time of trouble.'

Then Dad reappeared from the Westport and stopped dead when he saw Rosie.

Bella started her tirade again, 'You've a hard neck, Johnny Neill, for not asking Rosie to go with you – and her aye helping you out.'

It was Rosie's turn to look embarrassed but, as usual, Bella wouldn't give up. So, as a result of this stramash, the company on Sunday now comprised of Hattie, Danny, Lily, Rosie, Dad and me – and Uncle Tom Cobley and all.

Before the big occasion Rosie asked me to her house for some advice. She was excited but nervous. 'What will I wear on Sunday, Ann?'

She opened her wardrobe and I was dismayed.

It held quite a few dingy-looking clothes in shades of brown, sludgy beige and one particularly old-fashioned-looking frock in a horrible muddy green. It was a wardrobe more suited to her mother. She held up one disaster of a frock after another. Her hair hung heavy on her shoulders and she smelled of carbolic soap.

I decided to take the bull by the horns. 'Rosie, as it's a special thank you to Dad, why not treat yourself to a new frock in a bonny colour and in a modern design?'

She gave me a look as if I was mad. 'But I've got loads of frocks here. I don't want to squander money on another one, Ann.'

'But for this special occasion, Rosie – please?'

She gave me another queer look and shook her head. I knew I was beaten.

On the Sunday, we made our way to Margot's house in two groups. Dad had said he didn't want us all descending on her like Attila and his horde of Huns so Rosie went with Lily and Dad while I went with Hattie and Danny. It was so good to see Danny again. I had missed his company so much but I also wanted his advice on Margot.

It was a lovely warm autumn day and the house had a tranquil air as we approached it through a garden full of colourful autumn tints.

Hattie was almost beside herself with pleasure. 'This is the kind of house I would love to live in.'

Danny gave me a sidelong look and his eyes were filled with laughter. We were all so used to Hattie and her ideas of grandeur.

Margot opened the door in her usual elegant manner. Her dress was a beautiful, bias-cut model in a rich shade of russet red. She had a lovely string of pearls around her throat and a matching pair of earrings. A slim gold watch encircled her narrow wrist and the effect was stunning. Even Hattie was dumbstruck.

The interior was as I remembered it except that the large bowls of roses were now filled with autumn arrangements – a riot of multicoloured leaves and berries.

A few minutes after our arrival, Dad appeared with Rosie and Lily. Poor Rosie had decided to wear the horrible green frock and she had chosen her most comfortable pair of shoes. She looked like a frumpy old woman next to the delicately beautiful Margot. Margot however was charming to us all and we sat in her elegant lounge with glasses of sherry while the two men had beer.

I found it amusing that we were all sitting around her. Like she was the queen and we were mere peasants at her court. She provided a lovely afternoon tea but I managed to catch her on an unguarded moment when everyone was either eating or talking. She was summing us up. I suppose she had already dismissed Lily and me but I didn't like the amused gleam in her eyes when Rosie kept mentioning Dad's name. No, I didn't like it one bit.

I could see that she was unsure of Hattie and with good reason. For a start, Hattie, in her fashionable royal-blue suit with matching shoes, was better dressed than she was and Hattie was also better spoken than the rest of us. As for Danny ... well, she could barely keep her eyes away from him and I was thankful he was far too young for her. But was Dad?

After tea she made a little speech about the sad death of her husband. She ended by saying, 'I would never have managed if it hadn't been for Johnny. He's been a tower of strength to me and I won't forget it.' She threw her arms around him and gave him a kiss.

I glanced over at Rosie and she was white faced. Her lips clamped together in a thin annoyed-looking line which, for some reason, only emphasised her untidy hair.

Later, after we'd said our goodbyes to Margot, I walked back with Danny. The day was truly beautiful and all the gardens and trees were a mass of colour.

'What did you think of her, Danny?'

He didn't speak for a moment or two. Then he turned to look at me. 'What do you want me to say, Ann? That she's got your Dad truly hooked or is she mourning the death of her man? Well I think the answer is that your father's well and truly smitten and she's the coolest widow woman I've seen in a long time.'

He had only confirmed my own impressions.

The following week, Rosie came to visit me when Dad was away at Margot's. She said, 'I just want to thank you, Ann, for trying to help me with my clothes. I know now why you wanted me to buy something more fashionable and I just wish I had listened to you. But your dad told me Mrs Connors was an old woman.' She shook her head and I saw tears in her eyes. 'And he was lying to me.'

7

One morning in late December, Danny suddenly appeared in the shop. The weather had turned much colder and the lovely golden autumn was now a fond memory. He was well wrapped up against the bitter east wind which blew coldly into the shop every time someone came through the door. Although the bell above the door was meant to ring when a customer entered, on this particular morning, the wind added strength to it and it jangled noisily.

Connie was getting a bit tired of this noise and she had threatened more than once to bend the coiled spring which supported it. 'I'm going to sort out that ruddy bell once and for all,' she said as it clanged noisily once more. She scowled at the door and Danny hesitated.

Then she smiled. 'I'm not scowling at you, Danny – just that damned bell.'

He glanced upwards then said, 'I'd like a quick word with Ann. Do you mind, Connie?'

'No – go ahead.' She picked up a pile of papers and began to scribble names on the top with a stub of a pencil.

He hesitated again. 'Can Ann come outside for a minute?'

By now I was totally mystified and Connie was totally agog.

'I mean if that's all right? I don't want to keep

her away from her work.'

Connie nodded and I went outside and stood on the freezing cold pavement.

'What on earth's the matter, Danny? What's so secret that you can't speak in front of Connie?' I had a sudden dreadful thought. 'It's not your transfer is it?'

'No. It's just that I wondered if you would come to Lochee with me tonight?'

I was as mystified as ever. 'Lochee? Why do you want me to go there?'

'I can't tell you here because I have to get to work but will you come with me after you leave Lily with Granny?'

His face was white above his woollen scarf and he looked worried.

By this time so was I. 'Has something happened, Danny? Is it Ma?'

He shook his head. 'It's a long story but I can't say much at the moment but will you come?'

'Of course I'll come, Danny. I'll see you later.'

He gave me a thankful look and hurried away down the Hill.

When I got back into the shop I was grateful for the warmth. The heat was provided by an ancient paraffin heater which was smelly and you had to be careful not to knock it over during what we laughingly called our rush hours. Still, I didn't bother about its smell this time because I was grateful for its heat. It had been freezing standing on that pavement.

Connie gazed at me when I entered but she didn't ask any questions. That's what I liked about her. She didn't pry and, apart from the trivial chitchat of the street, she didn't really gossip. If she got a confidence from someone, then it was sacrosanct. In spite of that, she was a woman who knew almost everything about the people who inhabited her own little world but, as I didn't know why Danny wanted me to visit Lochee with him, I couldn't mention anything.

Instead I said, 'Danny was just reminding me that I promised to go to Lochee with him tonight.' It was a little white lie but, if she guessed it, she said nothing.

She smiled at me. 'I like that laddie Danny – something couthy about him.'

Young Davie the paper delivery boy arrived and, to my dismay, I saw he was still in his short trousers. His legs were red with the freezing cold and he had large holes in the heels of his woollen socks. I was wild at myself for forgetting to ask Hattie about some of Danny's cast-off clothes that would fit Davie perfectly. I made a mental note to ask her for them the next time I saw her.

As Davie filled the well-worn canvas bag with his newspapers, Joe appeared. He was rubbing his hands briskly. 'Heavens, it's cold enough to freeze a brass monkey,' he said. He took a couple of pennies from his pocket. 'I'll have a single fag, Ann, and a paper.'

I got one cigarette from the box under the counter and handed it to him. He opened his tin and placed it beside the many stubs which littered its base.

Connie saw this and laughed. 'Still saving up your nippers, Joe, I see.'

He smiled back. Showing a row of yellow teeth.

'Aye, in these hard times, I can aye make another fag out of my stubs. It saves a wee bit money and fag papers are cheap.'

'I don't think it's really good to do that, Joe. You're just smoking pure nicotine when you put the stubs together.' Although she sold tobacco and cigarettes, Connie was a non-smoker.

Joe made a sound between a laugh and a cough. 'Och, Connie, I've got to die of something. It might be with old age or maybe with nicotine poisoning but when you're dead what does it matter what caused it?'

We stood in silence and he continued, 'Look at the news. There's another war coming and it'll not be men of my age that'll be going but all the younger laddies.'

My heart went cold. Would that be Danny and Greg?

'Now there's this Spanish Civil War. I'm telling you, Connie, if I was twenty years younger, I would go and fight there. At least it will be sunny and warm in Spain and not cold and miserable like this place.'

As he left Connie remarked, 'Well, if you're dead or injured, does it matter if it's in the sunshine or the rain?'

'Do you think there will be another war, Connie?' I asked, fear still clutching my heart.

She shrugged her shoulders. 'Well, it certainly looks like it'll get worse before it gets better with this Hitler chappie but surely it'll not come to a full-scale war. After the last war, you would think the world had had enough of killing off all its young men.'

As the day wore on, I tried not to think about the trip to Lochee that night. Although I tried not to show it, I was worried about the urgency of it all. I had been to see the Ryan family a few times since Dad Ryan's funeral and, although they were all still so desperately hard up, I couldn't think what this urgent summons was all about. As with any worry, the day seemed to crawl by slowly and I was glad when Lily and I reached the Overgate to find Danny waiting for me.

For a brief moment, I thought Lily would kick up a fuss and want to come with us but she was tired and seemed pleased to sit by the fire with her comics and books.

In spite of my thick coat and woolly gloves, the wind seemed to penetrate the fabric and I was freezing cold as we waited at the tram stop. I had asked Danny what the urgency was all about but he said it would wait till we reached Kit's house. We huddled together to keep warm and he asked me if I had seen Maddie.

I shook my head. 'But I hope to see her soon, Danny.'

He gave me a rueful look. 'I was really stupid.'

I nodded but said nothing.

'I just wish I could see her because my feelings haven't changed for her but it's my own fault so there's nothing to be done now.'

I was annoyed. 'Don't be daft, Danny. I've told you over and over again to go and see her and tell her how silly you've been then tell her the truth.'

His voice seemed to come from far away as he gazed at the approaching tramcar. 'Aye, maybe one day I will.'

'Let me tell her that you want to see her and you can arrange a meeting,' I said, my voice full of hope.

He shook his head. 'But she's found somebody else. Have you forgotten that?'

I was about to argue with him but the tram was full of people and we couldn't get a seat together. I had no option but to hold my tongue, at least for the time being. When we reached our stop a few of the passengers got off along with us but they hurried away into the shadows, leaving the street almost deserted. A couple of brave souls scurried past but it wasn't a night to be outside.

I expected to see the entire Ryan family but, to my surprise, only Kit, George and Ma Ryan sat around the fire. When we entered, they threw Danny a grateful look. If they were surprised to see me, they didn't say so. Kit's fire was its usual meagre self but the kitchen was quite warm, at least compared to outside. The teapot sat on the gas cooker and we were soon seated with a hot cup of tea to warm our hands.

Ma sat very quiet but I noticed Kit's face was white and strained looking. On the other hand, George seemed angry to me but, as he was normally such an easy-going man, I thought I must be wrong in this assessment.

Kit spoke. 'Thanks for coming Ann and Danny. We don't know what to do for the best.' She looked at me. 'You don't know yet, Ann, but young Kathleen is expecting a bairn.'

I was shocked. Young Kathleen, who had looked so beautiful on the night of her grandad's wake, what was her age?

Kit answered my unspoken question. 'She's just sixteen although she'll be seventeen next year.'

George interrupted her. 'It's not really her age that concerns us – although we think she's too young to be settling down – it's the father we're worried about. He's the big problem.'

'Are you still sure it's Sammy Malloy,' Danny asked. 'Has Kathleen told you it's him?'

George looked unhappy. 'She wouldn't tell us to begin with but, aye, it's that toerag Malloy.'

I recalled the leering look he had given her that night of the wake and I didn't like him either but, if he was the father of the child, then it was too late for dislike.

'Her dad and I have been telling her to have the bairn and stay with us without getting married,' said Kit, pushing her hair behind her ears. 'We'll help bring it up and she can maybe get a job later.'

Although it wasn't really any of my business, I said, 'Does she not want to do that, Kit?'

George burst out, 'It's not what she wants that seems to matter. It's what the ruddy Malloy family want and they want their grandchild to be born in wedlock.' His face was white with anger and I could well imagine his distress. 'I ask you! Wedlock's the word that's being bandied around and that's a laugh. I don't think Mick Malloy ever married his wife. I'm sure she's a common-law wife and now he's going around holier than thou. Yapping on and on about illegitimacy like he's some priest or something.' He stopped. He had run out of breath after this outburst.

I was quite surprised at Ma's reticence. She

hadn't spoken a word except for her initial greeting when we arrived.

Again, as if reading my mind, Kit turned to her mother. 'What do you think will happen, Ma?'

Ma gave it some thought then said, 'She's not the first lassie to be in this condition and she'll not be the last. I think she should stay unmarried and bring the bairn up with all our help but I don't think this will happen. If it's meant to be, Kit, then it'll happen.'

I thought she was being too complacent but it wasn't my business to butt in or give my opinions. How would I feel if it was Lily in this position? Not very pleased that was for sure.

Kit seemed to take this advice quietly but I could hold my tongue no longer. After all I was here at Danny's invitation so he must have wanted my ideas on the situation. 'What does Kathleen want, Kit?' I asked. 'Does she want to marry Sammy or not?'

Kit looked at me and I saw the dark circles under her eyes. I felt she had enough to cope with during all these years of bringing up her family on the poverty line. Apart from Kathleen there was Patty, Kit's youngest child, and, looking round the tiny flat, I doubted if there was any room in it for another baby.

Kit slumped in her chair and she looked defeated. 'Quite honestly, Ann, she doesn't know what she wants. I'm not saying she's frightened of Sammy because she's not but she feels she has to go along with his wishes. Then, at other times, she says she wants to stay with us.'

Danny said, 'If I have a word with her, Kit, do

you think she'll listen to me? I can ask her outright what she wants to do.'

To be honest I was really disappointed with Ma. She was supposed to have the sixth sense and she had certainly warned me of the danger at Whitegate Lodge when I was working there. But now she seemed to want to stay out of the argument.

Kit and George both looked gratefully at him. 'That would be a big help, Danny. That's why we asked you over tonight because Kathleen has aye been fond of you and looked up to you.'

'Where is she now? Maybe I can have a word with her and get her true feelings into the open.'

He stood up and was just putting his coat on when the door suddenly flew open. Kathleen stood shivering on the doorstep while Sammy Malloy swaggered in. He glared at us and I could smell the alcohol on his breath. This was because I was nearest to him and he thrust his aggressive face close to mine. He quickly guessed what the topic of our conversation had been. 'What's my bairn got to do with you?' He almost spat the words in my face.

Both George and Danny sprang towards him but Kit was quicker. She stood in front of Sammy.

'Don't hit him, George – he's not worth it.'

Sammy puffed out his chest at these words and glared at the two men as they went back to their seats. Kit took Kathleen's hand and led her towards the fire. She handed her a cup of tea and made her sit down.

She glared at Sammy. 'Your bairn indeed. You leave my lassie standing in the freezing lobby

195

while you come bouncing in here, you snottery wee toerag.'

Sammy took one step into the room but faced with Kit's wrath he thought better of it and swaggered out. But he wasn't going to let Kit have the last word and he shouted so loud that the entire close must have heard him. 'The wedding will be on the second of January. You can come if you like but you'll not be missed if you don't.'

The minute he disappeared, Kit, George and Danny all began to speak. In the jumble of words Kathleen suddenly broke into a flood of tears. She was dressed in the same skirt and jumper she wore on the night of the wake but I could see the slight swelling under the skirt.

I was so angry that I could have hit Sammy Malloy myself. Kathleen was growing up to be a beautiful young woman and goodness knows what she could do with her life. Now it all lay in tatters because of this obnoxious man.

Danny was talking to her quietly and she kept nodding in response to his words.

I sat beside Ma. 'You think I can work magic, Ann, don't you?'

I was taken aback. Could she read my mind? I nodded. 'Well, I think Kathleen might listen to you,' I said truthfully.

The old woman shook her head. 'That's where you're wrong. I know I get these feelings about folk but I've always tried never to influence my family so, for some reason, I get very few hunches about them. But I'll tell you this – although I don't want Kit to hear...' She glanced over at the trio who were trying to drum some sense into

Kathleen. 'Aye, I'll tell you this. Young Kathleen will get married to that rotter but it'll not ruin her life like you seem to think, Ann.'

I was amazed because those were the very words that were in my mind – that her life was ruined.

'The thing is this,' Ma continued. 'We're all heading towards a dark horizon – it's around everyone at the moment – but we just have to get on with our lives.'

I was upset. 'What do you mean by a dark horizon, Ma?'

'It'll be different for everybody. Some will find it darker than others and some will hardly notice it but it's there, mark my words.' She gave me a keen look. 'I hope you're not looking for a wedding ring next year, lass, because it'll not be forthcoming.'

My face fell. Did that mean Greg had found someone else?

'When will it come, Ma? If ever?'

'I can't say any more, lass, than what I've already said because I don't always see the entire picture if you get my meaning.'

Kit came over. Her face flushed with emotion. 'I think Danny has talked Kathleen out of marrying that besom, Ma. She's made up her mind to have the bairn next year and stay with us.' The relief on her face was evident.

So much for Ma's prediction, I thought. I looked at her with raised eyebrows but she merely nodded to Kit.

'Well, that's grand, Kit. What a relief for you and George.'

I went over to speak to Kathleen and almost collided with her dad and Danny. We all started to speak at once but, like all conversations, it was a bit noisy. Then, I heard Ma speaking to Kit. 'Danny will do well. He'll be in another country ... but he'll be fine...' I strained my ears to hear more but George was now talking loudly about Sammy Malloy. Danny in another country? I couldn't bear the thought of that but maybe I had misheard Ma's whispered words.

Danny and I left soon afterwards. Kit asked me to keep the news to myself and I promised I would. It would all come out soon enough. One thing in life was sure – when a baby was on the way, it couldn't remain a secret for long.

I asked Danny when we were on our way home. 'What about Granny? Are you going to tell her?'

He nodded. 'Aye, Kit did say I could tell her because she doesn't want her finding out through Bella or any other nosy parker but they want to keep it quiet for the time being.'

'Do you think Kathleen will take your advice, Danny?' I didn't mention Ma's words.

'Oh, I hope so. Imagine being married to that rotter.'

I mentioned Maddie again but he didn't want to discuss it – at least not tonight. 'Just give me a wee while longer, Ann, then I'll go and see her ... maybe.'

I gave up. There was just so much one person could do and I felt I could do no more. In fact I was turning into a proper old nag.

It was the same with Dad. For the past month now, there were nights when he didn't come home from Margot's house. It was only a matter of time before Rosie found out and she wouldn't be pleased. And, to be truthful, neither would I. Harry was hardly cold in his grave and now Dad was staying the night in his lovely house. It didn't seem right.

Danny had left to go home when I suddenly remembered the clothes for Davie. I explained this to Granny.

'Och, the poor laddie. Don't worry, I'll ask Hattie tomorrow if she's got any of Danny's clothes put aside. I would give you some of Grandad's but they wouldn't suit a young laddie.'

I smiled, trying to visualise Davie in some of Grandad's cast-offs. It didn't bear thinking about.

Granny saw the smile. 'What are you smiling about, Ann? Tell me the joke.'

I couldn't hurt her, not in a million years, so I made an excuse. 'I'm just thinking of Sammy Malloy's face when Kit started on at him. He was dead scared I can tell you, Granny.'

She chuckled loudly. 'Kit can fair sort out the men. You should have seen her in her younger days. She looked just like Danny and Kathleen but what a firebrand. She would stand up to folk much bigger than herself and she was magnificent.'

I tried to bring this description to life but failed. This magnificent firebrand with the lovely red hair and beautiful face was now worn away to a grey shadow of her former self. Was that what marriage and poverty did for the young? Turn them into shadows?

Granny chuckled again. 'Well, I suppose it's fine

199

that we can still get a laugh out of this terrible situation.'

I wondered if, at this moment, Kathleen was smiling and laughing? I doubted it very much.

I knew Kathleen wasn't alone in her predicament. There were hundreds of girls like her but they didn't have Sammy Malloy as the father of their baby. Still, I had to be charitable and hope there was a nicer side to his nature because I was biased against him and his father for all the trouble with Danny. I had never met Mrs Malloy and maybe she was a good soul. Maybe Sammy had inherited some good points. Nothing was impossible.

I didn't see Danny all that week but Granny handed me a parcel one afternoon. It was some of Danny's outgrown clothes. I was amazed Hattie had kept them.

'Och she's a hoarder is our Hattie,' said Granny when I expressed my delight with them. 'She kept them in her blanket box and she was aye meaning to throw them out but never got round to it.'

There were two pairs of long trousers in wonderful condition, three shirts, a jacket and two hardly-worn woollen jumpers. I reckoned they should fit young Davie perfectly. There was just the one obstacle – I didn't want to hand them over in the shop. I always thought charity should be given unseen. I had a vague idea where he lived and I made a mental promise to deliver them as soon as possible but I didn't know his surname. I would have to ask Connie in a casual way.

I got my chance the next morning when he

arrived for his delivery. His jumper was so short that a good four inches of his arms poked out from the sleeves.

For once Connie hadn't managed to finish her pile of papers which meant Davie had to stand by the counter and wait. Fortunately the shop was empty so I had my chance. 'You know, Davie, after all this time I don't know your second name.'

He looked at me in astonishment and Connie twirled round. I was highly embarrassed by her attention. Especially when she laughed and said, 'He's a bit young for you, is he not, Ann?'

I felt myself blush and the harder I tried to stop it the worse it became. I had planned to get his name and address but there was no way I could find out now.

Connie chuckled loudly. 'Och, I'm just kidding you. Tell her your name Davie and put her out of her misery.'

It was his turn to blush. He stuttered slightly, 'It's ... it's Chambers – Davie Chambers.'

I gave a sigh of relief. It wasn't a common name so I should find no difficulty in finding his mother's house tonight. I had planned my strategy well. Not wanting to give her the parcel in front of him I had decided to make my visit when he was busy with the *Evening Telegraph* deliveries. It would mean taking Lily along with me because I could never be sure when Dad would arrive home – especially now that Margot was on the scene.

After school and just before our tea we set off. Thankfully, it was dark and I felt like some spy from a film. In fact, it was Lily who said this as we searched through the warren of houses that

201

lay beyond the front facade on the Hilltown.

The close leading from the street was narrow enough but it opened out into a large backland full of tenement houses. I was dismayed. It would take all night at this rate.

Lily said, 'Where does he live, Ann? Do you know what house he lives in?'

I shook my head. 'No, Lily, I don't know. I suppose I'll just have to hand him the parcel tomorrow.'

I saw an old woman. She seemed to appear from nowhere. One minute it was just a mass of dark shadows then this figure hurried by, clutching her message bag and pulling her coat tightly around her body. She stopped when she saw us. She looked uncertain and I had the foolish notion that she thought we were about to rob her.

Before she moved off, I spoke. 'I'm looking for Mrs Chambers. Can you tell me where she stays?'

As the woman moved towards us, I noticed she was really old but she had sharp, dark eyes.

'Mrs Chambers bides over there – those houses on the far side.' She pointed with a thin finger in the direction of another shadowy mass. 'She bides three stairs up but her name is not on the door.' She peered at us both again. 'You'll be wanting your stairs washed, no doubt.'

On that reproving remark she departed. If she gave a backward glance I didn't see it. We moved towards the houses she had pointed out. Finding Mrs Chambers was difficult because most of the gas lamps on the stair were either broken or not lit.

Lily held on to my hand tight in case she got lost. 'It's really creepy here, Ann. I hope there's no ghosts.'

I laughed. 'Of course there's no ghosts, you daft wee lassie.' Although I sounded jokey, I wasn't too keen on these dark stairs myself. Another problem was the number of unmarked doors on the third landing. I decided to knock on the first door. It was opened by a young mother who was carrying a small child. The smell of cooking wafted out and I could see she was harassed.

'I'm sorry to bother you but I'm looking for Mrs Chambers.'

The woman pointed to the far end of the dark lobby. 'It's the door facing you.'

The child began to howl, no doubt wanting its tea, and the woman went back inside. Once the door was closed the lobby became black as night. We literally had to feel our way towards the door but it was opened on our first knock.

'Mrs Chambers, can I come in for a minute?' I asked.

The woman held the door open. 'Aye, come away in.'

She was a tall woman, gaunt faced and grey haired. She showed us to the chairs beside the fire and I could also smell the cooking on the tiny gas cooker by the side of the sink.

'Is it your stairs you want washing?' she said, pulling a small book down from behind the clock on the mantelpiece. 'I have to keep a note of my customers and the times.' She smiled and her face was transformed into a more youthful look. 'I call this my social diary.' She laughed and I liked her very much. It didn't look as if she had got a great deal out of life. The room was small and sparsely furnished and her clothes, although clean, were pretty threadbare. Still, she still had her sense of humour.

I explained I didn't want my stairs washed and her face fell as she replaced her book. I had the parcel on my knee but I didn't know how to begin about the clothes.

Before I could speak, however, Lily said, 'My sister Ann works in the same shop as Davie and she's got some clothes she wants him to have. They belonged to my cousin Danny but he's too big for them now and his mother was going to throw them out but Ann thought about your laddie.' She stopped for breath and I was mortified. I had intended to approach the subject warily – after all, some poor people didn't like the idea of charity in the shape of discarded clothes or discarded anything.

Mrs Chambers, who had remained silent throughout Lily's speech, now burst out laughing.

I said, 'But only if you want them, Mrs Chambers. My auntie was thinking of putting them out like my sister said.'

'Well, that's right kind of you both and, if they fit my Davie, then they'll be a blessing indeed. That laddie seems to eat me out of house and home and he's growing at an alarming rate. This room will soon not be big enough for us both.' She gave another deep chuckle and I marvelled once more at her great spirit.

I knew she was a widow and I also knew that she travelled around the town on her stair-washing chores. This was a job that people hated and some were quite prepared to pay a small sum for the privilege of someone else doing it – although it had to be said that her employers were mostly people with a bit of money. The majority of people I knew, myself included, washed their own stairs – it was simply a case of having to.

We found our way back through the darkness and we had just emerged into the Hilltown when we met the old woman trudging along with her heavy message bag. She peered at us. 'Did you find Mrs Chambers?'

'Aye, we did. Thank you for helping us,' I answered.

As she walked away, I had to smile. She was muttering to herself, 'Young lassie like that wanting old Mrs Chambers to wash her stair! Bloody disgrace when I've got to trauchle down with my bucket and brush and wash my own.'

I could have put her right on two points – the stair washing and the fact that Davie's mother wasn't old. She just looked like thousands of women who were old before their time. The entire city was full of women who had once been pretty and full of life but were now worn down by husbands without work and children having to be reared on little money. No wonder their faces showed the strain and gave them old expressions that belied their years.

Next morning, the look on Davie's face gave me a moment of pleasure. The clothes fitted him perfectly and he wore the trousers, shirt, jumper and jacket. What a difference it made to him and I was reminded once again of the russet cashmere coat, Mrs Barrie's gift to me – it had given me such delight and confidence in myself.

Connie was speechless when he entered. 'Goodness me, Davie, I didn't know you! What a toff. You could go straight to Buckingham Palace in those togs, I can tell you.'

He glanced shyly over at me but I shook my head. I had told his mother last night that no one knew about the parcel and she could tell anyone she liked that she had bought them. Then I noticed that, although his gloves were cosy and hand-knitted, his shoes were really old and done. Blast it, I thought. I hadn't thought about shoes but I would remedy this later in the day. I also knew that Hattie had never spared any expense on Danny and all his things were good quality.

After he had gone, Connie said, 'Thank goodness the laddie has some decent clothes. His mother must have joined a clubbie to get him kitted out but I'm really pleased for him. I've often thought that if I had kiddies of my own then I could pass things down but, as you know, Ann, I've never been married.'

She gave me such a searching look and I could have sworn she knew. I remained silent and she went back to her papers. She was certainly a good judge of human nature was our Connie. It came from all her years of serving the public, I thought.

I was on my way home after leaving a note through Hattie's door regarding the shoes when I bumped into Minnie and Peter. He wasn't eating ice cream today – it was too cold for that. Instead he had a bag of sherbet dip and his little face was concentrating on dipping the liquorice stick into the paper bag full of sugary yellow sherbet.

Minnie looked pleased to see me. 'I was hoping to run into you, Ann.'

I smiled at them both. 'Hullo, Peter.'

He lifted his head briefly and gave me a smile.

The wind whistled around our feet as we stood at the junction of Westport and Tay Street.

'Come on up to Granny's house, Minnie,' I said. 'It's far too cold to be standing outside.'

We set off towards the house with Peter still mesmerised with his sherbet. I hoped Bella wouldn't be in the house and, thankfully, she wasn't. Although Minnie liked her, I don't think she would enjoy a third degree inquisition from her.

Granny had made some tea for Grandad but he was dozing in his chair and she hadn't wanted to wake him.

When we entered, her face lit up. 'Heavens you must've smelt the teapot, Ann!'

We sat at the table and Peter said, 'Where's the box of comics, Mummy?'

Granny went over and took them from the fender box. This was Lily's favourite place to sit. The brass fender, with its twin padded seats at either end, was one of the warmest spots in the room.

He placed his precious sherbet beside him and sat quietly by the fire.

'He can take them home with him, Minnie, because Lily has finished reading them. I don't like throwing them out when another bairn can get some pleasure from them.'

Minnie thanked her but then said, 'I'm sorry, Mrs Neill, but my mother would just throw them out because she doesn't like clutter.'

Granny nodded. 'Well, we'll keep them here for Peter and he can read them when he comes to visit.'

Minnie looked sad. 'That'll not be for a long time I think, Mrs Neill.' She turned to me. 'I've had a letter from my man and he's been shifted to a branch in Clydebank and he's managed to get a house organised. He's looking forward to seeing us again.' She didn't look very happy about it.

Granny was concerned. 'If you're not happy, Minnie, well, don't go back. After all, it's your life – although I have to say that a man with a job these days is very rare.'

'That's what my mother aye says. She keeps telling me I don't know when I'm well off but, as I was saying to Ann, I don't make friends very easily and it makes for a lonely time.'

'Aye, it's not easy, lass, settling into a new place,' said Granny, 'but I'll give you a grand tip. When you meet your new neighbours, ask them about themselves and before long they will be telling you all their problems. Most folk like to chatter about themselves and, before you know it, you'll have made friends. Just you try it, Minnie – believe me, it works.' She gave her an encouraging smile.

'Thanks, Mrs Neill, I'll try that because I've really no choice but to return. It's a terrible thing to say but I can't stand my mother any more. She's driving me barmy.'

She drained her cup and there was a ring of black tea leaves left clinging to the cup. She gazed at them and said, 'You don't read the tea leaves, do you, Mrs Neill?'

Granny said that she didn't.

'Well, that's a pity because these leaves are arranged in some strange-looking patterns.' She gazed into space, her face wearing a sad expression. 'I would really like to know what the future holds.'

Granny patted her hand. 'Maybe it's better if none of us know that, lass. Just put your faith in the future and it'll work out for you all – your man, the bairn and yourself.'

Peter was in the middle of a comic and he wasn't happy about leaving. Small as he was, he liked this house with the warm chatty people and the old man snoring in his chair and the seats by the fire and the big box of comics. At least that was what Minnie had told them – that he was always chattering about his visit for days after.

Granny rolled up the pile of comics. 'Here, Peter, you take them.' She looked at Minnie. 'If your mother throws them out, it'll not matter because I don't want them back, Minnie.'

I walked as far as the foot of the Hawkhill with them. Minnie stopped when we reached the foot of the street. 'Do you mind if I write to you, Ann, when I'm in my new house?'

'Of course not, Minnie – in fact, I was going to suggest it myself. You can write and tell me all your news or any problems and I'll give you all my news.'

We said goodbye and I watched with a heavy

heart as she climbed the hill. She carried the comics in one hand while Peter clutched his bag of sherbet in his little fist. After a few steps, they both turned and waved and I felt an overwhelming feeling of sadness.

8

Margot was selling her house. Dad arrived home at the end of January with this news. He looked tired and I was concerned for him.

'Margot has decided to put her house up for sale,' he said.

When I looked surprised, he continued, 'Well, she feels that although the verdict on Harry's drowning was an accidental death, she doesn't want to stay in the house on her own.'

I knew everyone had been so kind to her. The police had told her he had probably tripped over some obstacle on the dock and fallen in. It was a simple but tragic accident. Seemingly his favourite walk took him along a very cluttered path and, although it was a safe enough place, you had to watch your step if you decided to stroll along the many wharves.

Dad was still explaining. 'Aye, she said she doesn't feel happy in the house now that he's gone.'

I was about to suggest that, if she was so lonely on her own, then perhaps she could take in a lodger as company. But, before I could speak, Dad said, 'Another problem she has is the fact she needs money now that Harry's wage has stopped.'

'But surely, if he was on the point of retiring, then his wage would have stopped anyway?' I said, suddenly confused by this apparent lack of money. Judging from her beautiful home and elegant clothes, I thought she must be comfortable if not exactly rich.

'Aye, a lot of folk thought there was money but all she has is the house and a wee insurance policy Harry took out years ago.'

He quickly ate his dinner then got ready to leave. 'I've got to go with her to see a flat in Victoria Road that she fancies. It'll cost her a few bob but she'll have the balance of her money from the sale of her bigger house.'

'Will that not take a long time, Dad? Selling her house?'

He shook his head. 'No. There's folk seemingly been round to see it and they've put in an offer. She'll be flitting next week.'

Next week, I thought – she hadn't hung about after Harry's death. I knew hardly anything about buying a house. On the Hilltown most of us had a big enough problem buying a loaf of bread. Still, I thought it was a very quick move.

'Aye, she was lucky,' said Dad. 'My boss John Pringle has helped her with everything and Maddie's dad is handling the legal side of things so, between them, they've hurried things along when she told them she wasn't happy in the house.'

A bitchy thought entered my mind and I was ashamed of myself. Lucky Margot, indeed – she seemed to have loads of men running around her, all falling over themselves to help her and make her happy. Still, as Granny often said, there were women like this all over the world. Instead of working their fingers to the bone like most of the women I knew, these lucky ones swanned around while men danced attention on them.

As Dad hurried from the house, I was grateful he couldn't read my uncharitable mind. I hoped he would give me all the details about the new flat but, if he didn't, then I would bring the subject up.

As it was a Saturday, Lily was still at the Overgate and I was just putting on my coat to go and collect her when there was a knock at the door. To my amazement it was Maddie. She looked cold. Her hands were thrust into the deep pockets of her dark coat and her blonde hair was tucked into a bright red beret. I thought her face looked thinner but she smiled brightly.

'I've got a few hours off, Ann, and I thought I would catch you in.'

I was so pleased to see her. 'Come in, Maddie.'

I had cleared the table prior to leaving for Lily but I offered her some dinner.

'No, a cup of tea will be fine.'

I made some cheese sandwiches and I noticed she ate most of them. I was worried about her thin appearance and I asked her, 'Are you getting enough to eat at the infirmary, Maddie?'

She laughed. 'Oh, it's not that. There's always enough to eat but the food all tastes the same – soup, meat and puddings all with the same taste.'

I was shocked. 'What? Everything tastes the same?'

She laughed again. 'No, it's just us pernickety nurses who think that. No, the food is fine.' She made a funny face when she said it so I didn't know if it was true or otherwise. 'Still, I haven't come to visit you to tell you about the infirmary kitchens, Ann. Tell me all your news.'

I told her about Dad and Margot and I mentioned the sale of her house. 'In fact you've just missed Dad. He's away to look at a flat in Victoria Road with Margot.'

Maddie seemed surprised. 'Is your Dad really so friendly with her?'

I nodded. 'It's really your uncle's fault because he got Dad to help her right after Harry went missing and I suppose she still needs some help. Dad was saying that your dad and uncle are also doing their bit for her – your dad is selling her house for her.'

'I really don't know a great deal about her, Ann, although I overheard my parents discuss it last September when I had the weekend at home. She wanted to sell the house because she doesn't like living in it on her own.'

I was taken aback. Last September – that must have been just after the funeral, I thought.

'What does your dad think of her, Maddie?'

She gave this a moment's thought. Her hands curled around her cup of tea. 'He's hardly said anything about her – just that he's selling the house. My uncle John doesn't know her very well either. Although Harry worked for him for loads of years it was his first wife that he knew quite well. I don't think he ever met Margot before Harry's disappearance.'

And now they're all running circles around her, I thought wickedly.

After a moment's silence she asked, 'How is Danny?'

Although she sounded casual I wasn't fooled. 'Still being a stupid fool, Maddie. Granny says he needs his backside kicked.'

She laughed. 'So he's fine?'

I nodded. What else could I tell her?

She avoided my eyes. 'I did hear that he has put in for a transfer to Glasgow. Is that true?'

I nodded. 'But I hope he doesn't get it, Maddie. Minnie and her wee laddie Peter are going back to the west coast. Her man has got a shift to a branch of the Home and Colonial at Clydebank but I haven't heard from her yet. She did say she would write.'

Maddie was surprised and I told her of my meetings with Minnie. 'She's not interested in Danny. She's got enough problems as it is and I feel sorry for her. I just hope she settles down and is happy.' How could I explain the strange feeling that came over me when I said goodbye to them? Especially to Maddie who would think I was mad. I smiled. 'Anyway how did you hear about Danny?'

She blushed. 'I get mum to quiz Hattie. She doesn't like doing it but I've begged her to find out as much as she can.'

'Has Danny been in touch with you?'

She looked sad. 'No, he hasn't.'

I suddenly felt very old and weary. What a prize idiot he was. I told Maddie this but she just shrugged her shoulders.

'What can I do? Do I go and see him and beg him to get engaged again?'

'I wish I knew the answer to that – believe me.'

She stood up. 'It's time I was off but it's been

215

great seeing you again, Ann. I don't know when I'll see you again – I'm working really hard these days because my final exams will be this summer.'

'Will they be difficult?'

She nodded. 'It seems to get harder every year and these exams are so important because, if I don't pass, then I don't qualify.'

'Well, I hope you do pass, Maddie. You deserve to succeed.' I put my coat on. 'I'll walk with you to the infirmary. I have to go and bring Lily home. She's really doing well at school and I'm proud of her. How is Joy? Does she like the school?'

'Yes, she does. She's in a small private school and she seems to be very clever. She wants to be a solicitor like Dad.' She smiled at the thought. 'What about Lily? What does she want to be?'

'At the moment, it's a toss up between a film star and a spy.'

That made Maddie laugh.

We set off along Constitution Road with the wind blowing coldly against our faces.

'How's Colin?' I asked.

Maddie looked sad. 'I'm not seeing him very much these days. I had to be honest and tell him I'm still in love with Danny and it wouldn't be fair to keep going out with him.' Suddenly she laughed and all the sadness disappeared. 'Mind you, he didn't take it as badly as I thought and he's now seeing one of the girls from Dad's office. So much for missing me! It seems to be my thing in life. Missed by no one – neither Danny nor Colin.'

I stopped walking and looked at her. 'Don't you

216

believe that, Maddie. Danny misses you very much but, as I said earlier, he's just an idiot.'

'Does he?' She became serious. 'Well, why doesn't he come to see me and tell me what this is all about? It's been two years since we split up and I still don't have a clue why.'

I had no answer to that thorny question but, thankfully, we had reached the infirmary gate.

She glanced at her watch. 'Heavens, I'd better run.' She made a face. 'We never seem to have time to see or speak to each other these days, do we?'

'No, Maddie, we don't but it'll be better after you qualify. You'll maybe get more time off.' I didn't add that we were all getting older and time seemed to be slipping away from us.

Before reaching the door, she turned and called across the expanse of the driveway. 'I forgot to ask how Greg is. Is he still in Glasgow?'

'Aye, he is. We write to each other every week and I see him when he manages through for the day.'

'But no marriage plans yet?'

It was my turn to make a face. 'How could we, Maddie? I've got Lily to bring up and I couldn't ask a man to take on a ready-made family.'

'Well, if he loves you, then he should!' On that note she turned and ran towards the porter's window. I knew she had to report back in before resuming her duties.

Her last statement stayed with me all the way to the Overgate. Did he love me enough to take on Lily as well? Obviously not.

I gave Granny all Dad's news and, like me, she

was puzzled by Margot's behaviour. 'He said she was needing money?'

I nodded.

'Well, she'll get a good price for that great house and, with her new flat costing much less, she'll have a grand wee nest egg.'

The next day was Sunday and we were having a late breakfast because Dad didn't have his work to go to. He wasn't very forthcoming but I was determined to ask him.

'Did you see the new flat yesterday, Dad?'

He stopped eating his toast. 'No, Margot had to stay in her own house because the buyers wanted to measure the windows for curtains. She was really mad but there was nothing she could do. She wants me to have a look at it this afternoon.'

'Is she going to meet you there?'

He shook his head. 'No, she can't. The folk are coming back today to agree a price for the carpets. Their first offer wasn't enough so they said they would tell her today if they want to buy them or not.' He looked at me. 'I've got the key in my pocket because the flat is empty. Do you want to come with me and we can both look at it?'

I wasn't very happy with this idea but, on the other hand, I was dying to see it. 'What if Margot arrives and sees me there? She'll not want me poking my nose into her business.'

'No, no, she'll not be anywhere near the flat this afternoon because the folk are coming at three o'clock to see her about the carpets. We can quite easily go and see the flat and you can give me your opinion of it.'

I was taken aback by this. Why should my

opinion count?

As if reading my thoughts, he said, 'Not that anybody's opinion will count because it'll be Margot's choice as it's her money.'

Well, that was all right then. I still had my misgivings. After her lovely house and garden, how would she like to live in a flat that overlooked a busy main road?

Lily arrived with the Sunday paper. She had offered to run down to Connie's shop for it.

'What about Lily?' I said softly when she was out of earshot. 'We'll have to take her with us.'

Dad seemed uncertain but he said, 'Only if she promises not to say a word about it to Margot.'

Suddenly she was at his side. 'What have I not to say, Daddy? Where are we going?'

Dad picked up the paper and his toast. 'Never mind. You'll find out soon enough. Now eat up your porridge.'

She sat down and chattered between each mouthful. 'Davie came in and he was wearing a great pair of shoes. Connie said they were brogues and they were shiny and polished. Connie said he looked like a country gent and all he needed now was a gun dog. He was really pleased at her and he laughed.'

I said nothing but I was inwardly pleased as well. The pleasure on Mrs Chambers' face when I delivered the three pairs of shoes from Hattie was still fresh in my mind.

I thought they might be too big for him but she had laughed as she said, 'Och, I'll just stuff some newspaper in the toes and they'll fit him just fine.'

Whether she had done this or not, Davie was obviously wearing them and showing them off to Connie. What would her comments be in the morning? I wondered.

Later that afternoon, the three of us went to view the new flat. After the cold wind of the previous day, it had turned a bit milder and the sunshine felt quite warm on our faces. It was a pleasant day for a stroll and having a good old nosey around someone else's house.

We turned left at the foot of the Hilltown and walked along the left side of Victoria Road. We had almost reached the Eagle Jute mills when we saw the block of flats. The tenement block looked well cared for and the windows were quite large. The entrance close was cleanly scrubbed but a bit dowdy with its dark brown paint. The flat was on the third landing and I thought that three was my number this week. Mrs Chambers also lived on the third landing.

There were two doors at the top of the stairs, facing one another. Each had a smart coat of paint, a brass handle and a bell at the side. Dad opened the door on the right. It led on to a small square lobby but when he opened another door to the right, this was the living room and it was flooded with sunshine which streamed through the large window.

'It's only got the one bedroom,' Dad said, sounding like a house factor showing a tenant around.

We looked round this one bedroom which was also sunny and then saw the small bathroom and tiny kitchen. To be quite honest, I couldn't see

Margot being happy there after her lovely house and garden in Clepington Road but, if she needed the money ... well, she would just have to like it.

'Well, Ann, what do you think about the flat?' Dad asked.

I was amazed. Why did he want my opinion? 'It's a lovely wee flat, Dad, but will she not miss her great house?' I answered truthfully.

'No, she says she won't. She says that house belonged to Harry and his first wife and she never felt it was hers. But this place will belong to her.'

I must have put on my cynical expression because he became flustered.

'Another thing – she wants to get away from her sister-in-law. She stays a few streets away and she's aye going round and poking her nose into Margot's affairs. Margot is getting really cheesed off with her.'

I bet she is, I thought sourly.

'What is the sister-in-law saying about Margot?'

Dad seemed flustered again. 'Och, she's aye harping on about Harry. She said that Harry told her that he was unhappy before his accident – as if Margot can be blamed for that...' His voice trailed away when he recalled Harry.

While we had been chatting, Lily was happily looking out of the window. Watching the traffic go by. She had a good view of the road and she suddenly exclaimed, 'Here's Margot coming up the road.'

Dad marched over to the window to haul her away. 'Don't be daft, Lily. Come away from there.'

Lily pointed down the road.

Dad almost collapsed. 'Oh, it is Margot. Quick you two, down the stair.'

He ushered us out and we quickly ran down the three flights of stairs like scared rabbits.

'She'll meet us in the close, Dad,' I said breathlessly.

'No, she'll not. There's a back door that leads on to the washing green. You can both go out that way.'

We reached the back door, Dad tugged it open and we all darted outside.

Dad said, 'Right, you two stay here and I'll go upstairs and make it look as if I've just arrived. Give me a few moments then you can both head for home.'

What a palaver I thought but Lily's face was flushed with excitement. 'This is like being a spy,' she said, her eyes gleaming with pleasure.

But I couldn't help thinking of Dad in that terrible state. He was never terrified of any other woman he knew, even my late mother.

We decided to go to the Overgate. Lily related the story to her grandparents and they both laughed heartily – in fact, Granny had to wipe her eyes on the corner of her apron. 'Och, that's the best laugh I've had in ages.'

Even Grandad chuckled. 'It looks like our Johnny has met his match at last. She sounds just like Hattie.'

Lily was in her element. 'We belted out the back door, Granny, and we were in this wee back green and we had to hide like spies until Margot went upstairs.' She turned to me. 'What would have happened if she had looked out her back window?

She would have seen us lurking like spies.'

I laughed. 'Then that would have been Dad's problem. She was supposed to be seeing the buyer of her house about the carpets.'

Grandad said, 'Come on, Lily, you can take your old grandad for a walk but promise you'll not be a spy.'

She gave him a serious look. 'Och, I can't promise that, Grandad. After all, that's what I'm going to be when I grow up – a spy!'

He smiled. 'Well, I suppose I'll just have to put up with it if I want my favourite lassie to take her old grandad for a walk.'

She took his hand. 'Come on then, Grandad.'

After they left, Granny said, 'That lassie reads too many books. Her head is filled with nonsense.'

'It's Dad's fault,' I explained. 'He was telling her about a spy called Mata Hari one night and she's been like this ever since.'

Granny became serious. 'I feel sorry for Rosie. She never sees your dad these days.'

I didn't know what to say.

She went on, 'I've told her that she's far too good for him. She deserves a man who thinks she's the bee's knees – no' a man that only thinks about her when it suits him.' That was the truth. He had used Rosie all these years and now he had discarded her.

Granny was right to be outraged.

Then she said, 'Goodness! I nearly forgot with all this laughing at Lily's story. Danny was here and he wants to see you as soon as possible.'

'Does he want me to go to the Westport?' I was mystified.

She gave this a bit of thought. 'No, I think he meant he would see you here. He knew you would bring Lily this afternoon.'

I decided to wait. An hour later he appeared. He looked tired and Granny was concerned.

'You need to look after yourself Danny.'

'I'm fine, Granny. I'm just a bit tired because the shop is busy – especially on a Saturday when we work late into the evening.'

Then he said, 'Let's go for a walk, Ann.'

The early evening was lovely and mild but I knew the cold weather wasn't too far away. These unseasonable spells should be enjoyed. A large moon shone over the streets, turning the smoke from hundreds of chimneys into a grey gauzy mist.

I told him about Maddie's visit. 'She's stopped seeing Colin. She told him she was still in love with you.'

I waited for his answer but he remained silent.

Annoyed, I went on, 'Do you hear me? I'm telling you what she said.'

His voice sounded tired. 'I know it's my own fault and I just wish I could maybe bump into her and it would be quite the natural thing to start talking but I can't get up the courage to go and see her – not after what I've done to her. Anyway what would her parents think? They must hate me.'

'No they don't, Danny. Maddie hasn't told them too much. They think you're both waiting till her final exams are over. She sits them this summer.'

He suddenly smiled. 'Well, I promise I'll sort myself out before then. But, in the meantime, there's Kathleen.'

'But she didn't marry the awful Sammy on the second of January like he said, so that's one blessing, isn't it?'

He agreed. 'I just hope we've sorted her out about getting married. She's agreed to stay with her parents until the bairn is born.' He sounded relieved.

'When will that be?'

'Sometime in May according to Kit.' He stopped and I saw the gleam of anger in his eyes. 'I get so angry with Sammy Malloy. He messed up my life after Dad Ryan's death and now he's messed up Kathleen's.'

If it was any consolation to him, I felt the same. I told him so. To cheer him up I told him the tale of our flight from the flat. 'I should get Lily to tell it. She makes a better job of it than me.'

He laughed and I was glad to hear it. Then I remembered Granny's reaction to Lily. 'It was such a laugh, Danny. Lily was prattling on and on about being a spy and I told Granny about Dad's story of Mata Hari then, in the next breath, she mentions Rosie.'

We both laughed at this. Then, like Granny, I had to wipe my eyes. 'Do you think Rosie looks like this Mata Hari?'

'I doubt it. But, as I don't know what Mata Hari looked like, maybe Rosie does look like her, this seductive spy.'

On that cheery note we returned to the house.

Three weeks later Danny was far from being cheery however. Once again we were on our way to Lochee after Danny got the bad news. Kathleen was getting married after all.

The house was full of people when we arrived – a contrast to my earlier visit. Apart from Kit, George, Kathleen and Ma, the Malloy family were also in residence. When I say the family, it was Mick and his wife plus the obnoxious one – Sammy. For some reason, the men seemed subdued which surprised me. Then I realised it was because of Mrs Malloy.

Maggie Malloy was a very tiny woman – four feet eight inches and very thin. Her grey hair was extremely frizzy and it looked as if she had just removed a hundred dinkie curlers. Her sharp-featured face was softened slightly by dark-brown eyes. They looked shrewd.

Kit and George looked exhausted while Kathleen was as beautiful as ever.

Her father looked at her and asked, 'Is this what you really want, Kathleen? This marriage?'

She looked over at Sammy.

Her father said, 'Don't look at him. I'm asking you, do you want to marry him?'

She nodded but she didn't look happy.

As usual Ma sat in silence and I wished she would speak out. Then I remembered she had forecast this wedding.

Maggie came over from her chair and stood beside Kit and George. 'It's got to be your decision, Kathleen. Your parents and I can't make up your mind for you.'

Sammy butted in, 'Nobody's asking me if I want to get married. After all, she turned me down when I had it arranged for January and I'm seeing another lass now.'

Maggie turned on him with venom in her eyes.

'Shut up, Sammy. In that case, you're not to see this other girl again – Kathleen is your priority now.'

He sat back in his chair with a sullen look but he kept quiet. I was at a loss to understand Kathleen's change of heart. Especially now that Sammy had changed his mind.

Kathleen said, 'It was Father James that said I had to be wed.'

Kit was annoyed. 'That priest should keep his big nose out of this.'

Maggie was shocked. 'But that's his job, Kit. He is, after all, a man of the chapel.'

Mick Malloy then butted in, 'Well, is there to be a wedding or is there not?' It was obvious that this meeting was taking up some of Mick's drinking time.

Sammy sat and glared while Kathleen stared at her hands. Then she looked firmly at him and said, 'Aye there is.'

Her parents didn't look pleased at this statement but they remained silent.

Meanwhile Maggie started the bandwagon rolling by announcing, 'Well, you'll have to get the banns read and that will take three weeks so you'd better get your skates on, Sammy.'

Sammy muttered something under his breath while his parents put on their coats.

At the door Maggie turned to Kit. 'We'll be in touch about the wedding plans later.'

After they had gone, Danny asked Kathleen why she had changed her mind.

'I don't want my bairn being born illegitimate, Danny – without a father.'

Her Dad exploded, 'Heavens above, Kathleen! It's Sammy Malloy we're talking about here.'

Ma suddenly spoke up from her corner by the fire. 'It's just like I've told you, Kit – what's meant to be will happen.'

On that cryptic note we stood up to leave. Danny was far from happy about the outcome of the evening but Kathleen had made her decision and she had finally settled for marriage – to give her baby a name.

'Where will she stay when the bairn comes, Danny? Will it be with Sammy's folk or Kit and George?'

He shook his head in bewilderment. 'I've no idea and I don't think Kathleen knows either.'

I was perplexed but for a different reason. 'Why do you think she changed her mind when she knows Sammy is no longer interested in her? Do you think that's the reason?'

'Kathleen is a lovely lassie,' said Danny, 'but she's aye been a bit perverse – even as a bairn. I think, if Sammy had been begging her to marry him, she would have turned him down but, now that he's no longer interested in her, she suddenly thinks he's marvellous. Then there's Father James. She's aye looked up to him and listened to every word he says.'

I thought the same thing but I sincerely hoped she wasn't making one gigantic mistake.

The wedding took place at the end of February in St Mary's Roman Catholic chapel in Lochee. It was a terrible day of snow showers and high winds and the weather seemed to imitate the feelings of most of the congregation.

Kit and Maggie had been busy with the arrangements and a small wedding breakfast was to be held in Kit's house after the service.

Dad, Lily and I went with Hattie who to my relief had deliberately dressed down for the occasion. She wore a suit in flecked tweed, a brown hat and plain shoes. The suit had a well-worn look and she resembled a middle-aged matron – so unlike her usual elegant self.

Danny went with the Ryan families and we all trudged through the snow which was now covering the pavements to congregate in the lovely but cold chapel.

I saw Ma. She looked like a black Buddha while Kit wore a winter coat in brown and Maggie was decked out in fawn. The majority of guests were dressed in various styles but they all had one thing in common – their outfits showed how hard-up they were but they were determined to look their best for the wedding.

Then the bride appeared in a simple white wedding dress that had been designed to hide her bump. The material looked cheap and shiny and she had a tiny veil on her lovely red hair. She was one of the loveliest brides I had seen in a very long time. Her bridesmaid was an old school-friend. She was dressed in the same shiny material but in a shade of blue that didn't do anything for her plain, podgy face.

One of Sammy's brothers was the best man and they both wore dark suits. I had to admit that they were both very handsome men and I suppose any young girl's head would be turned by them.

Although I wasn't a religious person, I made a mental prayer that day. Hoping they would be very happy with one another and the coming baby.

I found the chapel lovely and soothing and the solemnity of the wedding service was another delight. I hadn't expected to enjoy this part of it but an inner peace flooded over me as the priest's voice intoned and echoed against the walls. I glanced at Lily and she was taking it all in. It was as if her eyes were photographing the entire scene so she could relive it in her head.

Later on, we all went back to Kit's house – apart from Dad and Lily who went back to the Overgate. Just as she had done on previous occasions, Kit had done the best she could. As there wasn't enough room for all the Malloy children, they were taken to Lizzie's house and fed there.

Kit was so glad to see Hattie. She gave her a hug and, if Hattie was surprised, then she didn't show it. 'It's lovely to see you Hattie. Thanks for coming and giving us your support.'

Hattie seemed overcome by this warm statement and she hugged her sister-in-law in return. 'I hope Kathleen and Sammy are happy for years and years, Kit – just like yourself and George.'

Kit glanced over at her husband. He was standing with the Malloy family and, although they weren't all laughing together, at least they weren't arguing.

Kathleen came over to Ma's chair. She had taken her veil off but she still had on her wedding dress. It had been hand sewn but very well done I noticed. Although the material was a thin shiny satin, the dressmaker had sewn the waistline with shirring elastic and there was a gathered overlay in front, similar to an apron.

'You make a lovely bride, Kathleen,' I said truthfully.

She smiled and blushed.

My heart ached for her. Please let her be happy, I thought.

Ma had taken off her black coat but her dress was also in black. She looked more suitably dressed for a funeral than a wedding but, as this was her usual mode of dress, no one took any offence.

Maggie appeared and spoke to Kathleen. 'Chrissie is wanting to see you, Kathleen.' She indicated the bridesmaid in the blue frock.

She gazed fondly after her. 'Aye, she's a right bonny bride, Kit.'

Kit returned her gaze and said, 'Aye, she is – although she wasn't so blooming in the early days of her pregnancy because of morning sickness.'

Maggie made a sympathetic face. 'Bad was she?'

Kit nodded. 'Mind you, I was the same when I was expecting my bairns so she probably takes it after me.'

'I liked her dress, Kit,' I said, trying to change the subject away from the perils and trials of morning sickness.

'We got it from Maggie,' said Kit.

Maggie then launched into the origins of the dress. 'Aye, old Mrs Morris made it a few years ago for my first laddie's wife and it's been used by the other two brides. Now it's Kathleen's turn.'

'Well, it's lovely,' I replied.

Maggie laughed. 'Aye, Mrs Morris had to make it to accommodate my first daughter-in-law's waistline because she was expecting a bairn as well. Then, lo and behold, did we not find out that the other two brides were in the same condition?'

Looking at the four Malloy men and their father I could well believe it.

I noticed the small back bedroom had been turned into a bar. The women had all been offered a small glass of sherry but the men had a crate of beer for themselves. Memories of the night of Dad Ryan's wake swam into my mind but I pushed them away. This was a celebration and not a death I said to myself.

The men were getting merry and I saw to my dismay that Sammy was almost legless. He kept coming to the door and shouting over to his new bride. Meanwhile, she ignored him and stood chatting with Chrissie and Danny. Chrissie kept glancing at Danny with large eyes that were the best feature of her plain face. Maybe she was secretly hoping that it would be her turn next.

'Where are they going to stay, Kit?' No one had mentioned this thorny question that had hung in the air for the last few weeks.

Still, it seemed as if a solution had been found as Kit explained. 'Well, for the time being, they are going to stay with Ma because she has the wee spare back room.'

Maggie butted in, 'I was just telling Kit that old Mrs Morris is not long for this world. Now I'm really chummy with the rent man and I thought of asking him if Sammy and Kathleen can get her house.'

What a world, I thought – the old woman wasn't dead yet but already there were plans being made for her house. Then I realised that, in this world of little money and no prospects of work, you had to stay one step ahead all the time. These people didn't have the luxury of taking life slowly.

Maggie was still chattering on. 'Aye, Mrs Morris is on her last legs, poor soul. Her house is tiny and just the one room but it would do the young couple for the time being. Mrs Morris is the woman who made the wedding frock. She was a great dressmaker in her day and she worked in a big house – a seamstress to a lady something or other who had this whole army of servants.'

I glanced at Kit and she looked tired. She had taken off her brown coat and she was wearing a wool frock in a deep shade of green that, in her youth, would have suited her deep auburn hair. Tonight she simply looked pale and slightly faded. Did she have high hopes for Kathleen or did she view it as a wasted life? At not quite seventeen and now married and expecting a baby?

A roar of laughter exploded from the back room. Hattie said brightly, 'The wedding breakfast is a huge success, Kit!'

Kit nodded but I could almost read her mind. 'It is for some folk.'

Maggie had now attached herself to Danny and she was telling him some story, her arms moving around as if to emphasise her words.

Kit smiled. 'She's not a bad sort is Maggie and I suppose the men in the family are not all bad either. It's just when they get a drink inside them then they become demons. If only they would stay sober.'

Hattie looked at me over the top of Kit's head. She said nothing but her expression said it all.

I asked, 'Has Maggie just got the four laddies, Kit?' I wasn't really interested but it was merely to break the spell of Hattie's look and the ensuing silence.

Kit nodded. 'Aye. Although she had twelve bairns, most of them died in infancy. Aye, she's had a hard life – just like the rest of us.'

At that point, Kathleen's three new sisters-in-law crowded around her and I noticed with sadness that they all looked worn out and dowdy. Kathleen's beauty shone out like a beacon but was it her lot in life to become like them? No doubt these three women had all been lovely on their own wedding days.

Another roar of laughter came from the back room and Sammy staggered out.

'Where's my wife?' He glared at the guests then collapsed on the floor.

His father came out and lifted him up. He smiled apologetically to Kathleen. 'He's not aye like this.'

Maggie's voice was shrill. 'He bloody better not be.'

I tried not to look at Hattie or Danny. I knew they would be appalled and Danny would be very angry.

There was something I was dying to ask – something that had been sparked by what George had said on my last visit. I said to Kit, 'George said that Maggie wasn't married to Mick. He said

234

she was a common-law wife. What's that Kit?'

For the first time that night, Kit laughed. 'Och, you're no' to believe George. He might think it but look at it this way. Do you honestly believe Maggie would still be with Mick Malloy if she wasn't legally married to him?' She stopped and looked over at Maggie who was now gesturing some command to her daughters-in-law. 'Oh, no, she's married to him. A common-law wife is one that lives with a man but doesn't get married to him. It's quite common and, although the union is not legally binding, most of these couples do live together for years.' She gazed at me intently. 'You're not thinking of doing that with that young man of yours, are you, Ann?'

It was now my turn to be appalled and I turned a bright red. 'Oh, no, Kit. I was just ... curious...' I stammered.

'Och, I'm just kidding you on, Ann,' she laughed.

It was now time to leave. Hattie, Danny and I said our farewells to the assembled company – well, everyone except the groom. He was snoring loudly on the bed in the back room, surrounded by empty beer bottles.

Kit said, 'Tell your Dad that we appreciate him coming – and Lily as well.'

Hattie had considered getting a taxi home but she didn't like to show this display of money in front of people who had so little so we caught the tramcar back to the Overgate. When we were seated in its dubious warmth, Hattie turned to me. 'Where is your father, Ann? I thought he would come back for the wedding breakfast but he left as soon as the service was over.'

'He took Lily back to Granny's because he thought Kit would have enough to feed without them, Hattie.'

Thankfully, she accepted this explanation but consideration for Kit's feeding arrangements had nothing to do with it. After depositing Lily with her granny, he was rushing off to Margot.

The flat was taking shape but he said he had a hundred and one jobs to do for her. It was totally insane this new image and I wished he was back to the old father I knew and loved.

Hattie turned to Danny who was sitting behind us. 'What do you make of the groom, Danny?'

His lips were firm and he didn't smile. 'I'll tell you this – he'd better treat Kathleen right or else he'll hear from me.'

For the remainder of the journey we sat in silence, all of us with our own private thoughts and recollections of the day that was almost over, of Kathleen's wedding day – a day that saw the radiant bride in a hand-me-down, cheap, shiny dress and a groom who was legless in the back bedroom. Some wedding night!

9

It was strange but, for years afterwards, I was able to recall every detail about the thirtieth of April – the day Dad and Margot arrived at the house to inform us of their wedding.

I was on my knees, washing the kitchen floor, while Lily sat at the fire with her colouring book and crayons – just a normal Saturday afternoon.

Dad appeared first, looking handsome and slightly flushed. To my surprise, he was dressed in his new suit.

'I've got some news for you both,' he said, stuttering slightly in an effort to impart something important. 'Margot and I have just got married!'

He went to the door and his new bride was waiting to come in. She looked stunning in a pale lilac dress with a matching hat, a tiny confection of tulle with a spotted veil.

I, on the other hand, was conscious of my old skirt and tatty apron plus the fact my hair was held back from my face with two large Kirby-grips.

She stepped into the room and immediately everything looked shabby and worn. It was as if a diamond had been set in a lump of lead.

Lily sat in silence and gazed at them with eyes as large as saucers while I stood by the side of my bucket like Cinderella.

Dad chided us both, 'Well then, Ann and Lily,

are you not going to welcome the new Mrs Neill?'

How did one welcome a new stepmother? With a kiss or a nod or a cup of tea?

I stepped forward and shook her gloved hand. Noticing with dismay the wrinkled state of my fingers. They resembled ten prunes.

Lily ran forward at the same time but she ignored Margot. Instead, she threw her arms around Dad's legs and uttered something we couldn't make out.

Meanwhile, I took advantage of this encounter to empty my bucket down the sink. Thankfully the house was clean and it smelled fresh as I had been on the last chore of the weekly clean.

I plumped the cushion up on the fireside chair. 'Sit down, Margot, and I'll make a cup of tea.'

She sat down delicately, looking as if she had been invited to Buckingham Palace and had stumbled into the garden shed by mistake. Although her expression gave little away, I could well imagine her comparison with her last house and this new unknown flat. Still, she wouldn't be staying here.

Dad remained standing. 'Don't bother with tea for us, Ann. We're having a quiet day today but we're planning a get-together next Saturday for all the family.' He stopped and looked at his new wife.

She resumed the story. 'Yes, it'll be in our house in Victoria Road. I'll write the address down and we'll leave it to you Ann to invite your grand-parents, Hattie and Danny – Greg too if he can manage.'

Lily opened her mouth to speak but I gave her

238

a warning glance and she remained silent.

Dad said, 'We're going away for a couple of days. I'll speak to my boss and get Monday off work so we'll see you all next week.' On that note they departed, leaving behind a fragrant scent of some expensive perfume.

As our kitchen window overlooked the Hilltown, we looked out after they had gone. I was sure Lily was going to shout out at their retreating figures so I held her back. I expected to see them walk away down the hill but, to my amazement, they got into a taxi which had obviously waited for them – what an expense.

Then, as I closed the window, the reality of the situation hit me. Dad normally worked on a Saturday morning and got his wages at the end of the shift. On a normal weekend, this meant I would have my housekeeping money by now – but not today. He had gone off with his new wife and left us with my small wage from the shop. That was enough to pay the rent and keep some pennies for the gas meter but it wouldn't stretch to a week's shopping.

Lily had her own thoughts. They didn't hinge on money but she was very unhappy. 'What will happen to us, Ann? Has Dad left us on our own?'

I tried to sound cheerful. 'No, of course he hasn't, Lily. When folk get married they go off on a honeymoon and that's what Dad and Margot have done. He knows you've aye got me to look after you.'

Lily looked doubtful and I didn't blame her.

'Come on – we'd better give Granny and Grandad the good news.'

There was no taxi for us as we made our way to the Overgate. It was a strange day of sunshine and showers. One minute the sun shone brightly with a brilliant glow and the next it was blotted out by black clouds that bunched up like dirty cotton wool.

Lily said, 'We don't need her address, Ann – we know where she lives.'

'Aye, we know that but she doesn't. Now remember not to tell her that we've been in her house before. Now mind that, Lily.'

Childlike, she clapped a hand over her mouth. 'Och, I forgot.'

'Well, as long as you don't forget when we visit them next week.'

My grandparents were just finishing their dinner when we arrived and Lily eagerly accepted a bowl of broth.

Granny was surprised by our visit. 'I wasn't expecting you today. Did you leave your dad with his dinner and decide to come and see us?'

Before we reached the house I had also warned Lily to let me tell them the news first and, although she hadn't looked happy about it, she agreed. I hadn't made up a speech on my way here and, because there was no way I could break the news gently, I just stated quite bluntly, 'Dad and Margot have just got married, Granny.'

I then realised I should have broken the news more subtly because her face drained of all colour and she sat down. Grandad's cup clattered against the saucer.

He was angry. 'He's done what?'

I went to sit beside Granny and she began to

regain some colour in her cheeks.

'I'm sorry, Granny – I shouldn't have been so blunt.'

'Och, it's not your fault, lass,' said Grandad crossly. 'It's that idiot son of ours who should have had the sense to make plans like everybody else. Running away like a thief in the night to marry a woman whose man is hardly cold in his grave...'

I was surprised by this outburst because he was normally so reticent about matters in the family. He poured out tea for Granny and me and, by this time, she had recovered her composure.

Lily, obviously thinking she had honoured her side of the silence bargain, now chattered on about what had happened. 'Ann was washing the floor and I was colouring my book when Dad appeared and said he was married. Then Margot came in and she was dressed in a lovely bonny frock and hat in blue – no lilac. Well, she looked down her nose at Ann because she was looking like a tink and her hands were all wrinkled and prune-like and she shook Ann's hand but I'm sure she didn't want to do it.' She took a deep gulp of air and, before I could stop her, she carried on, her eyes large with the excitement of the story. 'Well, when they left, Ann and me, we hung out the window and what do you think, Granny?'

Much to Lily's delight, Granny said that she couldn't even begin to imagine.

'They were in a taxi and it had waited on them. Ann said what a terrible expense. We're all invited to a party in her house in Victoria Road next Saturday – just the family so I don't think we can invite Rosie.'

It was a true saying, 'Out of the mouth of babes...'

Rosie. The name fell like a bomb on our ears. Granny looked at me with dismay. 'Who's going to tell her, Ann?'

Although I didn't relish the job I knew it had to be me. Poor Rosie – she worshipped him like a god. A flood of anger swept over me at this off-hand treatment by the both of them – Dad and Margot. Dad wasn't some single man without any ties and they should have told us about their impending marriage – if only to allow us to make our own plans. Still, he was besotted by her so what could we expect?

Lily began again, 'Ann's told me I've not to mention that we've been in her house so I'll have to watch I don't chatter too much.'

Granny laughed and I was glad to see she had got over her initial shock. 'Och, just you chatter as much as you like, Lily. It'll do Margot the world of good to see what she's taken on.'

I decided to go and see Hattie and Danny first – glad of anything that would postpone my meeting with Rosie. Before leaving, I made Lily promise not to blurt out the truth should Rosie or Alice appear.

Hattie was over the moon at the news but that was to be expected. Anyone with a lovely house and clothes was to be admired and welcomed into the family. 'Well, I'm glad your father has at last got the sense to marry someone decent, Ann. When I think of some of the women he's known since your mother died well, I shudder. Remember that Marlene Davidson?' Hattie's shoulders shook in response to the memory.

Marlene had been a good friend of his after mum's death and he had lodged with her for a time but, when she realised he wasn't going to marry her, she put him out.

Hattie was still waxing lyrical. 'I mean, look at her lovely house and her manners. Just compare her with Rosie – there's no contest.'

I was annoyed by her remarks. Marlene had been a good friend to him and as for Rosie ... well, Rosie was a gem and I would have been happy if he had married her and not this other unknown woman. I told Hattie this and she didn't seem pleased but she stayed quiet.

'There's to be a family party next Saturday in the house in Victoria Road. You've been invited along with Danny.'

She sighed. 'I've never understood why she sold her lovely house to buy a flat in a tenement. Surely she has money because she certainly didn't marry your father for his wealth.'

That was true so maybe she was as besotted with him as he was with her.

'Danny works late on a Saturday night so I hope the party will be in the evening,' she said.

I had no idea what time it was due to take place. Margot had said Saturday but had given no time.

'I'll let you know when I see Dad, Hattie. No doubt he'll be up to see us during the week.' Although I didn't tell her, I was as much in the dark about my own father as she was.

To my dismay, when I returned to the Overgate, Bella was there. She launched a tirade in my direction the minute I opened the door. 'Well, he's finally got himself hitched has he? And I expect I'll not be getting asked to the jamboree next week, will I?'

I could have killed Lily with her chattering but I had only mentioned to say nothing to Rosie or Alice. So I shrugged my shoulders, feigning a nonchalance I didn't feel.

'They did say family, Bella, and, as you're part of the family, then you're invited as well.'

Her face lit up with pleasure. 'Well, that's real nice of you, Ann.'

Granny raised her eyebrows but I was in no mood for a confrontation. Dad deserved all he got in my opinion and, if that included Bella at the party, then so be it. After all, as I'd said, Bella was family and, if Margot hadn't actually mentioned her by name, that was too bad. I still had Rosie to see and my patience was becoming sorely tried. How typical of my father to leave all the running about to others. There he was, swanning off on his honeymoon while we had to explain everything and even invite the guests to the wedding party.

But, before I could make a move next door, Bella piped up. She pointed with her head in the direction of Rosie's house. 'How do you think she's going to take this news after all her attempts to marry your father?'

'I've no idea, Bella. Have you any suggestions?'

She beamed with pleasure again. It had been a long time since anyone had asked for her opinion. To my surprise she gave this a bit of thought and, after a moment or two, she said, 'Well, if it was me who had to do the dirty deed then I would come straight out with it and tell her she will just have to accept it but, as it's you, Ann ... well, I expect you'll be more tactful.'

So I was on my own it seemed. I marched firmly to the door.

In an attempt at humour, grandad said, 'Wait and I'll see if Jeemy's Emporium has a suit of armour to protect you, lass.'

No one laughed and even Lily stayed quiet. Although she wouldn't quite understand the exact situation, she must have felt the tension in the room.

'Will I come with you, Ann?' she said in a small voice.

I went over and gave her a hug. 'No thanks, Lily, but it was good of you to offer.'

Grandad put his jacket on and took her coat from the peg at the back of the door. 'Let's go for a wee stroll, pet. It's not a bad day and I'll buy you some sweeties.'

She needed no second invite and she shot out of her chair. 'Can I have a bag of cinnamon balls, Grandad?'

He nodded and they both disappeared through the door.

Granny gave a huge sigh. 'Poor Ann – there's no cinnamon balls for you, is there? Just Rosie's wrath.'

For a brief moment I almost burst into laughter. Rosie's wrath would make an excellent title for a book but the thought of the coming visit dampened my faint flicker of humour.

Granny stood up. 'I'll better come with you,

Ann – it's not fair sending you in alone.'

'Oh, no, Granny, it's not your problem. In fact, it should be Dad that does his own dirty work and, if I thought I could get him here this minute, then I would make him do it. But I can't let Rosie hear this news through the gossip channel. It's just not fair to her or her mother.'

Thankfully, Granny sat down beside Bella and both women stared at me as I went out.

Rosie and Alice were both surprised to see me. I saw a strange expression flit over Alice's face and I'm sure she guessed the news I carried wasn't good. I was torn between telling Rosie there and then and maybe asking her to go out to a cafe for a cup of tea. But I finally decided to tell her in the house. I knew she would be terribly distressed and it was better to be like this in her own home and not in front of strangers or, even worse, some nosy neighbour.

She was dressed in her usual combination of colours and fabrics. She gave the impression of being fat and frumpy when I knew she was neither. She smiled and her face beamed while my heart sank. 'Och, it's yourself, Ann. I'm just waiting for your dad to come for his tea.' She saw my face and she stopped. 'Is there anything wrong? He's not ill, is he?'

Although I hadn't been aware of it before, I now noticed that I was twisting my hands as if wringing out the weekly washing.

Alice saw it and gave me such a strange look.

'Rosie, I...' My mouth was dry.

Rosie butted in. She sounded annoyed. 'He's not coming, is he? He's sent you to tell me that he's working for that woman, Margot?'

She couldn't have known how grateful I was for the mention of Margot's name. It didn't make my job any easier but at least we were on the same wavelength.

'Rosie, I'm sorry to have to tell you...'

'So he's not coming?' she said. 'I was right?'

Alice sat beside her daughter. She said gently, 'Let Ann tell you her story, Rosie. She's come with bad news, I think.'

Rosie went white. 'Oh, don't tell me he's dead?'

Would that news be better for her than the truth? I wondered.

I took a deep breath and looked straight at her. 'Rosie, Dad got married to Margot this morning. I can't tell you any more because Lily and I know very little ourselves.'

She looked perplexed. 'Married?'

I nodded unhappily and appealed to Alice. 'I'm really sorry but that's what he's told us. They've gone away for a honeymoon over the weekend but I expect he'll be back in time for his work on Tuesday.' I was blabbering but I couldn't help it.

Rosie said, 'He's married?'

Alice said quite firmly, 'Aye, it seems so, Rosie, and, if you ask me, he's not worth worrying over. Good riddance to him, I say.' She stopped as if suddenly realising she was talking to this monster's daughter.

But she needn't have worried – I was almost as angry as she was. 'If it's any consolation to you, Rosie, we're all very angry about it and I think he's made one gigantic mistake.'

Rosie was crying silently. Large tears rolled

247

down her face and if I could have got my hands on Dad at that minute I would have given him a few home truths. What a dirty rotten trick to play on Rosie. She was rocking back and forth in her distress and Alice and I both put an arm around her.

Alice's voice was soothing. 'Don't upset yourself, lass. You'll get over him in time and you'll find a far better man. Just you wait and see.'

To be honest, I also had tears in my eyes. 'Rosie, we always hoped it would be you he married. I thought he just needed time.'

Rosie remained silent but still rocked in her chair. The tear drops were now soaking the neck of her sludgy-green, hand-knitted jumper.

Alice looked at me and made a motion for me to leave.

As I stood up, she said, 'It was good of you tell her, Ann, but I'll not forget your father for this dirty rotten trick he's played on my lassie – no, indeed I'll not forget.'

I had no option but to leave. I turned around at the door to see the two women huddled together. Alice calm and very angry and Rosie, poor Rosie in her mismatched clothes, still crying silently. On the stove, a pot of soup bubbled away and I saw the frying pan sitting with a packet of sausages beside it. Obviously it was Dad's tea.

Granny was also angry when I got back to the house as was Bella. Bella spoke first. 'I suppose the lassie is heartbroken?'

I was too choked up with emotion to answer but I nodded.

Granny brought out the bottle of sherry. 'I

think we need this to settle our nerves.'

Bella gazed at the sherry with disdain. She pulled her medicine bottle from her message bag. 'I think we need something a bit stronger than sherry, Nan.'

She poured them both a measure of whisky but I settled for a cup of tea. Granny brought out the biscuit tin with her homemade scones inside. 'Bad news is aye easier to take in if you have something to eat.'

And so Dad's wedding day ended, not with a peal of happy bells and a flurry of confetti but with a flood of silent tears and a very deep anger that, apart from Hattie, ran right through two families.

Although I hadn't said a word at the time, I intended to catch him at his work the following week. I knew what time he took his dinner and I planned to accost him then.

Mondays and Tuesdays were always busy in the shop. Millworkers popped in on their way to work and it was usually a cheery time with all the local news and gossip. I wondered if the news of Dad's wedding had leaked out but it didn't seem to have. I decided to confide in Connie.

She looked at me in utter surprise. 'You mean to tell me that your father got married without telling you and Lily?' She sounded as angry as the rest of the family.

I nodded. 'I was going to ask a favour, Connie. As well as getting off for Lily can I also get a wee while off to go and see him during his dinner break at the warehouse? I've got loads of things to ask him.'

'Aye, you can,' she said, 'and make sure you get the right answers.'

On Tuesday, I could hardly wait till twelve o'clock and, when it came, I set off at a run towards Dock Street and the warehouse.

It was sunny when I left but I soon got caught in a heavy shower of rain which soaked through my clothes. I was fuming when I reached the open door. The warehouse was a large shed-like building, stacked high with boxes and pallets of fruit and vegetables. At the far end lay the boxes of flowers. I loved the smell in this shed with its mixture of aromas and, as I stood beside the door, the sun came out again. A thin shaft of sunlight squeezed through the small musty window high up on the wall, its beam sparkling against the hundreds of cobwebs that covered the roof.

I didn't see Dad but one of his workmates appeared. 'You've just missed your Dad, Ann. He's gone home because he forgot to bring his piece bag. Have you brought it?'

'No, I didn't see it, Bill. Has he gone to the Hilltown or the Overgate, do you know?' I'm not exactly sure why I didn't mention Margot but I had the sneaking suspicion that this man didn't know of the marriage.

'He's gone to the Hilltown because I offered to share my piece with him but he said he would go home and have his sandwiches there.'

He was nowhere near the Hilltown, I thought. He knew I would try and see him and this missing piece bag was simply an excuse. He also knew I couldn't keep asking for time off from Connie and he thought he was safe. Well, he was – at least until the party on Saturday when I would tackle him then. And that was another thing. What time was this party to take place? Morning, noon or night?

I was determined to get this uncertainty settled and I would do so on Saturday – even if I had to kidnap him at his own wedding party. There was no way he was going to dodge me forever.

Connie was concerned when I arrived back in my soaking wet clothes. 'You'd better get those wet things off, Ann, and don't bother coming back to work because I don't think we'll be very busy this afternoon.'

I didn't tell her I hadn't seen Dad. That would have made her really mad.

When I got home I found the house very cold and I quickly put a match to the fire. As I watched the flames shooting up the chimney, I glanced around the tiny kitchen. I loved this house with its brightly patterned curtains and the black-leaded grate with its wooden mantelpiece holding ornaments that had belonged to Mum. It wasn't fancy or well furnished but it was ours.

What would happen now with Dad away with his new wife? It hardly seemed real that it was barely forty-eight hours since he had sprung his surprise on us – and just when I thought the future looked brighter for us.

Then I realised I was shivering violently so I went in search of dry clothes. I wasn't looking forward to another soaking at the school gate so I made sure I was warmly wrapped up. May was turning out to be just as fickle as April but with the added problem of a blustery cold wind. April had been a wickedly deceiving month. One moment warm sunshine, the next freezing rain. And May was taking a leaf out of April's book.

That evening, we were sitting at our tea when Lily put into words all the things I was worried about. 'Is Dad not going to live with us ever again, Ann?' Her small face looked so innocent that I almost cried. 'Will he not bother with us and is he going to forget us?'

I looked her in the eye. 'I don't know what will happen, Lily, but you've always got me to look after you – no matter what happens.'

The look of relief on her face was heartbreaking to watch. 'You'll always be with me, Ann, won't you?'

I made a great show of licking my finger and making a huge cross on my chest. 'Cross my heart and hope to die.'

She smiled and began to eat her meal.

I was just thinking to myself that this was only Tuesday and already my anger was rising and wondering what I would be like by Saturday when, out of the blue, Dad bounced in the door. For a moment, I thought the wedding on Saturday had been a bad dream but it wasn't because he was looking sheepish.

'Bill was telling me you were at the work today, Ann. I had to go home because Margot likes me to have my dinner at home – at least for the time being.'

I was annoyed. 'You told Bill you were going home, Dad, and he thought that meant here. Have you not told your workmates yet about the wedding?'

He blushed and tried to avoid my eyes but I

was fed up with his evasiveness. He shuffled his feet. 'Well, that's the reason I went home at dinner-time because Margot doesn't want the men to know just yet. She thinks they might be annoyed because Harry was so popular. The only people who know at the work are Mr and Mrs Pringle. Margot told them.'

I was totally perplexed. 'What has Harry's popularity got to do with your wedding?'

He didn't answer at first. Then he said, 'Well, it's Margot's idea and it's just for the time being.'

I hated cross-examining him in front of Lily but I had no choice. 'And when is this party on Saturday? At what time?'

He was looking at the pot on the stove. 'Is that soup? I wouldn't mind a bowl of it, Ann. Can I help myself?'

He came over to the table with a huge bowl and three thick slices of bread. He said, 'Margot has planned the party for the evening because she thinks most of you will manage then.'

'Oh, by the way, I've asked Bella,' I told him.

His face fell. 'Ann, you haven't?'

Undeterred I continued, 'Well, Margot did say close family and she's your old auntie so why not?'

He shrugged. 'Well, if you've asked her, there's nothing I can say.' He went over to the stove and refilled his bowl. 'I'll have another plate of this braw soup if you don't mind.'

It was time to tackle the thorny subject of money. 'What about Lily and me Dad? What will we use for money now that your wages will be going to Margot?'

He avoided my eye again but I wasn't about to let him off the hook. 'Well, then, Dad, what do I use for the bills?'

He looked at me. 'I know my marriage was a big shock for you both and believe me I had no intention of doing it like that but Margot wanted it to be quiet with the least bit of fuss. As it is, she doesn't know that I'm here at this minute because she's going to discuss everything with you after the party.' He looked at Lily who was gazing wide-eyed at him. She looked worried and I could have hit him for all this upheaval in our lives – and all because of Margot.

After a moment's hesitation, he went on, 'The thing is, Ann, you'll have to give up this house and come and live with us.'

'What?' I shouted, unable to stop myself. 'She's only got the one bedroom in that flat or have you forgotten? Where are we going to sleep? In the lobby cupboard?'

He looked at me sadly. 'There's no need to be sarcastic. It doesn't suit you. No, she has a bed settee in the living room and you can both share it.'

Lily began to cry. 'I don't want to live with her, Dad. I don't want to sleep on a bed settee. I want my own bed here.'

I glared at him. 'Never you heed your dad, Lily. There's no way we're going to live with Margot.' I went over and stood beside him, a fierce expression on my face. 'I think you'd better get away home to your wife, Dad, and leave Lily and me alone.'

He protested. 'But you'll not have enough

money to live on – to pay the rent, the food and the bills. You'll not manage all that on that paltry wage you get from Connie.'

Suddenly a wave of tiredness swept over me. 'Look Dad, away you go home to Margot and let me worry about the bills. Tell her thank you very much for her concern but we'll manage on our own.'

He looked defeated. 'Well, for heaven's sake, don't tell her I was here. She'll be speaking to you after the party about the arrangements she's made for both of you.'

He darted out the door before I could answer. I was so angry that I could barely speak so maybe it was just as well he wasn't in the room. What right did Margot have for making arrangements for us behind our backs? I was a grown woman and, as far as Lily was concerned, she was my responsibility and not hers. And I would tell her that on Saturday.

It took Granny and me ages to get Lily settled in her bed that night. She kept crying and saying she didn't want to stay with Margot. All our reassurances didn't help.

Finally, in desperation, I took hold of her shoulders and looked directly at her. 'Have I ever told you a lie, Lily?'

Still sobbing she shook her head.

'Well, there's no way we're going to live with Dad and Margot now. From now on, it's just you, me, Granny and Grandad.' That seemed to settle her and she was soon fast asleep.

Meanwhile, Granny was seething. 'You know something, Ann? I'm beginning to believe that it must have been your mum's good sense that stopped your father becoming a prize idiot because that's what he's been since she died.'

I had to agree with her. I loved him dearly but, over the last seven years since mum's death, he had been one huge problem. I couldn't help but think how happy we would all have been if the blushing bride had been Rosie.

'How is Rosie?' I asked.

Granny shook her head sadly. 'The poor soul didn't go to work today because she was so upset but Alice is trying to persuade her to go into the mill tomorrow.'

I was filled with sadness at this news and hoped Rosie would soon get over her unrequited love for my father. Then I remembered the party. 'It's to be held in the evening, Granny, so I hope we'll see you and Grandad there.'

She didn't look happy about it. 'Well, I'm not looking forward to it but I suppose we'll have to put in an appearance.'

Quite honestly, I was glad to get to bed that night – I felt so weary. My mind went round in circles with permutations of how I could manage the bills. Even my dreams centred around money and I awoke the next morning with a sore throat, shivery and aching joints and a bad headache.

Connie looked concerned and I began to think I was turning into a liability for her. She seemed to have this expression on her face whenever she looked at me and I hoped she didn't think I was a burden in my job.

Before she spoke, I said, 'It's just a cold I've got, Connie. I'll feel better in a couple of days.'

But, by the Thursday evening, I wasn't feeling any better. I was sitting in Granny's kitchen listening to Hattie. She was prattling on about the forthcoming party. She made it sound like a royal command. 'I've not made up my mind what I'll wear but I'd better look my best. We must keep our side of the family up and not give Margot the impression we've no style.'

To be truthful, Granny and I couldn't care less what Margot thought but we kept quiet about it.

Then there was an almighty thump outside in the lobby. The door was flung open and Grandad stood on the threshold. He looked flushed. 'I've just bought a wedding present for Johnny.' He pulled a deep green pedestal into the room then hauled a huge flowerpot in beside it. 'I got it from Jeemy's Emporium and it came from a big house. It's called a jardinière – whatever that is. It looks like a flowerpot to me. What do you think?'

For a moment I experienced a feeling of déjà vu. It was similar to the time he brought the old pram home from Jeemy's when Lily was a baby. Hattie had even been in the same chair then as she was now.

We all gazed at him, speechless. The thing was enormous. Then, as she had done with the pram, Hattie spoke. 'You can't give that to Margot for a wedding present. It's too garish and ugly.'

Grandad was hurt. I could tell by his face. 'Why not? It came from a big house and she likes flowers.'

'They don't have a big house now, Dad – just a one-bedroom flat.'

He was in the huff. 'I'm not in my dotage yet,

257

Hattie. I'm not daft.'

Granny went over and walked around it. 'Actually I think it's great and just what Margot would like.' She gave me a huge wink behind both their backs and I could hardly keep my face straight. 'Aye, Dad, you've made a grand purchase there and it can sit in her window with a bunch of flowers in it. It'll be the toast of the tenement – you wait and see. The neighbours will be beating a path to Jeemy's door in search of another one.'

Grandad was pleased but Hattie wasn't. 'What on earth is she going to think when we turn up carrying that thing between us?'

Grandad looked triumphant. He had the answer. 'Jeemy said he would deliver it for me since I'm a good customer and it'll not cost us a toss.'

If this was meant to impress Hattie it failed miserably. In fact she looked enraged. 'Don't you let that grubby old man near Margot's house!' she stormed.

It was now Grandad's turn to be outraged. He spluttered, 'Grubby man. What are you talking about Hattie? Jeemy's maybe not the handsomest man around but he's not grubby.'

She retorted, 'He's filthy and his clothes smell of mothballs.' She turned to Granny. 'Don't let him get it delivered from Jeemy.'

Granny promised and, to our relief, Hattie left. We gazed at the green flowerpot. As a wedding present, it left much to be desired but, as I hadn't thought of buying them one, then this jardinière would have to do.

On the Saturday, Lily and I spent ages getting ready. We didn't want to let Dad down by being dowdy. Lily was lucky because she had a new dress and shoes but I didn't have anything fancy. I didn't feel like going out because my cold wasn't any better. I still felt shivery and my throat was very sore. Also an annoying cough that came in spasms seemed to attack me at the most awkward times.

Earlier that afternoon, I had sent Lily to the chemist for a cough mixture. I had written it down for her. 'Ask the chemist to make up tuppence worth of lemon, a pennyworth of glycerine and a ha'pennyworth of epickeky wine.' This mixture had eased my throat but I still felt ill.

I chose my best blue dress and black shoes while Lily looked a picture in her red woollen dress with its white lacy collar. I tied her hair up in a red and white polka dot ribbon and she was almost dancing for joy as we set off for the party.

I hoped that Danny would manage after his work – if only for a short time. No doubt Hattie would be dressed to the nines.

When we reached Victoria Road I warned Lily, 'Now mind and not mention that you've been in the house before. Make it look like you're seeing it for the first time.'

She was so excited that I'm sure she would have agreed to anything.

When Margot opened the door, Lily ran in. The living room seemed to be full of people – most of them our family. To my surprise, I saw Dad's boss and his wife, Mr and Mrs Pringle, were also there. Granny, Grandad and Bella were all sitting together by the fire while Hattie sat beside the Pringles.

Dad then appeared from the tiny kitchen. He was carrying a tray of sherry glasses. Each small glass holding an inch of wine-coloured liquid. I also noticed that Margot had prepared a small buffet on the table. Everything was small, dainty and delicious looking and she certainly had the knack of doing everything well.

The room also looked different now that it was furnished and I recognised a few pieces of furniture from her previous house. The carpet was new – a lovely soft green which matched the wallpaper and lampshades. It was all so elegant that even Hattie was impressed.

Margot handed me a glass of sherry and said, 'Would you like some lemonade Lily?'

Lily nodded eagerly. 'Yes, please.'

'Well, go into the kitchen and see your dad because he has the bottle in there.' After she left, Margot said, 'Thank you for the lovely wedding present, Ann. It was just what we wanted and I've already thanked the rest of Johnny's family.'

I thought she was merely being polite but she pulled back the curtains and the jardinière stood beside the window. It looked so grand set against the deep green patterned curtains and she had placed a mass of yellow daffodils and green leaves in the pot. The effect was stunning.

'It arrived yesterday from all the family so thank you again.'

Surely Jeemy hadn't delivered it. I went over to my grandparents and they looked like fish out of water. Bella gazed sourly at her empty glass. No doubt she had drained it in one go and, if there was a refill, then it wasn't in sight.

The Pringles and Hattie sat on the bed settee and I couldn't imagine Margot letting anyone sleep in this elegant room – no matter what she said.

Mrs Pringle looked bored and kept glancing at her watch. An extremely plain-looking woman, she had her hair very fashionably done in a Marcel wave but this scull-skimming style didn't suit her heavy-jawed face. It also made her large nose look even larger but her eyes were beautiful. Deep pools set in quite a nice complexion, it was a pity her face was so solidly square. She was wearing a very understated dress which I'm sure cost her a lot of money but she looked dowdy compared to Margot or even Hattie.

After an hour of this surreptitious watch glancing, Mr Pringle stood up. 'Let us all drink a toast to the happy married couple – Mr and Mrs Neill.'

We all raised our glasses. Margot looked amused while Dad looked besotted. To give her her due she was looking stunning tonight in a cream crêpe-de-Chine dress that skimmed her ankles and matched her strappy sandals. She was wearing pearls at her throat and ears and she was a study in monochrome but a glowing one.

Hattie had tried to outdo her new sister-in-law but had failed by a hair's breadth. She was also in an ankle-skimming dress but hers was a deep wine colour which suited her complexion and dark hair. She wore no jewellery but then she hardly ever did.

Margot nodded regally. 'Thank you for coming and making our wedding a happy occasion.'

It was obvious she didn't know the family's true feelings but we raised our glasses again. To my amusement, I noticed Bella was still clutching her empty glass.

Then there was a knock on the door. To my amazement Greg appeared with Danny. Margot gave them both an appraising look but she did that with all the male population.

I had written to him after the wedding last Saturday but I hadn't expected him to come. He put his arm around my shoulder. 'I thought I'd better come to give you some support, Ann,' he whispered. 'I couldn't remember the address so I waited on Danny at the shop.'

'Oh, Greg, it's good to see you! Are you here for the weekend?'

His face fell. 'No, Ann, I've got to go on a course on Monday which means leaving from Glasgow tomorrow so I'll have to catch a late train back tonight.'

This was the story of my life but it was good to see him even for a short time like this. In a perverse way I was glad he was returning that night because I felt terrible and not in the least bit sociable. I wasn't sure if it was due to the heat from the fire or not but I was feeling woozy.

Then the Pringles stood up. 'We have to go, Mrs Neill. This is Dorothy's bridge night,' John Pringle said while Dorothy looked annoyed at him.

Margot saw them to the door and I heard her murmuring seductively, 'You must call me Margot.'

Bella still had her empty glass while my grandparents looked tired. As if pulled by strings, they all stood up and Margot brought their coats. Hattie glared at them as they left and I could see she was ashamed of us not being party people and she was right. The only person bouncing around and eating everything in sight was Lily.

Dad refilled our glasses and I thought it a great pity that Bella had lost out on this extra drink. He ushered us towards the buffet table and urged us to eat up. I put a small sandwich and a sausage roll on my plate but everything tasted like sawdust. It was this horrible cold which I couldn't seem to get rid of.

Danny went over to Margot and handed over a gaudily wrapped parcel. The look of delight on her face was well out of proportion to its size but I was feeling churlish and a bit fed up.

It was a damask tablecloth and Margot showed it to us all. 'It's lovely, Danny! Thank you.'

I was annoyed to see him blush. Such was the charm of this woman.

Greg said quietly, 'Now your Dad's got married, Ann, does that mean it's our turn soon?'

He saw me glance in Lily's direction. 'Won't Lily be staying with them?'

I shook my head. 'How can we live here, Greg? Just look at this room? Margot will not be wanting two people to camp on her settee in spite of what she says. And I promised Lily that I wouldn't abandon her.'

'We can get married and take her to live with us in Glasgow, can't we?'

By now, my head was splitting and I thought I was going to faint. 'Can we talk about this some other time Greg? Let's just give Margot and Dad some time to settle down in their marriage and we'll make plans then.'

Once again we were parting on these terms and at this rate we would never get married. Still, on this particular night, I couldn't think of anything other than my aches and pains.

Thankfully, it was soon time to say our good-byes and we set off into the cold starry night. Greg had only half an hour to catch his train and he told me to go home to my bed. 'You'd better take a hot-water bottle with you, Ann, because that's a terrible cold you have. Don't come to the station with me. I'll write to you tomorrow night.'

He set off with Danny and I realised I hadn't had the chance to speak to my cousin all night. Were we drifting apart? Even worse. Were Greg and I also drifting apart? I said a small mental prayer that this wasn't the case and Lily and I headed off down the road with Hattie.

She was full of the evening's event. 'I'm glad your father has settled down with such a lovely decent woman, Ann. What a delightful house she keeps and she's so well dressed.'

I think she expected a reply or a confirmation of the wonderful Margot. 'Aye she is.'

'And didn't our present go down well? I couldn't believe it when I saw how well it went with her gorgeous curtains and the lovely room.'

I was mystified. 'Did Jeemy deliver it, Hattie?'

She was shocked. 'Indeed he did not!' There was a smug look on her face. 'I had this brilliant idea. Mrs Pringle gets her deliveries from this posh shop in town and they have this super shiny

264

van in deep green with gold lettering. It looks almost regal. Well, I know the driver quite well and I asked him to do me a favour.'

I looked at her and she was almost beside herself with pleasure.

'I bought a suitable card and some gold twine. Wrapped it around the jardinière and got him to deliver it for me. Margot thinks it came from that shop.'

'Well, let's hope she doesn't find out it came from Jumping Jeemy's Emporium.' This was the shop's nickname, earned because most of his stock was so old and mouldy that it was highly possible to inherit a couple or twenty fleas with your purchase.

She shuddered at the thought. 'She'd better not find out from anyone in the family or I'll be very angry.'

'That was good of the driver to deliver it for you, Hattie.'

'Actually it wasn't all goodness from him – I gave him a half crown for doing it.'

By now we had reached the foot of the Hilltown and we watched her as she set off for her own house.

As she disappeared into the night Lily and I climbed wearily up the hill. I could have sworn I was climbing Everest and by the time we reached the close my breath was coming in great gasps and I was sucking at the cold night air like a starving man greedily eating from a plate.

Lily gave me a concerned glance but I managed a wan smile. 'It's just been a long night, Lily.'

10

The news on everyone's lips seemed to be about the threat of war. Old people who had remembered the last war were fearful. Mrs Halliday was one such person. 'They said it would never happen again. That the last time was the war to end all wars.'

Connie was reassuring. 'Och, it might not come to anything. You've been listening to Joe too much.'

After she left, Connie said, 'Let's talk about something more cheerful, Ann. How did the party go? Did you have a good time?'

I was still feeling dreadfully ill but I tried to tell her about Saturday night.

After I described it she said, 'It must have come as an awful shock when your father got married so suddenly?'

'Aye, it was, Connie – a huge shock.' She studied me for a moment then said, 'Will you both be going to live with your new stepmother Ann or will you stay in your own house?'

'I'd like to stay where I am at the moment, Connie, but it'll all depend on the money situation. I don't know if I can keep it on my wage alone.'

She was sympathetic. 'I just wish I could give you more hours, Ann, but I can't. We're not that busy at the moment, I'm afraid.'

I was flustered. 'Oh, I didn't mean to sound as if I'm needing more work. I know you would offer it if you could.'

A few people entered the shop and I was grateful to end the conversation. Ever since Dad's wedding, I had been doing my sums and I knew I couldn't keep on the house without his pay. I had flirted with the idea of asking him for a small sum each week for Lily but I had dismissed it from my mind. If he had been keen to help, then he would have offered.

By now, I could hardly breath with the pain in my chest and my head was aching again. I hardly slept at night with all this mental working out of household sums so this added to my feeling of lethargy. I was so glad when it was time to go home and I huddled in front of the fire with a hot-water bottle on my lap.

The postman had delivered two letters. One was a long one from Greg. He wrote about the party and asked me again if I would consider moving to Glasgow with Lily. Maybe I should, I thought. It would take away this endless worry of making ends meet but I lay back in my chair, too weak to worry about answering it.

The second letter was from Minnie. She wrote:

I wasn't very happy at the start, Ann, but I've settled in well now. The folk here are really very friendly, especially the old couple from next door who dote on wee Peter and he loves them. My man is much happier in this new shop than he was in the last one. Give my thanks to your granny for all her help and advice and tell her I'm glad I came here. Love to yourself and Lily.

I was so relieved for her. I still remembered the feeling of sadness that had swept over me at our last meeting but now he had settled in and was happy. Was that what I should do? Move to another city to be with Greg?

My head was throbbing so I gave up thinking of all my troubles and fell asleep. It was a fitful sleep as I kept waking up to look at the clock. I didn't want to be late meeting Lily at the school gate. At ten to four, I got up, feeling very stiff and sore. By now, the room was warm and, as I glanced around its cosy interior, I knew I could never give it up without a struggle.

I had been toying with an idea all week and, as I made my way towards the school, I made up my mind. I decided I would pay a visit to Maddie's father, Mr Pringle. He looked after my legacy and had invested it for me. Mrs Peters had also done the same. I would draw some money out of it to tide us over and I felt better. I was planning to look for another small job in the evenings. With my hours from Connie plus a few hours elsewhere, then surely I would have enough to pay the bills. However, before I could think about that, I knew I had to get over this horrible cold first as it seemed to be sapping all my energy.

Lily ran through the school gate with Janie. They parted with such ceremony that it looked like they were parting forever instead of seeing one another the next morning.

'Lily, I have to see Mr Pringle in his office. You can come with me and we'll get chips for tea.'

She was excited. Anything different in her small life seemed to please her and her pleasure often far outweighed the project.

Mr Pringle's office was in Commercial Street. His large windows with the firm's name printed in bold letters on them gave the small premises a rather grand look. The small outer office had two desks with large typewriters on them. Two middle-aged women sat at these desks. Lily and I sat on the two armchairs. One of the women detached herself from her typewriter to attend to us. I stated my mission and she departed quietly into the inner sanctum.

She came back within a minute. 'Mr Pringle has a client at the moment but he'll see you as soon as he's free.' She sauntered back to her desk but before she sat down, she said, 'You should have made an appointment, Miss Neill.'

I apologised to her for my thoughtlessness and we waited. Lily was very quiet. I think she was afraid to speak in this church-like silence with only the gentle tap-tapping of the typewriters breaking it.

It was a good half an hour before Mr Pringle appeared. He saw us and smiled. 'How lovely to see you both.' He bent down towards Lily. 'And how's this little girl getting on?'

With a serious expression she gazed at him. 'I'm doing great, Mr Pringle, and thank you for asking.'

For a moment I thought he was going to burst into laughter but instead he said, 'Well, I'm glad to hear it, Lily.' He looked at me. 'Come into the office, Ann.' He then turned to Lily again. 'Will you be a good girl and sit here until your sister comes out?'

She nodded solemnly.

The chair in his small office was slightly more comfortable than the one outside and I gazed at the three walls lined with fat, leather, heavy-looking books. It was not unlike Connie's lending library room.

'Well, what can I do for you, Ann?' he said pleasantly.

Before going into his office, I had decided to be frank. 'I would like some money from my legacy, Mr Pringle.'

Over the years since receiving my legacy from Mrs Barrie, I had drawn some money out but he had always tried to make me understand the good policy of keeping most of it invested to make interest on it.

He lifted my file down from the shelf. 'How much money do you want, Ann?'

'Fifty pounds, Mr Pringle.'

His head came up sharply from the file and he gave me a piercing look. 'Fifty pounds?'

I wasn't going to mention losing Dad's money every week but he must have guessed.

'I forgot to say congratulations to your father, Ann. I believe he got married to Mrs Connors last week. Mrs Pringle and I were sorry we couldn't manage to go the wedding party on Saturday but it was our bridge night.'

Bridge night? The other Mrs Pringle, Dorothy, also had her bridge night on the same evening. It was a revelation how the other half lived.

'Thank you, Mr Pringle. It was a surprise about

271

the marriage but it's done now so that's that.'

He studied me once more. 'Fifty pounds is a lot of money, Ann. Are you sure you want so much?'

I nodded. 'Lily needs some things and I thought I would keep the money for a standby – for the odd emergency. It'll save me coming back for more if I get enough out now.'

He didn't say anything for a moment then he wrote in the file.

'I won't be able to get the money tonight, Ann, as the bank has closed. Can you come back tomorrow?'

Whether it was the disappointment or my cold but a spasm of coughing shook my body. I gasped, 'I'm sorry, Mr Pringle, but I can't seem to get rid of this cold.'

He left the office and came back with a glass of water.

'I think you should see a doctor, Ann. You look white and shaken. Do you want me to get a doctor for you?'

I took the water and sipped it. The spasm passed. 'No, honestly, Mr Pringle, I'll be fine. It's just a really bad cold.'

He looked worried. 'I wish you had made an appointment, Ann, and I could have had the money waiting for you instead of you having to come back tomorrow.' He took out his wallet. 'Let me give you some money in the meantime and you can get the balance tomorrow.'

I was mortified with shame and my face turned a deep purple. 'Oh, no, Mr Pringle, that will not be necessary. I don't need the money right now as it's just for Lily or the odd emergency.'

He gazed at me sternly. 'Well, if you say so, Ann, but you would confide in me if you were having any problems, wouldn't you?'

I nodded. If only he knew the truth. At that moment I had only enough money in my purse to get Lily her tea from the chip shop and that was all.

I tried to smile but even my jaw ached. 'Of course I would, Mr Pringle.'

He stood up. 'Well I'll see you tomorrow afternoon, Ann, and I'll have the money waiting for you.'

I was glad to escape and I grabbed Lily's hand and we hurried out into the street.

'We'll take your chips to Granny's and you can eat them there, Lily.'

She smiled at me and placed her small hand in mine. Once again, I was furious at Dad for abandoning her. To make up for this, I asked her, 'What do you want from the chip shop for your tea?'

She gave this some thought and then she said, 'Can I have a fishcake supper, Ann?'

I had to laugh. This was her favourite dish from the chip shop – especially when the small Italian man who owned the shop shook loads of salt and vinegar on it. He would ask her in his broken English, 'You, wee lassie, want some salt vinegar on your chips?'

Lily would nod solemnly and he would make a big show with the two containers on his counter. Normally I made soup every day and things like mince and tatties so this fishcake supper was a huge treat for her.

The chip shop was crowded but, as it was only a tiny shop, we didn't have too long to wait. The wonderful smell of cooking made my hunger even more acute and I was kicking myself for not taking the kind offer of money from Mr Pringle. It was, after all, my own money so why should I feel so much shame for being hard up? Still, I would have my fifty pounds tomorrow.

The owner leaned over the counter and beamed at Lily. 'Och, it's wee lassie, Lily. What you want tonight?'

Lily looked important. 'A fishcake supper, Mr Nettie.'

This was her nickname for him. When she had been very small his Italian name had been too difficult for her to pronounce and the name had stuck.

The rain started as we made our way up the Overgate and I carried her chips under my coat to keep them dry. On reaching the house, I was grateful to see the cheery fire in the grate but less cheerful to see Bella sitting at the table with Granny. They were conducting a post mortem on the party.

As Lily ran ahead to get her plate from the cupboard, Granny turned to Grandad. He was sitting at the fire with his pipe and evening paper. 'Bella and I were just saying that your jardinière went down a treat. Margot was fair pleased with it.'

Grandad looked pleased. 'I knew she would like it because I've got a good eye for a bargain.'

'Does she know you bought it from Jumping Jeemy?' Lily asked as she sat at the table.

274

'It doesn't matter where I bought it from, wee lass – it was still a grand bargain and why Hattie didn't want him to deliver it for me is a mystery.'

Bella hadn't enjoyed the party. 'I didn't think it was that good,' she said sourly. 'There was no sing-song or any drink – just those wee dinky glasses of sherry that have no kick – and as for those sandwiches ... well, there was hardly a mouthful in each one. You wouldn't have had to be hungry, that's for sure.'

Granny tried to be more charitable. 'Och, well, Bella, that's the way some folk are. They do everything in wee drops. It's supposed to be artistic or so I'm told.'

'Well, it might be bonny when it's set out on the table but we all want a good feed at a party. A good plate of steak pie, peas and tatties then rice pudding or custard or something sweet.' She smacked her lips as she imagined this feast. 'And we should get a good drink. Farty wee glasses like that are no use to man or beast, that's for sure.'

Grandad shook his head then retreated behind the newspaper while I had this mental image of Bella with a pint glass of sherry.

Then Granny noticed I was leaving Lily to tuck into her fish-cake and chips and wasn't having anything myself. She raised her eyebrows at me but remained silent in front of Bella. She then stood up. 'I think I'll make us something to eat, Bella.'

Bella stared at her and Grandad dropped his newspaper in his lap. He said, 'But we've just had our tea and I expect Bella had hers before she came.'

Bella shook her head. 'It was more like a wee snack so I wouldn't mind a bit of supper, Nan.'

Grandad was outraged. 'Supper? It's only six o'clock.'

Granny moved over to the stove and didn't reply. After a few moments, the wonderful smell of soup filled the air and she lit the grill. Placing thick slices of bread under it she stood with her back to us until the meal was ready. She then moved over to the table. 'Hot soup and toast,' she said. She looked at Lily. 'I don't expect you'll be wanting anything, wee lass?'

'No, thank you, Granny. I'm full up with Mr Nettie's chips.'

I was starving and I realised I hadn't eaten anything since early that morning. The hot soup warmed me up and the toast was thickly spread with butter. Granny detested margarine and so did I.

My body felt as if it had been kicked by an angry horse. I had aches and pains in every joint and my headache was beginning to come back.

Granny reappeared with the teapot, more toast and some Rich Tea biscuits.

Bella, quite overcome by this unexpected feast, looked at the biscuits. 'This is what I call a party – the only thing missing is the drink.'

Grandad muttered under his breath, 'Well, you've scoffed all my soup so you're not getting my bottle of beer.'

Undaunted by this remark, she pulled her famous medicine bottle from her bag. 'Will you join me, Nan?'

Granny declined so she filled a glass and

hobbled over to the sink to put some water in her whisky. Lily couldn't take her eyes off her. Bella gave her a huge wink. 'It's just my medicine, Lily. The chemist makes it up for me just the way I like it.'

Lily, who hadn't been hungry a moment before, was now gorging herself on the biscuits and looked relieved while Grandad still muttered darkly behind his newspaper.

I hadn't planned on telling Granny about my visit to Mr Pringle – at least not yet – but Lily began to chatter on about it. 'I sat on the chair outside while Ann went into the office. The lassie behind the desk kept looking at me in a snooty way but I didn't make any funny faces at her because I knew Ann wouldn't be pleased. You've got to behave in a solicitor's office, haven't you, Ann?'

Bella was agog at this story while Granny raised her eyebrows again. It was obvious that Bella wanted to know the whole story but there was no way I was going to broadcast the fact that Dad had left us almost penniless.

'I just went in because he likes to see me every now and again,' I explained before sipping another cup of warming tea. I made it sound like an illicit meeting – something shady and underhand. Bella didn't believe me. I could see that by her sceptical expression but she poured herself another cup of tea as well and sandwiched two Rich Tea biscuits together with a thick layer of butter.

Grandad saw this move and his paper shook with annoyance. Bella was eating him out of house and home and he didn't like it – and I was

277

the cause of it. Granny had seen how hungry I was but had made Bella the ploy for making this early supper. Poor Bella – not only was Grandad begrudging her this treat, she wasn't even the reason for it. I made up my mind to replace all this food the next day when I got my money.

To get back on safer ground and away from Grandad's wrath, Bella mentioned the party again. 'I thought Margot looked really bonny in that frock, Ann. And Hattie's face was put out of joint even though she tried hard enough to dress smarter than her.'

We all chuckled at the memory. Then I remembered Rosie and I asked how she was.

Granny shook her head. 'Well, she's gone back to her work but yon lassie is not well. She's heartbroken over your father and, although we've all told her she'll get over him in time, she won't listen to reason.'

I wondered what Dad was doing this minute. Lily and I were penniless at least until tomorrow and Rosie was beside herself with grief. What a world, I thought.

We all sighed with relief when Bella stood up to go. 'I'd better head for home, Nan. I like to be in the house before it gets dark. It gives me a chance to light the gas mantle when I can still see it. If I do it in the dark I often break the damn thing and have to buy another one.'

Grandad muttered, 'Aye and it's not before time.'

Thankfully, she was so busy wrapping a gigantic scarf around her neck and she didn't hear him because it covered her ears and half her head.

I was slowly thawing out with the warmth of the room and I didn't relish going out into the cold street and back to the equally freezing cold flat. The fire would have long gone out and, although it was the month of May, the wind made it feel more like January. Shakespeare certainly had it right when he mentioned the rough winds shaking the darling buds.

Granny noticed my shiver as I thought of the journey ahead of me and she suggested, 'Why do you not stay the night, Ann? You can cuddle down with Lily in her bed.'

Lily's eyes lit up and she looked disappointed when I shook my head.

'I've got some things to do so I'd better get away home.'

Granny came with me to the top of the stairs. 'I didn't want to say anything in front of Bella or the bairn but are you getting enough to eat, Ann? I noticed that Lily had her tea but you had nothing.'

I was feeling too weary and tired to lie to her. 'I was at the solicitor's office to see Mr Pringle. I'm taking some money out of my legacy to tide us over. The day Dad got married I was expecting his week's wages but he's obviously got to hand them over to Margot now.'

She was so angry that she shook with rage. 'That's a bloody disgrace. Do you want me to see him and knock some sense into him?'

'Oh, no, Granny, don't do that. You see he wants Lily and me to go and live with them to sleep on the bed settee in yon living room. Can you see Margot wanting us messing up her bonny green room?'

Granny was still fuming. 'It doesn't matter what they want. He should still support Lily and he can't toss away his responsibilities like that.'

I tried to defuse her anger. 'But, if he has to give us money every week, then maybe Margot will insist that Lily goes to live with them. This way I can keep us both and they can't ever take her away from me.'

She still wasn't convinced – not totally. 'It's still a disgrace that a laddie of mine can completely forsake his bairns for this flashy woman. Although I didn't say much to Bella, I don't like Margot very much. I think she's a bit on the scheming side but I hope I'm wrong. When you think of what a great person Rosie is, it would make you cry.'

I agreed with her and set off home. Another heavy rain shower was bouncing off the pavement and I pulled my coat tightly around me. It seemed as if I was forever getting soaked – no wonder I couldn't get rid of this cold. Back at the house, although I had intended to answer Greg's letter, I changed my mind and went straight to bed with my hot-water bottle. But, in spite of its warmth, I couldn't stop shivering and, when I finally fell asleep, it was a restless kind of slumber filled with vivid and weird dreams.

When I woke in the morning, I was glad I had made my appointment with Mr Pringle for the early afternoon. That way I could pick up my money then head for the school to collect Lily. We would do a grocery shopping on the way home and I would get the cupboards stocked up again. The coalman was also due and I would get the coal bunker filled up. If I could get a large fire going then I would soon feel better.

Mr Pringle seemed pleased to see me again. He handed over a white envelope. 'I've kept the money in low denominations, Ann.'

I looked puzzled.

He explained, 'I've got the money in ten shilling and pound notes except for two five-pound notes. It will be easier for you to spend them.'

I never thought of that and he was right. Not many people knew of my legacy and it would look strange if I started to flash five-pound notes around the Hilltown.

I thanked him and got to my feet.

He motioned me to sit down again but I kept an eye on the big clock on the office wall.

I started the conversation. 'How's Maddie? Her final exams can't be far away, Mr Pringle.'

He smiled. 'No indeed they aren't and she's getting a bit worried about them. We tell her she can only do her best and no more so she shouldn't worry about them.'

I nodded. 'Well, I hope she passes. She's worked so hard these last three years.'

Then he got to the subject I was dreading. 'Now, Ann, has your father made any plans for you and Lily? Are you going to stay with him and your new stepmother?'

'No, Mr Pringle, we're not. I'm looking after Lily and that's why I need the money – to make us independent.'

He seemed dubious. 'But surely it would be better to live as a family with them instead of carrying on alone?'

I shook my head. 'No, Mr Pringle, it wouldn't be a good idea because there's not really room for us in their house.'

He clasped his hands together and looked serious.

Meanwhile, I went on although, afterwards, I realised I had been blabbering. 'I know the money will not last forever but, if I'm careful, it'll last a good while. It's the best I can do at the moment but I'm looking for another job with more hours and that will be a big help.'

'Your legacy has been invested wisely, Ann, and what you've taken out today is merely the interest on the initial sum but, if you do keep dipping into it, the capital will slowly diminish. But you know that, don't you?'

I nodded. 'This fifty pounds will last me for a long time Mr Pringle. I get my wage every week from Connie so this will just be for the food. My wage covers the rent and a bag of coal.'

He smiled. 'You've got it all worked out and I admire you for it but I also hope your father is providing for you both. Regardless of his marriage, he still has a financial responsibility for your sister and a moral responsibility for you.'

Just to escape, I assured him that Dad was providing for us. I knew Mr Pringle had our best interests at heart but I was now responsible for Lily and that was the way it was going to stay.

After tea, I found time to answer Minnie's letter. I gave her my limited news and told her how delighted I was to hear her happy news.

I didn't write to Greg because I didn't know

what to say to him. How could we ever get married while I had Lily and he was miles away in another city? Fate seemed to conspire in keeping us apart.

I was on my way to the school to pick up Lily when another heavy shower fell from a dark clouded sky, sending thin sheets of cold water against my face and once again drenching my coat – a coat that didn't have much chance to dry out between these daily soakings.

I had planned to visit the grocer's shop before going home but, when we reached the door of Johnston's Stores, I suddenly felt so ill and weary. I gave the shopping list to Lily and I sat down on the wooden chair which was strategically placed for customers at the side of the counter. Lily was in her element reading from the list and she watched as the woman assistant danced to her commands. I could think only of my bed and I planned to go there as soon as Lily was safely delivered to the Overgate.

We carried the two bags of groceries between us and although I felt too tired to cook I knew Lily would need her tea. It was such a struggle to go through all the motions and I was grateful when I finally deposited her with Granny. I tried to put on a cheery face in front of Granny as I knew she would worry but it was with a huge sense of relief that I made my way back home, getting another soaking on the return journey. I lay down on my bed and I didn't even bother to remove my clothes as I felt so ill.

I awoke in a panic. I couldn't think where I was. It was a place I had never been before – this dense green jungle with enormous trees that spread high above my head. It was very hot and I could see steam rising from the wet leaves before it swirled in a white mist into a blue sky which seemed miles above my head. Thick green fronds of foliage dripped with moisture and they bent down with the weight of the water. I was totally alone in this alien place but I thought I could hear voices from a faraway spot. Were they calling my name? I wasn't sure.

My legs felt weary as I trudged through the dense undergrowth.

Then I remembered Lily. Where was she? I called her name over and over again but she was nowhere to be seen. The faint voices still carried on the warm wind but they seemed no nearer than before. I pushed aside thick branches of a tree but the wet fronds slipped from my hands and I felt a stinging slap on my face.

I called again for Lily but I was all alone. Where were Granny and Grandad? Or Greg and Danny? Surely I wasn't the only person alive in this horrible green and wet place. Then suddenly the jungle disappeared and I was in a desert. A vast empty tract of sand as far as the eye could see. I looked at the sky and a bright golden sun shone mercilessly on my upturned face. It was so hot that it burnt my eyes and I looked around for some kind of shade. There was none – just miles and miles of gritty sand that felt like shards of glass against my bare feet. The voices were still muffled in the distance and I stopped walking. I tried to catch a familiar word but, if they were indeed voices, they sounded more like muffled waves on the shore.

The memory of the sea made me thirsty and I was gasping for a drink of water. Then I saw the trees and a small blue pool about a hundred yards ahead of me and I ran towards it. I saw my reflection in the water but as I lay down to take a drink, the water disappeared and became a pool of sand. I lay down and cried bitterly.

The sun grew hotter by the hour and I made for the shelter of the trees but they also disappeared before my eyes. My face and neck became so hot that I was sure my hair would catch fire. I couldn't bear the hot sand against my bare feet either. I looked around for some shade but there was none – just a vast, hot and yellow desert with a baking sun beating down.

It was then I knew I was going to die in this wilderness. Then I remembered Lily and I got to my feet. I knew the trick was to keep moving but I was so tired and my legs felt as if they didn't belong to my body. I lay down a few times, not caring if I died, but then Lily's image would appear. I knew I had to find her and look after her.

Then night came and a freezing wind blew over me and I couldn't help but shiver. The desert was an eerie place full of deep shadows and bitter coldness. I had thrown my clothes away during the intense heat of the day and I was now regretting it. I thought of my wonderful cosy quilt at home and I wished I had brought it with me. After what seemed like hours spent shivering among the deep sand dunes, the sun came up and I was immediately overwhelmed by the heat. Vast waves of shimmering sunshine swept over me and I felt as if I was being fried like Mr Nettie's chips.

I had to find the jungle again. At least there was shade there and not this relentless and intolerable heat that seemed to drain my spirit and make the sand shimmer. My feet sank into a deep pit of sand and I had only travelled a few yards when I knew I couldn't go on. I thought, if I just have a small rest, then I would be fine.

The fine particles of sand were like red-hot needles against my skin and, although I knew if I fell asleep I would never ever wake up again, I let my head drop on to the sand. I just didn't have the energy to resist this final sleep.

Then suddenly a dark shadow swept over me and a disembodied face hovered over me. It was a sharp-featured man's face with dark piercing eyes. I opened my mouth to scream but it was too dry and I realised my mouth was full of gritty sand. His face appeared again and this time I managed to make a sound although it came out as a feeble groan and not a full-scale scream.

The man pulled me to my feet and pointed a long slender finger towards the horizon. I tried to follow it with my sand-encrusted eyes but the heat haze had distorted the far off distance. He pointed once more and I stumbled forward. When I looked back he was gone. The horizon seemed so far off and a long sandy wasteland lay before me. Then I saw the oasis. A fringe of green palm trees and another blue pool of water. I ran towards it, my feet dragging in the deep sand but with a great deal of sweating and willpower I soon reached it.

Lowering myself into the deep pool was a wonderful sensation and I let the cool water cover my face and hair. I planned to stay there forever but someone was helping me out of the water and I saw it was Granny. I tried to speak but she held her finger to her mouth. She had a big towel and she began to dry me off. It was then I noticed that the oasis had turned into a sweet smelling meadow. I lay down amongst the damp grass and the buttercups and a strange peace settled over me. The jungle and the desert were gone. I could smell the meadow flowers and I slept deeply.

I opened my eyes and I saw Greg. He was sitting by the side of my bed. I knew it was my bed because of the faded crochet cover that had belonged to Mum. There was also my cosy quilt and my chest of drawers with the mirror over it. Sunlight slanted in through the window and I knew it was the late afternoon and I was back in my own room. I thought Greg looked tired but when he saw that I was awake he smiled.

'Welcome back to the world, Ann.'

What did he mean? Then I remembered the jungle and the desert. My voice sounded croaky and my throat felt like sandpaper. 'Greg, where have I been?'

Before he could answer, Granny bustled in. She also looked tired. 'Now you're not to tire yourself out by speaking, Ann.' She propped me up and gave me a lovely drink of cool water.

I didn't realise how parched I was till I gulped the water greedily. 'It was the desert, Granny,' I whispered. 'That's why I'm so thirsty.'

Greg gave her a look but he said to me, 'That's

right, Ann, but you're back home now.'

Later, Granny gave me some thin soup while Greg still sat by the bed. Why was he here?

My mouth felt so much better now but I was still extremely tired. After Granny left with the bowl, Greg took my hand.

I whispered, 'Are you on holiday, Greg?'

He nodded. 'Yes, I got a few days off to come and see you.'

I was surprised. 'To see me?'

His face was certainly haggard-looking in the sun's rays. 'You've been very ill, Ann – with pneumonia.'

Granny reappeared. 'Aye, lass, we thought we had lost you but you held on till the fever broke. Our prayers were answered.'

At that moment, Danny and Dad came in. Danny tried to smile but he didn't quite make it. Meanwhile Dad sat on the edge of the bed. 'You've had a rough time, Ann, but you're on the mend now,' he said.

Danny finally managed a grin and I tried to match it. Then I remembered Lily. I asked where she was.

Dad said, 'She's staying with Margot and me but we'll bring her up to see you tonight.' He turned to look at Granny who was coming in through the door. 'I mean if that's all right with your granny.'

She nodded. Her face had a cool and unusual expression. 'But just for a quick visit because Ann may be over the worst but she's still not better yet.'

Later that evening, Lily came bounding through the door while Margot stood at the door.

For a moment, I thought she was maybe afraid of catching something infectious from me but maybe I was being uncharitable. If I was back to thinking these thoughts, then I was truly back in the land of the living – that was for sure.

Margot was as beautifully dressed as usual with a tweed suit and a fox fur around her neck. She said, 'This is just a quick visit, Ann. We'll come again another day.'

Lily snuggled down on the bed and whispered in my ear. As a whisper went it had all the soaring qualities of a true stage whisper. 'I want to stay here with you, Ann, now that you're better.'

Margot glared at her and went to pull her off the bed. Lily dived under the quilt and refused to budge. Margot pulled her out roughly and, although I tried to protest, my words came out with a croak.

'Look what you've done now, Lily! You've upset your sister.'

Lily began to cry and I put a weak arm around her shaking body. I whispered softly to her, 'It won't be long till I get better, Lily, so go with Margot just now and I'll get you back home very soon – believe me.'

She gazed at me with her dark solemn eyes then climbed off the bed. 'Will it be less than a week, Ann, before I come back here?' she said, her voice still full of sobs.

'Aye, it will – just as soon as I get stronger, Lily.'

On that promise, they departed. I wished I could have kept Lily with me but I was in no position to do so at the moment.

Granny popped her head around the door. 'It's

certainly your day for visitors, Ann. Do you feel like seeing Connie for a few moments?'

I nodded and Connie appeared with Davie. He was carrying a bunch of flowers wrapped in a newspaper and he looked worried.

Connie sat on the chair by the bed. 'Well, young lassie, what a fright you gave us all. Lying at death's door like that.'

I was alarmed. 'Death's door Connie?'

'Aye, it was touch and go for a while but you're on the road to recovery and that's a blessing.'

She pointed to Davie who was standing behind her. 'The laddie here wanted to bring you some flowers.'

Davie blushed as he handed them over. 'It's just a wee thank you from Mum and me. I got them from a neighbour who has an allotment at the foot of the Law hill.'

'Thank you, Davie, they're lovely.'

Granny took the flowers and returned with them in a vase which she placed on the chest of drawers.

'There, now,' she said, 'that'll cheer you up.'

Connie laid a pile of magazines on the bed. 'Something for you to read if you feel up to it.'

I was worried. 'Connie ... about my job...'

She took my hand. 'I don't want to hear another word about that. I'll see you back at the shop when you're feeling better and not before. No doubt your granny will tell you when that is.'

Granny nodded grimly. 'Aye, I will and it'll not be for a while yet.'

After Connie and Davie left, I said to Granny, 'I would like Lily to come back here as soon as possible. I don't think she's happy with Margot.'

'I'll speak to your dad about it, Ann, and tell him what you've said – see what he says.' She stopped and smoothed out my quilt. I knew she was angry about something. 'If I had been quicker off the mark when you took ill, I could have got Lily safely under my roof but your grandad and I were so worried about you when we found you lying almost dead on the bed ... well, Lily was forgotten. Then I heard that Margot had gone to the school to pick her up and she's been there ever since.'

Hearing this made me wish I had the energy to go to Victoria Road and take Lily back home with me but I still felt so very tired.

Dad appeared later that night on his own.

I was upset. 'Did you not bring Lily with you?'

'No, she's getting her hair washed. Margot likes to do the cleaning on a Saturday which is tomorrow and she likes to get the hair washing and the bath done the night before.'

I was suddenly overcome with sadness at Dad's statement. In all the time I had known him this was the first time I had heard him describe cleaning and washing so succinctly. Margot had certainly trained him in her own mould. Another thing struck me. If the next day was Saturday, how long had I been ill for? I tried to think and another feeling of tiredness washed over me but I was determined to ask about Lily.

'I want her here, Dad, and not with you and Margot. She's my responsibility.'

He made soothing noises. 'You have to get your strength back, for heaven's sake, and not get yourself in a tizzy over your sister – especially when she's fine and enjoying herself with us.'

For some reason this statement upset me and I felt choked up with tears. Was I jealous? I wondered.

He looked sheepish. 'There's just the one thing bothering Margot about Lily. She needs shoes and some more clothes and she was wondering if you had the money for them.' He gazed at his hands as he said this and I was too tired to argue. 'To be truthful, she eats like a wee horse and my wages are not enough for us all.'

If my mind had been more alert I would have argued with him. If his wages had been enough for the three of us before his marriage why weren't they enough now? But I was weary and longing to close my eyes again – to drift off into a deep sleep. 'If you look in the tin box on the mantelpiece you'll find money. Take what you need.'

Then Granny came in with Greg. He was carrying a small suitcase. Dad went out and I was reminded of a small weather house that Mrs Barrie had in her garden – the one where the woman went in as the man went out and vice versa. Granny bustled around for a few moments and then she left.

Greg held my hand. 'I have to leave soon, Ann, as I have to be back to work tomorrow but I'll be back next week – I've asked for a week's holiday.' He stopped and gave me a serious look. 'When you get better, Ann, let's get married and I'll ask for my old job back here. Then we can be together with Lily. Mind you, your dad says she is very happy living with them.'

Another pang of pain – or was it jealousy?

He continued, 'We all thought we had lost you last week and I don't want to lose you again. Will you say yes?'

'Of course I'll say yes, Greg.' I tried to sound happy. 'But just give me a bit longer to get my strength back and then we'll make our plans.'

All this speaking and planning plus all the visitors had really tired me out and I lay back on my pillow. Greg lingered for a few more minutes then he reluctantly said goodbye.

'Till the end of next week, Ann. I'll see you then.'

I tried to raise my hand but it felt like a dead weight.

But, as it turned out, Greg wasn't my last visitor. The sun was setting and the room was growing dim when Danny arrived with Maddie. I thought I was dreaming but they were both standing there as large as life and they were both beaming. Maddie came so close that I could smell the carbolic soap from her hands. Danny stood at the bottom of the bed and, although he looked tired, there was a strange glowing look about him.

After the usual sentiments about my health, Maddie almost shivered with excitement. 'Ann, we have something to tell you. Danny and I are engaged again and we're to be married later this year – after my final exams. Isn't it wonderful?'

I smiled. 'Maddie, that's great news.' I looked at Danny and he winked at me.

Maddie went on, 'I know it's a terrible thing to say but it was your illness that brought us both

293

together again. We both sat through the night with you to let your granny get a rest and we got talking. Danny told me about his father and somehow it all seems so silly and so far away now.'

I was perplexed. 'You sat up all night with me. Was I really as ill as that?'

Their faces clouded over. Maddie said quietly, 'Yes, Ann, you were. I got Mum's doctor to come to see you and he said the fever would either break or it wouldn't. Thankfully, it did and you're here to tell the tale.'

'A doctor?' I said weakly. 'What did he look like?'

Maddie was surprised by my question. 'Doctor White is middle aged, thin with a long gaunt-looking face and very bony hands.' She was still uncertain of my question but she had just described the man in my dream.

After they left I had a sudden thought – I hoped that Dad hadn't taken all the money from the tin. I had put the money, minus the amount Lily and I had spent in the grocer's shop, there and I knew I would need this money to keep us when Lily came home. Then, as I was falling asleep, I suddenly wondered what had happened to Lily's new shoes that I had bought for her a mere month ago.

11

I was getting better each day and was now able to get out of bed and limp into the kitchen to see Granny. It upset me to see her work so hard.

One day, I asked her, 'Who's looking after Grandad when you're here with me?'

She placed a rug around my knees and patted the cushions. 'Now you're not to worry about him because Alice and Rosie are looking after him.'

On the following Monday morning, Greg appeared. He was on a week's holiday but he was minus his suitcase. He explained, 'I've got lodgings with my ex-landlady in Victoria Road.' He laughed. 'She's still an old dragon but her cooking makes up for it.'

Granny looked amused. 'Well, they do say that the way to a man's heart is through his stomach so you better get your skates on, Ann.'

She then took advantage of Greg's visit to go to the Overgate to see Grandad.

After she left, Greg became serious. 'I've got the loan of my friend's old motorbike. Do you remember it, Ann?'

Did I remember it? It broke down on our very first time on it and we had to get the bus back home. I smiled.

He went on. 'I thought I would pay a quick visit to see my parents later in the week but if you would like to come with me we could catch a train or a bus.' He looked at me eagerly and his face fell when I said I didn't feel well enough for the trip. 'I thought not,' he said. 'It would have been a trip out for you, Ann, but I know you're not back to normal yet.'

'Although I feel better every day, Greg, I still feel a bit weak and my legs are still wobbly.'

He nodded then changed the subject. 'It's good news about Maddie and Danny, isn't it?'

I laughed. 'And it's my fault I believe. They got back together when they sat up through the night with this old invalid. Still, I hope they plan the wedding as soon as her exams are over. I don't want any more hitches in that relationship.'

'We must think seriously about our own wedding some time.' Again that flush of weariness came over me but I tried to ignore it. I always seemed to get this feeling when faced by a decision these days.

'We'll have to wait till their wedding is over because two weddings at once will be too much.'

'As I said, Ann, I'm hoping to get a transfer back to the library here but my boss said it will take some time.'

Time – there was that word again. Greg and I never seemed to have time to see one another let alone plan a wedding.

We heard Granny's step in the kitchen and she stuck her head around the door.

'What would you like for your tea, Ann? A boiled egg or scrambled egg?'

I wasn't feeling hungry but I didn't dare tell her that. She was trying her best to build up my strength.

'It doesn't matter, Granny – just make whatever you want.'

She looked at Greg. 'What would you like, Greg?'

He stood up. 'Nothing, thank you, Mrs Neill, I have to go – my old dragon is very fussy about mealtimes. If I'm not sitting at the table on the dot then she goes in a huff.'

I called after him as he left, 'When you see your parents, tell them I'm asking for them and I hope to see them sometime soon.'

By the end of the week, I was feeling almost normal again although I still needed a rest in my bed every afternoon. But I was back on my feet and looking forward to going back to work.

The days had flown by in with Greg's company and we planned a visit to his parents as soon as I felt up to it. Then, one day, to my delight, he produced a lovely ring with a red ruby and pearl twist. It fitted like a glove.

'Now we're finally engaged,' he said. 'I didn't mention it to my parents as I thought we could announce it together. They were very sorry to hear how ill you've been.'

'How did you manage to get a ring that fitted so well?'

He looked a bit sheepish. 'Your granny gave me an old ring you've had for years and I asked the jeweller to match the size. Do you like it?'

I was over the moon with it. 'Oh, Greg, it's beautiful!' I twisted my finger around to let the ruby catch the light. It twinkled like a burst of red stars.

Then Granny came in and wished us a happy future.

I said, 'It'll not be for a while yet, Granny, as we want to wait till after Maddie and Danny's wedding. We don't want to steal their show so we're keeping it a secret for the time being.'

She looked at Greg but he merely shrugged his shoulders as if to say it wasn't his decision. She became quite stern. 'Now I know you, Ann, you're thinking about Lily but she's settled with Margot and your Dad. Let her live with them and get on with your own life.'

I was stricken. 'Oh, no, Granny, we want her to live with us. I would never forgive myself if I let her down now because I promised her I would always look after her.'

So it was on this note that Greg returned to Glasgow. We would keep our engagement a secret until he returned to work in Dundee – whenever that would be.

Before he had left the house on that last day I had overheard Granny telling him, 'You'll have to make her understand that she's entitled to her own happiness. She's taken on the whole burden of her family since her mother died and now she can't let go of the reins.' If Greg answered, I didn't hear him.

Was that what I had become? Someone who couldn't let go of the past? I knew Granny meant well but I had solemnly promised Lily that we would be together till she grew up and I wasn't going to let her down.

One bit of good news was that I had seen Connie and I was planning to start work again the following week. I had also checked the tin and I saw that Dad had taken twenty pounds.

Surely if Lily needed new clothes and shoes, they couldn't possibly come to that sum? Never mind, I thought, I've still got twenty-seven pounds left.

I had told Granny to take money for my food but she had refused. 'If I can't feed my grand-daughter without taking money for it, then I shouldn't be doing it.'

I made my plans for the following week. As soon as I started work, I would have Lily back with me. I had my money to tide us over and I felt a great deal better than I had done in a long time.

Because I was feeling so well, Granny spent some time at her own house and only came to spend the night with me. I tried to tell her this wasn't necessary but I think she was afraid I would have a relapse. I learned later that she had been the one who had found me when I was ill and she almost fainted on the spot because she thought I had died – poor Granny.

I gazed at the engagement ring on my finger. I would tell Lily but swear her to secrecy.

I was having my afternoon nap when Lily bounced in from school. Margot was with her and I made a conscious effort to like her. Maybe I was wrong about her and she certainly always made sure she met Lily from the school. I was grateful for that.

Lily jumped on the bed as usual. She planted a huge wet kiss on my cheek. 'Ann, can I come and stay the night with you?'

I glanced at Margot but she didn't seem to hear. She said, 'Can I have a glass of water? I feel parched.'

Lily watched her go and then she turned her

small face to me. She looked serious. 'Ann, I want to come back here to live.'

I hugged her. 'Of course you'll be coming back here but I'll have to have a word with Margot and Dad about it. But never mind that just now – just tell me what the bed settee is like,' I said, making it sound as if it had come from a far distant planet.

She giggled. 'Och, it's awful. You can feel the springs through the sheets and it's not squashy like this bed. I can almost disappear in this bed.' She threw herself on to the other side. 'See what I mean? I bet you can't see me!'

'Can you keep a secret, Lily?'

Her eyes were as large as dark moons. 'A secret?' she whispered.

'Aye, if I tell you something, will you promise not to tell a soul?'

She nodded her head violently. 'I promise.'

'Well, Greg and I have just got engaged, Lily, and we want you to be a flower girl at our wedding. Mind you, it's not for a while yet because we don't want to get married before Maddie and Danny.'

'I promise I'll not say a word, Ann. Will I be living with you when you get married?'

'Aye, you will, Lily – cross my heart.'

I showed her the ring and she gasped. 'It's the bonniest ring I've ever see, Ann.'

Then Margot reappeared. 'Time to go, Lily, and get the tea on.'

She was reluctant to leave but I gave her a gentle push. 'Mind what I told you,' I whispered.

She nodded and then set off with her stepmother, not looking very pleased about it either.

It was a few days later when I got the letter from Jean Peters. She wanted to meet me in our teashop in town that day.

I had no choice but to go. She was waiting for me under the clock at the foot of Reform Street. When she saw me she looked surprised.

'Heavens, you've lost a lot of weight, Ann. Have you been ill?' I told her the story and she was annoyed with herself for dragging me out. 'I never gave it a thought. I just wanted to see you.'

'Don't worry about it, Jean. I feel so much better now and the trip into town has done me the world of good.'

We set off for our favourite teashop but to our amazement it was packed with customers.

Jean remarked, 'It's not often this place is packed like this.' Then she said, 'I know why the town is so busy – it's market day and the farmers will be in most of the cafes and restaurants.'

Although I had felt fine when I had left the house, I was now feeling a bit weak and could have done with a seat. Still, the sun was shining and overnight rain had scoured the pavements clean. The street looked as if it had had its face washed and the air was fresh. It was a lovely day.

Jean looked uncertain. As we had walked along the road, we chatted and soon we were now outside the Royal Hotel.

'Come on,' Jean said, 'let's go in here for our tea.'

I must have looked dubious because she added, 'It's my treat.'

We made our way to the posh-looking coffee lounge. The carpet was thickly luxurious and the atmosphere calm and quiet. There were no farmers in here all debating about the current price of potatoes or animals. A clock chimed loudly from some unknown source but the chimes were melodic. The coffee lounge was really a small part of a grander cocktail lounge and we sat down at a table in the alcove by the door.

A young waiter appeared and took our order before silently drifting away towards the unseen kitchen. It was such a contrast to our usual tea-shop that we looked at one another and almost burst out laughing. At our usual place, the noise was deafening as the sounds of customers' chattering voices mixed with the clattering sounds of the waitresses carrying trays of crockery and cutlery.

The waiter soundlessly reappeared and placed two china cups and saucers in front of us along with a silver coffee pot.

I whispered to Jean, 'I hope you've brought a lot of money with you, Jean. What will this cost?'

'Och, it's just once in a blue moon that I'll ever be in a place like this and no doubt you're the same so let's just enjoy the experience.'

I nodded. It was very peaceful sitting in this quiet sanctuary and I slowly began to relax and to feel better.

Jean studied me. 'You must've had a rough time, Ann. I only hope you're not doing too much till you're fully recovered.'

I told her about Lily and how desperate I was to get her back.

'Just take one step at a time, lassie. Wait until you're truly better. Now tell me about Margot.'

I told her everything I knew. Even right down to her fabulous wardrobe. I added, 'I've no idea

302

what she saw in my father. I know he's still handsome but he hasn't any money and I have the feeling she loves money. But maybe she just fell in love with him.' I sounded dubious. I mentioned Rosie, and Jean shook her head in sympathy. I then mentioned Kathleen's wedding and the impending birth and the good news about Danny and Maddie.

Her eyes were shining with all the gossip. 'Och, I just love a good blether with you, Ann.'

I gazed at her with mischief in my eyes. 'I've left the best till last, Jean.'

Her eyes sparkled with interest.

I showed her the ring with its unusual twist of the ruby and the pearl. 'We're engaged but it's a secret at the moment.'

'What do you mean a secret?'

'I don't want to clash with Maddie's wedding plans because they've just got back together after that awful misunderstanding. And also we're waiting till Greg gets a shift back to Dundee and that could be a long wait. Plus I've got to sort out the problem of Lily. She'll be living with us after we're married.'

Jean sat in silence. After a moment, she said, 'Well, I wish you both all the best for the future. Now, I've got some news as well. I heard a couple of days ago that Miss Hood has died. She's being buried tomorrow at two o'clock.'

Miss Hood – my heart sank at the mention of her name as I remembered how miserable she had made my life at the Ferry and how she had even tried to kill me. Now here I was almost bursting into tears at the mention of her death.

Jean was still speaking. 'I'm going to the funeral, Ann. Not because I liked her but I think there will be nobody else there.'

I made up my mind and said, 'I'll come with you, Jean.'

She tried to make me change my mind but I wanted to go – if only to finally lay old ghosts to rest.

Jean called the waiter over and asked for the bill. We tried hard not to look shocked at the amount and Jean acted like a lady who was used to dealing with bills this size. 'Just keep the change, son,' she said.

I had my back to the door and was putting my coat on when a couple appeared and headed for a table at the far end of the lounge. To my utter surprise, I saw it was Margot. More surprising was the fact that her companion was John Pringle – Dad's boss. For a moment or two, I was totally confused. What on earth was Margot doing with Mr Pringle in this luxurious place?

Jean saw my confusion. 'What's the matter Ann? If it's the size of the bill, don't worry about it. I asked you to come in here.'

'It's not the bill, Jean. It's Margot. She's just come in with Dad's boss – Maddie's uncle.'

By now Jean's eyes were like saucers. She peered over at the couple but they didn't notice us. They were too intent with one another.

Margot was beautifully dressed as usual. She had on the yellow dress she had worn on the day we went to Clepington Road. Over this she was wearing a pale lemon jacket and her dark hair swept forward as she leant towards her companion. It was such an intimate scene.

Jean whispered, 'What if she sees you?'

I had been thinking the same. 'Oh, let's get out of here in case she does.'

But Jean wanted to witness some more. 'I don't think she's seen us because she's so intent on him.'

Still, I wasn't taking any chances and we made our escape. I found to my surprise that I was shaking.

Jean took my arm. 'Come on, Ann, I'll take you home.'

We sat in the kitchen of my house and had another cup of tea. My head was going around in confused circles and I had been unable to get the scene out of my mind all the way home.

'Are you going to tell your father?' asked Jean.

I was shocked. 'Oh, I can't do that. I mean maybe they were there for some innocent reason.'

Jean looked sceptical. 'Maybe you're right but they looked really chummy to me, Ann.'

I had thought the same but what could I do? I made up my mind to get Lily back here as quickly as possible. If Margot was romantically involved with John Pringle then Dad would soon find out and I didn't want Lily being in the middle of the stramash when it happened.

'Dad will just have to deal with it on his own Jean. I've had enough of his nonsense these past few years. He ditched Rosie who would have made him a lovely wife to marry Margot on the spur of the moment and now he's going to reap what he's sowed if you ask me.'

Jean stood up. 'Good for you! You look after

305

yourself and Lily and let the grown-ups look after themselves. Now I'll get away but I'll meet you tomorrow. I've booked a taxi so we'll pick you up here.' When she saw my face she hurried on. 'I know it's an expense, Ann, but it'll be a much more comfortable journey, especially for you, and again it's my treat.'

I watched her leave with a mixture of relief and sadness. The room was very quiet – especially after all my visitors over the past weeks. I missed Greg and Granny and Lily and my thoughts were in turmoil. Although I had sounded brave in front of Jean I knew there was no way I could abandon Dad when he found out about Margot. Would that be sooner rather than later? I also wondered whether I should confide in Granny. On that confusing note I went to lie down for an hour. I still seemed to need this afternoon rest but I knew it wouldn't last for much longer. I was getting stronger every day.

I dozed off but a noise from the kitchen woke me up. I lay on the bed wondering if I had imagined it because everything was now quiet. I called out, 'Is that you Lily?'

There was no answer but another faint sound like the door slowly closing. I got up and went into the kitchen. It was empty. I must have dreamt it, I thought, remembering the vivid dreams I had during my fever. There was a faint aroma in the room – a perfume. I wrinkled my nose but the smell evaded me. Perhaps it was Jean's scent, I thought, until I recalled that she never used any make-up or scent. She had told me years ago that she just used plain soap and water – God's own beauty treatment, she had called them.

I looked at the clock. It was almost four o'clock. Would Margot bring Lily to see me today? At half past four I knew she wouldn't and I made my tea. I felt so forlorn and alone, sitting at my solitary meal. Maybe I should have taken up Granny's offer to stay at the Overgate. After my tea, I wrote a letter to Greg and one to Minnie then went to bed.

The taxi arrived the next afternoon and it transported us swiftly to Balgay cemetery. I'd still had two pounds in my purse from the day before which I had taken to pay for our tea but, as Jean had paid the bill at the hotel, I had decided earlier that morning to buy two bunches of flowers – one bunch to put on Miss Hood's grave as a small gesture from Jean and me and the other to put on Mum's grave.

It was another beautiful day and I realised how lovely and peaceful the cemetery was. For some reason, all my previous visits seemed to be during snow or rain showers or, if it was dry, it was always cloudy. This grey depressing weather had coloured my view of the place but today it all looked so calm, peaceful and green and a warm golden haze hung over the weathered headstones.

Jean had been right in her assumption about how few people would be attending Miss Hood's burial service. Apart from ourselves, Maddie's father and the minister, the only people in attendance were two men who looked like they could have come from the hospital that had been Miss Hood's home for the last few years – ever since the night of Mrs Barrie's death – and I felt a great sadness at the waste of her life.

The warm still air made me feel sleepy but, as the minister intoned the sacred words of the burial service, I felt tears stream down my cheeks. Miss Hood who had hated me with an intensity I could never understand was now dead and I was shedding tears at her funeral. Emotion was a strange thing I thought.

I remembered her little boy and the tragic love affair with her West Indian actor and I was crying for all her lost years with them. As I said to Jean at the time, perhaps, if she hadn't lost them to the West Indies, her life might have turned out differently.

Then the service was over and Mr Pringle and the minister came over to thank us both for coming. Mr Pringle looked concerned and said, 'You should take better care of yourself, Ann. Don't go running around after everyone so much. No wonder you were ill and I just wish you had mentioned how you were feeling that afternoon to me.'

I promised to take his advice. Once again I was being told off for looking after Lily. Oh, I know he hadn't said it outright but I got the impression that he thought my devotion to Lily was bordering on being obsessive. Perhaps I should let go, I thought.

Back in the taxi, I had an anxious moment wondering what it would cost but Jean seemed unconcerned. It took me straight to the close. Jean stepped out on to the pavement with me while the driver stared into space. 'Have you heard any more about what we saw yesterday?' she asked.

'No, Jean, not a word but I'll keep you in the

picture if something does happen.'

I pulled out my purse to give her my share but she waved my hand away. 'No, Ann, I said it was my treat. I've only got my man and myself to spend my legacy on. You've got to bring up your sister so just you hold on to it.'

On that note, she disappeared back into the vehicle and it set off down the hill and I had the feeling of déjà vu. The last time I had watched a taxi like this was on Dad and Margot's wedding day.

As I was climbing the stairs, I suddenly realised I had forgotten to put the flowers on Mum's grave. Without thinking, I had placed both bunches on Miss Hood's.

'Well, Miss Hood,' I said aloud to the walls, 'that's a bunch from us and a bunch from Mrs Barrie.'

Lily didn't appear that afternoon either and so I made up my mind to be at the school gate one afternoon to see her.

I started work a few days later and Connie was comical. 'Do you want a chair to sit on, Ann?' When I said no thank you, she added, 'Well, if you get tired, please sit down.'

I didn't tell her that, if I sat down, the customers wouldn't see me behind the huge mound of papers but I was still touched by her concern.

It was good to be back in the shop. Davie blushed when I thanked him for the flowers and Connie laughed. 'I'd better watch you two.'

Then the three girls came in, full of laughs and smiles. 'Och, it's great to see you again, Ann. We all missed you and we had to get our sweeties and fags from Connie but it wasn't the same. We like getting served by a young person.'

Connie knew they were joking and she pretended to be annoyed. 'Away you go, you three besoms, or you'll feel the back of my hand.'

Oh, yes, it was good to be back.

At four o'clock, I was at the school gate. There was no sign of Margot as the children came screaming across the playground. I was worried. Had she stopped collecting Lily? I wondered. But there was no sign of Lily either.

Then I saw Janie and I went over to speak to her. 'Hullo, Ann,' she said. 'I told my ma that I thought you were dead.'

I ignored her childish curiosity. 'Is Lily not at the school today?'

She gave me a queer look. 'Lily doesn't come to this school any longer, Ann. Did you not know that?'

I was speechless and as she went to dart away I called her back. 'Janie, I've been ill and I didn't know that Lily had moved. Where is she now?'

Janie had to give this a bit of thought. 'I think it's the Victoria Road School, Ann – at least that's what Ma says. She said if you were dead then Lily must have gone to live with her father and stepmother and that's why she's changed schools.'

She was desperate to get home, especially as neither of her parents were at the gate so I let her go. What did this new development mean? Oh, I knew it was a bit further to walk here from Margot's flat but surely it wasn't that much further.

I felt the old tiredness sweep over me and I wished there had been a seat to sit on. Instead I leaned against the wall and watched as the children disappeared in all directions. For a moment, my mind was a blank. I knew I had to do something but what? Then I made up my mind. I would enlist the help of my grandparents.

They were both at home when I arrived and I was suddenly overcome with a feeling of emotion as I stepped into the room. Grandad was in his chair with his pipe and paper and Granny was sitting chatting to Alice. They all looked pleased when I walked in.

I had too much to tell them but my first worry was Lily. Any other time, I would have probably waited until Alice had left but I was too tired and concerned to bother about her knowing the problem. 'Granny, did you know that Lily has been taken out of Rosebank School and put into Victoria Road School?'

She went white and shook her head, her eyes suddenly fearful. 'No, Ann, that's the first I've heard of it.'

'Well, she has. Margot hasn't brought her to visit me for about a week now and I went down to the school this afternoon to see her. Janie, her pal, tells me that I was dead and her father and stepmother had put her into another school. What do you make of that?'

Granny was beside herself with anger. 'Did your father or Margot not tell you this, Ann?'

'No, they didn't and I'm not pleased about it either. As far as I'm concerned they were only looking after her while I was ill but I think it's time we had her back with us.'

Granny put on her coat. No matter how warm

the weather was, she always wore her coat. 'Come on – we're going round to Victoria Road to sort this out.'

Alice got to her feet. 'Just make sure you sort out both of them, Nan.' It was obvious that she still hated Dad.

We both headed for the flat and, by the time we reached it, I was out of breath. When was I going to feel better?

Dad opened the door and I was shocked by his thin appearance. He had just finished work by the look of it and he was still in his dungarees. At first he didn't seem keen to let us in but the gleam in Granny's eye made him stand aside.

Lily was sitting quietly in a chair in the living room. There were no toys or crayons or colouring books lying around. Everything was pristine and neat. Today the jardinière held a mass of mixed flowers and leaves and I noticed there wasn't a crease in the neat seat cushions.

Lily saw us and rushed over. She was crying. 'I want to come home with you and Granny, Ann.'

Margot rose elegantly from the bed settee. Again leaving no wrinkles on its surface.

'Well you can't go home with them, Lily. We're your legal guardians now, your father and I.'

Granny ignored her. 'Do you like your new school, Lily?'

After a fresh bout of tears, Lily said, 'No, I hate it. I've no pals there and I miss Janie and Gladys and Cathie. They were my best pals at Rosebank and I liked the teachers there as well.'

Margot pulled her away from Granny. 'Sit over there and be quiet.'

Granny looked her straight in the eye. 'We're taking her away with us. You were only looking after her while Ann was ill.' She looked at Lily. 'Get your coat on, lass.'

Margot immediately burst into a spate of anger. 'She'll do no such thing. Johnny, please see your mother and sister out of my house.'

Dad looked ill but he did as he was told. 'You had better leave now, Mum – after all, Lily is my responsibility and not Ann's.'

We found ourselves on the doorstep with the sound of Lily's howls following us to the foot of the close. I was beside myself with grief. 'We have to get her away from that awful woman, Granny. What will we do?'

'I know what I'd like to do but I would get the jail for it!' she said, looking fierce. 'Still, there's nothing we can do, Ann, because she's right. Lily is your father's responsibility and, just because he never took it on before, it doesn't mean he's lost the right. You get all the bother of bringing her up then along comes madam and she takes over.'

As we headed for the Overgate, she said, 'I'm beginning to think your father has bitten off more than he can chew with that woman.'

My mind was on the furtive meeting I had witnessed with Jean. I told Granny about it and it stopped her in mid stride. 'It's such a puzzle,' I said. 'Surely, if she's secretly meeting Dad's boss, you would think she wouldn't want to be lumbered with a bairn, would she?'

Granny set her mouth in a grim line. 'I think she's got some scheme on the go but what it is, goodness only knows.'

Alice came in as soon as she heard our steps in the lobby. Her face fell when she saw no Lily. 'What happened, Nan? Is the bairn not with you?'

'The new Mrs Neill has got us over a barrel, Alice, and there's nothing we can do.'

This upset me. 'I've got to get her back, Granny. I made a solemn promise to her that she would aye be with me.'

Alice voiced the same suspicions as me. 'But why does she want to hang on to a bairn if it's your father she wanted. You'd think she would be grateful not to have to bring her up.' Her face was like stone as she spoke. She hadn't forgotten that Dad had jilted Rosie.

What a mess, I thought.

'If we'd known that then, it would have made all the difference in trying to her back,' said Granny bitterly.

Grandad had been out when we arrived but he now appeared with a fresh pack of tobacco in his hand. He started to speak but stopped when he saw our faces. 'What's the matter? It's not Lily is it?'

Granny nodded. 'You know how Ann and I went down to see why Lily had changed schools?'

He nodded.

'Well, Lily is fine but we're trying to sort things out.'

If only we could I thought.

She told him the story and he was enraged. 'That son of ours has dodged his responsibilities for years and now it seems a matter of utmost importance to him and that new wife of his to

314

look after his bairn. I'm going over to sort him out and give him a piece of my mind.'

Dear grandad, I thought. Why, Margot would eat him for supper. I thought of Lily sitting like a statue on that pristine chair with nothing to play with. And I remembered Dad's thin, worried face. There was nothing I could do about him – he had made his bed and he now had to lie in it – but Lily was another matter.

Granny had a plan. 'If we ask Rosie to go to that hotel as a customer maybe she could overhear them and we could confront her with the evidence.'

I had a mental picture of Rosie in her mismatched outfits sitting in that elegant lounge. Secretly spy on Margot? Why, she would stick out like a sore thumb.

'That wouldn't work, Granny.'

She asked why not.

With Alice sitting there I had to be tactful. 'Well, Rosie has to work at the mill – she's not one of the idle rich like Margot. It has to be someone who can pass herself off as a customer without looking suspicious.'

I thought of Jean. Would she be prepared to come into town maybe twice a week in the hope of spotting Margot and Mr Pringle? I would reimburse her, of course, for her expenses. Briefly, I felt like a criminal at the thought of secretly spying on someone but I then saw Lily's small, sad figure and my heart hardened. My mind was made up and I wrote to Jean that night.

My initial euphoria at being back to work had evaporated with the crisis over Lily but I was

pleased when Danny appeared at the shop at dinnertime.

'Kathleen's had a wee girl, Ann. I'm going out
to see them tonight. Do you want to come with
me?'

Because of my illness I had almost forgotten
about Kathleen but I wanted to see her again –
and the new baby. I arranged to meet Danny at
the Lochee tram stop at eight o'clock.

It was a glorious evening with a golden sunset
as we set off. Danny filled me in with the missing
week from my life. 'Kathleen and Sammy are living in a single room in Louis Square and she had
the wee lass yesterday. I didn't want to visit last
night but it'll be good to see them both.'

Lochee was bathed in a golden glow when we
arrived. People were taking advantage of the
lovely weather and they were standing around in
groups, exchanging gossip. The sun shone like
amber on a few fortunate windows but Kathleen's
window wasn't so lucky. Her small flat lay at the
end of a dark lobby. Once inside, the gloom was
in sharp contrast to the golden sun outside and I
had to adjust my eyes to the dimness. The room
was tiny with a small black sink at the window
and a fireplace with a small fire burning in it. This
made the room feel warm and everything was
clean and tidy.

Kathleen lay in the small box bed inset in the
wall and she held her new daughter who was
wrapped in a shawl. Kit and Maggie were sitting
beside the bed. There was no sign of the new
father, Sammy.

We moved over to look at the new addition to

the Ryan clan. The baby was lovely. She yawned and gave us all an unfocussed look then made whimpering noises.

'We've called her Kathleen but we're going to call her Kitty,' said the new mum.

Maggie fussed over her new granddaughter, adjusting the shawl around her tiny body.

Danny spoke to Kit. 'Where's Sammy? We would like to congratulate him as well.'

Before Kit could answer, Maggie swung around, her eyes blazing. 'He's out wetting the bairn's head with his pals – damned wee besom that he is. Here's his wife just over a long hard labour and what does he do? Goes around like he's just had the bairn instead of his wife. Out celebrating the fact as well. Wait till I get my hands on him. I'll give him a piece of my mind.'

The whimpering from Kitty became a wail.

Maggie said, 'Are you needing a feed, wee lass? Are you hungry?'

Kathleen gave us a shy look and I realised she wasn't wanting an audience while she fed the baby.

'We'll wait outside, Kathleen.' I then steered Danny through the door.

We stood outside in the late evening sunshine. It was the time of night I liked best during the summer months when long slanting fingers of sunlight slowly faded into the deep indigo-tinged twilight.

I gazed with interest at the building. 'Is this the house that Maggie mentioned? The one belonging to the old dressmaker?'

He laughed. 'No it's not and Maggie is very an-

317

noyed about it as well – the fact that the woman didn't pop her clogs and leave her house behind. No, this is someone else who died. Another old body – a man in his sixties but he looked about eighty.'

No wonder, I thought – living in permanent gloom wouldn't do anyone any good.

'Luckily for Kathleen, Maggie was also chummy with the rent man for this building and she and Sammy had moved in to the empty flat a few weeks ago. I've heard that Maggie is still fuming that her original target is still alive and kicking and refusing to leave this world. In fact, I heard Maggie's even stopped speaking to her!'

'But if she's got this house why is she bothering?'

'Seemingly the other house has two rooms while this one just has the one room but she's told Kathleen that as soon as the other tenant dies then her house will be theirs.'

What a world, I thought. Even the poorest people couldn't die in peace without someone coveting their house.

Mainly to cheer myself up I asked, 'When is the wedding, Danny?'

He looked gratefully at me. 'It's booked for September but Maddie will be speaking to you and Lily because she wants you both to be bridesmaids along with Joy.'

The mention of Lily brought a lump to my throat but I didn't want to worry Danny now that he was so happy.

'We've got your illness to thank for us being together again, Ann. I've been so stupid that I can hardly believe it now. Maddie didn't bat an eye when I told her about my father's death. Oh, she was sorry about the sad circumstances but she said it was our lives that mattered and not something that happened so long ago. It was just as you said it would be and it was a shame that you almost had to die before I realised it.'

All this talk of dying was getting me down so I changed the subject. 'Will you be looking for somewhere to live, Danny, or will you be staying with Maddie's parents?'

He shook his head. 'No, we're looking for a flat.'

Suddenly I shook with laughter and had to wipe the tears from my eyes. Danny looked puzzled.

'Do you think that old woman will pass on in time for your wedding and that Maggie will get her house for you?'

We both laughed while I imagined Maddie being grateful to Maggie for being so chummy with the rent man.

Kit appeared and stood beside us. She gave me a concerned look. 'We were all worried about you, Ann. George and I came to see you but you'll not remember it because you were so ill.'

I felt terrible. How many visitors had I not seen during my long days of the fever?

Kit gave a sigh. 'Still, it's a blessing that you're better now.' She leaned wearily against the rusty railings that marched up the shabby stone steps. 'Maggie is a good soul but she can be a wee bit wearing. Still, she's been really good to Kathleen but we're all fuming at Sammy. He's hardly been in the house since the bairn arrived and, when he

319

has put in an appearance, he's been drunk.'

Danny was furious. 'I'd better not meet him then, Kit, because I'll give him a talking-to that he'll not forget.'

Kit shook her head. 'He's not worth it, Danny. When I think of all the lads that fancied our Kathleen and she goes and ends up with Sammy Bloody Malloy, I could cry. But she wanted to marry him and she's now got to live with the consequences.'

'How is Ma?' I asked.

Kit smiled for the first time. 'Och, she's just the same as usual. Nothing seems to put her up or down. She watches and waits and she says everything comes in God's own good time. Let's hope He has something good up His sleeve for Kathleen – like Sammy becoming teetotal!'

We all went back inside the gloomy room and Maggie was still hovering over the baby.

When it was time to leave, Danny and I left some money for the baby's bankie and we then said our goodbyes. There was still no sign of the doting father.

Later that week, I got a surprise visit from Jean. She was full of excitement over the prospect of spying on Margot. In fact, she wanted to start there and then.

'I'll pay your expenses, Jean,' I told her.

'No, we'll go half and half as I'll get my cup of coffee out of the trip. My man is busy at the moment with his joinery work so this wee ploy will keep me busy. When do you want me to start?'

'Granny and I thought twice a week, Jean, but we'll leave it up to you when you go.'

I had been feeling even more depressed at the plight of Lily but Kit's remark the other night about how Ma Ryan had said everything comes in God's own time had cheered me up. I really felt very cherished by all my visitors during my illness. As well as my own family and the Ryans, Maddie and her parents had also come and so had their doctor. Rosie was the only one who had stayed away but that was because she didn't want to run into Margot and Dad and I understood entirely.

As Jean sat at the table with her cup of tea, I said, 'I'll give you my share of the expenses now.'

I took down the tin, expecting it to hold twenty-five pounds but it was empty. I sat down so hard on the chair that Jean thought I had fainted.

'What's the matter, Ann? Are you not well?'

Much to my own disgust, I began to cry. 'The tin's empty, Jean. It had twenty-seven pounds in it the other day when I took out two pounds to join you at the teashop.'

She was shocked. 'Do you mean to tell me you've had a burglar?' Her voice was faint.

I shook my head. 'I've had a burglar Jean but I know who he is – my father.'

It was Jean's turn to shake her head in disbelief. 'Och, surely your own father wouldn't take the money, Ann. It must have been a sneak thief. Do you lock your door?'

'No, I don't because nobody around here would ever dream of stealing from their neighbours. No, it must have been Dad because he was the only person to know I had money in here, believe me.'

She still sat in disbelief. I didn't know what to

do. Whoever had taken my money had now left me penniless once more and I didn't want to go begging again to Mr Pringle.

I told Jean this and she was annoyed. 'It's not begging, Ann. It's your own money that you're asking for.'

'But he'll want to know how I managed to spend fifty pounds in so short a time.'

'F-f-fifty p-p-pounds,' she stuttered, the words coming out along with tiny beads of spittle which settled on her chin before she wiped them away. 'Fifty pounds? You've lost fifty pounds?'

'No, Dad asked me for money for Lily's keep and some new clothes and shoes and I told him to take it from the tin. When I looked afterwards the tin had twenty-seven pounds left. I took out two pounds and that should have left twenty-five pounds but it's gone.'

'Look, Ann, I'll fund the spying venture and you can settle up with me later.' She took a few pounds from her purse. 'In the meantime have this wee loan till you see Mr Pringle and if you take my advice you'll get another place to hide it in – especially if there's someone with sticky fingers around.'

She left to begin on her venture. She'd said there was no time like the present and I sincerely hoped she would be successful.

After she left, a memory came into my mind of that afternoon when I'd thought I heard the noise of someone in the house. Perhaps it hadn't been a dream. I knew it couldn't have been Dad as he'd have been at his work so was it a sneak thief? I hoped so.

12

At the end of the week Jean appeared with her report of the assignment. Before she arrived, I had made up my mind to stop her going to the hotel. I didn't feel happy about it and my first instinct had been right. At the time. I thought spying on someone bordered on the criminal and this view had been reinforced as the days went by. If Margot was up to no good then no doubt the truth would come out in time but I wanted no part in it this way. I would try and get Lily back by some other means.

Jean was bursting to tell me her news. 'I've been to the hotel twice but they only appeared on one day. They sat together like the last time – so intent on one another that they never looked to the right or the left. But I couldn't hear what they were saying even although I took a seat near them.' She sounded disappointed about her inability to hear everything. I suspected she would have liked to give me dramatic news and was annoyed that there was none.

I told her what I thought about the entire thing. 'I think we'll call it off now Jean because I don't feel that we're doing the right thing.'

She didn't argue and I got the feeling she was relieved at my decision although she didn't say so.

My main worry now, apart from Lily, was the

323

fact I would have to make another appointment to see Mr Pringle. Jean's loan had helped out as did my wages from the shop but I had dodged the rent man last Friday night and I knew I couldn't do it again. I'd never missed paying my rent before so he would have just assumed I was out that time but he would soon stop thinking that if I was never in.

I voiced my worry about meeting Mr Pringle to Jean and she was annoyed. 'Listen, Ann, it's your own money we're talking about here and, if you have to take some more out, then so be it.'

'But he aye seems so upset if I ask him.'

She snorted. 'Solicitors are aye like that. They like to think they're investing the money for you and that you shouldn't ever need it. They normally don't need it themselves so they don't know how the other half lives. Just you go and see him and tell him the truth – that your money was pinched.'

But it wasn't as easy as that. What if he asked me if I knew who took it? I couldn't mention Dad.

Jean was still talking. 'Would you like me to come along with you for courage?'

It was good of her to offer. 'I'll have to make an appointment today and go back for the money tomorrow. If you can come with me now I'll manage to go myself tomorrow.'

She shook her head. 'No, you'll not, Ann. Tomorrow is Saturday and I'm sure the office is closed at the weekends.' She didn't sound sure but I thought she was right.

I was almost in tears. As it was, I was going to have to dodge the rent man again that night and twice would certainly make him suspicious. He had once told me that he knew the people who dodged their rents and made it difficult for him to collect them. Now here I was joining that great evading brigade.

Jean said, 'Let's go down and make an appointment for Monday and I can lend you some more money and you can pay me back later next week.'

I tried to refuse but she wouldn't listen so we set off. It was another lovely day of warm sunshine and it was a pleasure to be out in the fresh air. I was feeling so much better now and more like my normal self.

The two efficient-looking typists blinked at us as we walked in and one came to the counter.

'I'd like to make an appointment with Mr Pringle, please.'

To our astonishment, she told us to sit down and Mr Pringle would see me as soon as he could.

Jean raised her eyebrows at me but I shrugged my shoulders. We both sat in silence and listened to the gentle tapping of the typewriters which, as usual, I found very soothing.

Ten minutes later, Mr Pringle appeared at the door of his office and he seemed surprised to see us both sitting there. The typist rose from her chair and spoke quietly to him. He nodded and smiled in our direction.

He came over. 'I was on the point of writing to you both. What a surprise to see you both here – you must be clairvoyant!'

We sat looking at him as if he had gone daft but he waved us both into his office.

Jean remained in her chair. 'It's Ann who wants

to see you, Mr Pringle – I'm just here to keep her company.'

'No, Mrs Peters, I want to see you too.'

He herded us both into his tiny office and we sat down, full of trepidation. What on earth could he possibly want with us both? I wondered fearfully.

He made a great show of pulling down a large folder from the top shelf. He placed in on his desk and began to inspect the contents.

I had this absurd mental picture of him blowing away cobwebs from it but it was pristinely clean and looked as if it had hardly been handled in years. In fact my own folder here was almost identical to it.

I was suddenly worried. Had we lost our money through a bad investment? He had explained all these things to me at the time of my inheritance but it all sounded double-Dutch to me and I was glad to leave it in his capable hands. Had it all gone wrong?

He saw my worried face and he smiled. I relaxed. I somehow didn't think he would smile if the news was bad.

He gave us both a serious look. 'Now, ladies, I have some important news for you both. You know that Miss Hood has died and thank you both for going to her funeral last week. I have her will here and she has left you all – yourselves and Mr Potter the gardener – a good sum of money.'

I gasped out loud. 'She couldn't have mentioned my name, Mr Pringle – she tried to kill me.'

He looked solemn. 'Indeed she did, Ann, and

you're right – none of the beneficiaries are mentioned by name. Her will is a strange one, I must admit. It was drawn up years before either of you went to work for Mrs Barrie.'

Jean piped up, 'Well, how come we're mentioned in it?'

He explained, 'As I told you, it was drawn up during her early days with Mrs Barrie. There is no doubt that she loved her very much and when the question of wills came up one day she asked Mrs Barrie for advice. Now this is the strange part. Mrs Barrie told her that she was leaving the bulk of her estate to one beneficiary but there was also to be a few minor ones.'

Jean was puzzled. 'What's that got to do with us, Mr Pringle?'

'Well, it seems that Miss Hood did the same. She decided to have exactly the same will as her employer. Now, I suppose she thought the minor bequests would be for some charities or something like that and I do believe she was very fond of dogs so she probably thought the money might go there. But, because her will states firmly that Mrs Barrie's minor bequests are also to be hers, you both now find that you're beneficiaries of Miss Hood – and Mr Potter, of course.' He took off his glasses and wiped them on a tiny chamois cloth.

I was quite upset at this news and I said so. 'I don't think I should take this money, Mr Pringle, because it wasn't meant for me to inherit it. She hated me.'

'I know all that, Ann, but the fact remains that Miss Hood being of sound mind and body copied

Mrs Barrie's will and that's how it stands.'

Jean said, 'But she wasn't of sound mind.'

'When this will was drawn up she was. I can't force you to take the bequests but I strongly urge you both to think carefully about this. You can both do with the extra money.' He looked at me. 'Especially you, Ann – you have your sister to bring up and that will take a good deal of money.'

Not in my neck of the woods it didn't. There were hundreds of families living on the breadline and they seemed to get by. Why should I take this money which obviously wasn't meant for me? If Miss Hood was still alive she would say so.

'What will happen to this money if we refuse it?'

'Miss Hood had a son and he is the main beneficiary so this money would be added to his. However, we have failed to trace him and, if this remains the case, after a number of years the money will go to the Crown.'

Jean looked pensive. 'Will this son get a lot of money even if we take ours?'

'I'm not at liberty to divulge this but what I can say is this – these three small bequests are just a small part of the estate.'

Jean made up her mind. 'Well, I can't speak for Ann but I'll take my bequest and say thank you very much, Miss Hood.'

They both looked at me. I was torn between my feelings for the late housekeeper and my urgent need of cash. I made up my mind. 'I'll take the bequest as well, Mr Pringle, but can this money be put into a post office account or something similar. I don't want it to be with my bequest from Mrs Barrie.'

'That can be arranged,' he said. He placed the folder back on the shelf. 'Now, what did you want to see me about?'

'I wanted to see you...' I said.

Jean stood up. 'I'll wait outside, Ann, and let you conduct your business in private.'

My mouth felt dry. 'I need some more money, Mr Pringle.'

He looked at me but said nothing.

Flustered, I continued. 'It's just that the money I got a wee while ago is finished and I need some more.'

He then lifted my folder down and I almost laughed. It was certainly a day for the poor folders.

'I'll need to go to the bank but if you wait till I come back, you can have it later. We're closed tomorrow and I know you must be desperate to have some more money so soon, Ann.'

My heart lifted at this news. I would have money for the rent man and the shopping and I could also repay Jean's loan.

'I'll wait outside, Mr Pringle, and thank you.'

Jean was sitting on the chair outside with a faraway expression. I knew she was thinking about Miss Hood. I was doing the same. Although I felt awkward about taking her money, I didn't bear the dead woman any bitterness – it was all in the past where it belonged. In fact, I had a great sympathy for her unhappy life.

Jean put into words what we were both feeling. 'Imagine giving us a bequest, Ann?'

I didn't add that it wasn't a personal thing. Miss Hood probably thought it was going to a dogs' home or a sanctuary for aged donkeys. It certainly wasn't meant to go to her arch enemy – me.

Mr Pringle was back within the hour and I re-entered his office. He handed me a brown envelope and, once again, it contained my money in small denominations – fifty pounds.

He said, 'It's your money, Ann, and you can do what you like with it but can I give you some advice?'

I nodded.

'Please don't be so generous with your father and his new wife. Your father has a job and he can well look after themselves and you and Lily as well.' He stopped and gave me a searching look. 'I don't want to pry, Ann, but I hope your stepmother isn't asking you for this money?'

'No,' I said but he wasn't fooled. I decided to be straight with him – well, almost straight. 'She doesn't ask for it, Mr Pringle, but my dad did get some of the last lot.' I didn't dare mention he had had most of it. 'But they're not getting any more.'

He seemed pleased with this. 'I'm glad to hear it. Now, I'll arrange to have your other bequest paid into the post office savings account and I'll let you know when you can pick up the book.'

I was almost at the door when he said, 'Don't underestimate your stepmother, Ann.'

I gave him a straight look. 'Don't underestimate me either, Mr Pringle.'

He smiled and said, 'Oh, I've never done that, my dear.'

Outside, Jean tried to make me see sense over this new bequest. 'Make the most of it, Ann. It'll make your life so much easier.'

I tried to explain, 'Oh, I'm not turning my back on it, Jean. Like I said, I just don't want it beside Mrs Barrie's money.'

We parted with Jean catching her bus and me walking slowly back home in the late afternoon sunshine, clutching my envelope. I would have to get a new hiding place for it and I knew just the place – the next day, I would ask Connie to look after it for me. There was no way that Dad or the sneak thief would ever know where it was. They could search all week and never find it. I was feeling very happy and I suddenly realised it had been a long time since I'd felt this contented. The one dark blot was Lily but I would get her back – I was sure of that.

Dad appeared that night at the same time as the rent man. Luckily for me I had put the two weeks rent in the book so he didn't see my envelope of money. I had been worried about having it in the house and, until I could see Connie, I had hidden the envelope down inside the packet of washing powder. Who would think of looking inside a packet of Rinso? I thought.

I had made a big pot of soup – enough to last me a few days – plus a pan of stovies as I was slowly regaining my appetite and I was feeling hungry. However, I was shocked by Dad's appearance. His neck looked so thin that the collar of his working shirt stood out and he had a half-starved appearance. A sharp worry hit me – was Lily also looking like this?

'What do you want, Dad?' I said without charm. I was totally fed up with him. 'I've got nothing here for you so you'd better get away home for your tea.'

He looked so ill and drawn as he turned to go back out the door that I suddenly felt so sorry for him. Was this to be my cross to bear in life? To be annoyed with him one moment then so sorry for him the next?

I ran after him and I almost collided with the rent man as he came from the landing above.

'Dad!' I shouted after him. 'Come back up and get some soup.'

He bounded up the stairs and I was taken aback when he sat down and ate three slices of bread and butter before I even put the bowl of soup in front of him.

'Is Margot feeding you, Dad? You looked starved.'

'Och, aye, she does make some meals but they're not like this nice thick soup or your stovies. It's usually just wee dainty bites of things and she never makes a dinner. It's just a couple of tiny sandwiches.'

My earlier worry about Lily surfaced again. 'I hope she's feeding Lily?'

He looked sheepish and it wasn't because he was on his third plate of soup either.

'Well, that's the reason I'm here, Ann. Margot says she needs more money to look after Lily – to keep her clothed and fed, she says.'

Should I tackle him about the missing money? I decided to leave that for the time being.

'I gave you twenty pounds not that long ago, Dad. How much does it take to look after a wee lassie? Surely Margot hasn't spent all of that money?'

He was now tucking into a huge plate of stovies and he had sliced more bread. He spread a thick layer of butter on his slice of bread before replying. 'Margot likes to keep her dressed in bonny things and it's aye the very best she buys for her and it costs money.'

I had made up my mind that afternoon and I was sticking to it. 'Well, she's not getting any more and that's final.'

He stopped eating. His fork poised in mid air. 'She'll take it out on the bairn,' he said sadly. 'Believe me, she'll make Lily suffer.'

I was so incensed that the words shot out of my mouth. 'What do you mean she'll suffer?'

He looked downcast at his plate. 'She'll cut right back on our food for a start.'

I looked at him. 'Are you meaning to tell me that she'll stop feeding you and Lily if I don't give her money? What does she spend your wages on?'

'Aye, I'm telling you the truth about the food.' He seemed resigned to this terrible state of affairs.

I couldn't believe my ears at this terrible news. I knew then that I had to get Lily back. I could do nothing about Dad but Lily was another matter – especially now that I knew she wasn't getting fed properly.

Dad sat down with another plate of stovies. 'Don't worry about her, Ann. I make sure she gets a good meal every Saturday when we go down the town together.'

'How do you manage that if you've no money?'

He grinned for the first time in ages and I could see he was still the handsome man I remembered

– albeit a thinner and hopefully a wiser one.

'It's true that Margot demands my whole wage packet but I've got this mate in the warehouse who's a dab hand at altering his payslip. He never gives his wife the entire amount although she's under the illusion that he does. Now he does the same thing for me. That way I can manage to sneak a few shillings for Lily and me. It was the same when you gave me that twenty pounds. I gave Margot eighteen pounds and we kept two for ourselves. It gave Lily such a laugh.'

Oh, I bet it did, I thought – turning her into a juvenile fraud.

'But even if I give you more money, Dad, it doesn't give you both a better life, does it?'

He stood up and said darkly, 'No but it makes life that wee bit more bearable.' He looked so unhappy that I felt sorry for him – much against my better judgement.

I had a sudden thought. 'If Margot had a lot of money, would she give Lily up and let her come back here to stay?'

He seemed dubious. 'It would depend on the amount and I'm not letting you give up your legacy and give it to her – no, indeed.' He put on his jacket. 'Leave it with me and I'll do my best to get your sister back here because this is where she should be.'

I was actually quite proud of him then. He hadn't dropped into Margot's pit entirely because he was sincere when he spoke of my legacy – I was sure of that. But there was still Miss Hood's bequest. Although I hadn't said it at the time, I felt that money was somehow cursed. I wasn't a particularly superstitious person but I felt uneasy about it. It wasn't meant to be mine and it hadn't been given with a loving thought and a kind heart. On the other hand, Margot wouldn't see it like that. If I gave her the post office book when it came, then I could demand Lily back. I had no idea of the amount of this legacy but Mr Pringle had said perhaps a couple of hundred pounds which, to me, was a fortune.

I was beginning to get the measure of Margot and I thought that money was her whole world. I knew she wasn't dependant on my handouts but it was clear she had no intention of spending her own money on anyone but herself. If she didn't spend money on essential things like food, what did she spend it on? Surely not clothes and flowers?

The next morning, Connie listened to my story and took the envelope, saying, 'I've got a wee safe in the back shop, Ann. Your money will be there if and when you need it.'

She seemed dubious when I outlined my plan. 'She might just take the money and not hand Lily over. That way, she'll aye be able to call the tune.'

'No, she'll not, Connie, because I'll go to Mr Pringle and get him to shift the money back into his control. I've got it all worked out and I'll put it to Dad this weekend. He's promised to bring Lily up for her tea tonight.'

Connie still seemed unsure. 'Well, for your sake, I hope you're right.'

Lily and Dad appeared at teatime. It was lovely to see Lily again but I was shocked at her thinness. She looked so small in the red dress I had bought her before the wedding.

I had prepared a big meal and it was great to see them both enjoy it. I had also bought a box of fancy cakes from the baker shop and we let Lily choose the first one.

I let her into a secret. 'You know that Maddie and Danny are getting married in September Lily?'

She nodded and I almost burst out laughing at the ring of cream around her mouth.

'Well, they want you to be a flower girl. What do you say about that?'

She was delighted. 'Oh, Ann, that will be great. Will I get a bonny frock to wear and a bunch of flowers?'

'Aye, you will. Maddie has her exams to sit soon but, when they're over, she's going to make all the arrangements for her wedding so she'll see you then.'

Her face beamed then I saw the tears in her eyes.

'What's the matter, Lily? Do you no' want to be a flower girl?'

'Oh, I do, Ann, but Margot won't let me. She doesn't let me do anything but sit in that awful room and look out of the window. I've not to make a mess, she says.'

Anger threatened to overwhelm me but I tried to stay calm. 'It'll not be long before you're back here to stay, Lily,' I promised her.

Dad gave me a warning glance but I had made up my mind. There would be no more nonsense from him or Margot and she was welcome to the cursed money.

I put my proposition to Dad later while Lily was sitting with a huge pile of comics that Connie had given her. 'I've inherited some money from Miss Hood's will, Dad.'

He almost choked on his cup of tea. 'You've what?'

I repeated it and added, 'You and Margot can have it in return for Lily.' I sounded like Al Capone from some gangster picture playing at the Plaza cinema.

Dad was dumbfounded and he remained speechless.

I went on, 'I don't know the right amount at the moment but it should be about two hundred pounds. Tell Margot what I've said and, when I get Lily back here, then I'll give her the post office book and change the name on it or, if you want, I'll put your name on it, Dad – whatever you both want.'

When it came time for them to leave, he was still quiet. But, then, as he went through the door, he said, 'I'm not having you give your money to Margot – it's not right and she doesn't deserve it. No, you keep it and I'll find a way to get things sorted out.'

'No, Dad, I want you to tell her what I've said. She's welcome to it.'

Lily was tearful and I felt terrible to see her go. She clung to me and her wet tears left a damp patch on my jumper.

I whispered to her, 'Now mind what I told you, Lily, you're to be at Maddie's wedding and you'll be a bonny flower girl – you and Joy.' I slipped her two half crowns. 'Keep this hidden from

Margot and get yourself some sweeties on your way to the school.'

'Cheerio, Ann,' she said through her loud sobs and my heart hardened further against Margot. If anyone deserved Miss Hood's tainted money, then she did.

As the days passed, I had no word from either Dad or Margot and, worse still, nothing from Lily. Then, one afternoon at the end of June, just a couple of days before the summer holiday, there was an urgent knock on the door. Lily and an older girl were standing at the door. Lily looked so ill and she almost fell into my arms. I carried her through to her bedroom where fortunately the sun was streaming in through the window, making the room warm.

Meanwhile, the older girl remained on the doorstep. I called her in. 'What's happened?'

The girl spoke slowly and quietly. 'I don't really know anything except that I was told to take her home as she's been sick in the classroom.'

But this wasn't her home – at least not yet. 'She lives with her stepmother and her father in Victoria Road. Did you not go there?'

The girl nodded briskly. 'Aye, I did but there was nobody in so the teacher told me to bring her to her sister's house on the Hilltown.' She became agitated. 'You are her sister, aren't you?'

'Aye, I am so don't worry – you've done the right thing.'

The girl left to go back to her class with a couple of chocolate biscuits for all her trouble.

Lily was lying on the bed. She looked so white and listless and when she opened her eyes they seemed too large and dark for her tiny face. I would have to get Granny – she would know what to do. But how could I tell her? I couldn't leave Lily alone in the house.

Then I remembered Davie. He had left school and he was searching for a job. Perhaps, if he was at home, he could take a message to the Overgate. I ran as fast as I could. Thankfully, he was in the house and he set off at once with my message. Lily was still on the bed and she was sleeping. I decided I would send for the doctor when Granny arrived because Lily looked really ill.

I saw that she had been sick down the front of her jumper and I gently removed it. I still had some of her clothes in the house, including a nightdress. I went to fetch it plus a basin of warm water to clean her up. I was carrying this through when Granny appeared. She was panting and out of breath. 'Davie told me that Lily isn't well.'

Davie stood quietly at the door. 'I'll get away home now, Ann, but, if you need any more help, just give me a shout.'

I went with him to the door and thanked him. I was on my way back when I heard an angry shout from the room. It was Granny's outraged cry and I hurried towards the sound.

Granny had removed Lily's jumper and blouse and I was shocked at her thinness but even more shocked at the state of her clothes. The blouse had holes under the arms and the vest and pants were the same. I also noticed that they were the same clothes I had bought her months before. If Margot was needing money to clothe her, then where were they?

But, as I moved towards the bed, I got a further shock and found out the reason for Granny's cry. Lily's body was a mass of bruises – some looked newly done while others had the yellow tinge of healing.

Granny's face was a mask of anger and her eyes were dark with outrage. 'Who did this, Ann? I just hope it wasn't her father?'

I shook my head violently. 'Oh, no, Granny, he would never do this to Lily. No, it looks more like Margot's hand.'

'I think you should send for the doctor, Ann – just in case something's broken.' She set about washing Lily's face and putting on the clean nightgown.

I ran down the stair towards Connie's shop. She would know what to do and she had a telephone in her house. I'd always thought they were a luxury but, now that there was this emergency, I was grateful to know that it was there and that Connie would be able to help me.

She was having a cup of tea when I ran in. She smiled as I darted past the counter. 'Where's the fire, Ann?'

I blurted out my story and she immediately leapt to her feet. 'I'll run round to the house and call my own doctor. He lives in Garland Place so he shouldn't be long in coming.'

'What about the shop, Connie?'

This stopped her in her tracks and she looked at me. 'I'll only be five minutes. Can you stay until I get back?'

I was impatient to get back to Lily but it seemed churlish to refuse when she was going out of her way to help. I nodded but added, 'Be as quick as you can, Connie, because I'm really worried about her.'

She was as good as her word and she was back within six minutes. 'I was in luck, Ann. The doctor was in and he's coming round at once.'

I can't remember if I thanked her. When I got back home Lily was awake but she still looked pale and lethargic.

'The doctor is on his way, Granny. He'll not be long.'

I went and sat on the bed. Lily looked at me listlessly. 'I've been awful sick, Ann – right in front of my teacher and my classmates.'

I made soothing noises while Granny tried to question her about the bruises. 'Did you fall down when you were sick, Lily?'

Her face took on a closed look and she shut her eyes.

Granny wasn't giving up. 'Did somebody hit you, lass? Come on, tell us.'

She still stayed silent and the questioning came to an end with the arrival of the doctor. He sat by the side of the bed and took Lily's wrist in his fat pink hand. He gave her a thorough examination. His eyes rested on her bruises but he gave her a smile which lit up his plump face. 'You've got a bad dose of tummy-ache, young lady. You've been eating something that's upset you.'

He got up and ushered us out of the room but before he left he gave her another smile and she managed a weak smile in return. When we were seated in the kitchen, he questioned us, anger written all over his face. 'Who is responsible for those bruises? That young lass has had a good beating. Which one of you did it?'

We were both stunned but Granny recovered her voice before I did. 'That wee lassie is my granddaughter and this is her sister,' she said, pointing to me. 'Up to a few minutes ago when she was brought back from the school, she was in the tender care of her stepmother so you'd better question her.'

The doctor was taken aback by this onslaught. He had suspected one of us and he now realised how wrong he was. He packed his bag and made to leave. 'Well, in my opinion, she must be kept here and not returned to that environment. I'll make out my report about it.'

After he'd gone, Lily seemed to be a bit better. I made her some milky pudding and some colour came back into her cheeks.

Granny asked her again about the bruises but she seemed reluctant to talk about them so I gave it a try, saying, 'Don't be frightened, Lily. You're not going back to live with Margot ever again. You're staying here with me.'

She stared at us with large frightened eyes. 'Are you sure, Ann? She told me not to tell anybody about it.'

I bet she did, I thought.

Granny asked her about the bruises again and Lily seemed to think about it. Then she said, 'Margot hit me because I didn't do the cleaning quickly enough. She has this big black belt and she'd skelp me with it. Then, yesterday, when I was washing the stairs, she came down and gave me a shove. I fell down the steps, Granny, and hurt my tummy.' She pointed to a large black bruise which almost covered her stomach and side. 'Then she got so angry because the bucket of water got spilt and I had to wipe it up. I had to clean the lavvie after that. Then she held my head under the flush and I thought I was going to drown. And she doesn't give us enough to eat and Dad is aye starving as well. She won't spend money on food and she just makes wee snacks that don't fill you up.' She looked pleadingly at me. 'Can I have a fishcake supper from Mr Nettie's shop, Ann?'

I tried not to look at Granny while this story was spilling from Lily's lips but I knew she would be beside herself with anger.

I tucked Lily up in bed. 'No, I can't give you a fishcake supper tonight, Lily, because you have been very sick but you'll get one tomorrow night if you're feeling better.'

To say Granny and I were incensed with this was an understatement.

Granny said, 'I'm going round to see yon madam, Ann, and give her a few home truths.' She went to put on her coat but I stopped her.

'No, Granny, you stay here with Lily and I'll go. If I set off now I'll catch her before Dad gets in from work and I'll tell her a thing or two.'

I set off for Margot's house, my anger almost boiling over and I was in a right state when I knocked on the door. She appeared in another lovely frock, a pastel floral creation, and she looked angry. Her face was screwed up with annoyance and, before I could open my mouth, she launched into a tirade against me. 'Did you pick Lily up from the school?' she asked quite sharply. 'She wasn't at the gate when I called and someone told me she was with her sister.'

I pushed her into the lobby. It wasn't a hard push – more like a determined shove. I was in no mood for her nonsense or her sharpness. 'Aye, she is and that's where she's staying for good.'

Margot opened her mouth to speak but I gave her no chance. 'She was brought home from school because she was sick. There was nobody in the house here which is a blessing because we've discovered she's covered in bruises. The doctor is making out a report and, if you know what's good for you, you'll keep well away from her in the future.'

She looked at me with a very haughty expression but I knew she was bluffing. 'I only gave her a tiny push, for heaven's sake. Your sister bruises so easily. I've only to give her a hug and she comes out in big bruises.'

Oh, yes, I thought, getting a hug from Margot was the equivalent of getting a good crush from a bear or an all-in wrestler. I said, 'I don't want to hear another word from you, Margot. The episode is closed but Lily is never coming back here to stay and, when I see Dad, I'll tell him the same thing. I've no idea what you've done with all the money I gave Dad but it wasn't used to dress Lily. She was dressed in ragged clothes and they were the things I bought her last year.'

The mention of money made her bristle. 'And where is that famous post office account that your father was going on about? He said it was to be mine but it's just another one of your confidence tricks. Your father told me before we married that you were an heiress. I imagined it was thousands of pounds but now I know it was merely pennies.'

If Dad had been in the vicinity of my foot I would gladly have kicked him. No wonder she had latched on to him. She thought he would be able to get his hands on the money with no trouble from me, in exchange for a share of the bed settee. Well, that had been her bad luck.

I shot her a last warning look. 'If you come anywhere near Lily, I'll get the police on to you. You've got a choice. Be happily married to my Dad and keep your nose out of our affairs and we'll do the same with you. If you don't, then the police will hear about your "tiny pushes" of a defenceless lassie.'

I turned on my heel and marched down the stairs. I knew I would have to keep an eagle eye on my sister because I didn't trust Margot one inch. I sincerely hoped my threats about the doctor's report and the police would make her keep her distance. One thing was clear in my mind – she wasn't coming near us ever again.

Lily was sitting at a cosy fire when I got home. She gave me an anxious look but I grinned at her. Granny was making tea and a super smell hung over the small kitchen.

Lily was surrounded by her books and comics and she now looked totally happy. Granny and I would have to revert to the same arrangement over the school holidays and it would mean her living between the two houses again but I didn't think she would complain.

She ate a huge bowl of soup, followed by a plate of custard and milk. 'Oh, that was great,' she said. 'I was really starving!'

Granny and I laughed at her comical face but I knew she was still as angry as I was over the day's events.

Dad arrived at the end of that week. He looked totally washed out. I glared at him but he seemed so depressed that I relented and made him sit down at the table.

He said sadly, 'You've got to believe me, Ann, I didn't know a thing about Margot hitting Lily. She was aye in her nightgown when I got in from work and Lily never said a word about it.' He looked angry. 'I only wish she had.'

Would he have stopped it, I wondered? Yes, he would have – I was sure of that. He may be a fool with women but he loved us.

13

Maddie's exams were over and she came to the house a few days after sitting them.

'Thank goodness they're out of the way,' she said. 'Whether I pass or fail, the wedding is the main thing now.'

I was confident she would be successful with her exams and I told her so.

'To be truthful, Ann, I really don't care.'

When I looked shocked at this, she said, 'Oh, I know I've put a lot of work into my training but I'm just so glad that Danny and I are getting married. When he was acting strange, I really thought he had found someone else but, now that I know the full story, I feel wonderful.'

Lily was now almost back to normal after her dreadful time with Margot and she was giving Maddie her full attention. Though Granny and I tried not to make a big thing out of it, Lily still had bad nightmares. Thankfully, however, these also seemed to be coming to an end – well, they seemed to be and those she did still have were less serious in their ability to make her wake up screaming.

Maddie was chattering on about the wedding. 'It'll be on Saturday, the first of October. We did try for September but this is the date we've finally chosen. Now I'll need you and Lily to come with me for your bridesmaids' dresses soon. Mother and I are having a few problems over the colours but I thought a deep blue for you Ann and paler blue for Lily and Joy. What do you think?'

Before I could answer, Lily piped up, 'Oh, I think that's wonderful, Maddie.'

I laughed. 'It's your wedding, Maddie, so you should just pick the colours you want.'

'Right then, we'll meet up in two weeks time and discuss everything.'

It was almost the end of the school holidays and Lily was so excited. She could barely concentrate on anything other than the wedding. She was almost driving us all daft with her constant chatter about being a flower girl. One day, she told Connie, 'I'm to be in a pale blue frock and shoes and I'm carrying a bonny bunch of flowers in my hand and I've to walk behind the bride in a sedate fashion along with Ann and Joy. I've also got to be on my best behaviour because everybody will be looking at me and I don't want to let myself down.'

Connie burst out laughing. 'You sound just like your granny, Lily, and I bet you're repeating her words.'

Lily looked outraged. 'No, Connie, it's me that's speaking the words – not Granny.'

Later on, after Lily had gone back to the Overgate, Connie asked with a smile, 'Is there going to be a bride at this wedding or is it Lily's show?'

We both laughed at this. To listen to Lily, anyone would think she was to be the star attraction but I was grateful to have her back to normal – constant chatter and all.

Connie asked about Margot and Dad. 'Have

you had any more trouble from her?'

Thankfully I hadn't. 'I never see them much. Dad appeared a few weeks ago but there's been no more sight of him since then. I'm a bit worried about him because he's got so thin and I know she doesn't feed him right.'

Connie was unsympathetic. 'Well, he's a grown man and he shouldn't let her get off with that sort of treatment. Still, some men are daft when it comes to a woman.'

She picked up a huge pile of papers and dumped them on the counter. The poor wooden structure groaned at this rough treatment.

She was obviously in the mood for discussing men. 'I aye remember my cousin's wife. She was a good-looking woman but a proper besom. He was a quiet man but when he told her something important she aye said she didn't remember it. But, if another man spoke to her, she could remember every word – chapter and verse *plus* all the commas and full stops. He gave her a lot of money one day to pay a big bill and she spent it on a new outfit then she swore blind he had told her to spend it on herself and that he'd never mentioned paying a bill. Aye, she was a carbon copy of Margot.'

This knowledge didn't really help me but it did prove that men sometimes picked the wrong qualities in women and often overlooked the gentler and kinder women such as Rosie.

Another constant worry was the talk of war. These rumours had been hanging around since 1936 when Germany invaded the Rhineland but, as far as our customers were concerned, it was going to happen sooner or later.

Joe seemed to follow Hitler's every move and he was always in the shop telling us about another of Germany's antics. 'He's planning to conquer Europe and he'll do it. Don't you folk forget it,' he warned.

Previously, when he had uttered these doom-laden statements, most of us had ignored him but the papers were now saying the same thing. It seemed as if the world was in turmoil.

But Maddie's happiness was infectious. Lily and I went to meet her in D.M. Brown's department store. Her mother was there with Joy who seemed pleased to see Lily but she was playing up about being a flower girl. Lily on the other hand could hardly wait.

'Look at Lily,' said Mrs Pringle. 'She's looking forward to being dressed up, aren't you, Lily?'

Lily's face was beaming and she nodded so briskly that it was a wonder her head didn't fall off.

Joy gazed at us for a full minute then conceded. 'Only if we're dressed the same.'

She was certainly being lukewarm about the whole event and Lily couldn't understand this attitude. She looked at Joy as if she'd just arrived from another planet.

We all made our way to the bridal department where the atmosphere was hushed and expens-ively perfumed. Long racks of white gowns filled three sides of this room while the fourth wall held a colourful kaleidoscope of bridesmaids' dresses. I had never seen anything like it and neither had Lily. We stood with open mouths and wide eyes.

An assistant appeared as if from nowhere and sidled over. She seemed to float rather than walk over the deep piled carpet and it was obvious that Mrs Pringle was a valued customer in this shop.

The assistant spoke. 'Madeleine, may I offer my congratulations on your forthcoming wedding?' Her voice was quiet and cultured. It matched her slender black-frocked figure. Her hands I noticed were softly white with slim fingers and she wore no rings.

Lily tugged my sleeve and said in a stage whisper, 'Who's Madeleine, Ann?'

'That's Maddie's full name, Lily, but she gets called Maddie for short.'

Maddie made a face at us. 'Thank goodness for that.'

The assistant wafted over to the racks of bridal dresses.

Maddie and her mother inspected the selection the woman produced.

'We'll start with these,' she said.

While Maddie and her mother were in the changing room, we sat on comfortable chairs. Joy still seemed a bit sulky but, after a short time, Lily's enthusiasm won her over and she was look-ing forward to trying on a dress when it was her turn.

Then Maddie appeared in one of the most beautiful dresses I had ever seen. It wasn't a fancy-looking dress with lots of lace or tulle but its simplicity was breathtaking.

We all gasped in admiration. She looked so lovely that I couldn't help but wonder what this lovely girl, with all her advantages in life, was doing marrying into our poor family. Then I thought of Danny and I knew why.

He wouldn't be an assistant with Lipton's shop all his life – I was sure of that. Still, I expect it was his handsome face that appealed more to Maddie than any ambitions in life he might harbour.

She twirled slowly and the heavy crêpe-like material moved in fluid lines around her slim figure.

'What do you think of this dress, Ann?'

'Oh, Maddie, it's beautiful.' I could think of no other description.

'I like it as well,' she said as she moved back into the inner sanctum.

A moment later the assistant emerged with the dress over her arm.

'I must say, Madeleine, that you have been one of the easiest brides to dress. Some girls take days to make up their minds but I have to say that you've chosen one of this year's best creations.'

It was our turn next. Maddie had said blue which was fine with Lily and me but Joy wanted a different colour.

I tried on a deep blue dress which was as simple as Maddie's and in the same material.

'Do you like it, Ann?' she said with a worried frown on her face. 'I don't want you to wear something you don't like or that you think doesn't suit you.'

I loved it. It was the kind of dress I could never hope to own even if I lived to be a hundred.

The assistant was beginning to see this wonderful sale wrapped up by teatime but then Joy threw a tantrum. She didn't want to wear the pale blue frock that the assistant produced.

Lily stood quietly on the sidelines in her frock. Like me, she would have been pleased to wear any of this shop's frocks.

Mrs Pringle was beginning to get annoyed at Joy's stubbornness. 'Look at Lily – she's wearing it and she looks lovely in it.'

Joy's face set in a rebellious frown.

Mrs Pringle said, 'Now try it on, Joy. Maddie wants you and Lily to be dressed the same.'

Joy shook her head. 'I want to wear yellow.'

The assistant whose name was Miss Carr, went over to the rack and brought back a pale lemon dress patterned with tiny white dots. She held it up beside my blue frock and although it looked very fancy against the severe simplicity of our dresses the contrast was lovely. Miss Carr knew her job.

'What do you think about the lemon dress, Joy?'

'I want to wear yellow,' she replied sulkily.

Mrs Pringle had had enough. 'This dress is yellow, Joy, and you're going to wear it if it suits Lily as well. After all, it's your sister's wedding and it's her big day – not yours.'

Miss Carr swept both girls off to the changing room and they emerged a minute later like two little dolls. Miss Carr then suggested blue and yellow flowers to bring the outfits together and the sale was completed.

Maddie said she would choose her veil and headdress at a later date and then Mrs Pringle suggested we should have our tea in the restaurant. Lily was beside herself with excitement as we made our way up in the lift. Joy was a bit quiet for a time but, once again, Lily's pleasure soon rubbed off on her and they were soon both chattering about the wedding.

We sat down gratefully at a table and Mrs Pringle picked up the high tea menu. 'Do you fancy a high tea or an afternoon tea?' she asked.

Before I could stop her, Lily said, 'Oh, a high tea, please, Mrs Pringle.'

With a red face, I said, 'Just order what you want, Mrs Pringle, and don't listen to my sister – she's aye hungry.'

Lily looked downcast but Mrs Pringle laughed. 'If the little flower girl wants a high tea then that's what we'll have. It will save me making a meal when I get home.' She looked at Maddie. 'Your father has a meeting tonight and he won't be home till after nine o'clock.'

The waitress appeared and took our order. I saw Lily glance in my direction before ordering fish and chips but I didn't really feel annoyed at her. She was enjoying herself so much.

Maddie asked her mother about her own outfit and her mother sighed. 'I'm not sure what I want but Hattie and I will come together one afternoon and we'll both choose our outfits and hats – maybe one day when Joy is at school,' she said darkly.

Hattie – I could well imagine her delight in being part of a grand wedding. This social occasion of a lifetime for me and Lily would be taken in her stride by my aunt.

I gave a fleeting thought to the total cost from

the bridal department and it would have kept a family for a year or maybe more if they budgeted. Still, Maddie's face was glowing with happiness and I was overjoyed that they were now firmly back together – her and Danny.

After our lovely high tea, Mrs Pringle picked up her bag. I felt I should offer to pay for it as it had been Lily's idea to have the high tea. 'Please let me pay for the meal, Mrs Pringle.'

She shook her head. 'Not at all, Ann – it's my treat. And, to be honest, it is such a delight to see a child eat so heartily.' She turned to Joy. 'I wish you would eat your food like Lily instead of picking at it and pushing it around your plate.'

Joy didn't answer.

Later that night when we were in Granny's house, Lily regaled her grandparents with the entire saga. 'Oh, Granny, you should have seen the shop. It was full of brides' frocks and also bridesmaids' frocks as well. They were in a lot of bonny colours but Joy didn't want to wear the blue one so we're wearing lemon ones with white dots. The woman said to wear blue and yellow flowers and then we had our tea in the restaurant and I had fish and chips. Ann glared at me because I said, "The high tea, please." But we think Mrs Pringle just wanted a cup of tea. Ann did offer to pay because she said I was a gutsy besom but I'm not really. I just like to eat.'

Granny chuckled while Grandad pulled her on to his knee. 'What are we going to do with you, young lady? Have you been eating D.M. Brown's out of house and home?'

She was outraged. 'I only had fish and chips,

three slices of toast, two scones and two cakes and a cup of tea, Grandad.' She turned to me and, in a loud whisper, said, 'I would really have liked to wear the blue frock, Ann, but I don't really mind because it's been a magical day.'

Her eyes were shining and I was so grateful to the Pringle family for giving this special day to her.

I asked Granny, 'Have you bought something nice to wear to the wedding?'

She shook her head. 'I thought I could maybe wear something from my wardrobe.'

'No, Granny, I'm going to treat you both to new outfits. A frock and hat or a suit for you, Granny, and a new suit for Grandad.'

It was his turn to look outraged. 'Och, I've still got that suit I've had for years and it still fits me like a glove. No sense in wasting money on a new one if the old one is still good.'

But the old suit didn't fit him as he had shrunk with age. The jacket hung from his shoulders and he looked comical in it.

He couldn't understand it. 'It used to fit like a glove away back in 1921.'

Lily was amazed. 'Have you had that suit since 1921, Grandad?'

He looked smug. 'Aye, I have, wee lass, and it's been a good suit. Of course, it's a good make and you can't disguise quality. It cost me thirty bob and that was a lot of money away back then.' He gazed morosely at the jacket. 'I can't understand why the suit's got too big for me.'

Granny laughed. 'It's not the suit that's got too big, Gandad – it's you that's got smaller.'

I had a hard struggle to get them to agree to new outfits. They never wanted to take anything from me as a small thank you for all their hard work and devotion to us both but, in the end, I made them see sense and I left them some money from my envelope.

I had taken my money with me as I wasn't sure if I should contribute to our dresses for the wedding but Mrs Pringle had insisted on meeting all the expense. Tomorrow my envelope would be back in Connie's safe.

It had been a relief that Mrs Pringle had picked up the bill because I had seen the price tickets on our dresses. Also it left me a bit of money to make sure my grandparents were nicely turned out for the wedding.

Maddie had said the invitations would be sent out at the end of that week but I had no idea how many of the family would be invited.

I wondered if Dad would be invited and, if he was, he would have Margot with him. I wasn't looking forward to seeing her again as I was still seething over Lily's ill treatment.

The wedding was to be in St Andrew's Parish Church – a lovely church right across the road from the King's picture house. The wedding meal was to be in a swanky hotel in Perth Road. It had originally been a mansion house, Maddie said, but it was now a hotel. It faced the river Tay and the garden was seemingly beautiful – just the very thing for the wedding photos.

Although the next few weeks were hectic, I still had time to make an appointment with Mr Pringle. I had changed my mind over Miss

Hood's money. It wasn't now going to Margot but to Dad. That way, he would have some control over his life because I strongly suspected he had no say in his present set-up. Margot ruled the roost.

Mr Pringle was dubious about this arrangement. 'What if your father doesn't get the benefit of this money, Ann? What if Mrs Neill gets her hands on it?'

'Then that's a chance I'll have to take. I want Dad to have some money he can call his own as I'm really worried about him. He looks so thin and I know his wife never cooks a proper meal.'

Mr Pringle listened carefully and then said, 'Well, if that is what you want, Ann, I'll go ahead and place the money which should be around two hundred pounds in an account in your father's name.'

We then chatted about the forthcoming wedding and he smiled. 'I'm in the middle of all these women, Ann. Why is it that women go daft at a wedding?'

I said I didn't know. One thing I did know however was the fact that my own wedding, should it ever take place, would be a more modest event.

Danny appeared one evening. He looked harassed. 'I've escaped from Maddie and her mother. Mr Pringle is the same but he hides in the garden.'

I made a face at him. 'Och, you don't mean it, Danny Ryan. I bet you're fair lapping up all this attention.'

He grinned. 'It's worth it to be with Maddie. I would gladly go to the moon to be with her and thankfully our separation is behind us now.'

'Who's going to be your best man, Danny?'

'I was going to ask Kit's son, Patty, but Kit thinks he's a bit young and she thought he wouldn't be able to cope with such a grand affair. I thought of asking Greg. Do you think he would agree?'

I was sure he would be delighted but I obviously couldn't speak for him.

'Just write a letter to him, Danny, and I'm sure he'll do it. He's coming home that weekend for the wedding.'

'Right then, I will.' He sounded relieved and I hoped Greg would accept the offer.

'How are the invitations coming along?'

He made a face. 'I'm sure Maddie has invited the entire city according to her father. All the Ryan clan from Lochee, and I hear Ma is really pleased about me getting married. Then there's your Dad and Margot, Granny and Grandad, Rosie and Alice, Bella and Connie.' He ticked the names off on his fingers. 'Kathleen is hoping that Maggie will look after Kitty to let her and Sammy come. Mind you, Kit is not looking forward to him being there. She says he'll get blind drunk and show them all up but Maddie says not to worry as she has folk like that on her side also. She says that's what weddings are all about – having a few black sheep at the party.'

I wondered if Rosie and Alice would go. I thought not. Rosie wouldn't want to meet Dad and maybe it was better if Dad didn't meet Alice.

Danny burst out laughing.

I looked at him. 'Share the joke, Danny.'

'I'm thinking of Mum. What a pickle she's in

359

about her outfit. On the one hand, she doesn't want to outshine Mrs Pringle but, on the other hand, she wants to be the star of the show – in the spotlight. She's going around looking worried and smug at the same time if you can believe it.'

I could well believe it. I changed the subject to the house that Danny and Maddie had been looking at over the past week.

'What about the house?'

'We both like it. It's a flat in Roseangle – the one that Maddie pointed out to you last week. When we got the key to view it, we really liked it. There's a small living room and one bedroom and a tiny kitchen and bathroom. Maddie's Dad can arrange the loan for us and I think Maddie has set her heart on it.'

'What about you, Danny? Do you like it?'

He nodded. 'Aye, it's grand.' He blushed. 'If Maddie likes it, then so do I. She calls it the love nest.'

His blush deepened and I decided not to tease him. Maddie had taken me to see the flat from the outside as Danny had said. She couldn't take me inside because the owner was still in residence and in the throes of moving. But we had admired it from the outside. The building was at the lower end of Roseangle and it had a view of the river. The stonework had been repointed recently, giving the building a fresh and almost new look.

Another thing I was amused by at the time was the entrance to the stairs. You went in through a spick-and-span tiles close. For years, the family joke was that Hattie had always longed to live in such a building with a tiled close. To her, it was the epitome of gracious living. Although she had never achieved that dream, it now looked as if it was coming to her in a second-hand way so to speak. From now on, Granny and I would have to listen to her singing the praises of the tiled close and it would drive us both barmy.

Danny was still speaking about the flat. 'You know it's on the second landing and the folk moved out a couple of days ago. We've been in to see it but I know Maddie wants to show it to you, Ann. She was wondering if tomorrow night would suit you and Lily.'

I knew Lily would be delighted to get a conducted tour around the new house and, to be truthful, so would I.

'That would be great, Danny. Will we meet Maddie at seven thirty?'

'I'll tell her and she'll meet you outside.' He turned to go but said, 'I've got another bit of good news. George has got a job in a foundry and seemingly they're looking for other workers so he's hoping tae get Belle and Lizzie's men jobs too. Kit was also saying that Cox's mill is taking on extra workers so she's hoping to get a job back there.'

I was pleased for them. After being jobless for so many years, it was marvellous that they might now all get on their feet financially. 'That *is* good news, Danny. What a difference it'll make to get a wage packet again.'

I had been thinking about the Ryan women and wondering if they could all afford outfits for the wedding but this good news would certainly help their morale. I had toyed with the idea of offering them some money to help them over the expense but, when I mentioned it to Danny, he shook his head.

'They'll not take it, Ann. I've also offered to help out but they say they'll manage and they'll not show me up. Kit says they'll be togged up like the other guests.' He smiled. 'As if I'm worried about that – it'll just be good to see them there.'

He went away back to the wedding fever and I waited to tell Lily the news of the house visit the next day. When I told her, she began to jump up and down with excitement. I warned her, 'It'll not be furnished yet, Lily. It'll just be the bare rooms.' This failed to quell her pleasure and that was the thing I loved about her – the ability to get excited about everything. Big and small things in her life were viewed with this magical mixture of wonder and pleasure and I hoped it would be something that would stay with her all her life.

People became jaded so easily in life but things seen through Lily's eyes had a freshness and a breathless quality that was so wonderful. I recalled Joy's sulky behaviour and I was thankful that Lily hadn't all her good fortune. Too much too early wasn't a good upbringing for a child, I thought. But then I remembered that it hadn't harmed Maddie. Perhaps it was just an off day for Joy.

I was hurrying to the Overgate the next day with Lily when we met Kit and her two sisters. I had met Lily at the school gate. She was now back at Rosebank school and the headmistress at Victoria Road School had been most helpful over the transfer – especially as she hadn't been in her

362

school very long. I still had the niggly feeling that Margot would turn up one afternoon but Lily was well warned not to go off with her. Not that she would willingly go but she might be frightened of the woman. Thankfully, however, it hadn't happened.

It was Lily who spotted the three women. 'Hullo, Kit!' she shouted across the street.

They came over. 'Hullo, Lily,' said Kit. 'Now tell us what you're wearing for the wedding because we're looking for our outfits.'

Lily looked important. 'Well, I'm in a lemon frock and so is Joy...'

I butted in. Lily would hog the entire conversation if I let her. 'Are you shopping for your outfits now?' I asked.

Kit said, 'Aye, we are. The men can wear their suits that they've had for years but we want to look smart for Danny and Maddie.'

They were standing outside Style and Mantle, a shop at the foot of the Wellgate, and they had been scrutinising the windows which held an assortment of ladies' wear.

'We've got ourselves a Provie check each but we're not sure if this shop accepts them.'

Lizzie snorted. 'Even if they do, Kit, it's too pricey for us. Let's look for something a bit cheaper.'

But Kit refused to be sidetracked. 'No I'm going in here and asking if their shop is on the Provident line list.'

At that moment if I had my hands on Miss Hood's money I would gladly have given it to them. They were always having to struggle and I knew Kit would want to be especially nicely dressed for her favourite nephew's wedding. But, as it was, I didn't have this money and I didn't know whether I should offer to help them out. I drew Kit aside as her sisters glanced at the window again.

As I didn't even want Lily to overhear, I whispered quietly, 'Let me help you out with the outfits, Kit.'

She shook her head. 'Och, no, Ann. Honestly we're having good fun deciding on something to wear and we've got the rest of the afternoon to find something.'

Still, as we said goodbye to them, I was pleased I had offered.

At seven thirty, Lily and I arrived at the close in Roseangle to find Maddie was waiting for us. She looked tired but I thought it was all the arrangements for the wedding that was making her face look white and strained.

She gave us a cheery wave, however, and we climbed the spotlessly clean stairs to the imposing looking wooden door with its shiny brass handle. She was a bit out of breath as she inserted the key in the lock. We stepped into a fair-sized lobby which had four doors – two on the right wall and two on the left – but the outstanding feature was a gigantic stag's head which seemed to be part of the wall. Lily jumped in alarm and I also got a fright.

Maddie burst out laughing and we joined in. 'Meet Hamish,' she said.

The stag had a large pair of antlers and his eyes seemed to be alive. 'Are you going to keep him,

Maddie?' I wasn't sure if I would had I been in her shoes.

'We haven't made up our minds yet but I suppose he could always act as a coat hanger.'

Lily shivered. 'Well, I don't like the beastie, Maddie. He keeps looking at you as if he'd like to jump off the wall.'

Maddie opened the first door on the left and we stepped into a square shaped room which over-looked the back of the building and had a won-derful view of the river. It was a lovely room, full of light, and I loved it.

'This is great, Maddie, and what a lovely view!'

Lily ran over to gaze out of the window while Maddie opened a door on the far wall. This was a tiny scullery just big enough for the sink and the gas cooker. We then looked at the small bedroom which faced the road and the bathroom which also faced the river.

She then opened the fourth door in the lobby to reveal a large cupboard then our tour of the house was over.

'We're hoping to get the carpets laid and the curtains up next week and the furniture will be delivered in a couple of weeks. The last owners decorated it not so long ago and we quite like the paper so we won't bother about that just yet.'

We were back in the living room. I gazed around me and said, 'It's a lovely flat, Maddie, and I hope you'll both be very happy in it.'

'It won't be long now till the wedding and I'm counting the days.'

The time had certainly flown in and we were now in September.

'You'll be hoping for good weather for your wedding day, Maddie?'

She smiled but the tension was still visible. 'I hope nothing goes wrong before then.'

'Nothing will go wrong, Maddie,' I said, trying to reassure her.

'It's just that everyone is saying there's going to be another war and the more times I hear it the more worried I become.'

I was worried myself because Connie was also sure that we would soon be at war with Germany. That would mean that Danny and Greg and boys like Sammy would all be called away to fight but I had to cheer her up.

'Don't worry about it, Maddie. Just you look forward to your wedding and leave your worries behind you – after all, it's supposed to be the happiest day of your life, isn't it?'

She smiled again. 'I know and I'm just being daft.'

As we set off down the stairs she said, 'Mum wants us to go to the church for a wedding rehearsal. It will be on the Friday night prior to the wedding day and she wondered if Lily and you could stay overnight with us. That way the cars could all leave from the one address.'

When my face lit up, she said, 'I'm looking forward to having a good chat and you'll be a big help when I get nervous about my big commitment.'

I pretended to look shocked. 'Och, you'll not be nervous, Maddie – you'll carry it off with your usual panache.'

On that note we parted.

The following weeks flew by in a whirl of wedding arrangements which left me bemused by all the things that had to be seen to. To be honest, I had always thought the only thing that had to be done was to turn up on the appointed hour and hope the bridegroom did the same. But, no – it was all a flurry of plans and a frenzied atmosphere.

Our shoes arrived late and Mrs Pringle was becoming quite agitated in case the shop hadn't dyed them the correct shade to match our dresses. In fact, when they finally arrived, they were superb and Lily was over the moon with hers.

'Do you think I'll be allowed to keep them afterwards, Ann?' she asked when the parcel arrived.

I was doubtful. 'Well, Mrs Pringle has paid for them but maybe if I offer to buy them after the wedding then she'll let you have them.'

Then there was the flat. The carpets had been laid and I went with Hattie to give her a hand to hang the curtains. Hattie was in her element as she handled the thick velvet curtains. The living room ones were in shades of wine, deep gold and pale peach and the effect was stunning. I thought of our little flat on the Hilltown and this glorious place made it look drab. I made a mental note to buy some cheery curtains for the coming winter.

Maddie's parents had bought the living room furniture as a wedding present to the couple and Hattie had done the same with the bedroom furniture. Maddie and Danny had chosen the pieces but both sets of parents picked up the bill.

Maddie rushed in as we were on the last curtain and she began to tell me of their good fortune with the wedding gifts. 'We're very lucky with Hattie and my parents' gifts. Not many young couples get off to such a good start so early in their marriage.'

I agreed with her. I had discovered that the traditional gift from the bridesmaid was china. Hattie had told me this. Either a tea set or a dinner set or, if you were well off, then perhaps both.

'Lily and I will get you some china, Maddie, so, if you want to pick something for yourself, we'll buy it,' I told her.

She tried to protest. 'Danny and I don't need any more presents, Ann.'

I shook my head.

'Thank you, then. Maybe we can go and look at a tea set. We better make it on a Saturday so that Lily can come with us.'

'Good, that's settled then.'

Meanwhile Hattie was still in raptures over the new flat and the tiled close. She told Granny later, 'I always said that Danny would do well for himself. Maddie and her mother have such good taste and the new flat is just a dream come true for me.'

Granny was unimpressed. 'Don't tell me you're going to move in with the young couple, Hattie? Will you give up your house in the Westport?'

Hattie looked at her mother as if she was daft. 'I'm merely describing the flat. I'm not proposing to move in.'

One thing that almost got overlooked in this frantic frenzy was the fact that Maddie had passed her exams. She was now a fully trained SRN. She seemed quite unconcerned about her achievement and she confessed this to me one day when we were at the flat. 'When I started to do my training, I thought it was all I wanted to do but, when Danny stopped seeing me, I realised he was the most important thing in my life. I'm just so glad we're getting married. Oh, I know I'll always have my training behind me if I ever need it but Danny is far more important to me than that.'

I could well understand her wanting to get married but I felt differently about marriage. I couldn't envisage a time when I wouldn't want to work except perhaps if children came on the scene. I kept my views to myself. Maddie knew what she wanted and hopefully it was this.

That day, she also said, 'Danny has got a letter from Greg and he'll be delighted to be our best man.'

'That's good, Maddie. I expect there will be a letter waiting for me as well. He normally writes three or four times a week.'

I was feeling quite guilty as I said this. I hadn't written to him for nearly a week now what with all the running around with Lily between the house, the school and the Overgate – not to mention the wedding. I hoped he would understand.

There was a letter waiting for me. It began with the words, 'Are you still in the land of the living, Ann?'

Full of remorse I sat down and wrote a short note, pleading overwork.

There had been no sight of Dad since the episode with Lily and I was dreading meeting

Margot at the wedding. Still, I reckoned there would be lots of guests and hopefully our twain wouldn't meet.

Connie was full of the wedding as well. Her entire conversations these days hinged on how lovely it was to have been invited and what she would wear when the big day arrived. As it was, I was grateful for all this frivolous talk because most of the customers were full of gloomy predictions of war.

Joe came in a few days before the wedding and as usual he was despondent.

Connie stopped him in mid flow. 'Och, well, Joe, maybe Mr Chamberlain will get the peace he's looking for. He's going to Munich to see that terrible Hitler.'

Joe snorted with derision. 'Aye, he'll maybe get a peace deal but what about the rest of Europe? Do we want to abandon them to that dictator?'

'Well, if it stops our laddies getting killed in another war, then let's hope Mr Chamberlain will get what he wants. I'm all for looking after number one in this life.'

Joe muttered something under his breath which sounded like 'Just like a woman'. Then he left with his five cigarettes.

I found this kind of talk depressing and I hoped that Mr Chamberlain would get a peace deal with Hitler – even if the German Chancellor was the toerag that Connie always said he was.

One good thing was the weather. It was not very warm but lovely and sunny – autumnal, in fact. The trees along the Perth Road were a delightful mixture of russet red, gold and brown.

On the evening before the wedding, Mr Pringle ran us to the church for the rehearsal. Mrs Pringle sat in front with her husband while Maddie, Hattie and I sat in the back. Maddie's uncle was bringing Joy, Lily and Danny and Greg was coming straight from the station.

The church was cool and dim, the wooden pews lying like shadowy masses at each side. There was a smell of old wood and candles and, for some reason, we all began to speak in whispers in this hushed atmosphere.

The minister was standing at the altar and he came forward to shake our hands.

I heard Lily's high voice saying, 'Pleased to meet you.'

The Pringles closed their mouths tightly and looked as if they would burst out laughing. I made another mental note to speak to my sister before the wedding with a list of dos and don'ts. Then I realised I was forever making these little mental notes to myself. I would try and relax I told myself – another mental note.

Then Greg arrived. He had been running and was out of breath.

'Sorry I'm late,' he said, smiling at the group but he didn't pick me out for a special glance.

Oh dear, I thought, he must be upset at my not writing.

The minister put us through our paces and it seemed to take forever. If Lily was walking the right way then Joy wasn't or vice versa but by nine o'clock we all knew our proper moves – at least I hoped so.

We stood in a tight bunch outside the church.

It was a lovely night – clear and starry with a sharp coldness in the air – and the weather was to be good for the following day we had heard.

Mr Pringle and his brother were rounding up their passengers. Greg and Danny decided to set off on foot while I went in the car with Maddie and Hattie. I tried to speak to Greg before he went but I didn't get the chance. As we passed them in the Murraygate, I gave him a wave and although he waved back I felt there was a lack of passion in his hand movement. Danny's wave had been positively vigorous in comparison. Still, there was nothing I could do until the next day when I would apologise for not writing.

The house at Perth Road was full of people when we arrived, most of them relatives of the Pringle family. After a quick supper, Joy and Lily were despatched to their beds while the rest of us sat around with a glass of sherry.

Maddie's uncle had come into the house with us where he joined his wife. I gave him a covert glance and wondered if he was still secretly meeting Margot.

'Thank you both for the beautiful Chinese rug, Uncle John and Aunt Dorothy,' said Maddie.

Uncle John looked as if he had been drinking something a lot stronger than sherry while Dorothy looked as if she might be missing a bridge night. Life might have been kind to her but her looks hadn't. Her long gaunt face was devoid of any make-up and the grey suit she was wearing didn't help her appearance one bit. I wondered if her snooty look was perhaps just a bad habit. Did she wear spectacles? I wondered. If she kept them off in public then that would account for the permanent haughty expression.

After a decent time in her family's company, Maddie excused herself and we escaped to her bedroom. She was highly flushed from the heat in the lounge and the sherry and she was looking morose.

'I know I should be overjoyed tonight, Ann, but I can't stop worrying about the talk of war. If it happens, then all the young men will be called up and that means Danny and Greg.'

This infernal rumour of war, I thought, it intruded into all our conversations and our lives and, if we were all honest enough to admit it, it caused real fear in our hearts. I thought about it all the time but had tried to push it to the back of my mind.

'Och, maybe it'll fizzle out, Maddie. Connie says that Mr Chamberlain will bring back a peace treaty and we'll not be at war with Germany.'

'The government are issuing gas masks, Ann. Did you know that?'

I nodded. There was no getting away from all the news in the shop. The daily headlines were in my full view every day and I was becoming more knowledgeable about the world situation with each lurid story but, as I had said, I had tried to avoid it – like an ostrich with its head in the sand. Still, one thing was clear – I had to cheer Maddie up. After all, it was her wedding day in a few hours and she shouldn't be worried like this about a war – whether or not it ever materialised.

I asked her, 'Are you going away on a honeymoon, Maddie?'

Her face lit up. 'We're not going away because Danny has only the three days off work. Now that he's one of the chief assistants, he has to be in the shop. He has tomorrow, Sunday and Monday off so we thought we would just stay in the flat. Then, later on, if he gets some time off, we will go away for a holiday.'

I tried to visualise what life would be like living with a man all the time and I couldn't. Was I too independent?

'Will you be getting married soon, Ann?'

I shook my head. 'We've not made any plans yet.' I showed her the ring Greg had given me.

She was excited. 'So it won't be long till you do get married.' She turned the ruby and pearl twist in her hand. 'It's a beautiful engagement ring, Ann. I wish you would wear it tomorrow.'

I said I would wear it although not on my engagement ring finger. No, I wouldn't wear it there – at least not until I saw Greg. A shiver ran up my spine as I recalled how distant Greg had been and the cool glance he had given me.

I awoke the next morning to a cacophony of sound and golden autumn sunrays streamed through the window. I lay for a moment, unable to remember where I was then it all came back as my senses slowly wakened. It was Maddie and Danny's wedding day and it was here at last.

There was a delicious smell of frying bacon coming from the kitchen and I realised how hungry I was. I dressed quickly and hurried downstairs. Joy and Lily were sitting side by side at the large wooden kitchen table. Joy was picking at a bowl of porridge while Lily was tucking into a plate of bacon, sausages and egg.

A plump woman stood at the cooker and I remembered that Hattie had said Mrs Pringle had hired her for the weekend to do the cooking and housework to allow Hattie to have the weekend off for her son's wedding. The woman looked up. 'Breakfast, Miss?'

I nodded. 'Please let me help you with it.'

I made the toast and tea while she put the food under the grill. As she turned to speak to me a large splodge of porridge hit her on her chest and dribbled down her spotless overall. Although she said nothing, she glared at the culprit – Joy.

I was at a loss myself. I couldn't possibly chastise my hosts' child. Then she did it again. I heard my voice before I gathered my wits about me. 'Joy, stop that. Now say you're sorry to the lady.'

Joy was taken aback with my sharp voice. She gave me a black look but she did say, 'Sorry, Mrs Patterson.'

I sat down with my plate and it was a very chastised little girl who faced me but I could see she hadn't liked my getting on to her.

After breakfast as they ran out into the garden to play I heard Joy say to Lily, 'You've got a right old dragon of a sister, Lily.'

Lily stopped dead in her tracks. 'No, I don't, Joy Pringle – I've got the best sister in the whole world, so there.'

Mrs Patterson grinned. 'You've got your fan club in that wee lassie.'

Before I could reply, Maddie and her mother appeared. They didn't want any breakfast and I felt like a gigantic glutton with my piled-up plate.

Mrs Pringle was fretting about the flowers. 'They should be here by eleven o'clock Maddie and I hope they're not late. The hotel phoned last night and thank goodness they have everything under control. The flowers for the table arrangements were delivered there last night so that gives them loads of time to do that and it's the same with the flower arrangers at the church.'

I felt quite faint by all this talk of flowers and I thought I should be pulling my weight here instead of sitting eating a huge breakfast. 'Can I do anything to help, Mrs Pringle?'

She smiled. 'No, thank you, Ann. I think everything is in order but my ankles are beginning to swell up and I hope I can get my new shoes on.'

'Why do you not go and have a rest and put your feet up? When the flowers arrive, I'll let you know.'

'Do you know, Ann, that's exactly what I'll do.' She set off for the lounge which was now bathed in warm sunshine.

The flowers didn't arrive till twelve o'clock by which time the entire household was going daft. In fact, Mrs Pringle was actually on the phone to the florist when the man arrived at the door with them.

Maddie's bouquet was lovely. It was done with white flowers mixed with a sprinkling of pale lemon blossoms while the bridesmaid and flower girls' posies had blue and lemon flowers in them. Mine was identical to theirs but slightly larger. There were also three circlets of flowers for our heads, again in blue and lemon flowers.

Then it was time to get dressed. I had a bath.

The water was perfumed with Maddie's bath crystals and I felt like a princess. Afterwards I dressed in Maddie's bedroom while the girls were in Joy's. Maddie stayed in her parents' room until the car arrived to take us to the church.

When she came out, the effect was breathtaking. Although I had seen the dress in the department store, it now looked so much better with the addition of a filmy veil and a white flowered head-dress.

Her father stood at her side and I could swear he had tears in his eyes but maybe it was merely a trick of the light.

Lily and Joy were like little dolls and I was delighted by my appearance. The deep blue of the dress went well with my dark hair and the circlet of flowers matched exactly the ones on the girls' heads.

Mrs Pringle came with us and we left the bride alone with her father to await the bridal car. It was traditional for there to be a 'scramble' when the bridal car set off for the church. This involved the bride's father tossing a couple of handfuls of low-denomination coins to the local children who would each do their utmost to pick up as much money as they could. In anticipation of this, a horde of children waited patiently in the street for Maddie and her dad to emerge from the house and head for the car. They were not disappointed. As the chauffeur drove off, Mr Pringle scattered a generous amount of money out of the car window. In their eagerness to collect the coins, some of the smaller children seemed oblivious to the possibility that they might get run over but the older ones had seen it all before and made sure this didn't happen.

At the church, loads of spectators had gathered. Everyone, it seemed, liked a wedding to look at. We stood inside the porch and I heard the rousing strains of the church organ. Suddenly I was filled with the sense of the occasion that had been missing. Up until that minute, I had been slightly cynical of all the religious trappings of a wedding but, now, in this lovely church, I felt overcome and touched by the solemnity of the building.

Then Maddie arrived. The organ soared into the 'Wedding March' and we began our walk behind her down the long aisle. I saw heads turning and gasps of excited breath. Ma Ryan and all her family sat beside Granny and Grandad. On the opposite side sat all Maddie's relations and friends. All had gathered there to witness the marriage of Maddie and Danny.

Standing at the altar were Danny and Greg. I thought they looked nervous but they both also looked so handsome in their dark suits. I don't think I had ever seen Danny looking so smart and good looking as he was that day. His red hair, normally so bouncy, was slicked down but I knew it wouldn't last like that for long. Before the day was over, it would be like a red halo around his head.

It was then that I realised how much I really loved him. Oh, not in the sense that Maddie loved him but more like a sisterly feeling of love. My mind flashed over all the years we had known one another – all the help and support he'd given me – and I knew then that we were truly grown-up. Our childhood lives were behind us.

Then he glanced at Maddie and all the nervousness left his face. He smiled at her and she responded with such a wonderful look of love that I just knew they would both be very happy always. He glanced at Lily and Joy and gave me a grin but his special look was for Maddie and that was how it should be.

Greg hadn't turned as I stood beside the bride and I became anxious. Something was amiss and, whatever it was, I had no doubt I would soon find out – nothing was surer. I glanced at my ring which I wore on my right hand. I had hoped that Greg would perhaps place it on the left hand at the wedding meal but now I wasn't so sure. But, for now, I let the minister's words wash over me and the voices of the congregation rose with the sound of the organ playing 'Love Divine'.

Then it was over – far too soon, I thought. We found ourselves out in the autumn sunshine with the crowds of spectators peering through the railings. There were more photographs here and I knew it had been planned that others would be taken at the hotel.

I was in the car with Maddie's parents and her mother was crying. But it was tears of joy, she said – just tears of joy.

14

The garden at the hotel was a wonderful kaleidoscope of autumn tinted trees and banks of gold, bronze and crimson chrysanthemums. We posed for more photographs against this backdrop. Lily took her role so seriously and did all the things she was told by the photographer and the sun shone on all the proceedings.

If Maddie and Danny were radiant, then so was Hattie. Mrs Pringle was smartly elegant in a navy suit and shoes with a picture hat in navy and white fabric. Meanwhile Hattie was gorgeous in a dress and jacket in almost the same colours as the crimson chrysanthemums. Her hat was a very simple cloche style that set off her dark hair to perfection.

The guests were either in the garden or inside the posh-looking hotel lounge with its thickly carpeted reception area. Once all the photographs had been taken, we went inside too. We stood in a line and welcomed the guests. I was proud of my grandparents. Grandad wore his new pin-stripe suit with a white shirt and a blue tie. Granny looked ever so smart in a dress and coat in royal blue and a blue hat with a cream flower pinned at the side.

Ma Ryan was dressed as usual in black but on this happy occasion she had livened it up with some white. Her close fitting hat looked like a remnant from the last century but everything she wore suited her and, although she hadn't planned it, she too looked elegant.

The Ryan girls wore an assortment of colours but they were also smart with their straw hats to match. Obviously the 'Provie' checks had stretched like a length of elastic because the men were all in dark suits with white shirts with starched collars.

Meanwhile Bella was outstanding because of her hat. It was enormous in proportion to her face but the shop assistant had told her it was a hat suitable for a grand society wedding and the social side of her nature had swamped her common sense. Still she was enjoying herself and that was all that mattered.

Then Kathleen appeared and I almost gasped. She was dressed simply in a pale green summer suit with her red hair tumbling on to her shoulders. Instead of a hat she wore a simple headband with tiny green flowers and the effect was stunning. There was no sign of Sammy but I noticed quite a few of the unattached males gazing at her with admiration – including Colin Matthews, the lad who worked in Maddie's father's office.

Connie was standing beside Dad and Margot. Connie looked smart in a suit with a fox fur around her neck while Margot as usual was well dressed in a deep gold dress with matching hat and shoes. Dad gave me a glance as he passed and I was shocked by his thinness. His suit, which he'd bought for Harry's funeral and which, at one time, had fitted him perfectly, was now almost hanging from his thin shoulders. Margot

looked bored with his company and worry tightened in my stomach.

Jean Peters and her husband were next and,
although she didn't say anything out of place, I
could well imagine her summing up Margot.

I'd almost resigned myself to not seeing Rosie
and Alice when this voice spoke as she shook my
hand. I didn't recognise the smallish man with
balding hair and a round cheery-looking face and
I almost didn't recognise Rosie.

After the introductions were all over, I made a
beeline for her. 'Rosie, I didn't know you – you're
looking great!'

She beamed and introduced me to her friend.
'This is Albert. He's a friend from the Salvation
Army and, when Mum couldn't make it, I asked
Maddie if I could bring him along and she said it
was fine.'

I almost laughed at her detailed description and
bona fide references for Albert. Did she think I
was the security officer detailed to throw out any
gatecrasher? I said, 'Rosie, you look wonderful.'

She had lost some weight and now looked less
podgy. Also her hair had been cut. Instead of the
heavy and ponderous bun at the back of her
neck, her hair now lay in a soft brown cap against
her scalp. Like Kathleen, she had also opted for a
hairband but hers had a tiny spotted veil
attached. Her outfit clung to her figure and it was
a smart dress in emerald green. What a difference
to the old Rosie I thought. I told her so.

Her face lit up. 'I decided to take your advice,
Ann, about changing my looks.'

'Well, it's worked wonders, Rosie.'

I stood up as I had my other duties as chief bridesmaid to attend to. Dad was sitting a few feet away and he heard my voice. He looked over and his eyes almost popped out of his head when he saw Rosie – and not Rosie alone but with another man. He called me over but Margot gave me a sullen look.

'I'll see you later, Dad – it's time to go into the dining room.'

We all went through and the room was beautifully done up with large bowls of flowers in shades of white, yellow and blue. The top table was spread out within the large bay window while the other tables were circular and held ten people. The tablecloths were sparkling white and the silver cutlery shone brightly while the glasses glittered in the shafts of sunlight.

For many, many years after, I was able to recall that scene. So much so that, every time I felt downcast or depressed, the remembrance of that day filled me with joy. As for Lily well she always referred to it as a magical, once-in-a-lifetime day.

But, although we didn't know it then, it was a golden sunny day of happiness before we all raced to our own dark horizons.

Before the meal, one of Maddie's uncles stood up and made an announcement. 'Mr Neville Chamberlain has returned with a peace treaty. It's to be peace in our time and there will be no war with Germany.'

A cheer ran around the room and Maddie looked relieved. She had thought her married life might be short-lived but now everything looked rosy for them. Our futures were all assured.

I caught a glance from Connie as she quietly listened and I saw her shake her head ever so slightly at the news. Then I saw Ma Ryan and she sat in silence with a strange look on her face when people cheered. Neither of these two women believed it but I wanted to – for all our sakes.

The waitresses brought round plates of delicious food. Lily cleaned every plate until it was shining and almost not needing washed but I sat next to Joy and she hardly touched a morsel. What a queer world, I thought. There were children on the Hilltown and the Hawkhill who would be grateful for even a fraction of this lovely food while Joy didn't seem to appreciate it.

Greg then made his speech and he was really humorous. He told the guests of how he'd first met Maddie at the infirmary and said that her cool hands had aided his recovery. He then made a couple of funny anecdotes about Danny before becoming serious.

'Today is a very happy day for Maddie and Danny. May they both have a long and happy life together.' He held up his glass. 'A toast to Maddie and Danny.'

Everyone in the room echoed those sentiments and, now that the threat of War had been removed, it looked as if the future was secure – at least I fervently hoped so.

During his speech he had said some words of praise to the bride's attendants but, while he did glance at me when he was speaking, I was alarmed to see his eyes had a blank look. Lily, however, didn't notice anything wrong and she visibly beamed at his admiring words. She was too young to realise nearly all weddings had these speeches and she truly believed he was telling her she was the best flower girl in all the world. But let her have her little illusions, I thought. Life was too serious and scary not to have a fantasy bolthole to escape into.

It was then that I noticed that Dad and Margot had been seated at the same table as Maddie's Uncle John and his wife Dorothy. Margot was hogging John all to herself as she leaned towards him and whispered in his ear. Dorothy was not amused by this behaviour and her thin gaunt face had twin patches of red on her cheeks. Dad also looked like thunder and I felt sorry for him – especially when it seemed that Rosie was having a whale of a time at the next table. She and Albert were having a great conversation with the rest of the table guests and the topic must have been funny because, every now and again, they all burst out laughing.

Dad glanced over to her table and his eyes lingered on her for a full minute. As if conscious of this gaze, she looked over and blushed at the intensity of his eyes.

Then the meal was over and we all drifted through to the lounge. The Pringles had booked a four-piece band for dancing but at the moment we were all waiting about as the band set up their instruments. It was a hiatus in the otherwise busy day.

I glanced around the elegant room. The Ryan families were sitting with some of Maddie's relations and they were all listening to Ma. Maddie and Danny were sitting with my grandparents and Bella while Dorothy was beside Joy and Lily. She didn't look happy.

I knew I would have to do my social rounds soon but the old weariness swept over me and, although these spells were now very seldom, I still had them from time to time. I suddenly felt so tired and realised I needed to sit down by myself for a while. I knew there was a room where the coats were being kept. In fact, the hotel had hired a woman to check them in for safe-keeping – not so much for our side of the family but Maddie's female relations had some lovely fur coats with them. I had noticed a small room next to this cloakroom. It had a couple of soft chairs so I decided to retreat there for a short rest.

The woman in charge of the coats had gone. Perhaps she'd nipped off for a cup of tea but the room was empty. So I didn't go into the small room because this room had a large bay window with a padded seat in front of it. The room also had a lovely view of the river.

I sank thankfully on to this window seat and gazed out at the view. The setting sun was casting a golden glow over the water. Everything was so peaceful and it was hard to think just how near we were to war with Germany. Thank goodness it had been averted, I thought.

I had seen so little of Greg but I knew he had his duties as best man to see to and I knew he couldn't help that. I heard the door open quietly and I turned, feeling not too pleased to have my reverie interrupted. But it was only Rosie and she moved almost silently over the thick carpet.

'I thought I saw you come in here. What a great wedding it's been and we've really enjoyed ourselves.' Her face was flushed with the heat of the room but it suited her.

I spoke quietly. 'You look like a million dollars, Rosie.'

She blushed a deeper red but she was pleased by my words, I could tell.

'I decided to tog myself up and although it's too late for your father, maybe another man will be interested.'

I was curious about Albert. 'What about the man you came with?'

'Och, he's a great man but he lost his wife last year and they were both good friends of mine in the Salvation Army. We met up again when I rejoined after your father got married but it's just a friendship.'

I opened my mouth to answer when we heard the angry words from the small annexe. It was Margot's voice. She was talking very loudly and she sounded angry. 'Well, I'm warning you, John, if you don't start divorce proceedings against that silly, cow-faced wife of yours, then I'll tell her everything about us.'

John's voice rose in anger as well. 'Tell her what, Margot? That I've been a stupid fool but now I've come to my senses? Will you tell her that I've now decided to stop playing a silly fool? Is that what you'll tell her?'

Rosie and I both got to our feet and made silently for the door. But before we reached it, Margot shouted, 'I'm still going to leave that stupid man I married. What a mistake that was!'

When John spoke, his voice was harsh. 'Don't you dare run down your husband like that. He's a decent hard-working man who deserves better than you.'

Her voice took on a pleading tone. 'I only married him to make you jealous – you know that. You know I only ever wanted you, and I thought, when Harry found out about us and it finished him, then we would be married. One thing I'm certain of is the fact that I'm not staying married to that idiot and his impoverished family a minute longer. Supposed to have an heiress as a daughter. Well, I've seen precious little of that legacy I can tell you.'

John's voice became quiet but it wasn't a pleasant sound. 'That's all you've ever cared for, isn't it, Margot? Money – you'll do almost anything to get your hands on it. I don't want to ever see you again and I must have been mad to think I ever did.'

Thinking that either Margot or John must come through the annexe door and in to the room where we were, Rosie and I darted for the cover in an alcove at the far end of the room.

As we reached the safety of our hiding place, we saw, to our dismay and horror, that a figure was sitting in a chair. It was Dad and he had tears in his eyes. He looked at us and we could tell by his face that he was in shock. Letting out a small cry, Rosie ran out of the room.

'You had better go as well, Ann. There's nothing you can do for me now.' He lay back in the chair and gazed dismally at the wallpaper.

I didn't know what to do but he repeated himself and then said, 'Just leave me alone, Ann – I've got a lot of thinking to do.'

I went back into the lounge and, thankfully, there was no sign of either Margot or John. My magical day had turned sour and I could gladly have hit Margot for all the distress she'd caused – not only to her poor late husband Harry who knew about her liaison with his boss but also to our family. To make matters worse, the whole scene had been witnessed by Rosie and that would upset Dad even more.

The band struck up a cheery tune. The bride and groom were already on the floor when Greg asked me to dance. I had been annoyed at his off-hand manner but now I had other things on my mind.

He said, 'You look lovely in blue, Ann – one of the prettiest bridesmaids I've ever seen.'

If he expected me to simper blushingly, then he was wrong. I didn't mean to be blunt but it just came out like that. 'Are you avoiding me, Greg?'

He gave me a sharp look. 'There is something I've got to tell you but I thought I would wait till after the wedding.'

I was not in the mood for any more nonsense and time wasting. 'Tell me now, Greg, and get it off your chest.'

He gave this a moment's thought and then said, 'I've got a transfer to London, Ann.'

I almost stumbled and I looked at him with amazement. 'To London?'

He nodded.

'London?' I knew I was repeating myself but I couldn't help it. 'I thought you had found another girlfriend. I didn't think it was this – a transfer to London.'

'Well, I have and it may last a few months or even longer. Don't be fooled by this peace treaty of Mr Chamberlain. We'll be at war with Germany sooner or later. London is being cleared of all the valuable items in their libraries and museums and I've been asked to go and help with the inventories.'

On that sombre note, the dance ended with a flourish. What a day it had turned out to be – first Dad's betrayal by Margot and now this. But, as it turned out, we had no more time together that evening. As the long golden rays from the sun slanted in through the large windows, Greg had to dance with all the unattached women in the party while I had to do my rounds of smiling and chatting to both sets of relations.

Lily was enjoying herself and that was one blessing – that and the obvious radiance of the newly married couple. Nothing could spoil their joy on this special day.

I went over to speak to Connie and told her Greg's news. I was hoping she would laugh at my fears but she didn't.

'Aye, it's coming, Ann, and we'll have to be ready for it. One good thing is the government is also getting ready as well.'

I was downcast but she said, 'Don't worry about it, Ann. Maybe it'll not last long when it comes. Anyway there's nothing anybody can do so just you enjoy this golden day and don't give it another thought.'

Easier said than done, I thought.

Kit then joined us and I complimented her on her outfit.

'Aye, it cost me a few bob but it's worth it to see Danny so happy. What a lovely family he's married into and Ma is over the moon by all the attention she's getting from Maddie's relations.'

'Where's Sammy?'

Her face dropped. 'He didn't come home last night and Maggie is hopping mad about it. She told Kathleen to come and enjoy herself with us and she's looking after Kitty.'

I didn't know what to say as I couldn't understand why she had married him in the first place. Lots of girls had babies without the blessing of a marriage and Kit and George had been prepared to look after them both. It was a mystery.

I glanced over to where she was sitting with Colin. She'd been on the dance floor all evening – either with him or Brian, John and Dorothy's son.

There was no sign of Maddie's aunt and uncle and I couldn't get the row between Margot and John out of my mind. Rosie was sitting with Albert but her laughter had gone and she now looked miserable so it was no surprise when they both stood up to go before the end of the dance and said their goodbyes to us all.

One blessing was the fact that my family had enjoyed their day immensely – especially Hattie who had flitted like a crimson rose amongst the guests, doing her social act.

Although there had been a reconciliation with the Ryan women since Dad Ryan's death, it was still funny to see them glance at one another as Hattie flitted past like the hostess of the year. She was certainly well pleased with her new standing in this well-off world.

All too soon, it was time to get Maddie upstairs and into her going-away outfit. This was a lovely mauve suit flecked with tiny particles of a deeper mauve and pink. She looked radiant in it. We stood in the posh bedroom that had been set aside for this purpose and we looked at one another. She gave me a big smile and, for a moment, I thought she was going to cry but she didn't.

Instead, she said, 'It's good news about the peace treaty, isn't it, Ann? I've been so worried that Danny and I would hardly have any time together before he had to go away to fight in a war.'

'Don't be daft, Maddie,' I told her. I remained silent about Greg's new assignment in London. After all, it might be a small storm in a large teacup so there was no sense in worrying her – or destroying her happiness on her special day.

'You know I told you we're just going to the flat, Ann?'

I nodded.

'Well, nobody knows that – they all think we're going away for a couple of days. You'll not tell anyone, will you?'

I was shocked. 'Of course not, Maddie! I wouldn't tell a soul.'

She gave me a large beaming smile and we then went downstairs to where Danny was waiting. He was surrounded by all the guests and some had cartons of confetti. A loud cheer went up when Maddie appeared and she blushed. Then they were swept away in a flurry of bodies and clouds of multicoloured confetti but she leant out of the taxi window and waved to me.

'Thanks, Ann. Thanks for everything!'

In a strange way, I knew she was thanking me for my illness – an illness that finally brought them together again as a couple – a couple who would go through life with one another. It was my turn now to almost cry. I felt the salty tears in my eyes and a dryness at the back of my throat. Greg came up beside me and I tried hard not to burst into a flood of tears. I didn't want him to think I was the sort of girl who cried at weddings.

The band played for another hour and then it was all over. The Pringle family had organised cars to take everyone home. Ma was in one of the cars with her family and I saw Colin quietly talking to Kathleen before she got in beside them. My grandparents, Bella and Connie were also swept away in a posh-looking taxi and Bella was almost purring. I overheard her, as she was shutting the door, say, 'Och, Nan, this is the way to travel, is it not?'

There was no sign of Dad and Margot and it looked as if they had left at the same time as John and Dorothy.

Then it was time for Greg, Hattie, Lily and me to leave. Lily was exhausted but jubilant. She had been told she could keep all her wedding finery.

'Make sure you hang it up in the cupboard, Ann – I don't want my lovely frock getting crushed. And will you keep my shoes in their box?'

I lay back on the upholstered seat and merely nodded at all her requests. It had been a wonderful day but I was just exhausted.

Hattie was also jubilant with the day's events.

'It's been one of the happiest days of my life,' she said. She looked at me. 'Did Maddie mention where they were spending their honeymoon?'

I gave her a wide-eyed innocent look. 'No, Hattie, she didn't.'

Greg was staying with his ex-landlady in Victoria Road so, after Hattie had been dropped off, he was the next one to leave the car. As he stepped out, he said, 'I'll be up to see you both to-morrow, Ann. Maybe we can go for the day out?'

I said that would be great and he disappeared up the close and was soon swallowed up by its gloomy interior. But, before he disappeared, Lily had called after him. 'When you and Ann get married, can I be your bridesmaid?'

He had grinned at her. 'You bet, Lily! You'll be our number one bridesmaid.'

When would that be? I wondered gloomily. It seemed as if our relationship was somehow doomed. I looked at the ring on my right-hand finger with dismay. I had forgotten in all the evening's events to show it to him. Maddie had said we could announce our own engagement at the dance but we had never got the chance.

I would go back to wearing it around my neck and I was convinced it would remain there – like some albatross … or a noose.

As I tucked Lily up in her bed she whispered, 'This has been the best magical day in the whole wide world, Ann. Hasn't it?'

I smiled at her tired but very serious looking face. 'Aye, Lily, it has.'

Her eyes were like pools of light in the dimly lit bedroom which, after the bright electric lights of the hotel, now seemed subdued.

She sighed. 'It was a really good day and I wish it could have gone on for ever and ever and ever.'

'Well, if really great days did go on forever and ever, Lily, they wouldn't stay great, would they? You would soon get fed up with them after a while so you just have to enjoy them when they happen.'

But she was asleep and hadn't heard my little moral tale. She still had her circlet of flowers on her head and I gently removed it.

I sat in silence for a while. Like her, I also wished that life could be full of weddings and flowers and magic. But, of course, it wasn't and we would all soon find out what lay in store – what perils, if any.

Greg appeared at ten o'clock sharp the next morning. There had been a touch of frost and everything looked sparkling in the early morning sunshine. We decided to go to Broughty Ferry beach. Lily wanted to visit Jean but I didn't think Greg would want to sit and chat as we had so little time together. And anyway we had seen her at the wedding although I hadn't managed to speak to her for long. There had been so many people to see.

Lily ran on to the beach with outstretched arms. She resembled a human kite. Greg and I sat on a bench and marvelled at her exuberance. The wind was cold but the sea was calm and blue. It was so peaceful. How could we almost be at war with Germany on such a lovely day as this? I wondered.

Perhaps Greg was wrong – and Connie and Joe. Maybe this peace treaty would last and Greg would soon be home from this new assignment in London. I mentioned these thoughts to him.

He sighed. 'Well, I hope you're right, Ann, because I was really hoping our wedding would be the next one.'

I turned to him with urgency in my voice. 'Let's get married straight away!'

He didn't quite jump for joy at this suggestion so I sat back on the hard bench. Up until then, I hadn't realised I had perched on a few inches of wood – almost as if ready to take off in flight.

'When we get married, Ann, I want it to be perfect – not some quick arrangement before I set off for London and maybe off to war.' He shook his head. 'Anyway, you have enough worries at the moment without the added burden of an absent husband. Hopefully, the war will be averted or, if it does happen, then maybe it will be short lived and then we can make our plans.'

Although I wouldn't admit it, I was secretly relieved by this. He was right when he mentioned my worries and I now had the additional anxiety over Dad.

He was speaking again. 'I was going to ask you if you and Lily would like to come with me to see my parents at the end of October?'

'That would be lovely, Greg. Lily will be over the moon about it.'

She was.

He told us, 'I have to do another couple of weeks at Glasgow then it's off to London so we'll go to Trinafour the last weekend of the month. Is that all right?'

He left on his train that night but we did have

the prospect of a weekend together to look forward to. Lily could hardly wait but she also had the added pleasure of telling her school chums about her day as a flower girl. No doubt it would grow feet and legs with the telling because she was such an imaginative child.

The next couple of weeks flew past. There were all the comments from the family about the wedding which seemed to hog every conversation. The general opinion was that a great time had been had by all.

I told Connie about Greg's move and the reason for it. 'I don't know the whole reason for it, Connie, but it's just in case there's another war.'

'Of course there will be another war, Ann. Look what happened to poor Czechoslovakia. The minute Chamberlain signs a peace treaty with Hitler, the Germans march into another country. How can anybody trust a man like that?'

She was right. Most people now knew another war was inevitable and lurking on the dark horizon – even Maddie who was now more worried than ever.

I told her what Greg had said about it maybe not lasting for long but her blue eyes were clouded with fear and I felt sorry for her.

'Look, Maddie, just enjoy your marriage. There's no sense worrying about something that might never happen,' I told her although I didn't believe the words myself.

Her face cleared. 'Of course you're right, Ann – as usual. It's just that Danny and I are so happy that I fear something must come along to break such happiness. No one's life could have such joy in it for long.'

Marriage certainly suited them both. I had teased Danny a few times that his waistline was expanding but he merely laughed.

'It's not extra food, Ann – it's happiness and contentment.'

Meanwhile I was keeping an eye on the weather. It had turned to rain after the wedding weekend but I was hoping the sun would shine for our trip away to the country. As if in answer to my prayers, it did. We set off on the train with Lily bouncing up and down in excitement. We soon left the industrial scene behind us and we were travelling through a countryside ablaze with autumn trees.

Lily was fascinated with all the tiny rural stations and she sat with her nose glued to the window. When we reached the tiny station at Struan, Greg and his father were waiting for us. They stood beside a small, decrepit-looking van.

'Hop in, Lily,' said Greg's dad.

She clambered in the back and sat on a cushion. I climbed in beside her while Greg sat in the front with his father.

Mr Borland asked us, 'Do you like my new transport, Lily?'

Lily was enchanted. 'Och, it's great, Mr Borland. Is it new?'

He laughed. 'Aye, it was new at one time but that wasn't yesterday.'

She gave this a bit of thought. 'Well, it's still a great van and I like sitting on this cushion.'

We went over a bump in the road and she howled with laughter. Oh, to be a child again, I thought.

Mr Borland chuckled. 'Well, young Lily, I've got lots of things planned for you. The sheep need to be taken down from the hill and Paddy the dog is wagging his tail at the thought of seeing you again.'

I couldn't see his face because my view was through the tiny back window but I was grateful to him for all these efforts on her behalf. She really enjoyed her visits here.

'So Paddy knows I'm coming?' she asked him.

'Aye, he does. I told him this morning and he's been wagging his tail ever since. Of course, he's also glad to see your sister as well.'

Lily took all this in her regal stride. Paddy's tail was really wagging for her alone but she was gracious enough to share the limelight with me.

'That's great, Mr Borland, and we're going to enjoy our stay, aren't we, Ann?'

I agreed that we were and that was all the comment needed from Lily's sidekick.

Mrs Borland had prepared an enormous meal for us and Lily began to eat like she hadn't seen food in weeks. She tasted everything from the soup to the pancakes.

Later, we went outside and the countryside was a delight. It was hard to believe that winter was just around the corner. There had been overnight frost here as well and white patches still hugged the fields and hills that had been untouched by the rays of the sun.

The grass crunched under our feet as we watched Lily and Mr Borland stride towards the sheep which seemed to cling to the hillside.

In the quiet air, Lily's childish voice carried

towards us.

'She's having a great time, isn't she?' said Greg. I nodded silently.

'I'll be away next week, Ann – off to London – but I'll write and tell you all about the big city. I just wish you were coming with me.'

'Well, let's get married right away, Greg. We can get a special licence. Connie told me about it and you don't need to wait till the banns are read.'

He gave me a tender look. 'If I really thought that's what you truly wanted, Ann, then I would do it but I don't think you do – at least not yet.'

I tried to protest. 'But I do – I really do...'

At that moment, Lily's voice carried down from the hill and she was crying. She had slipped on a patch of frosty grass and I ran up the hill towards her. Reaching her at the same time as Greg's dad. Fortunately it was nothing more serious than a badly scraped knee and a frosty damp patch on her knickers. I turned around and saw what Greg had always known – although a single woman I was as tied to my sister as if I was already married.

There was no more talk of quick marriages and thankfully no more talk of impending wars.

When dusk came and the curtains were pulled we sat by the light of the oil lamps. Mrs Borland made another huge meal for our supper and it was lovely and cosy sitting in the kitchen with the fire crackling in the grate and the soft glow from the lamps.

Outside an owl cried and Lily stopped eating, her eyes as large as the owl's. 'What was that?'

Mr Borland teased her. 'Oh, it's just the huge owl that lives across the garden from your win-

401

dow. You'll hear him all night long going twit-twit-twooooooo.'

She gave him a look as if she didn't believe him and returned to eating her third scone and jam.

I apologised for her appetite. 'You'll be thinking I never feed her?' I said to Babs Borland.

She laughed. 'Oh, leave the bairn to enjoy herself.'

Afterwards, I put Lily to bed in the tiny room in the attic.

She looked fearfully at the small skylight window. 'That owl won't be able to get in here, will he, Ann? I didn't want Mr Borland to think I was scared when he told me that story but I'm scared now,' she confessed.

I tucked her up. 'It's just a bird, Lily, and that's the sound it makes when it's calling to other owls so don't bother about it. It'll not touch you.'

She lay snuggled up in the bed with the flowery valance and pink quilt. 'It's really great here, Ann. I like staying here with the Borlands because they're so good to us.'

Suddenly, from outside the window, we heard, 'Twit-twit-twooooooo.'

I jumped in alarm and Lily almost fell out of the bed with laughter.

'So you're scared of it as well! Never mind, Ann, you'll be sleeping with me and I'll look after you.'

She was still laughing when I went down the narrow stairs.

Greg and his parents were discussing my father's quick marriage when I arrived back in the kitchen.

Like all women, Babs thought it was very romantic. 'Your new stepmother's called Margot?' she said cheerily.

I nodded. To be honest, it was a discussion I could do well without but it would have been churlish of me to say so – especially as they were under the false impression that they were both blissfully happy.

'Where did he meet her?' asked Babs.

I explained the tragic circumstances of Harry's death and Dad's later involvement with the widow.

'She sounds so glamorous – at least, according to Greg who's told us about her lovely house and her clothes,' she said.

I wished I could change the subject but Babs seemed to welcome this women's talk of weddings and fine clothes. It made a change no doubt from talk of sheep and crofting. It would seem like another world to her – especially in this small rural corner where she didn't even have a close neighbour.

I described Margot's wedding dress and her lovely house.

Babs said, 'You don't have a wedding photo, do you, Ann?'

I had but it was in my suitcase. Dad had given me one a week or so after the wedding and I don't know why I carried it around with me – probably because he looked so handsome in it and photographs in our house were few and far between. Dad looked so trim and young beside his glamorous bride but he didn't look so good these days.

I went upstairs to get the photo from my small

suitcase which lay beside the bed.

Lily was still awake. 'I'm speaking to the owl, Ann.' Her eyes were wide open.

I smiled at her. 'That's fine, Lily, but make sure you tell it not to make such a racket when we want to go to sleep.'

The photo was in a deep brown folder. It wasn't a large image but it had been taken by a photographer at his studio in the town. Margot didn't know I had it but Dad had given it to me a few weeks after the wedding – mainly because I asked him for it. The photographer had done a good job and the couple had come out very well. They were maybe a bit stiffly posed but it showed their faces and figures very clearly.

Downstairs, I showed the photo to Babs. Never in a hundred years could I have envisaged the reaction. At first Babs peered at it then she put on her spectacles and she peered at it again.

'What did you say her name was, Ann?'

'She's Margot Neill now but she was a Mrs Margot Connors before she married Dad.'

'I know this woman,' said Babs, 'but her name wasn't Margot in those days. It was plain Mary – Mary Farr.'

Greg seemed surprised. 'How do you know her, Mum?'

'Before I married your father, I was in service in a large house in Perth. Mary Farr arrived – from Ireland, I think. She came as a housemaid.' Babs studied the black and white photo which showed Margot clearly but didn't do justice to the lovely lilac dress and hat. 'Yes, it is her – I'm sure. She was a beautiful girl. That's the reason she caught the eye of young Charlie Cooper whose father had a string of ladies' dress shops on the west coast and in Glasgow, Perth and Dundee. Charlie was in charge of the Perth shop and, to cut a long story short, they got married very quickly – they had only known one another for a couple of months. Then, quite suddenly, Charlie's father died and he sold up the business and they moved to Edinburgh to live.'

I had gone cold. How many husbands did Margot have? I wondered. 'Her name wasn't Cooper when Dad met her. She was married to a lovely man called Harry Connors who worked with Dad in the warehouse. This Charlie Cooper must have died.'

Babs laughed. 'Charlie Cooper isn't dead. We get a Christmas card every year from him. He now lives in England and I always wondered why he never mentioned Mary. He did tell me years ago that she had squandered all the money he got from the sale of his shops but I assumed she was still with him. He must have got a divorce from her.' She shook her head in wonder. 'What a small world it is! Imagine Mary Parr turning up and looking as chic as she ever was.'

Mary Farr – also known as Cooper, Connors and Neill I thought bitterly. It would seem that the fair-faced Mary Farr had always been adept at squandering other people's money. It was an art form with her.

Babs suddenly looked stricken. 'Oh, Ann, I shouldn't have been gossiping about your stepmother like that. Perhaps she had a good reason to divorce Charlie. If she's happy with your father, then please don't tell her about me.'

In spite of myself, I blurted out, 'Dad is not happy with her. She still carries on about money like it was some god and I'm really worried about my father.'

The Borlands stared at me – even Greg. He said, 'You never mentioned this, Ann. How long has it been like this?'

Although I didn't go into any details, I did say there had been an incident at Maddie and Danny's wedding but, although Greg would have liked to hear the whole story, he also knew I wouldn't like to speak about it to his parents.

Babs looked at the photo again. 'Well, one thing's for sure – she's certainly aged well and I could understand what a man sees in her with her lovely face and nice figure, not to mention her fabulous clothes. She's kept her slim figure, not like me,' she said, patting her ample hips.

She handed back the photo and I went upstairs and put it back in my case. For some reason, I felt it had spoiled my weekend.

We left on the Sunday afternoon as Greg had to catch his train to London the next day.

Lily once again had her nose pressed against the window, and, apart from her chattering, it was a sombre journey. I knew I would miss Greg so much and he had said the same to me.

The incident with the photo had also unnerved me and I couldn't understand why Margot had changed her name from Mary. But surely lots of women did that if they disliked their name? I inwardly asked myself. There was no harm in it so why did I have this dreadful feeling of foreboding?

It was raining when we reached Dundee. The wet pavements and dark tenements looked so drab and grey and formed a sharp contrast to our memory of the frosty hills and autumn-tinted trees. People walked along the wet pavements but most of them didn't look happy. They had worried frowns as if the threat of war was hanging over us all like the sword of Damocles.

Then, when we reached the Overgate, we found Grandad in bed with a bad chest infection. Granny was making him some hot thin soup and I suddenly realised how old he looked. Granny was chastising him for wanting to smoke his pipe and he gave me a beseeching glance.

'Don't bother looking at Ann for help because she knows it'll make your chest infection worse.'

I gave him a rueful look and Lily, Greg and I set off for home. We said our goodbyes to Greg and he made his way back to Victoria Road.

Greg left early the next morning but he came to say goodbye at the shop and Connie went into the back shop in order to leave us alone – which was a laugh because she could overhear every word but the gesture was appreciated.

After he had gone, I felt so drained. The rain fell from a gunmetal-coloured sky and the wind was cold. Winter wasn't far away and I dreaded the return of the cold weather. This was the worst possible weather for Grandad's chest but, maybe, if he remained indoors, he would be fine. I certainly hoped so.

Meanwhile, Connie was reading all about the events unfolding in Germany. She would read out the headlines with an avid interest every morning.

In November she read one headline with disgust. 'Look at this, Ann. Those thugs in Germany have smashed all the Jewish business community's windows.' She showed me the picture in the paper that portrayed a crowd of people laughing and gazing at a row of smashed windows.

'They're calling it Kristallnacht or Crystal Night,' she snorted with derision. 'When is this country going to wake up and deal with that wee thug Hitler? Going to Munich to plead for peace is just damn stupid and Chamberlain should have known better.'

The news was certainly depressing and I was glad we didn't live in mainland Europe. We had freedom of choice which the poor Jewish people didn't seem to have.

Connie was still fuming. 'Hitler is devising ways to know who is Jewish. He wants this true Aryan race of blonde hair and blue eyes. And would you look at the wee gowk he is? He's like some ugly stunted gnome with that stupid black mouser on his upper lip. If there's anybody a million miles away from being blonde haired and blue eyed, then it's himself.'

To be honest, I was getting a bit tired of all this news of war. Either it came or it didn't but the papers whipped up this constant barrage of fear and even the children began to get worried.

Lily mentioned to me one afternoon after school, 'If there's going to be a war, Ann, will that mean we'll not be together?'

I squeezed her hand. 'Of course, we will. Don't worry about it, Lily, because it may never happen. And, if it does, then it's the young men who have to go.'

This seemed to reassure her and she didn't mention it again but, as far as I was concerned, the worry went on and on.

On New Year's Day, we were at the Overgate. Rosie and Alice were there and I was pleased to see Grandad was looking and feeling so much better. We were all discussing the year that had gone – remembering the good parts and skimming over the bad ones. Then, in the middle of all this chatter, Dad appeared. He looked so thin and ill and his white face had an ageing drawn look.

I leapt from the chair. 'Dad, what's the matter? Are you ill?'

I noticed that Rosie had also risen and she stood by my side, looking worried.

He drew a hand across his eyes then spoke in a soft voice. 'I've left Margot and I wondered if I could come back to live with you at the Hilltown.'

What did he mean? Had he left her for good or what?

I stared at him while Rosie led him to a chair by the fire. She said, 'Sit down, Johnny, and I'll get you a cup of tea.'

'Have you left Margot for good, Dad?' I asked him while Lily burst into tears.

While I comforted her, he explained, 'It's a long story but I've had enough of her nonsense.' He looked at me. 'Oh, by the way, I never thanked you for that gesture from Mr Pringle, Ann.'

Rosie and I gazed at him in horror. I was almost afraid to speak. 'What do you mean, Dad?'

'Maddie's father called me to his office last

month and gave me this.' He held up a small post office account book. 'Thanks, Ann, but Margot has demanded that I give it to her or at least half of it – I'm not quite sure.'

I relaxed. I thought he was referring to John Pringle.

'She's welcome to it all if it means you're rid of her,' I said with feeling.

Granny, who had remained silent up till now, said, 'I aye said you were a stupid idiot, Johnny, and now it's been proved.'

He looked sheepish but Rosie put her arm around his shoulder – much to Alice's annoyance.

Dad looked gratefully at her. She had kept her initial elegance since the wedding and hadn't gone back to her mismatched clothes or untidy hair. Tonight she was wearing a royal-blue pleated skirt with a soft woollen jumper in three shades of blue. It suited her and her short hair was like a shining cap.

Dad looked at her with admiration. 'I know I've been an idiot, Rosie – imagine passing you over for somebody like Margot...'

Alice butted in, 'Aye you did pass her over, Johnny Neill, and now it's too late. Albert has asked Rosie to marry him and she's thinking about it, aren't you?'

She blushed as we all looked at her and gave her mother an annoyed glance.

Undeterred Alice went on, 'Aye, he proposed to her at Christmas time but she's still thinking about it. Tell them, Rosie.'

She said very quietly, 'Aye, I am thinking about it.'

We all said our congratulations to her and I really wished her all the happiness in the world – she deserved it.

Granny then made a huge meal for Dad who looked as if he hadn't eaten in years. Meanwhile Lily was getting her oar in as far as Rosie's wedding was concerned.

'Can I be your flower girl, Rosie?'

For a woman on the verge of getting married, Rosie didn't look very happy and I hoped Dad's appearance hadn't spoiled her future plans. She deserved better treatment from a man instead of forever being passed over on his whims. Still, when did any of us ever get what we deserved?

Much later, after Alice and Rosie had gone, Dad said, 'I don't think I'll ever get rid of Margot. She says she wants my wages every week because I have to keep her.'

Granny made a sound between a snort and a laugh. 'She's not entitled to your entire wages Johnny but you'll probably have to make some kind of settlement to her as she's your wife.'

Granny said to me later that she almost told him to make the same kind of settlement he made to us – nothing.

Instead she carried on, 'Go and see Mr Pringle and he'll keep you right.'

Dad promised he would and we all left for the Hilltown.

After Lily was tucked up in bed, he said, 'What a bloody mess. She was going with my boss for over a year and long before Harry died. Mind you, I don't blame John Pringle. He was as big a fool as I was and just as stupid.'

'You know that Rosie also overheard her that night of Maddie's wedding?'

He nodded bleakly. 'Aye, I do.'

'And what about Dorothy Pringle? Does she know the whole story?'

'Aye, I had a word with him and he's told her the truth. She's really angry at them both but she's prepared to give him another chance. Dorothy's a great woman and, although she can't hold a candle to Margot in looks, she's worth a hundred of her kind. Then there's Rosie. I can cry when I think about her and how I've finally lost her to Albert.'

'Well, Dad, it's no use crying now. You heard what Alice said – Albert has proposed and, if Rosie is thinking about it, then she'll not let him down.'

He sat slumped in the chair and that is how we celebrated the first day of 1939 – with the threat of war now growing more certain, Dad arriving home with his tail between his legs and his wife Margot hanging like a millstone around his neck. She knew I still had the bulk of my legacy and she wouldn't let Dad go until the money was all hers – this Mary Farr, one-time housemaid in Perth.

15

It was good having Dad back home. Meanwhile Margot, true to form, was acting like Shylock but instead of a pound of flesh she was demanding the entire body.

Dad had taken Granny's advice and had been to see Mr Pringle. He suggested a small weekly settlement from Dad's wages but that didn't suit madam.

Dad came home one day very depressed. He had just been to see Mr Pringle. 'Margot wants more money than I'm giving her and she also says she's entitled to half your legacy, Ann.'

I gasped in astonishment.

He held up his hand. 'Just a minute till I tell you what Mr Pringle said. He told Margot that she has no claim on any money belonging to you and, as she's had over a hundred pounds from Miss Hood's money, she's not entitled to another penny – except her weekly settlement.'

'Well, that's fine then, Dad.'

'I'm still annoyed that she got some of Miss Hood's money because that was yours.'

'Don't worry about that. It'll be worth it if it gets her away from us.'

He rubbed his eyes. Although now getting decent meals, he was still thin and tired looking.

It was none of my business but I asked him about John Pringle. 'Do you think she's bothering him for money as well?'

'I haven't a clue but it wouldn't surprise me. He's had another word with me about it and we both agree what total fools we were and he's very kindly said he'll put a wee bit extra in my wages to cover what Margot gets – although she doesn't know this.'

Once again I couldn't get over how generous the members of the Pringle family were.

'That's very decent of him, Dad.'

'Aye, he's a decent bloke. Like me, he was dazzled by Margot and I don't blame him for that. Still, his wife has been a great rock to him and he was telling me he's never going to hurt her again.' He looked sad. 'Another thing that's bothering him is the fact of Harry's death. He blames himself for it because Margot told him that Harry found out about them before he died. Thank goodness I only met her afterwards.'

I was appalled by Margot's cruelty – not only to Harry but also to John Pringle.

'Do you think she's lying about Harry finding out about her and John Pringle?'

Dad shook his head. 'Goodness knows but Mr Pringle will have to come to terms with it. At least he has his wife – not like me and Rosie. I've burned my boats well and truly now that she's marrying Albert.'

There was nothing I could add to that.

Greg's letters were full of news about the big city and, although the war was never mentioned, I could read between the lines that the government was now planning for a war.

Joe seemed delighted that his predictions were coming true and, when he arrived at the shop every morning, he had long discussions with Connie about the latest developments.

He said, 'I hear the government is to issue air-raid shelters to the towns that would be the biggest target for enemy bombing.'

My heart grew cold as Connie nodded and added, 'Aye, it's the youngest men that will be called up first and then the older ones later, I suppose.'

I thought of Maddie and Danny. She had got a part-time job in a private nursing home. She loved the work and it kept her busy while Danny worked long hours in the shop. He was up for promotion to under manager and Maddie's pride in him knew no bounds. I just hoped and prayed that their life together wouldn't be cut short by a war.

Hattie loved to visit them. She told Granny, 'I just love walking through that lovely tiled close and the flat is such a delight.'

Grandad, who had recovered from his chest infection but still refused to give up his pipe, butted in, 'Aye, we know it is, Hattie. Your mother and I have been to visit them as well.'

Although Hattie said nothing, I knew she wasn't pleased by the fact that all the family had been invited since the wedding. Bella had gone with Granny and Grandad while Kit and her sisters and their families had also gone for a Sunday visit. They all knew it was an open door to them and that they were all welcome at any time as Maddie had no side to her. The only person who hadn't gone so far was Ma but she enjoyed hearing about the news from Kit. As I said, this seemed to annoy Hattie who would have liked to keep the flat as somewhere only she was invited to go to. Granny had also voiced this view to me but had very sensibly remained silent about it to her daughter.

Then, in April, the government planned to introduce conscription. A compulsory list of young men under the age of twenty-one was drawn up and Sammy's name was on this list. As it was, Danny was really angry with Sammy because a rumour was going around Lochee that he was seeing another girl and that she was also expecting a baby.

'Maybe it's the best thing that can happen to him is to be in the army,' said Danny one night when I was sitting in their lovely living room.

The view from the window was spectacular as the setting sun cast a molten gold glow over the water. Maddie also gazed out at the scene with a faraway look in her eyes. When she spoke her voice was soft. 'It seems so strange to be approaching a war on such a lovely night as this, doesn't it?'

Danny didn't want her upset so he said, 'Och, it'll maybe not come to anything, Maddie.'

I felt we were all wishing on the moon with this ostrich-like view. I also felt that, if war did come, then it would last a lot longer than the prophets were saying and, like all wars, it would be a nasty conflict with some people surviving and others who wouldn't. But of course I couldn't voice this to Maddie who was holding fast to the wish that it would all go away in some magical puff of smoke – if only.

Sammy was called up and he went to a training camp near Perth. On the day of his departure, Maddie and Danny asked me to go with them to see Kathleen and Kitty.

'She'll need some support,' Maddie said.

We made our way up the narrow stair that led to Kathleen's poky flat. We heard a baby crying before we reached the door. The thin wails echoing down the dark lobby. It had to be Kitty's cries.

Danny opened the door and the cries became louder. He shouted out, 'Kathleen, it's Danny!'

The baby wailed even louder as we all crowded into the small room. Kathleen was lying on the bed and she looked really ill.

Danny made a rush for her but Maddie held him back and she quietly approached the bed. Kathleen was crying softly and her hair and face were streaked with blood and sweat. Maddie smoothed her hair away from her face and lifted the slender body into her arms.

'What's happened, Kathleen? Have you had an accident?'

Meanwhile, I lifted Kitty from her cot and, although she didn't stop crying, her sobs weren't quite so loud now.

Maddie said quietly, 'Tell us what happened, Kathleen?'

She turned and we saw the bruises. Her face had a large black bruise down the left side and we could see other marks on her body. She was wearing just her vest and pants and her arms and legs were also a mass of bluish bruises.

Danny was almost speechless with anger. He said, 'Who did this to you, Kathleen? Was it Sammy?'

She nodded tearfully. 'He told me I've not to see any other man while he's away so he gave me this beating to show me what would happen if I did.'

At that moment, I swear that, if Danny could have got his hands on Sammy, he would surely have given him the beating of his life – just to let him see how he felt about a smashed face. But Sammy was in his training camp and away from Danny's anger.

Maddie got Kathleen dressed and I carried the toddler while Danny set about packing her things into a suitcase. We then made our way to Kit's house where she would be looked after and would hopefully remain – even if Sammy did return.

Like Danny, when George saw his daughter and his granddaughter, he went white with anger. 'If that wee bugger has any sense, he'll not come back here or I'll sort him out once and for all.' There was no doubt of that and, if Sammy should return, I knew he would be in big trouble. He must have hoped that Kathleen would cover her injuries up and say nothing. Just like countless women who took the beatings and said nothing, thinking it would bring shame to them if they told the community what their lives were like – as if the fault was somehow theirs.

Kit was appalled by Kathleen's injuries but Maddie thought most of them were superficial.

'Thankfully her skin is so white and translucent

that some of the bruising looks worse than it is.'

Kit looked at her in astonishment.

Flustered by now, Maddie explained, 'Oh, don't get me wrong, Kit. That brute certainly gave her a bad beating but I don't think anything is broken and hopefully the bruises should subside in a week or two.' She took Kit's arm and led her over to where I stood, still clutching Kitty who had now fallen asleep in my arms.

'Although the bruising will heal, Kit, I don't know what damage has been done mentally and I strongly advise her to stay away from her husband. A brute like that never changes.'

Kit's eyes were blazing. 'Don't you worry about that, Maddie. If George or I ever set eyes on him... Well, he'd better watch out, that's all I'm saying.'

Although it was never voiced, we all still wondered why in heaven's name she had married him. Maybe she had loved him but one thing was crystal clear – she didn't love him now.

The story of Sammy swept around Lochee at the speed of light. Even Maggie, his mother, was gunning for him. As she said, perhaps it would be better for him if Hitler got his hands on him first instead of her.

Joe came rushing in one lovely day in May. 'Have you heard that Hitler's signed a pact with Mussolini?'

Connie nodded. 'Aye, it's not far away now, this war.'

It was a strange summer, that year of 1939. On the surface, everything looked normal. People strolled in the warm sunshine and went about their daily chores as usual but the underlying feeling was one of fear for the future. Wives worried about their husbands and mothers feared for their sons.

Minnie wrote to me that summer. She was also worried about Peter, her husband. He was in his late twenties but the general rumour was that all the male population under the age of forty would be called up. Still she seemed reasonably cheerful in spite of this and she was determined to remain where she was. After all, as she said, young Peter was now at the primary school and he was loving it.

I wrote back with my news which wasn't much. I mentioned Maddie and Danny's wedding but I couldn't say much about Greg because I had only seen him twice since the wedding.

I couldn't help but think my life was in some sort of limbo. I did the same tasks each day – took Lily to school then worked with Connie. Would this all stay the same if war was declared? I wondered.

In August, it all changed. Greg was coming back to Dundee as his work in London was now over. Then we heard through Maddie's father that Margot had sold her flat in Victoria Road. She had moved away from the town but Mr Pringle didn't know her whereabouts which was a huge relief.

However, Dad didn't see it that way. 'I'm still married to her,' he said sadly.

'Can you not get a divorce?' I knew divorces were very rare and I had no knowledge of what they entailed but it sounded like a good idea, just to finally get rid of her.

Then there was Rosie who had still not made up her mind to marry Albert. Granny told me in confidence that she wouldn't marry him if she thought there was even the slimmest of chances with Dad. But he was still married and Rosie could see no possible end to the problem. It was getting her down and the fact that Alice kept harping on at her to seize her chance of happiness with Albert – that didn't help.

'You know,' said Granny, 'this is a strange time. We're waiting for a war that never comes and, for the first time in years, people have got jobs. Look at Danny's relations in Lochee. The men are all working at the foundry and Kit's sisters are back in the mill. Kit's looking after wee Kitty to let Kathleen go out to work and they're all making some money for the first time in ages.'

I agreed. It seemed as if prosperous times were just around the corner and it looked like the hard days of joblessness and the inquisition of the means test were now a relic of the past.

Lily and I went to the railway station to meet Greg. He was coming back to his old job at the library and his lodgings in Victoria Road. At first I didn't see him on the crowded platform but Lily spotted him. She ran forward. 'Here we are, Greg – over here!'

He heard her voice and smiled. 'Hullo, Lily. My what a big girl you're getting!'

I stood quietly waiting. For some strange reason, I didn't know what to say to him. I had only seen him on two very brief occasions since

421

last October and, for all I knew, he could have met someone else when he was away. Then he grinned at me and I knew he hadn't.

We decided to go for our tea to the restaurant in Union Street. As usual, Lily was thrilled by all the attention from us both. We told each other all our news and what the families were doing.

Lily was enthralled by all his talk of London – especially when he mentioned the underground trains. 'Oh, I'd love to go on them, Greg – they sound super!'

'Ann and I will take you there one day, Lily, and you can see the palace where the King and Queen live and lots of exciting places.'

Lily gave him her wide-eyed look before tucking into her huge ice-cream sundae which he had ordered for her. As it turned out, it was fortunate her attention was taken up with demolishing the sundae because she wasn't listening when his face became serious. 'I have to tell you that I'm not back for good, Ann.'

My face fell and I felt so depressed by this news.

'I have to be honest with you, I know I won't be one of the first men to be called up because they're taking the youngest ones first. Then there's the problem of my gammy leg. I don't think I would pass a medical test for the forces.'

My heart leapt and my depression lifted. He was telling me good news – not bad.

Then he said, 'I've made up my mind to join up when this war starts. Oh, I know I'll not be fighting on the battlefront.' He paused before continuing, 'Well, at least I don't think I will but you never can tell. One thing I do know is that I would be a great help with the administration side of things.'

I was confused. 'So you're telling me that, even if you don't get called up, you're still going to join?'

He nodded. 'I hope you're not angry?'

What could I do? Being angry wouldn't help. After all, if the war did start, then all the men would be away and Greg was just looking ahead.

'But we'll have some time before that happens?'

'You bet we will!' He looked at my hands. 'Have you still got the ring?'

I pulled it from under the neckline of my summer frock.

He put it on my finger. 'Now I'll know that you're thinking about me when I'm away.'

Lily overheard this part of the conversation but only because the ice-cream dish was empty. 'Ann's aye thinking and speaking about you, Greg,' she said seriously.

He smiled at her. 'Well, just make sure, Lily, that she doesn't change her mind.'

Lily just loved this sense of responsibility. She sat up straighter in her chair. 'Oh, I'll do that, Greg – you can count on me.'

We both laughed. As we made our way home through the busy streets, I prayed that, should the war start, then please don't let it happen soon. I had just got Greg back and I didn't want to lose him again – at least not just yet although I admired his decision to join up in spite of his bad leg. He would feel he was doing his bit for his country and I was proud of him.

As it turned out, we had barely three weeks together before the calamity burst upon us. Hitler invaded Poland and we were all told to tune our wirelesses to one wavelength. Chamberlain had issued an ultimatum to Hitler to withdraw his troops by the deadline of Sunday, third September. Hitler had ignored this and we were now, after months of speculation, at war with Germany.

It was a brilliant weekend of sunshine and high temperatures but the weather didn't register with us as we all had our own private thoughts.

Greg and I went with Lily and Dad to the Overgate where we listened to the news along with my grandparents. It was so hard to believe that we were entering a period of hostilities in such lovely weather. The flowers were blooming in the parks and we had planned to spend the day at the beach at Broughty Ferry. Instead we all sat in Granny's kitchen.

Dad said, 'It's the same bloody caper as last time. We were told that the last war was the war to end all others and here we are again with that bloody megalomaniac, Hitler. We should have put his gas at a peep years ago instead of letting him march into any country he chose.'

Still we were lucky that Lily was still with us as children were being evacuated from the schools. The scenes outside the railway station had been heartbreaking as queues of children lined up to say goodbye to their parents before being taken to a safer place. We were all told that Germany would invade from the skies and it was in the children's interest to get them away from populated areas. But, as it was, Lily had taken a dose of chickenpox a few days earlier and I hadn't wanted her to be evacuated just yet. Lily didn't want to go at all but, if it meant her safety was at stake, then I would make her go. Greg suggested I could perhaps send her to his parents' house and I was relieved to know I could always fall back on that if the going got too tough.

Greg had been as good as his word. He had joined up and he hadn't passed the medical but, because he had already done some war work in London, he was passed fit for administration duties. Three weeks before he had come back home and now he was on the verge of leaving again.

The day after war was declared I was in the shop when Joe came in. 'Have you heard what Hitler has done now? We thought he would arrive from the skies but his ships have sunk the *Athenia*.'

Connie nodded, her face frowning deeply. 'Aye it's in today's paper that a U-boat sunk it off the Hebrides and they didn't give the ship any warning. It seemingly happened just a few hours after Chamberlain's speech on the wireless.'

'Aye,' said Joe with disgust. 'And it wasn't even a navy ship. Just a liner going to Canada and those buggers go and torpedo it. I believe lots of folk drowned?'

Connie said that they had. She had read that as well.

This made me all the more determined to move Lily to a place of safety. She was still unhappy about this idea but I told her she should go after the blisters were better. I put calamine lotion on

425

them every night but she wouldn't stop scratch-
ing them and I feared they would never heal.

Every night she would burst into tears. 'I don't
want to be evacuated, Ann – I want to stay here
with you and Dad.'

Just to placate her, I told her about Greg's plan
for her to go to the Borlands' farm but even this
didn't soothe her.

'I'll miss my pals at the school if I go away. I
love going to see the farm on my holidays, Ann,
but I don't want to be there on my own.'

'Well, lots of your pals at school will be evacuated too so, even if you do stay here, you won't be
able to see them, Lily. So it won't do any harm to
write to the Borlands, just in case you have to get
away from Dundee.'

That night I sat down and wrote to them and
hoped they wouldn't think I was lumbering them
with my sister. Still, time would tell.

As the weeks passed people began to call this
the phoney war but there we were all in a state of
readiness, with gas masks at the ready in case of
a gas attack and Air-Raid Precautions Wardens
and fire-fighters in place. Then there was the
blackout. I had bought a length of black material
to make a blind as it was an offence to show even
the tiniest of lights. I had heard through Connie
of some officious wardens telling people off in no
uncertain language.

Greg was leaving. At the beginning of October,
almost on the date of Maddie and Danny's wedding anniversary, I went with him to the railway
station. The platform was heaving with hundreds
of men being whisked away to camps all over the

country. When the train arrived, it was also packed with people and it looked as if Greg would have to stand all the way to his training camp.

I felt so sad at our parting but not entirely surprised. It seemed as if our relationship had been a series of goodbyes, ever since day one when we had met in the infirmary.

'Keep wearing the ring,' he called from the window. 'I'll write as soon as I arrive.'

The steam train gave a mighty snort of black smoke as it moved slowly along the track and it drowned out the rest of his words. I saw his mouth open and close but I couldn't hear what he was saying. I stayed on the platform for a long time, well after the train had disappeared from my view, then slowly made my way back to the Overgate to Lily and my grandparents.

I had heard from the Borlands by return of post. They had said they would be delighted to have Lily any time she wanted to come. But, as the weeks passed and although the Luftwaffe had bombed several places in Scotland, most of the evacuees wanted to come home and most of them did.

I asked Lily if she wanted to go to Trinafour but she was unsure. 'I like going there but I would rather stay here with you, Ann. If the Jerries bomb us, then we can always go into the air-raid shelter.'

So it was settled. I wrote back to the Borlands and told them the position. I did add, however, that, if things got bad in the town, then Lily would be coming to them whether she liked it or not.

Dad joined the Home Guard and he regularly

went out to training courses in the Drill Hall in Ward Road. The Tay Rail Bridge was a possible target for German bombers and he would regularly patrol it with his workmates – the ones who were too old to be called up.

Meanwhile Hattie was moaning about the food rationing. 'What are we meant to make with one egg a week? I remember one party at the Pringles where I made a pudding with a dozen eggs.'

Granny had no sympathy over her shortages. 'We're all in the same boat, Hattie, so you'll just have to make the best of it.'

That was the last thing Hattie was prepared to do. 'I hear that some folk get things on the black market – if you know the right people to ask.'

Granny was annoyed. 'Oh, is that folk with money you're talking about?'

Hattie was outraged. 'No, it isn't. I would never do such a thing and neither would Mrs Pringle. They've cut back like the rest of us and I'm forever making meals with vegetables.'

Granny didn't look impressed as she went to make a cup of tea.

Hattie's voice became soft with a memory. 'Do you remember that delicious meal we had at the wedding? Wasn't it the most wonderful day?'

Granny wiped her eyes as she waited for the kettle to boil. I knew she was thinking of Maddie and Danny. He was waiting for his call-up papers and Maddie was almost distraught with worry.

'Aye, it was a wonderful day, Hattie. It was a different world last year and now we've been plunged into another war,' she replied quietly, busying herself with the cups and the saucers.

428

We had heard nothing about Margot since she moved from the flat. It had seemed she had sold it in the nick of time because people weren't buying houses during these worrying times. Not for the first time I marvelled at her nose for survival. It would seem she was an expert at it.

I hadn't mentioned the story about Mary Farr to Dad. For one thing, Babs might have been mistaken about her but, if she was indeed Mary Farr, then it wouldn't do Dad any good to know about her past life. That's why it came as a huge surprise a few days before Christmas to get the visitor.

I noticed the stranger before he came into the shop. He had looked through the window a few times as if making up his mind whether to enter or not. Connie had spotted him as well. 'What's that bloke looking at? Do you think he's some official from the Ministry of Food?'

I was just saying I didn't know when the three girls bounded in through the door.

'The usual things, Ann,' said Sylvia. They were all giggling and it was refreshing to hear some laughter in these sombre times.

Connie took her eyes away from the window to look at the girls. 'What's the joke girls?' she asked.

'Well, we're hoping to meet loads of soldiers at the dancing now that there's a war and we were just describing our ideal soldier before we came in here,' said Sylvia as I weighed out the sweeties.

Amy called out, 'Hurry up, Ann, or we'll be late for work again!'

As they darted through the door Connie called after them, 'You lassies will be late for your own funerals!'

She then looked shocked. 'What am I saying? I shouldn't speak like that in these bleak times.'

I knew she was thinking about young Davie, the paper lad. He had now left the school and had got a job with the Caledon shipyard. His ambition however was to join the navy. Before he left, Connie had caught hold of his hand and said to him, 'Just stay where you are for as long as you can, Davie. There's plenty of time to join the navy when this war's over.'

During all the fun with the girls, the man had disappeared but now he was standing in the door-way. I noticed he was very well dressed with a thick woollen overcoat, a soft hat and good quality leather gloves. He raised his hat in an old-fashioned gesture and Connie visibly beamed at him. 'Can I help you?' she said.

He hesitated. Then said, 'I'm looking for a Miss Ann Neill.'

I had a sweetie in my mouth and I almost swallowed it whole. Was there something wrong with Lily? Or Greg?

Connie was surprised too but she pointed to me, saying, 'This is Ann.'

The man seemed uncertain how to begin. Then he said, 'Can I have a private word with you Miss Neill?'

I cast a worried eye in Connie's direction but she quickly came to my rescue.

'Can you tell her what it's all about Mr...?'

'My name is Charles Cooper and it's a private matter.'

My mind was in a whirl. Where had I heard that name before. Then I remembered. Charlie Cooper

– Mary Farr's ex-husband.

I said to Connie, 'Oh, I think I know what Mr Cooper wants, Connie. Can I have a wee while off?'

She nodded and I took him up to the house. Thankfully the flat was warm because I had lit the fire before going to the shop that morning.

He sat down and placed his hat on his knee. He didn't want any tea so I sat opposite him and waited patiently for him to explain this unexpected visit.

Once again he seemed unsure how to begin. 'I've ... I've heard from Babs Borland that your father has married my wife, Mary?'

I was puzzled. Surely he meant his ex-wife. It must be a slip of the tongue, I thought. I nodded. 'But she's left Dundee and has just sold her flat. She and Dad are separated and we don't know where she's living now.'

He frowned. 'When will your father be home? I would like a word with him.'

'He gets home about five thirty but he does his guard duty tonight so he won't have much time to see you.'

He rose from his chair. 'Then I'll be here at five thirty sharp.' He put on his hat. 'Thank you for seeing me.'

I went back to work feeling confused. Why did he want to see Dad? Surely he didn't still care for his wife? Or did he just want to see one of the men she had married after divorcing him?

Connie gave me an inquiring look when I went back to the shop but I told her it was Dad the man had really wanted to see, not me.

I said no more about it – not even to Granny when I went to pick Lily up for the school.

When Dad arrived home in the evening I told him about the man's visit. For some reason, I didn't mention the connection with Margot. After all, the man might be in the town on business and had decided to pay her a visit. He certainly didn't look very happy when I told him she had gone away. Was he still in love with her and hoping for a reunion?

A few minutes later he appeared at the door again. Dad was just sitting down to his tea so I offered our visitor something to eat.

He declined with a charming smile. 'No, thank you. I'm staying in a guest house in the town and I get my meal at seven thirty.'

Dad looked quizzically at him. 'Well, what can I do for you, Mr Cooper? You're not with the Ministry of War, are you?'

He laughed. 'No, I'm not. I'm the husband of your wife, Mary.'

Dad looked as if he had been hit with a ton of bricks. 'Mary?'

Mr Cooper nodded. 'Oh, yes – she's still my wife. We never got a divorce although there's been many a day I wish I'd never met her, let alone married her.'

Dad looked stunned. 'But we got married two years ago and before that she was married to a great bloke called Harry Connors. He died in an accident although I've since heard it could have been a suicide.'

It was now my turn to look stunned. 'A suicide?'

Dad held up his hand. 'It's a long story, Ann, and I'll tell you about it later.'

Charlie Cooper looked serious. 'I always said Mary would drive a man to drink or an early death.'

Dad nodded. 'It seems likely she drove poor Harry to his death. As for me, well, I survived but it was touch-and-go, I can tell you. Many a night I almost walked out on her but it's not easy when you're married.'

Charlie agreed. 'She spent all the money I got for my father's shops and then one afternoon she just disappeared. I'd heard nothing of her until Babs Borland wrote to me.'

Dad was surprised. 'How did you manage to find me? Surely you've looked for her before now?'

Charlie chuckled. 'Indeed I did not. To be honest, I was too glad to be rid of her. I have a lady friend now who understands that I'm still officially married and, to be blunt, up until now, the arrangement has suited us both. As a result, I never gave Mary – or Margot, as she now calls herself – another thought. But now I intend to divorce her so I have to know her whereabouts.'

The penny finally fell with Dad. 'Let me get this straight. If you're still married to her, does that not mean I've committed bigamy?'

For the first time that night, Charlie burst out laughing. 'Yes, it does! You were never legally married to her and nor was your friend Mr Connors or indeed any other sucker she may have met in between.'

Dad didn't jump for joy but he looked ecstatic.

'What a relief!' He then looked unhappy. 'But she's left Dundee now.'

'It doesn't matter – the police will find her and then I can serve the divorce papers on her. One thing is clear, Mr Neill – you're not a married man and, as far as Mary or Margot is concerned, you never were.'

He stood up to go. 'I may not see you again as I hope to return home at the end of the week. I live on the south coast of England now and travel is so terrible these days with all the troop movements. The way they're packed into trains, it's like travelling in a cattle truck.'

Then it dawned on Dad. How had Babs Borland known about Margot and Charlie Cooper?

Charlie seemed surprised by the question. 'It was your daughter's doing. She showed Babs the wedding photo and she recognised Mary. Babs got in touch with me to say how sorry she was to hear we had parted and got divorced. Of course, I knew nothing about this and it wasn't until she told me the whole story that I decided to come and see you.'

I saw him to the door but Dad went downstairs with him. On his return, I said, 'I should have told you but I thought Babs was mistaken about Margot being this Mary Farr. But it seems she wasn't.'

I told him the entire story that Babs had told me and he looked dazed. Then he let out a huge whoop of joy. 'Did you hear what Charlie said? That I'm not married to her?'

I was so pleased for him. Who would ever have guessed it? That the fair Margot had committed bigamy – not once but twice. Or maybe even more. Who knew the whole story?

As I put a cup of tea on the table, I asked him, 'You said that Harry committed suicide. Did you mean that?'

'Nobody will ever be able to prove it but I've been to see Harry's sister, Olivia, and she's told me a few home truths.'

'What truths?'

'Well, for instance, the fact that Harry had a big bank account when his first wife died. She was a thrifty woman and they saved money every week. Then, just before his death, he discovered that the account had almost been cleaned out by Margot. Poor Harry got into a state and told her they would have to survive on a wee pension from now on. Well, the bold Margot wasn't having any of this so she told him she was leaving him and she wanted the house sold and the proceeds split right down the middle. Poor man, he couldn't take any more so Olivia is sure he drowned himself.'

I was shocked. 'But how does she know this now? Harry wouldn't confide in his sister surely?'

'That's where you're wrong, Ann. Oh, he didn't go round and tell her all his problems but she got a letter from the solicitor after his death. Harry told her everything about Margot in it.'

I was still puzzled. 'But why has she left this news until now?'

Dad looked unhappy. 'She didn't. Do you remember I mentioned before I married Margot that Olivia was saying some awful things about her? I didn't believe her so she tried to see me at the work but I kept dodging her.' He gave me one of his sheepish looks.

I knew how good he was at dodging me, never mind poor Olivia.

'Well, she knew she couldn't come to the flat at Victoria Road so after a few months she just gave up. She told me last week when I went to see her that, if I was fool enough to believe Margot's fairy stories, then it was my own fault.'

'I see.'

But Dad was full of joy now and very cheery. 'I'll have to get away to my guard duty but do you know the first thing I'm going to do afterwards?'

I couldn't guess. 'Surprise me, Dad.'

'I'm going to see Rosie and tell her the good news that I'm not married.'

I wasn't pleased. 'Leave Rosie alone, Dad. She's finally found a man to marry so don't you go and break things up for her. When you don't have her on a string, then you want her but, if you know she's waiting in every night for you, then you either ditch her or treat her terribly.'

He smiled and his whole face lit up. 'Not this time, Ann. When I saw her at the wedding looking so bonny, it suddenly struck me that I've loved her since your mother died. I was just some bloody fool but I'm not going to remain one. I'm going to sweep her off her feet.'

This was something I had to see so, after his Home Guard stint, I went with him to the Overgate. Rosie wasn't in. She was out at the pictures with Albert.

Dad's face was a picture of dejection.

I made a mental prayer. 'Please don't accept

Albert's proposal tonight, Rosie.'

Although it was none of my business, I left her a letter, telling her the good news about Dad. She could then make up her own mind and do whatever she wanted to do.

Good for Rosie, I thought. She now had two men interested in her and, although they weren't at daggers drawn, perhaps it would come to that.

As it turned out, there was no drama – much to my disappointment. When she read the letter after her return from the pictures, she rushed up the Hilltown to see Dad. Both Dad and I were surprised to see her. Her cheeks were flushed with the cold wind and her eyes were bright. Not knowing about the note I'd left for Rosie, Dad was taken aback but he also looked pleased.

'That's wonderful news about Margot,' Rosie said, trying to catch her breath.

He gave me a sharp glance but I looked innocent.

'I'm really so pleased that you're now a free man, Johnny – I really am.'

Dad looked so smug and I wished I could wipe that look from his face. He really was the end at times.

He looked Rosie straight in the eyes. 'Rosie, I'm asking you to marry me. We can get the banns read then get married as soon as possible. What do you say?'

She gave him an astonished look. 'But I'm married, Johnny. I got married to Albert last week. Did your mother not tell you?'

The smug look vanished and I thought he would burst into tears. 'Oh.'

I turned to her. 'Congratulations, Rosie! I hope you and Albert will be very happy in the future.'

Dad looked stunned and I couldn't help thinking it served him right. 'Oh, aye, Rosie – congratulations from me as well.'

He made his way wearily to the bedroom door. 'I'll say goodnight then, Rosie.'

She winked at me. 'Oh, Johnny...'

He stopped and looked at her. 'What?'

'Come back here, you daft gowk. I'm just kidding you. I'm not married to Albert or anybody – at least not yet. Of course, I'll marry you and as quick as you like.'

Dad rushed over and scooped her up in his arms. 'You wee witch,' he said laughingly.

I noticed he had a relieved look and it would have served him right if she had been married. Still, I was glad she wasn't. I tried to look innocent but I couldn't keep it up.

'That was your idea, wasn't it, Ann?' he said accusingly.

'You deserved it, Dad. It would have been a disaster if Rosie had married Albert and then you would have lost her for good.'

He became serious. 'Thank God I didn't lose you, Rosie. I just got lost somewhere along the way – I took a side turning, so to speak.'

He left to walk her home and I went happily to bed. It had been a long time since I had been this happy. The last time had been at Maddie and Danny's wedding.

16

Danny had received his call-up papers and he was on the verge of leaving. Maddie was distressed but she was trying to put a brave face in front of him. They had invited me to the flat on the eve of his departure. The thick velvet curtains were drawn against the dark wet night and the room seemed smaller and cosier.

Maddie had a tense white face but Danny seemed cheery enough although I thought that was simply a cover for his true feelings.

It was a strange feeling to see how everything looked so normal and comforting in this topsy-turvy world that had been turned on its head by this war.

Danny was worried about leaving Maddie alone in the flat. 'I'm trying to get her to stay with her parents, Ann, but she'll not listen to me. Will you, Maddie?'

She looked at him stubbornly. 'I want to stay here till you come home, Danny.'

I could understand her point of view. 'Once a woman is married, Danny,' I said, 'she likes to live in her own place and not go back to her parents' house unless for a visit or an emergency.'

'Is this not an emergency?'

'It is but Maddie will have all the family to call on if she needs any help.' I smiled at her and she returned the smile.

'There, I told you, didn't I, Danny Ryan, that Ann would side with me?'

'Oh, I'm not siding with you, Maddie. It's just that, if you want to stay in your own house, then that's that.'

Maddie then began to tell me about their visit to Lochee the previous night. 'Danny's family are so upset at him leaving and Kit was crying. George told her to stop being so pessimistic and she told him to stop using such big words and that she couldn't help but worry.'

Danny laughed. 'Poor Kit, I felt so sorry for her. There's been no word from Sammy and that lassie he was supposed to be seeing hasn't heard a word either.'

'Maybe he's lying low after giving Kathleen that beating. He'll know he'll not be welcome in Lochee for a long time to come.'

I asked Maddie about her job. 'Are you still at the nursing home?'

'Yes, I am. I'm grateful to have it as it will keep me busy. Maybe I'll not worry about Danny so much if I have a lot to do every day. I've heard there's a list being drawn up for nurses – just in case we're needed.' Her face fell at the thought of the possible casualties of war being ferried to the infirmary. Seemingly, some wards were already being set aside for injured men returning from the war.

I tried to change the subject away from the topic of the war but we were soon back on it. Danny didn't know where he would end up. His warrant travel card was for the south of England and he had to report to an army camp there.

Then Maddie looked stricken. 'Heavens, Ann, we've never asked about Greg. How is he?

'He seems to be fine. He's in the south of England as well – in some office at a place called Bletchley Park. He never mentions what kind of work he's doing but I think it's administration duties.'

Danny laughed and touched the side of his nose. 'Oh, I see – it's hush-hush, secret work, is it?'

We all laughed at the thought of Greg being a secret agent and maybe being parachuted into Germany or the war zone like some Hollywood film star. But this wasn't fantasy with some actors playing their parts. This was real life in 1940 and nobody had any idea how it would all end. Every country that Germany had invaded had lost thousands of its civilians so would we be any different? One good thing was the fact that Neville Chamberlain was no longer the Prime Minister. Winston Churchill was now in charge and he was taking on the enemy – head on with no appeasement. Like thousands of families across the land we were all praying for the safe return of loved ones. If anyone had to be killed, then please God let it be someone else.

It was time I was home and as I said my goodbyes, Danny said, 'Will you come to the station with Maddie and me tomorrow night, Ann?'

I was surprised by this request. Surely Maddie would want the last few precious moments alone with her husband? I said so.

'You can leave us alone for the last five minutes,

Ann, but I would like you to be there with Maddie when I leave. You're such a tower of strength to everybody and I'll feel better if I leave her in your good hands.'

I looked at Maddie. Was this what she wanted?

'I didn't like to ask you, Ann, but I would dearly like you to be with me.'

Although I didn't want to impose on their last time together, I reluctantly agreed.

Maddie's face looked less tense and Danny smiled. 'Thanks, Ann,' he said.

It was a sombre little party of three who set off for the railway station the following night. The weather was mild and murky – more like November than January. Still, we were all well wrapped up against the weather and the thought of the emotional hurdle ahead of us.

The station was packed with people, just as it had been when Greg was leaving. Like us, families were seeing off their husbands and sons. It was a scene of emotional upheaval. Danny had already said all his goodbyes to both sides of the family and we were a small party compared to others who seemed to have the entire population of a small village in attendance. Although Maddie and I were upset about Danny's departure, these clusters of human beings cheered us up and we shared a secret smile about it.

I felt I was in the way. They should be alone together tonight, I thought, to have their last few precious moments as a couple without my presence. I planned to say a quick cheerio to him then leave them alone – not that they would be alone on this crowded platform but they would be alone mentally. In peacetime, people noticed one another in situations like this but, on that murky night, no one noticed anyone but their own. It was a strangely insular crowd.

I stood with my hands in my pockets, feeling miserable and cheerless. I knew Maddie was feeling worse but she tried to keep the tears at bay.

With fifteen minutes to go until the arrival of his train, I said my final goodbye to him. My beloved cousin who had been my strength and mainstay for most of my life was on the verge of leaving – going to his own personal dark horizon.

'I'll be praying for you, Danny,' I said. Now why did I say that? I wasn't a religious person but maybe a little divine help would see him through the months ahead – or, worse still, the years ahead.

He grinned. 'Thanks, Ann – I'll need all the help I can get.'

Maddie gave me a weak smile and her eyes had the watery look that heralded a flood of tears.

I walked to the far end of the platform and waited for her at the door to the buffet. Like the station platform, this cosy corner was also packed with people. It was almost impossible to see through the windows as they were all steamed up with condensation and had long rivulets of water streaming down.

I stood with my back to the wall and tried not to think about Danny – I had my own worries about Greg. But he was in some administration building and Danny would be on some foreign battlefield – of that I was sure.

I heard the high-pitched, tinny voice from the

tannoy and then the sound of the mighty steam train as it stopped briefly to pick up its cargo of fighting men, all going to war with their own feelings of horror and anxiety about the unknown. Human nature being what it is, I thought, some would have a higher degree of apprehension than others. Probably, for a tiny majority, this war was an adventure – one that would take them away from the depressing years of unemployment. Connie had said that a vast number of jobless men had enlisted at the start of the war. It had been reported in the papers.

I said another mental prayer for Greg and Danny. Then I remembered Sammy and said one for him as well, even though he should be ashamed of himself for hitting Kathleen.

Then I saw Maddie walking towards me. She was wiping tears from her eyes and my heart went out to her – not very long married and now this enforced parting. I went over to her and linked my arm through hers. She gave me a grateful glance and we made our way into the street. It was pitch black as we slowly walked to her flat. The pavements felt slippy with drizzly rain and we felt rather than saw the swirling mist that left our faces wet with moisture.

I would have been quite happy to keep silent on our way to Roseangle but Maddie seemed to want to talk. 'Do you remember the first time I met you, Ann?'

'Aye, I do, Maddie. It was Hogmanay and, when your mum asked you to play the piano, you played "Horsey, Keep your Tail up".'

She said nothing but gave my arm a squeeze.

'Do you mind when we made the camiknickers before making the frocks?' I asked her.

She gave a small laugh. 'Yes, I do. Life was such fun then, wasn't it, Ann?'

I agreed it was although I recalled it wasn't much fun working for the dreaded Miss Hood.

'I feel as if part of my life has gone, Ann – that the world has turned upside down but we're still trying to stand upright. Do you know what I mean?'

I nodded in the darkness. 'Aye, I do, Maddie.'

'I've told myself that, even if I never see Danny again, he'll always be the best and biggest thing that's happened to me.'

I had to stop her thinking that Danny would never come back. I stopped walking and turned to her. Her face was an indistinct white blur in the darkness. 'Look, Maddie, you've got to hang on to the hope that Danny will survive this – for his sake as well as your own. The minute you stop believing that, then there will be no hope for you both. Just hang on to the thought of meeting him again when this awful war is over.'

She sounded doubtful. 'Do you really believe that, Ann? That, if I give up hope, then it will be the end for us both?'

'Aye, I do. This war will not last forever and just think what life will be like when Danny comes home...'

We had reached the entrance to her close and we climbed up the darkened stairs. Inside the room was warm and bright with her golden shaded lamps. The velvet curtains cut out most of the light but she also had her blackout blind down.

I said, 'You sit by the fire and I'll make some tea and toast.'

She sat down and kicked off her boots. Within five minutes, I was placing the tea tray on a small side table beside her. The tea was hot, strong and sweet for me and weak and sugarless for her.

'Would you like me to stay the night with you, Maddie?'

'It's good of you to offer, Ann, but I have to get used to living alone from now on. Mother wants me to stay with them while Danny is away but I want to stay here.'

'Do you think that's a good idea, Maddie?' I said dubiously.

She gazed into her teacup for a moment as if daydreaming. 'It's like this,' she said dreamily. 'I feel if I stay here then Danny will know where I am when he comes home. This is my home now. Not with my parents.'

I admired her for her brave stand. She was standing on her own two feet and, although she would need some emotional help from her family, she was also saying, 'Look at me – I'm grown up now and I'm a married woman.'

It was time for me to leave. The dark streets held no terrors for me but I couldn't help but recall the Overgate and Hilltown before the war. The area was always crammed with people and children, all gossiping, playing or generally just adding to the nightly cacophony of noise. But, that night, those streets lay dark and still. Maybe the weather was to blame for the dearth of humanity but I somehow didn't think so. Most people were glad to be inside – away from the thoughts of war, away from anything unpleasant.

Dad was in the house when I got back. He had not long returned from walking Rosie home and he was busy stoking up the fire. 'Has Danny gone?'

I nodded, unable to speak. I had had to be brave for Maddie's sake but now the full implication of his departure hit me. My eyes filled with tears but I didn't want to burst out crying. I went over to the stove and put the kettle on. As I poured out the two cups of tea, I almost burst out laughing. Was this our panacea to all kinds of trials and tribulations? A cup of tea?

I asked Dad about his wedding.

His face fell. 'I've been speaking to the bobbies and they suggest waiting a wee while. They want to speak to Margot.'

I was astounded. Was this another of Dad's ploys to keep Rosie waiting again? 'But it might be years before the police find her. Does that mean Rosie has to wait till then?'

He seemed unsure. 'I don't think so but I also don't know much about the charge of bigamy. I'll give it a week or two and then Rosie and I can make our plans.'

On that depressing note I went to bed. Since my illness I had suffered from nightmares but they had lessened over the past year. That was why the dream, when it came, was vivid and shocking. I was at the edge of a large green field and I saw Danny in the middle of the long grass. Suddenly the ground opened up and he disappeared – just as if the earth had swallowed him whole. I searched and searched for him but the field was empty – just full of long green grass and meadow flowers. I woke up in a panic. I knew I had been screaming but the house was quiet. Was it possible to scream in a dream but still remain silent?

I tried to go back to sleep again but the image appeared again. Full of dread, I rose silently and moved to the kitchen. The fire was almost out but the room was still warm. I sat in the fireside chair with my feet curled under me and tried to shake the image of horror from my mind. I told myself firmly that dreams weren't prophetic. After all, I had spent the evening with Maddie and Danny and our sole topic of conversation had been the war. My brain was saturated with it as it was the only thing I heard every day in the shop. That would explain my bad dream. I made some cocoa and, after I'd drunk it, I went back to bed and didn't wake up until the alarm clock went off with its usual loud clatter.

I had a letter from Minnie the next day. She wrote, 'Peter has been called up. He went away last week and we're both missing him terribly. Still, I've made lots of new friends and my neighbours are great so I've made up my mind to remain here and not return to Dundee. As I told you earlier, Ann, Peter is at the school and he's loving it. How are Greg, Danny and Maddie? All well I hope.' I wrote back by return of post and gave her my scanty news – such as it was.

During the following weeks it was as if I was living my life in limbo. Life went on much as usual and, apart from trying to make meals from the rations, nothing seemed to change very much.

Danny wrote to Maddie nearly every day. He

had been taken to a training camp down south because seemingly the Scottish training camps were all full. Because his letters were censored she didn't know the exact location. He told her he was missing her a lot but life wasn't too bad. Then the letters became less frequent and she began to worry.

Hattie consoled her, saying, 'He'll be on training sessions, Maddie, and he'll maybe not have enough time to write like he did before.'

I said the same and this seemed to reassure her although she wasn't totally convinced.

Then, on the last weekend in March, he suddenly appeared at the door. I was in the house with Maddie when he just walked in. For a full minute we both looked at him in silence, as if he was a ghost. Then he smiled and we realised it was Danny – and he was home.

Maddie ran over. 'Oh, Danny, is the war over? Are you home for good?'

He shook his head. 'No, Maddie, I've just got a forty-eight-hour leave but it's great to see you again.' He turned to me. 'Hullo, Ann. How are you?'

I said I was great. He looked so handsome in his uniform but the army had tamed his hair and it was cut really short.

I picked up my coat. 'I'll say cheerio for now but it's great to see you, Danny.'

Maddie said, 'Oh, you don't have to leave right away, Ann. Stay a bit longer.'

I knew she was just being polite and she couldn't wait to be alone with Danny.

'No, you'll both want to be on your own as

forty-eight hours isn't that long.'

I left them and made my way home. What a lovely surprise for her and it was good to see Danny again. The memory of my bad dream had faded into the back recesses of my mind but seeing him in his uniform now brought it all flooding back. I shivered as if someone was walking across my grave. To shake off this morbid feeling, I turned my thoughts to Greg. Although he wrote every second night, I hadn't seen him since he left. Did he also get forty-eight-hour leaves? Seemingly not.

As it turned out, it was a night of surprises as one was hovering on my horizon. Later that night, I opened the door to find a young burly police constable standing on the step. I must have turned white because the young man gave me a concerned look.

'Is Mr Neill at home, Miss?'

I relaxed. If it had been bad news about Greg I doubted very much if it would come via Dad.

I stood aside and he came in. Dad was at the kitchen sink. He had been shaving but he was now wiping his face with a towel. He glanced at the policeman with surprise.

The man took out a notebook and once again my worry came flooding back. He said, in stiffly formal words, 'You were married to a Margot Connors, née Farr, formerly known as Mary Cooper?'

Dad nodded. 'I knew about her marriage to Harry Connors but not to the other bloke.'

The policeman studied his notebook as if it held all the secrets of the world. When he spoke his voice was flat and official sounding. 'Yesterday, the said Mrs Mary Farr Cooper was arrested in Edinburgh.'

We both gasped out loud. 'Arrested?' said Dad. 'For bigamy?'

'Initially she was arrested for deception and theft but bigamy will be added to these alleged crimes. Can you accompany me to the station, Mr Neill, as we have enquiries to make?'

Dad went white but he put on his jacket and left with the constable. As they set off down the stairs, I was mortified. Would the neighbours see him getting into a police car? Would they think *he* was being arrested?

It was a bright clear evening and the Hilltown would be busy with people taking advantage of a nice night. The weather had been cold and wet for most of the month and we had just spent our first winter with the blackout. It was good to be out in the fresh air although the lighter nights now brought the added danger of bombing raids by German planes.

Oh, yes, the street would be busy – I was certain of that.

I had asked the policeman if I could go with my father but he had said no. They wouldn't keep him long, he said, as it was merely routine.

To make matters worse, they met Rosie and Lily on the stairs and they were both in a state when I opened the door to them.

'Where's that bobby taking Dad?' Lily had cried with tears streaming down her face.

I looked at Rosie who was also visibly upset. I said to her, 'It's that damn Margot again. She's

451

been arrested in Edinburgh and the police want Dad to help them with a few enquiries.'

She nodded dumbly while I wiped Lily's eyes.

'Come on, Lily, you can help me make Rosie a cup of tea.'

Although still tearful the thought of doing something useful soon cheered her up.

I quietly told Rosie what the bobby had said but I also added that we didn't know much about the arrest or where the offence had taken place.

Rosie decided to wait till Dad got back from the police station. 'I've got to find out what's going on, Ann. That Margot was a real besom and I feel sorry that your father was married to her.'

I felt sorry for him also but I still couldn't understand how he could have been such a fool to get in tow with her in the first place. But, never mind, I thought, hopefully it would all be behind him and he would settle down with Rosie. He had learned a hard lesson.

It was midnight when he returned. Unfortunately the street was deserted and our neighbours wouldn't have witnessed his return. They would think he was still in the jail. He looked tired and drawn.

As I made some supper, he said, 'Margot was arrested yesterday for deception and theft, just like the bobby said.'

As the next day was Saturday, Lily was sleeping in her own room instead of at the Overgate which meant I had to keep a watch in case she heard Dad's voice and maybe wandered through.

Rosie was puzzled. 'Where did Margot go when she sold her flat, Johnny?'

452

'She ended up in Edinburgh where she got a good job as a housekeeper to a retired judge – using a forged reference, I believe. Imagine Margot with a judge?' His lips twitched and it was good to see him smile – it transformed his whole face. 'But it seems she didn't know he was a judge. She thought he was just some doddery old man that didn't know his thumb from his pinky but he was far from being dottled. He noticed that large sums of money were going missing. Every time he went to the bank he locked the money he withdrew in a drawer in his desk. Of course Margot was full of sympathy and she even went round the house with him, suggesting how a burglar might have got in.'

At that point he did burst out laughing, much to Rosie's surprise. 'Och, I'm sorry, Rosie, but it's priceless. I can see her floating around full of sunshine and light – sweet Margot with her employer's welfare at heart. But she made one big mistake. She got greedy. Instead of being happy with the money she had already pinched she had to steal some more. What she didn't know was it was a trap set up by the police. She always swore blind that she never went into this room on her own but the old man had a good sense of smell and he could identify her perfume. Well, the police found the money under a mattress on her bed but she's still denying it. Of course Margot would because she thinks she can get off with anything.'

The story stirred a memory in my mind. The smell of scent – the day I thought I heard the noise and found the twenty-seven pounds missing.

'She must wear her scent awful strong for the man to smell it,' Rosie said doubtfully.

'Aye, she did and it wasn't a flowery scent she wore. It had a strong musky smell but I've no idea what it's called.'

'Probably something expensive,' I said. I mentioned the money I had lost. 'Do you mind when I wasn't well, Dad, and you asked me for money for Lily?'

He nodded.

'Did Margot know where it was? In the tin I mean?'

He looked dubious. 'I don't think so – unless Lily mentioned it but I can't see that.'

'I found twenty-seven pounds missing a few days after you'd gone and there was a faint perfume in the room although I couldn't place it.'

Dad suddenly said, 'Come to think of it, she could have known. When I got home that day, I told Lily that there would be no more money from the tin. I wonder if she overheard it?'

'It doesn't matter now but I think she pinched my money as well.' I didn't add that, for ages, I'd thought he was the culprit.

He was very angry. 'She was a bad woman right enough but hopefully she'll get her comeuppance. I think she thought that your legacy would land in her lap, Ann. She thought you would be some placid wee lassie that she could hoodwink into parting with the money but she came up against the wrong person. You stood up to her and she didn't like it.'

I knew that. At least I had only lost a few pounds and it had been worth it to get rid of her.

Dad walked Rosie home while I got ready for bed. The next day was Saturday and Danny would be leaving on the Sunday. In the evening, he would probably catch the night train back south. Then what?

I soon found out on the Sunday afternoon when they both appeared at the house. Maddie didn't look as ecstatic as she had done on the Friday night but Danny looked much the same. I soon found out the reason for Maddie's downcast face when he mentioned this forty-eight-hour pass was actually embarkation leave. He didn't know his eventual destination but it was to be overseas.

'I'll probably get sent to France,' he told me. 'The French army is fighting the Germans and loads of regiments are being sent to help, I believe.'

I glanced at Maddie and she returned my look with sadness. Her blue eyes were shadowed and she looked miserable.

'Hopefully, it'll not be for long, Danny,' I said cheerfully, which was an act as I felt far from being cheerful.

'That's what I keep telling Maddie but she won't believe me,' he said with a smile.

I wouldn't have believed it either if I was in her place but I wasn't going to say that.

I told them the story of Margot and their eyes widened with shock. At least it was a diversion from the talk of war.

'She's been arrested?' said Danny.

I nodded while Maddie looked on in disbelief.

'What will happen now?' he asked.

I shrugged my shoulders. 'I've no idea, Danny. Maybe she'll get carted off to jail.'

Maddie spoke. 'But your father will still be able to marry Rosie?'

I said I hoped so – for Rosie's sake more than anything.

Then it was time for them to leave. I said another goodbye to Danny and told Maddie I would see her soon. I then watched as they set off down the Hilltown and my heart was heavy with sorrow. Danny was maybe going to France – going to some unknown horror and fear that Maddie and I could never even begin to fathom. Going to his own dark horizon.

17

Maddie was expecting a baby. The Pringles and Hattie were over the moon with her news, as we all were. It was the end of May and the baby was due around the end of the year – or Hogmanay, according to Bella.

The dark blot on her happiness was Danny. He had gone to France and, although she had received a few letters from him since his leave, she hadn't heard for over a month now. As a result, he didn't know about the baby.

She had given up her work at the nursing home because she hadn't been feeling well. Most mornings she suffered from morning sickness that was so bad it left her weak and trembling. Still, she was adamant she wasn't going to stay with her parents so I spent every night with her. After leaving Lily with Granny, I would head to the flat at Roseangle to keep her company until I had to go to work early in the morning.

Hattie would then arrive as soon as I left which meant she had to cope with the symptoms of the sickness. She was telling Granny one day, 'Poor Maddie is so ill every morning. It lasts until midday or even the early afternoon.'

Granny was sympathetic. 'Aye, the morning sickness is a beggar, right enough, Hattie. Still, most expectant mothers suffer from it and few escape it.'

I knew this was true. Although I had no first-hand knowledge of it, I remember hearing our neighbours Rita and Nellie suffering from it. Even my own mother had experienced a few months of feeling unwell when she had been expecting Lily. The only good thing about it seemingly was the fact it didn't last long.

'She'll feel much better after three months, Hattie,' Granny said, trying to sound helpful.

Every morning, Maddie went to look for a card or a letter from Danny and each time she was disappointed. We tried, Hattie and I, to explain how hard it would be to write while being in France but she fretted every day.

Hattie would make some delicious little snacks for her but as soon as she ate them she was sick. I was worried about her and that was the truth. I told Granny my worries. 'She's not eating enough to keep her alive, Granny, never mind keeping the baby nourished.'

To my surprise, Granny wasn't in the least alarmed. 'Och, don't you bother about Maddie. She'll be keeping enough food down for the two of them, believe me.'

'I wish Danny would write. That would make her feel better – I'm sure of it.'

'Well, it is a war, Ann, and I'm sure he would write if he could. He's not doing this out of spite or anything like that.'

I knew that but it didn't help.

Then, in June, the news came through about Dunkirk. Connie was white faced one morning as I went into the shop. The papers were still lying in their bundles on the counter. 'Are you all

458

right Connie? You don't look well.'

She sat down and I hurried to make her a cup of tea. She pointed to a paper on the counter. The headlines were stark – 'British Army Retreat from Dunkirk'.

'My neighbour's laddie is in the army and he turned up at the door at four o'clock this morning.'

I was about to ask if he had a forty-eight-hour pass but the look on Connie's face stopped me.

'The laddie was wearing an old pair of trousers and a jersey. He didn't even have on a pair of socks – just an old pair of sandshoes. He was at Dunkirk and he told his mother he was one of the lucky ones. He was in the water for hours. The Germans were shooting at the retreating men but seemingly a fleet of small boats crossed the English Channel to get the soldiers back to Britain. As I said, young Jack was lucky because he was picked up quite quickly but he thinks most of the men didn't make it. He says the death toll will be high.'

I felt sick. 'Oh, no, Connie! Danny is in France as well.'

Connie looked sad. 'Well, Ann, unless he's got out like Jack...' She stopped because to continue would have brought me even more horror.

I thought of Maddie and the coming baby and I almost cried. But tears wouldn't do any good in these circumstances. She would need all the help and support we could give her.

Connie continued, 'The Germans managed to cut off the troops and then the Belgian Army surrendered on orders from King Leopold and

459

that left a huge hole in their defences. Jack was telling us that the Germans are shooting refugees as well as men from the forces. According to him, it's just one big massacre.'

Then Joe came in, his face as white as Connie's. 'You'll have heard this awful news, Connie?' he said. 'Still, it's a miracle that they've managed to save thousands of men from the beaches because of the armada of wee boats.'

Connie nodded. 'Aye, so Jack said. He was picked up by a holiday cruiser. It could only carry a dozen men but he said there was hundreds of small boats coming over the channel. Jack's clothes were ruined but the voluntary women were handing out spare clothes to let the lads travel home for a few days.'

Joe was pessimistic. 'You wait and see, Connie. France will be the next country to surrender to the Jerries. Yon Hitler is just tramping over everybody and the amount of folk getting killed is horrendous. In the last war, it was the men on the battlefront that got killed but not this time.'

'Jack was telling his mother that there's a big battle going on at St Valery and those soldiers haven't managed to get out. He saw lots of men being treated in a casualty unit at Dunkirk and said that the doctors are drawing straws to see who goes and who stays. Jack said it was full of badly injured soldiers and the only reason he saw it was because one of his mates had a broken ankle. He managed to get him to the beach but he was in so much pain that he took him to the hospital unit and he had to leave him behind. He was crying when he told his mother that.'

I couldn't listen to this horrible saga any longer and I asked her if I could go to see Maddie for a half hour.

'Aye, you can, Ann. I only hope Danny has also been one of the lucky men and is sitting at home.'

As I was putting my coat on, I overheard Joe speaking. 'Of course, the men who are injured will be taken to prisoner-of-war camps – that's what the Geneva Convention says.'

Although I hadn't long left Maddie, I knew I had to be with her when this dreadful news broke.

She had been sick again and Hattie said quietly, 'It's been on the wireless but I don't know how to tell her.'

When she emerged from the bathroom, looking white and ill, she knew something was wrong. 'What is it? Is it Danny?'

I sat her down and as gently as I could I told her about the retreat from Dunkirk. I added, 'Danny is more than likely still in his camp somewhere or even on his way home like Connie's neighbour, Jack.'

She shook her head sadly. 'You don't really believe that, do you, Ann?'

I was saved from telling her a lie because she suddenly rushed towards the bathroom from where I could hear her retching.

Hattie had tears in her eyes. 'What a bloody world it is, Ann.'

I was taken aback by her language. In all the years I had known her, I had never ever heard her swear. It would seem there was always a first time for everything.

I quickly told her the news of Jack. 'It was

461

seemingly traumatic, Hattie. The poor laddie was standing in the water for hours and he had to leave his pal behind with a broken ankle. He says there are thousands of men dead. Dear God, please don't let Danny be one of them.'

Maddie reappeared and she looked drained of colour and energy. I was now extremely worried about her because she was so frail and wan looking. How would she ever get through this pregnancy?

I had to go back to the shop but I was dreading it. All the customers would be talking about this latest news and I didn't think I could cope with it but I couldn't leave Connie to do all the work. The comments were all the same. If France did indeed surrender to the Germans, then we would be on our own – one small island against the hard jackboots of the ever-powerful and conquering Germans.

Connie said that civilians from the overrun countries had either been killed or carted off to labour camps but how she knew this I wasn't sure. Perhaps she had access to other newspapers. She had certainly known about the Duke of Windsor and Wallis Simpson long before it appeared in the papers. I suddenly longed for that far-off world of a few years ago when life was simple and we all lived in peace – at least in our neck of the woods.

Connie asked about Maddie and the baby. 'Is she keeping fine?'

I nodded. 'Aye, she's bearing up, Connie.'

To my distress, I noticed that Joe was still hanging around the shop. Every customer who came in had a long discussion with him about

Dunkirk. Up until that moment, I couldn't have told anyone the whereabouts of Dunkirk but I don't think a single person in the country could be unaware of its location after this terrible blow – this retreat.

In the afternoon I was glad to reach the peaceful atmosphere of my house. Dad was no longer working in the warehouse now. Mainly because of the dearth of vegetables and the almost extinction of fruit, Mr Pringle had reluctantly had to let half his workers go but Dad had got a job with the Caledon shipyard as a labourer. He seemed to like this new job but the case hanging over Margot was making him tired. She was due in court later in the year. I just wished he could marry Rosie and forget all about Margot. She wasn't worth bothering about.

I made up my mind to voice these thoughts to him in the evening. After all, if the Germans did overrun our country there might not be enough time to do all the things we wanted to do. I felt then as though life were somehow more precious and short. We shouldn't waste a moment of it.

I wrote to Greg, telling him we thought Danny was either missing or dead. After I read over it I tore it into tiny pieces and threw them into the cold grate and put a match to them. I rewrote my letter but left out the news of Danny.

When I went to the flat that night, Kit and her sisters were there. Their faces were all downcast and I thought how we had all aged a lot since this awful war had started.

It was a strained conversation as we all skirted around any mention of Danny. Kit tried to be cheerful but very soon we lapsed into silence.

Maddie always felt better in the evening but without the topic of Danny to keep us going we found very little to say. There was only so much Maddie could tell us about her pregnancy.

Then, in the middle of this silence, Maddie said to me, 'Do you think Danny was at Dunkirk, Ann?'

I was taken aback by the directness of her question. 'I'm not really sure, Maddie. He could be anywhere. Even back at his camp in England.'

She smiled ruefully. 'I don't think so.'

The Ryan women were at a loss as to what to say so they remained silent.

In an effort to bring some talk into the room, I asked Kit how Kathleen was coping with Kitty.

Kit smiled, her pale face lighting up. 'Och, she's coming along fine. She's into everything – even the coal bucket. The other morning she resembled a wee black lassie from Africa and she looked so funny. Kathleen is doing really well in her job. You know she's seeing a lot of Colin Matthews?'

I didn't know but it was good news nevertheless.

Kit continued, 'He's been called up but he's asked her to write to him...' She stopped when a spasm of pain crossed Maddie's face. 'Och, I'm really sorry, Maddie. I shouldn't be chattering on like this. You'll be wanting to go to your bed?'

Maddie shook her head. 'No, I'm fine – honestly. I like the company.' She swept her hair back from her face. 'Is there any news of Sammy?'

It was Kit's turn to look distressed. 'No, there's been no word – either to Kathleen or his mother.

And seemingly that rumour about the lassie he was supposed to be seeing being pregnant turned out to be a load of hogwash. Oh, he was seeing her all right but there was no baby on the way.'

Maddie spoke quietly, almost to herself, 'Danny's missing and Sammy's missing. Lots of wives and mothers will be mourning their men tonight – and every other night.'

We all stayed silent again and it was so quiet in the room we could hear the loud ticking of the clock which had been a wedding present from one of Maddie's relations.

My mind went back to the day of the wedding and how joyous it had been but then I remembered how the threat of war had hung over us even then.

Soon the Ryan women got up to go and we were left alone. It was then that Maddie broke down in a flood of tears. I held her tightly until she became quiet and I put her to bed.

'I don't think I'll be able to go on without Danny,' she said.

Although near to tears myself, I had to stop her feeling morose like this. 'Look, Maddie, you're having Danny's baby so try and look to the future with a bit of happiness. Danny wouldn't want you to be unhappy like this – especially at a time like this with a baby on the horizon.'

She suddenly smiled and it was so much like the old Maddie I remembered. 'You're such a tower of strength, Ann. Danny always said you were – even as a little girl.'

'Right then, Maddie, if you think that, then listen to what I tell you.'

After she fell asleep, I sat in the living room in the dark but I left the curtains open. The river lay like a silver blur in the distance but everything else was in darkness. Although I hadn't admitted it to Maddie, I would also find life hard without Danny. For all my days, he had been my lifeline and, although I knew our lives were destined to go down different roads, I still hoped he would be part of my journey. I went to bed with these thoughts in mind and prayed so hard to a God I hardly knew but hoped would be a forgiving one.

Maddie's morning sickness stopped as if by magic. It was late June and she began to look so much better – blooming, in fact. I also thought she suited the extra weight.

There was still no word of Danny in spite of Mr Pringle having written to the Ministry of War. Dunkirk had been so chaotic although the small boats had miraculously ferried over three hundred thousand troops to safety. Every day that came and went was a blow to her hopes and her parents wanted her to give up her house and go and live with them. As usual, she had been horrified at this suggestion. In an effort to avoid the mounting pressure from her mother, she turned to me to back her up.

'If I give up the flat now, Ann, it would be just like admitting that Danny is dead. Do you know what I'm trying to say?'

'Aye, Maddie, I do.'

'Well, will you tell my mother that I've got to stay here until there's no doubt about Danny's fate? When that day comes, I'll face it then.'

Faced with this implacable tone the Pringles

had to give in but I knew they would keep on trying. I also knew that, in their opinion, Danny was dead.

Joe was also full of the war news. 'I see the RAF is fighting the Jerries in the south of England,' he told Connie. They're calling it "The Battle of Britain" and I bet the Spitfires will fly rings round the Luftwaffe. Then there's that bombastic Mussolini joining his pal Hitler...'

One evening in the late autumn when Maddie resembled a hippopotamus, she asked me what I thought had happened to Danny.

'I don't know, Maddie. Maybe he got caught up in the fighting at St Valery or even in the retreat. The truth will come out one day soon – I'm sure of it.'

'But you think he's dead?'

I don't know why I did it but I shook my head. 'No, I don't.'

Her face lit up.

I immediately tried to backtrack. 'But don't listen to me, Maddie – I could be wrong.'

'But you don't think you are?'

'It's a difficult thing to put into words.'

I hoped she would drop this line of conversation but she didn't.

I said, 'Well, it's like this. Ever since we were bairns, Danny and I have always known what the other one was thinking of. It's a kind of intuition, if you like. If I thought Danny was dead, then I would feel it – I'm sure about that.'

She nodded thoughtfully. 'Still, there's no word from him.'

'That's why I could be totally wrong, Maddie, so don't listen to me.'

Then she changed the subject. 'I can feel the baby kicking.'

'Can you? Is it sore?'

She laughed. 'No, it isn't. It just feels funny or should I say strange.'

I was pleased the way the conversation was going so I wanted to prolong it. 'You'll not have long to wait now, Maddie. Are you hoping for a boy or a girl?'

'I don't care. I just wish Danny was here.'

She started to cry silently and huge tears were rolling down her cheeks. This was how she had been since Dunkirk. France had surrendered and we stood alone at war with Germany and we were still mourning Danny. Quite honestly, it was difficult to believe we were at war as life went on regardless. It was a strange situation because people who had been out of work for decades were now earning a wage packet. The Ryan family in Lochee was one such example. Belle and Lizzie were back in the mill while all the men worked in the foundry.

One reminder of the war was the siren. At the start of the war, every time we heard its wailing and eerie note, we headed for the air-raid shelters which were clustered in the back green behind the tall tenements in Rosebank Road. But it was such a trek in wet or cold weather that we stopped.

Granny said she would make sure Lily was taken to their shelter should the siren sound but this bothered me very much. I was worried about my grandparents having to trail out in all kinds of weather so I told them to stay inside as we all felt quite safe in our own homes. However, in November, this all changed. A German bomb fell on a tenement house in Rosefield Street and demolished it, killing one woman. This was a taste of the damage the German Luftwaffe could inflict on us and I had to review my plans regarding Lily.

I was still staying with Maddie at nights so I asked her if I could bring Lily with me.

She looked mortified. 'Oh, Ann, I've been so selfish having you here with me and you have to look after Lily as well. Look, I'll be fine on my own. You stay at home with Lily.'

'Is that what you want me to do, Maddie?'

Her face crumpled and she shook her head. 'No, I feel so safe when you're here, Ann.'

'Well, that's settled then. I'll bring Lily here with me and we can both sleep on the bed settee. There's plenty of room.'

'Oh, but I don't want to be selfish. Lily has to come first with you.

I went over and gave her a hug. 'Don't be daft, Maddie. I can quite easily look after you both.'

Lily was delighted to be with us at the Roseangle flat and she giggled as she snuggled down on the settee that first night. 'I hope we don't have to leave this cosy bed if the siren goes off, Ann.'

As it was, it put me in a bit of a quandary as because of her size, I never knew if I should take Maddie out of the house.

She was getting so big that she often despaired. 'Do you think I'll ever be thin again?' she often asked, as she tried to see her feet.

'Aye you will, Maddie. Just as soon as the baby is born, you'll get back to your normal size.'

Lily was fascinated by her large tummy with the voluminous, coral-coloured smock covering it – a smock which, in my opinion, merely highlighted the bump.

Meanwhile back in the shop Joe was still full of doom and gloom and I dreaded going into work every morning to face another barrage of bad news.

'I see the Jerries have launched a blitzkrieg on London. What a devastation the Luftwaffe have caused – houses on fire and hundreds of folk killed.' He stopped for breath and also to light his cigarette stub. 'Have you seen the mess in Rosefield Street? It's as if somebody has cut the tenement in half.'

There was also the problem of Maddie. She was becoming even more morose, if that was possible, as she neared the end of her pregnancy. Some days she would just sit quietly at the window with large tears running down her cheeks. We were all becoming more alarmed. The Pringles were almost out of their minds with worry but still she wouldn't budge from the flat.

I was in the lobby one evening when I overheard Hattie saying, 'You've to think about yourself and the baby, Maddie. It would be much better if you went to live with your parents. They have an air-raid shelter in the back garden so you won't have to walk so far – especially at night.'

Maddie's voice was soft but firm. 'We never go to the shelter now. I think if a bomb is meant for me then it'll find me – no matter where I am.'

Hattie was shocked and almost speechless. She spluttered, 'Do you mean to tell me that, after that bomb in Rosefield Street, you still stay inside after the siren goes off?'

If Maddie answered, I didn't hear it.

'Well, I'll have a word with your mother. Ann shouldn't allow it.'

At that point I should have moved into the living room or gone outside but I did neither. I was so upset by Hattie's implication of neglect.

Maddie retorted harshly. 'It's not Ann's fault, Hattie, if I want to stay in my own house. What do you want her to do? Pick me up bodily and carry me out?'

For one moment, I had the intense urge to laugh as that would take some doing considering the size of Maddie now.

Maddie added, 'Until I know for sure that Danny is truly dead, then I'm staying here. Ann doesn't think he's dead.'

I groaned inwardly.

Hattie's voice was soft. 'Listen to me, Maddie. I know Ann thinks she has this telepathic thing with Danny and maybe she does but you can't possibly rely on it. Now can you?'

'No, I can't but it's the only hope I have. Call me superstitious if you like, Hattie, but I feel, if I leave our flat, then I'm somehow abandoning Danny. I know it sounds stupid to you and my parents but it's the way I feel.'

When Hattie replied her voice sounded tearful. 'I miss Danny as well. He's my only son – my only child.'

Maddie started to cry as well. 'Oh, Hattie, I

471

know that and I also know the pain you're going through, just like me, but your pain must be worse than mine because you've had him all his life while I've only had him a few years.'

I quietly opened the door and went downstairs. There was a small shop at the top of the road so I took refuge there until I saw Hattie hurry away along the pavement. To my distress, I saw her dabbing her eyes with a hankie.

Maddie was sitting at the window when I walked in with large tears streaming down her face. She tried to stand up but she wobbled slightly and grabbed the back of a chair for support.

'You've just missed Hattie,' she said, through her tears.

'Maddie, I'm sorry but I did overhear your conversation. I didn't mean to listen but by the time I thought of going out I had heard every word.'

Maddie was tired looking and white faced. 'Hattie thinks Danny is dead and so do my parents,' she said wearily.

I had to make her listen to me. 'I think you should go and live with your parents, Maddie – just until the baby's born.'

'What about Danny?'

'Well, that would be what he would want, Maddie.'

She studied my face for a moment then sat down heavily in the chair.

'I'll just stay for another few weeks but I'll make up my mind soon about going when the baby comes – I promise.'

There was nothing else I could say. Maddie was

certainly one stubborn woman in spite of her fragile and gentle nature.

To take her mind off her problems, I told her the latest developments with Margot. Maddie's eyes were round with amazement when I told her that Margot was standing trial for theft and bigamy.

I said, 'She's in jail at the moment, awaiting her trial. She'll not like being in there because she'll not get to flounce around in her bonny frocks while being in a cell.' For some reason, there was a tinge of sadness in my voice. Oh, I knew she had a criminal streak in her but I also knew that prison would be a terrible experience for her. In a way, I felt a little bit sorry for her – not real sorrow but more a tinge of sympathy.

Maddie noticed this and commented on it. 'Don't feel sorry for her, Ann. She ruined your Dad's life and all her other husbands' as well.'

I nodded. 'OK, Maddie – no more sympathy.'

This was an easy promise to keep because we all had bigger worries on our plates. The news on the war front was becoming more and more grim by the day.

As usual, Joe regaled us with the latest casualty figures in the London Blitz.

Connie glanced at me. She knew Maddie's time was near at hand. She had just another few weeks before the baby was due and the last thing we wanted was to be always reminded about the war, especially with Danny missing – or dead.

After Joe left, she said, 'I can't stop him talking about the war, worst luck.'

'It's not your fault, Connie, that he gets great

pleasure in mentioning every new development.' Also I knew that Danny's fate wasn't Joe's fault.

Connie laughed. 'I've nicknamed him "Winston" because he seems to know more about the war than Churchill!'

The newspapers were now much thinner due to the paper shortage which meant the pile of papers on the counter didn't loom so high and we could see the new delivery girl, Betty from the next close, waiting patiently. Because of Joe's gossiping we were running late. The next hour flew past quickly.

While Connie went to put the kettle on for her morning tea, I went to collect Lily from Maddie's flat.

They were normally asleep when I left to go to work but I knew Lily would be up and ready for school when I arrived. Maddie had offered to walk her to school but I felt it was too far for her at the moment. As I hurried towards the flat I felt I was forever running here and there. Time was a thing I was always running out of. With Dad now working at the shipyard, his overalls were dirtier than usual which meant I had to spend more time at the wash-house. I normally went one afternoon a week when Lily was at school and I tried to time it so I could be at the school gate at four o'clock.

Lily would help me to push the pram and bath full of wet washing up the Hilltown then, after our tea with Dad, we would put the washing on the pulley before setting off for Maddie's house.

It was now December and I couldn't believe how quickly time had flown. It only seemed like yesterday when Maddie had told us of her pregnancy. Now she was in her last few weeks and all our worries were intensified.

Her moods had swung between highs and lows during the last months but she had become really withdrawn and depressed during the last month. We all tried so hard to cheer her up but nothing seemed to make her feel better. All she thought of during these long winter days and nights was Danny and she would sit at the window with her wedding photo in her hand and cry silently. When I tried to shake her out of these black moods, she would become ashamed of herself and try to enter into the conversation. Yet, after just a few words were spoken, she would drift off again to her secret place.

Mrs Pringle sent for me one day. 'Ann, we really need to get Maddie to come here and stay. Can you help us?' The poor woman was worried and anxious looking.

I was honest with her. 'I've tried, Mrs Pringle, but she'll not listen to anybody – not even Hattie or me.'

'Still, you will try again to make her see sense?'

I promised I would. As I walked down the road a sharp, heavy shower of sleet fell from the steel-wool coloured sky. Even the weather was in a miserable mood which matched most of the citizens of the town. People passing on the street hurried by with their hands deep in their coat pockets and they had their headscarved or bonneted heads tucked into their chests like half-emerged tortoises. Their worried and frowning faces looked so pasty grey in the fast-fading light of the December afternoon.

Lily decided to stay with Dad that night – partly because of the cold sleety weather but mainly because of the unexpected gift of a pile of Christmas annuals that Connie had unearthed in one of her cupboards. So I set off alone into the dark winter's night. Although it was barely seven o'clock, the street was deserted and I could hear the noise of my heels as they echoed against the slippery pavements.

When I got to the flat, I had just missed Hattie by a few moments. Maddie sat in her usual chair but the thick velvet curtains were pulled across the window to shut out the weather and the light. She looked white faced and there was a tightness around her mouth.

'Are you feeling all right, Maddie?' I asked although I could see that she certainly didn't look fine.

She didn't answer and I became worried. I started to ask her the same question when she turned an anxious face to me. 'Ann, I think the baby's coming.'

I almost fell over in shock. 'Oh, Maddie, why did you not tell Hattie? She would have been able to get your parents here to help you.'

She gave me another anxious look and I saw the beads of sweat on her upper lip and her forehead. 'I wasn't really sure when she was here and I didn't want to cause a false alarm.'

'But you don't think it is a false alarm? Is that what you're saying, Maddie?'

She nodded then her face contorted in a spasm of pain. I jumped towards her, unsure what task to do first.

Thankfully Maddie's voice was clear. 'We did midwifery during my training – not a lot but I have an idea of what to expect. The pains weren't regular when Hattie was here. That's why I said nothing but they're getting quite regular now.'

'What do you want me to do first, Maddie?' I tried to calm down and said a silent blessing for Connie's annuals as at least I didn't have to worry about Lily.

Another spasm of pain came and the sweat was more distinct now as it ran in small trickles down her neck. When the pain passed, she said, 'I've got my suitcase all packed. It's in the bedroom.'

I darted across to the bedroom and found the case sitting beside the wardrobe and I carried it through.

'I'll have to phone your mum, Maddie. What's her number?'

The one item I always thought was a luxury in this flat was the telephone but the previous owner had installed it and Maddie and Danny had merely taken it over. Now it was proving to be a blessing. She called out the number and I quickly dialled it. Thankfully I had learned to use a telephone when employed by Mrs Barrie at the Ferry so I wasn't a complete novice. Mr Pringle's cool and calm voice answered and I was aware of my own excited and high-pitched tone.

'Mr Pringle, it's Ann. Maddie's baby has started to come and I don't know what to do.'

He was calm and that helped. 'Now listen, Ann. Tell Maddie that we're coming for her in the car to take her to the nursing home. Just keep her calm and we'll be there in a few minutes.'

477

Maddie was really distressed by now and she was pacing back and forth across the floor. I repeated her father's message. I also knew petrol was scarce and rationed but he must have kept some in his car for this very reason.

I laid her case on the chair and went into the tiny bathroom to get her facecloth and tooth-brush and paste. There was a small flowery case on one of the shelves so I put the things inside it.

Suddenly she started crying for Danny. 'Where is he, Ann? Where is...' She stopped as another pain swept over her.

I felt so helpless as I put my arm around her shoulders but I couldn't answer her question.

'I'm leaving the house and I haven't heard from him. I feel as if I'm betraying him by going away. Where is he?'

I tried to get her to sit down but she said walk-ing around was more comfortable so I walked beside her, trying to soothe her cries for the missing Danny. 'He'll turn up, Maddie – just you wait and see. He's a survivor.'

Oh, my God, I thought, why did I say that? And at this crucial time as well.

Thankfully I didn't have time for more regret-ful thoughts because her parents came hurrying through the door and took charge. Before leaving with her, Mr Pringle said, 'Can you wait till I've taken Maddie to the nursing home, Ann? I'd be very grateful.'

I nodded wordlessly.

I wandered into the small kitchen and made myself a pot of tea. I switched the light off and opened the curtains. The sleet clouds had passed

478

away and the sky was now clear. A pale silver moon shone over the river and although it looked lovely I had read about the dreaded 'bombers' moon'. It was ideal weather for the Germans to fly their planes and drop their deadly cargo of death on the cities and their innocent populations.

I kept hearing Maddie's cries for Danny and I wished I had stayed silent when she had asked me months before if I thought he was dead. Why, oh, why had I pinned her hopes on my stupid intuition? Had I wanted to impress her with this secret thing I shared with her husband? Had I wanted to show off?

My thoughts were interrupted by Mr Pringle's return. I quickly closed the curtains and switched the light back on when I heard the key in the lock. He looked tired. 'Thank goodness you were here, Ann, and we're both so grateful for all the help you've given Maddie over these awful months.'

I muttered that it was no problem.

'Well, now that she's out of the house at last we are hoping she'll stay with us. Can you pack all her clothes, Ann, and I'll take them with me? Then we'll lock up and I'll get the plumber to turn the water off.'

'How is Maddie?'

He seemed rueful. 'Well, you know what matrons are like – they whisked her away and told us to phone tomorrow morning.'

I was shocked. 'Tomorrow morning?' I said in amazement. One thing was clear as crystal – I was terribly naive when it came to childbirth. Then I remembered Mum. I had thought at the time what a long drawn-out process it seemed to be and I also remembered how astonished I had been then.

I gave a small laugh. 'Oh, I thought the baby was coming there and then – in this room.'

He smiled. 'If only it was that quick!'

I did the packing for him and we both stood on the landing as he locked the door.

'This is the second time we've both locked up a house, Ann, but maybe you've forgotten?'

But he was wrong. I remembered the time quite clearly when we had locked up Mrs Barrie's house after her tragic death. I also recalled how I knew at that moment I would never again go back to her house. Would this be the same? Would I ever be back in this flat? More painfully, would Maddie?

18

Maddie had a son. Hattie arrived at the shop just before dinnertime, red faced and out of breath, and it was clear she had been hurrying around with the news of her grandson.

'Maddie had a son this morning at eleven fifteen,' she said. 'He weighed seven pounds, eight ounces and his name is Daniel James Patrick Ryan.'

Connie laughed. 'That's a big mouthful for a wee bairn, Hattie.'

Hattie smiled weakly – it was her social smile. 'Well, he's named after his father and his two grandfathers.'

'How does it feel to be a granny, Hattie?' asked Connie.

Hattie's face was a mixture of emotions – obvious joy at the baby's birth but annoyance at Connie for calling her a granny. 'It's a new experience for both me and Mrs Pringle – it's her first grandchild as well.'

I finally managed to get a word in. 'Is Maddie feeling fine? When can I go and see her?' I still remembered her distress from the night before.

For the first time, Hattie's social mask slipped and she looked tired and drawn. 'Maddie is fine. She's very tired but the nursing staff are very happy with her. The baby is lovely and she's over the moon with him.'

I noticed she hadn't answered my question. 'When can I go and see her then?'

Hattie gave me a disapproving frown. 'Oh, not today, Ann. I'll speak to the sister in the nursing home and she'll maybe let you visit her next week.'

I was really unhappy with this and I said so. 'I would really like to see her as soon as possible. I'll not stay long and I'll not tire her out, I promise.' By now, we were out on the street, standing on the wet pavement with a cold, vicious wind swirling around us.

Hattie didn't seem to notice it. She whispered, 'It's like this, Ann. She's been crying for Danny ever since she was admitted. She keeps calling out for him and asking where he is. Quite honestly, her mother and I are at our wits' end with her. I didn't want to say too much in front of Connie because she's such a gossip.'

I almost stuck up for Connie but I was too worried about Maddie to say anything. I felt my throat become dry with anxiety. 'Well, that's all the more reason for me to see her as soon as possible.'

Hattie didn't give me much encouragement. 'The staff don't want her to be disturbed. She needs all the rest she can get and it's only the close family that are allowed to visit.'

'Oh, thank you, Hattie! And what am I? Some far-flung relation from another planet?'

She gave me another disapproving frown and hurried off down the hill. She was soon lost behind a crowd of people and my heart sank at her parting words. I had hoped Maddie's distress last night had merely been her labour pains and that she would feel better when the baby was born but it seemed her stress hadn't gone away.

After leaving Mr Pringle last night, I had hurried home to tell Dad and Lily about the imminent birth. Lily was so excited and began asking all kinds of questions.

Dad said, 'She's a bit early, is she not? I thought she was due on Hogmanay.'

Later that night I told them the good news of Maddie's son. 'He's to be called Daniel James Patrick Ryan,' I told a wide-eyed Lily.

I didn't sleep very well that night. Then, in that strange time of black stillness just before dawn, a dim memory surfaced in my brain – something I had overheard a few years ago and had forgotten. It was just a snatch of conversation but it all came back to my mind. That was why I was planning to visit Lochee that afternoon. It had crossed my mind that Hattie may have already called there with the good news but, if she hadn't, then I could be the glad messenger. I could hardly wait for the morning to pass until I was finished in the shop.

Ever since Hattie's arrival with the news, Connie could speak of nothing else. 'Seven pounds, eight ounces is a good weight for a bairn. He'll have a good start in life at that weight.'

To be honest, I wasn't really listening to her. My mind was full of Maddie's distress at her missing husband. Then, as soon as I finished work, I didn't even bother to go home. Instead I hurried off to Lindsay Street and the Lochee tramcar.

It was a typical December day – cold, wet and murky – and the pavements were slicked with rain. Huge black clouds hung overhead in the sky and the amateur street weather prophets were forecasting snow before the evening.

I remembered the day of Lily and Joy's births – how hot it had been with a blue cloudless sky and a bright beaming sun. Still, that had been July and this was December. Christmas was almost here and then it would be Hogmanay. It would be quiet again this year – no bells or hooters or any celebrations at New Year and no greeting the midnight sky with fun and frolics. We were at war and all the things we'd enjoyed before were only a dim memory. There would be no sound of bells until this war was over because that would be the signal should Germany invade our island.

I tried to forget this depressing image and concentrated on the task ahead of me. I sat huddled in the cold tramcar and it seemed to take ages to reach my stop but, when it did, I hurried up the street towards Kit's house. She came to the door, carrying Kitty who had obviously just had her dinner. Her little mouth was stained orange. Kit laughed. 'She loves beans on toast.'

She gave me a quizzical look but, when I told her about Maddie's baby, she gave a loud yelp of joy.

'A wee laddie – that's grand news. What's his name?'

I said, with a laugh, 'Well, Connie says it's a mouthful, Kit! He's called Daniel James Patrick Ryan and he weighed seven pounds, eight ounces.'

'Heavens, that's a good size especially when she was nearly a fortnight early.' She looked at Kitty. 'Do you hear that, my wee pet? You've got a brand-new cousin, isn't that braw?' She turned to me. 'Ma will be chuffed by this news, Ann.'

I sat at the fire while she put the kettle on. Kitty was put into a large wooden playpen which took up almost all the floor space in the small kitchen.

'Is Maddie fine? I hope she didn't have a long or hard labour because it's a right bind, I can tell you, Ann.'

I repeated my story of being with her. 'I honestly thought she was having the baby there and then, Kit, but Hattie said he wasn't born till eleven fifteen this morning.'

She gave me a rueful look. 'Aye, bairns don't come till they're ready, that's for sure.'

I was hesitant about my request. 'Kit... Kit, Maddie is really distressed about Danny and she keeps calling out for him. She did it last night and now Hattie tells me she's still the same. I don't know what I can do to help her but, during the night, I remembered something I heard in your house years ago.'

Kit's eyes were wet when she faced me and I knew they missed Danny as much as we did. 'What was that, Ann?'

I hesitated again, unsure how to begin. 'Well, do you mind when I came here one New Year's Day with Danny? It was years ago and Ma warned me about being in danger from a blackbird. Do you mind that?'

Kit nodded.

'Well, I was wondering if I could ask her about something she said on another day. She was speaking to you and I overheard a wee snatch of the conversation.'

Kit seemed puzzled but she said, 'She's in her own house but, if you keep an eye on Kitty, I'll run over and get her.'

She darted through the door and, within five minutes, was back with Ma in tow.

'Kit's told me the braw news, Ann. Maddie's had a wee lad and he's named after his father and grandfathers.'

I noticed she didn't say his late father which was encouraging.

When she was seated with a cup of tea in her hand I said, 'Ma, I was here one night with Danny and as I left I overheard you telling Kit something about Danny and a foreign country. Now I didn't hear the entire story because George was arguing with Sammy Malloy on the night we heard about Kathleen expecting the baby and I only caught a few whispered words.'

Ma gazed at me for a full minute. I wondered if she was debating whether or not to tell me. I knew she didn't like to broadcast her sixth sense – not unless it was important which it had been in my case because I was in real danger at the time.

As the silence grew I became more desperate. 'It's just that Maddie's breaking her heart about Danny and I don't know how to help her, Ma.'

She continued to gaze at me, her dark eyes inscrutable. Then she said, 'You don't believe he's dead, do you?'

I said that I didn't but that I wondered how I could justify this feeling. What if I was wrong?

'I heard you tell Kit that Danny would be in another country but that he would come home.

Is that what you think, Ma? You see I have either to give Maddie some hope for the future or else tell her he's dead. She would have to accept it then and try and rebuild her life.'

Ma gave a huge sigh. 'Aye, it's true what I told Kit. I don't think he's dead because I could see him coming home in the future but I don't like to say too much about this feeling because I sometimes only see snatches and not the whole story.'

My face fell.

'Still I have to say I feel it in my bones that he's still alive.'

I could have kissed her. That was enough for me. I stayed about another hour, catching up on all the news of the family.

Thankfully Belle, Lizzie and the men were all working now and they had wage packets coming into their houses after years in the wilderness of the Depression. Just having money for everyday items once more – it was a pleasure they had almost forgotten.

Kit chuckled. 'How's the granny? How is Hattie?'

'Well, Connie says she's pleased with the baby but not so pleased about getting older. Still, if Mrs Pringle doesn't mind being called a granny, then I think Hattie will be the same.'

Both women laughed.

'Aye, she's a great case is Hattie,' said Kit but it was said with affection and not rancour.

Thank goodness the bad old days of the family feud were over. It didn't mean that Hattie was forever visiting them or living in their pockets but relations between them were now friendly.

'When can we go and see Maddie and the baby?' asked Kit.

I repeated what Hattie had said – that it would probably be next week some time. What I didn't say was that I intended to visit her the next day, no matter what Hattie or the nursing home sister said.

On that note, I made my departure. I had got what I came for and, although I had no firm foundation for my intuition or Ma's sixth sense, I still felt strongly about Danny's survival.

The next day saw me at the nursing home and there was some bother about going in to see Maddie.

The sister had a well scrubbed but stern-looking face and she was prepared to stand her ground. 'No visitors except close family,' she told me in her clipped voice. 'You can come back next week and visitors will be allowed in then.'

What a dictator, I thought. Sister Napoleon. I was just on the verge of leaving and feeling most unhappy about my non-visit when Mrs Pringle came out through the foyer.

She looked tired but smiled happily when she saw me. 'Oh, Ann, are you going to visit Maddie? She'll be so glad to see you.'

'The sister won't let me in, Mrs Pringle,' I told her truthfully while the woman almost went as white as her uniform.

'Oh, Sister, you must let Maddie's friend in. She was the one who lived with my daughter all those months and she looked after her so well. It was Ann who called us out when Maddie went in to labour.'

The woman gave me a smile. It didn't reach her eyes but I didn't care – I was going to be admitted.

Maddie was in a lovely bright room and there was a large bunch of bronze and yellow chrysanthemums arranged in a crystal vase by the side of her bed. Her face lit up when she saw me although her eyes had that red-rimmed look as if she had been crying recently. Still, she gave me a bright smile.

'Oh, Ann, it's good to see you.'

'How are you feeling Maddie? How is wee Daniel?'

She laughed. 'Well, let's just say I'm glad to be able to see my feet again!'

It was my turn to laugh. 'Aye, you were really big but it's been worth it to have wee Daniel, hasn't it?'

'Yes, it has. He's a lovely baby and maybe you'll be able to see him shortly. He's in the nursery but he's due for a feed in half an hour.'

That was good – just time for a short visit and Hattie couldn't accuse me of tiring her out.

Maddie clutched my hand and her eyes became watery. 'You're the only person who understands how I feel, Ann. Everyone is telling me to pull myself together for the sake of the baby. It's almost as if they're telling me to forget Danny but I can't. If only I knew the truth about him, then I know I could cope. It's this not knowing...' She wiped her eyes with the back of her hand.

I was in a quandary. I didn't want to mention my recent visit to Lochee to see Ma Ryan. What if

Hattie was right when she said Ma's sixth sense was all mumbo-jumbo? Also Hattie didn't believe in my feelings about things. Was that also mumbo-jumbo? Worse still, was I deluding myself too thinking I knew about Danny?

Maddie heard the footsteps before I did. A nurse popped her head around the door.

'Can your visitor leave in twenty minutes as it's time for baby's feed?'

Maddie nodded. 'Can she see Daniel? Just for a moment?'

The nurse looked at me but she remained silent, her face a closed book.

'Ann is my husband's cousin – she's the one who's been looking after me,' explained Maddie, giving the nurse her charming smile.

The nurse relented. 'Just for a brief moment before baby's feed.'

She disappeared from the door and went away down the corridor.

'I have to be careful not to let the nurses see me crying, Ann, because they tell me off. My mother is the same – they just tell me to buck up and look after Daniel.' Her face twisted with annoyance. 'As if I wouldn't look after him properly in spite of grieving for Danny.'

The nurse reappeared carrying a white wrapped bundle. Daniel James Patrick Ryan looked bored with life as he gave a huge yawn, showing a tiny pink, moist cavity. His face was also screwed up with all the effort he had put into the yawn. He was lovely.

'Oh, Maddie, he's gorgeous. What an adorable baby!'

Maddie perked up and tried hard not to look smug. 'I think so as well.' Then her face fell and she whispered, 'If only Danny could be here to see his son, then life would be perfect. I hate this awful war and all the killings that are taking place.' She began to cry silently and I couldn't bear it.

'Maddie,' I said, 'I don't think Danny is dead.'

She gave me a strange look and wiped her eyes.

'I just have this feeling and I can't explain it but you have to believe that he's alive.' I decided to be frank with her – mumbo-jumbo or not. 'Do you remember I told you I didn't think Danny was dead?'

She nodded. 'Hattie says it's just superstition.'

I waded in deeply. 'I went to see Ma Ryan yesterday to ask her about something I overheard a long time ago.'

Maddie looked puzzled.

'I heard Ma tell Kit that Danny would be in another country for a few years but he would come home again and that he would be all right.'

There was a glimmer of hope in her blue eyes. 'Is Ma really reliable with her predictions?'

'It can't be proved one way or another but she was spot on with the warning she gave me years ago.'

For the first time since Danny's disappearance, she looked like the Maddie I remembered. She grinned. 'You've made me feel so much better, Ann, but then you always do.'

I thought a small warning should be given. 'Maddie, remember it's just my feelings and admits she doesn't always get the entire pict

491

just fleeting images – so please give this a bit of thought and don't take my word as gospel.'

She smiled. 'No, I won't but what you've told me has helped me a great deal. Anyway who knows where Danny is? A bit of mumbo-jumbo isn't going to turn me into a raving lunatic, is it?'

I left the magazines I had brought and the brightly drawn card that Lily had made. She had been learning about Samson and Delilah at school and her card reflected this. It showed a tiny Delilah who looked like Maddie and she was holding a gigantic Samson of a baby. He was drinking from a huge bottle and this made Maddie smile.

The nurse appeared again and it was time to leave. I said goodbye to Maddie and Daniel James Patrick Ryan.

When I reached the door, she called out, 'Thanks for everything, Ann!'

'I'll be back to see you soon so keep your chin up – promise me.'

Daniel let out a loud wail that drowned out her answer and I left.

Dad and Rosie got married on the first Saturday in March. It was a simple ceremony at the registrar's office but it was a very happy occasion for us all. Alice did sniff a little bit at the thought of her daughter marrying Dad because she hadn't truly forgiven him for his earlier cavalier treatment of her. Still, by the time we were all sitting ꞉e office, she seemed to cheer up.

꞉ie looked lovely in a deep blue dress with a beaded bolero. She wore a matching hat with a small veil that had tiny blue velvet spots doted over its filmy surface and I thought how young she looked with her short haircut. Gone was the ageing and ponderous bun at the nape of her neck.

I was the bridesmaid and although Lily wasn't an attendant she was still dressed up with a flower pinned to her new frock.

Kit's husband George was the best man. Because of the rationing, it was a bit of a struggle to put on a decent wedding meal but we all combined coupons and contributed to it.

The reception was held in Granny's house and there were fourteen guests. Granny and Alice had set out the table with a selection of small sausage rolls, sandwiches and cakes. There was even a little wedding cake which Hattie had donated to the occasion.

Rosie was radiant and Dad looked chuffed. Before we toasted the happy couple with small glasses of sherry, Dad made a speech.

'I want to thank my new wife, Rosie, for standing by me all these years – she's never let me down, bless her. Here's to many happy years together.'

Rosie blushed and Alice looked pleased and we all toasted them and agreed about the sentiment.

I noticed how Kit and George seemed less tired and pale faced. Having a job had injected George with a new lease of life – not only for himself but for his whole family.

Connie was sitting next to Bella who was, as usual, drinking something stronger than sherry. She had her medicine bottle in her hand and

Connie was shaking her head over something Bella was saying.

Hattie was truly elegant but she made Rosie feel special when she commented on how lovely she looked.

I was so proud of Granny and Grandad as they stood beside Lily. It had been almost ten years since Mum's sudden death and we had all been through so much but they had been towers of strength.

Lily was excited at the thought of having Rosie live with us but I didn't tell her we would have to look for somewhere else to stay. It wasn't fair on the new bride to have two lodgers in the next room. But, for the moment, it was all love and joy.

Margot's name wasn't mentioned but her shadow was there all the same – at least it was with me. She was awaiting trial and how it would end no one knew. Still, she was a beautiful and resourceful woman so she would survive – I was sure of that.

Maddie came towards me and I didn't know what to say to her. There was still no word about Danny and I now regretted my impulsive talk with her in the nursing home.

Daniel was almost three months old and the Pringles were looking after him for a few hours to let her come to the wedding. Her initial spark of hope had now gone and, although she never chided me for raising her spirits with my silly story of intuition and sixth sense, I sometimes felt it lay between us like a dark unspoken thought.

And now she was coming towards me. I tried to

smile but failed. Instead, I looked at the bride. 'Rosie's looking lovely, isn't she?'

She nodded but I knew her thoughts were elsewhere.

'I'm glad that Dad has come to his senses but sometimes you just need a bit of time to work things out for yourself.'

She sat down beside me and folded her hands on her lap. For the first time ever since I'd known her, I wasn't sure what to say to her so I took one of her hands and held it tightly. No words were spoken but we both knew we were thinking of Danny.

After a few moments, she said she had to leave. 'Daniel will be needing his next feed.' She smiled. 'The little glutton, he's always eating.'

I looked over at Lily. She was stuffing a huge sandwich in her mouth and we both laughed at her.

'I think it's a family trait, Maddie.'

Then she was gone.

In the early evening when most of the guests had gone home, Dad and Rosie left for an undisclosed destination. Much to Lily's outrage, they wouldn't say where they were going – and this was despite her questioning them with a third-degree interrogation that would have made a Hollywood detective proud.

When they left, she turned to me in disgust. 'Imagine not telling me – their own wee lassie.'

Granny gave me an affectionate look and we were both grateful to Rosie for making Lily feel like she was her lassie.

It was the thirteenth of March and Dad and Rosie were back from their few days' honeymoon. We were sitting in the kitchen when the sirens went off. We all debated about going down to the shelter.

Dad said, 'Let's give it a miss but we'll maybe have to go later.'

We went to bed full of apprehension. The sirens kept up the eerie wailing sound and, at about three o'clock in the morning, we decided to get dressed and just lie on top of our beds, in case we had to move quickly.

'Somebody is getting the Luftwaffe's rage tonight,' said Dad.

But, as the night wore on, we realised Dundee wasn't on the Luftwaffe's agenda and we fell into fitful sleeps. Although Rosie was still working in the mill, she had taken a few weeks off for her wedding so she was able to see Lily off to the school.

I set off for work feeling bleary-eyed and still half asleep and I wasn't alone. Connie and Joe were the same. No one knew who had been bombed during the night but Joe guessed it was Glasgow. Later that day came the news that it had been Clydebank. I felt ill and prayed that Minnie and Peter were safe. They lived right bang in the middle of the bombing target.

In the afternoon, Rosie and I went to the Overgate and I thought of going to see Mrs McFarlane, Minnie's Mum. Before I got the chance, we met one of her neighbours.

'You were a pal of Minnie's, weren't you?' she asked.

I nodded, too afraid to speak – afraid of what was coming next.

'You'll have heard that Clydebank was razed to the ground last night and poor Mrs McFarlane hasn't had any word about Minnie or her wee lad Peter. She hasn't stopped crying since last night and the grapevine says there are lots of people dead.'

I felt faint and my face went white. I remembered the last time I had seen Minnie and Peter and how I had felt that overwhelming sense of sadness. Would I ever see them again? It would seem not if there was all that carnage throughout the night.

I felt this deep anger rise in my throat at this stupid and futile war. Hitler fighting more countries but at what cost? Millions of innocent lives lost for a piece of land.

Granny was also shocked when we told her. 'Poor lassie and her poor wee laddie,' was all she could say. But what else could be said? Just another two casualties of war.

There was a letter waiting for me from Greg when we arrived back home. He wrote, 'The skies of London are ablaze with fire and I hear the damage is terrible in both lives and property. We're lucky where we are if lucky is the right word.' He went on to say he was missing me and he signed off with his usual flourish, 'See you soon, I hope.'

I didn't answer that night. I tried to keep my letters as cheerful as possible but, at that moment, I felt far from cheerful.

We were listening to the wireless in the evening

when the sirens went off again. We looked at each other in horror.

Rosie said, 'Do you think it's our turn tonight, Johnny?'

Dad nodded and we trooped downstairs to the concrete shelter. Although we were all warmly wrapped up, it felt cold and damp. Still, once it filled up with people, the temperature rose slightly.

Much later, when the all-clear sounded, we walked home under a cloudless sky with the moon shining – a bombers' moon. We were just inside the door when the sirens went off again but we decided to stay where we were and repeat our routine from the previous night. I wondered if we would get any sleep during this war and it crossed my mind that maybe Hitler was trying to kill us all off with insomnia.

Joe seemed a bit chirpier the next morning but Connie gave him a warning glance. I heard her whisper to him, 'Don't mention Clydebank, Joe. Ann's pal and her wee laddie lived there and she thinks they've been killed.'

Joe gave me a sad look. They then began to discuss the uncomfortable conditions in the shelter.

Connie said, 'I was in that awful shelter for most of the night and I've made up my mind, when the siren goes off, I'm staying in my bed. I'm getting too old to be haring off to any shelter with all the dampness and cold. No, from now on, if a bomb hits me, it'll hit me in my bed.'

Joe agreed with her but she looked at me and added, 'Mind you, if I had bairns, then that would be different – you have to put their welfare before any discomfort.'

The rest of the day passed in a blur of animated discussions between Connie and her customers but, to give her her due, she made sure Clydebank wasn't mentioned.

When I got home that afternoon, tired and worn out with sadness and sleeplessness, I found the house empty. I knew Rosie would be standing in some long queue somewhere on the Hilltown. Everywhere there were queues – at the baker, the butcher and the grocer. Still, I was grateful that Rosie did the shopping now. I felt that maybe I could get on with my life without the worry of Lily or Dad as they were now in Rosie's safe and capable hands.

I decided to go to the Overgate. Perhaps seeing Granny would cheer me up. She was sitting at the window, chatting to Alice but there was no sign of Grandad.

She poured out a strong black cup of tea but didn't mention the war or the bombings. My mind was in a turmoil over the recent happenings in Clydebank. I recalled Ma's warning of our dark horizons and I now knew what she meant. She had warned me we all had to face them but that some people would be luckier than others.

Was I one of the lucky ones? And Lily. Obviously Danny, Minnie and Peter had been the unlucky ones. I felt tears spring into my eyes but didn't want to cry in front of Granny. She had enough to contend with without my weeping and wailing.

Suddenly there was a commotion on the stairs and Granny darted from the window. 'I don't believe it!' she said.

I became alarmed. 'Is it the German army?'

She chuckled. 'Och, no – it's good news. Anyway the Jerries won't invade this country because they know they've been beaten.'

Well, maybe they wouldn't invade I thought but they were doing a grand job of destroying it.

Granny threw open the door and Bella stood on the threshold. Then to my utter joy and delight I saw Minnie and she was clutching Peter's hand. They both looked worn out and their clothes were dusty and torn. But they were both alive. I ran towards them and threw my arms around them both. I realised I was crying but I didn't care.

Granny was crying as well – as were Bella and Alice. 'Och, it's great to see you both again. We all thought you were dead in the bombing.'

As she went over to put the kettle on, Minnie sat down wearily while Peter ran over to the box by the fireside for the comics. Thankfully there was a pile of them and he sat down with his nose against the pages.

Once we were all sitting with cups of tea, Minnie told us about her lucky escape. 'I have to thank the old couple next door because they were the ones that insisted we went to the shelter. Peter had this bad cold so I was going to stay in the house but they wouldn't listen to me. The old man picked Peter up and carried him to the shelter so of course I had to follow, didn't I? To start with I wasn't pleased with them but, when we came out in the morning, the entire street had vanished. And not just our street either – there's hardly a house left standing.'

We were shocked by the ferocity of the German attacks. And it wasn't only Clydebank that had been hit. Places like Glasgow, Greenock and other towns had also been badly bombed.

There were tears in Minnie's eyes and I was crying at her story.

'We were taken to this refuge centre but it was crammed full with folk so most of us who had families elsewhere decided to leave.'

Granny asked her, 'Where are your neighbours now, Minnie? The old couple who saved you both?'

'They've got a married son who works on a farm in Fife so they've gone there.' For the first time since she'd come in, I saw her lips twitch with a semblance of a smile. 'And I've come home to my mother. She says she's so grateful we're both alive that she'll never clean her house again. Still we'll see.' She became serious again. 'I'm just so grateful that we're still here – me and wee Peter.'

Bella, who had been strangely quiet during the story, asked, 'What about your man, Minnie?'

'Well, I'll have to write to him and tell him we're safe but will he get the letter? That's the question.'

'Do you know where he is?' asked Granny.

She shook her head. 'His last letter was posted in England but it was censored so much that I don't know what to think. Reading between the lines, I think he's maybe overseas now.' She sighed. 'What a terrible war this is.'

She then asked about Maddie and Danny and cried when I told her Danny was missing, presumed dead.

'Oh, that's terrible for Maddie and Daniel!' She shook her head as if words failed her and we knew how she was feeling.

She stood up. 'I'll have to get more clothes as what we're wearing is all we have – everything is gone.'

Granny said softly, 'Oh, I think you'll find that folk will help you out and you can get Peter into the school.'

I gave them both another hug at the door. Peter was pleased he could take the comics home with him. I walked down to the end of the close with them and watched as they walked away towards the Hawkhill.

Suddenly I didn't feel sad any more. It was a strange feeling but I felt, from now on, they would be all right.

Rosie was back at work and it was my turn to do the shopping. A large woman stood in front of me in the butcher's queue. She was bemoaning how hard it was to feed her six children on the measly rations. This sentiment was echoed by the rest of the queue whose members were becoming restless.

The reason for this wait became clear when a tiny elderly woman began to argue with the butcher. 'Do I have to get all that fat with my bit of meat?'

I couldn't hear the butcher's voice but the wee woman's anger came out loud and clear. 'Well, I'm not paying good money for all that fat.'

We tried to peer inside and listen to the butcher's reply, only to see him lift up a large knife. A loud collective scream arose from the women at the head of the queue. To their relief, or maybe disappointment, whichever way you looked at it, he merely trimmed a sliver of fat from the piece of meat.

The wee woman emerged from the shop and we all stared at her. Then someone began to clap and we all joined in with the applause.

The woman had a twinkle in her eye. 'That's the first time I've had a round of applause for standing up for myself.'

After that, I noticed the butcher trimming more thin slivers of fat from the meat but the woman in front of me wasn't impressed. 'He'll just put it into the mince and the sausages,' she proclaimed.

I was glad to get home as I was weary and my legs were tired. For the past week, I had been having vivid and upsetting dreams about Danny. I could see him lying in a field and he was pleading with me to help him. He stretched out two arms and, to my horror, I saw they were bandaged almost to his shoulders. When I moved towards him, I could also see a thick white bandage around his head but what upset me most was the fact that he disappeared when I ran to him. One minute he was lying there and the next I was left alone in the field, crying.

I decided not to mention these dreams to Maddie. They were so upsetting to me and I could only guess how distressing they would be to her.

On my day off I went to see her at Perth Road where she had been staying since the baby was born. Daniel was thriving and, although he had her blonde hair, he had the same vivid blue eyes as Danny.

Maddie was restless. Seemingly she had to wait in for a registered letter from the postman. 'It's a letter to do with Dad's business but for some reason it's being sent here.' She sounded annoyed.

I could see why she was disgruntled. It was a lovely April day and, although there had been a heavy shower earlier on in the morning, it was now sunny and quite warm. We could have gone for a walk if she hadn't been tied to the house.

'Mum and Hattie have had to go into the town – that's why I'm on my own.' She gave me a strange look and no doubt she was wondering why I had decided to pay a visit in the late morning but she didn't say anything.

As it was, I couldn't have told her why I had decided to come. I didn't normally visit her so early in the day. My only reason was I simply had to see her and Daniel.

We sat in their sun-filled lounge and I looked at the river flowing, sparkling bright, beyond the garden. Maddie was giving Daniel his bottle and I heard his loud sucking noises mixed up with little roars of rage when he found his feed was finished.

We spoke about the lucky escape Minnie and Peter had. 'It must have been a terrible experience for them to come out from the shelter and see her entire house demolished,' said Maddie.

I nodded. 'Not only her house, Maddie, but the whole area – it's all gone.'

Maddie shuddered. 'Somebody's just walked over my grave,' she said.

The doorbell sounded, a series of gentle peals

504

floating throughout the house.

'That will be the postman,' Maddie said, handing Daniel to me.

I could hear muffled voices in the hall. I carried Daniel to the window to let him see the flowers and the river. He gazed at me with his bright blue eyes and gave me a smile. A smile so wide that milk started to dribble from his mouth. My heart turned over in emotion and I almost burst into tears as I wished with all my heart that Danny could be here to see his lovely son.

Maddie didn't reappear and I became worried. Surely it didn't take as long as this to sign for a letter? I sat down and jiggled Daniel on my knee but there was still no sign of Maddie. I was really worried by now so we went out into the hall. There was a padded seat beside the telephone and Maddie was sitting on it, tears streaming down her cheeks.

I suddenly felt very cold. 'What is it Maddie?' I couldn't say, 'Is it bad news?'

Maddie gave another huge sob and, as if catching the emotion, Daniel began to cry loudly. To be honest, I wasn't far away from tears myself.

Then she looked at me and I suddenly realised she was crying with joy. 'It's Danny,' she said, 'he's alive!'

I moved quickly towards her and she held out a sheet of paper. I then saw the registered letter on the hall table.

'This letter has come from the Red Cross!' She handed the letter to me and scooped Daniel up in her arms. 'Your daddy is alive! Your daddy is alive!'

I quickly read the letter. It said, 'Private Daniel Ryan is a patient in a hospital in Germany.'

I looked at her. 'He's in hospital, Maddie.'

She nodded, tears still streaming down her face.

I read on. 'He was very badly injured in France. He has two broken arms, a broken leg and a fractured skull and he'll stay in hospital until he's fully recovered.' It went on to say how pleased they were to send this news. There was another sentence. 'Another soldier was also injured at the time but he has recovered. He will be taken to a prisoner of war camp. His name is Private Sam Malloy who we believe is a relative of D. Ryan.'

The signature wasn't very clear but the message was. Danny was alive and so was Sammy. Danny was badly injured but alive.

Then Mrs Pringle and Hattie arrived back to a scene of utter happiness and, when she heard the news, Hattie burst into tears. I had only ever seen her cry once before and I realised then the awful strain she had been under, over her only son. Although she had never put it into words, Hattie, along with everyone else apart from Ma and me, believed he was dead – killed during the chaos of Dunkirk.

Well, the news spread like wildfire around the Hilltown, the Overgate and Lochee. My grand-parents were overjoyed, as was the whole family. I went to Lochee to see Kit but I really wanted to see Ma Ryan. Maggie was there and she was over the moon to hear of the two men's survival – especially when so many soldiers had died.

Kit said to me on the quiet, 'Kathleen's not

going back to live with Sammy when this war is over. She plans to make a new life for herself and Kitty and, although the Catholic faith doesn't believe in divorce, I think that's what'll happen.' She looked over at Maggie and smiled. 'Mind you, although I don't want him back as a son-in-law, I'm really pleased the wee sod isn't dead for his mum's sake. As for Danny...' Her eyes filled with tears.

In the middle of this commotion, I noticed Ma sitting by the fire. 'It's great news, isn't it Ma?'

She nodded wisely and her dark eyes sparkled. 'You and I knew he wasn't dead, didn't we?'

I nodded happily.

'He's in a strange place and he's very badly injured,' she said.

'And our dark horizons, Ma, what about them?' I asked.

She patted my shoulder. 'One step at a time, lassie.'

I left them all rejoicing and went home to our own elation. Rosie and Dad were trying to help Lily with her homework. A large pile of books and annuals lay on the table beside her school jotters.

Lily's face lit up when she saw me. 'I'm giving Peter all my books, Ann, because he lost all his toys when his house was bombed.'

Darling wee Lily.

Rosie caught my glance and gave me a secret little smile.

Oh, I hoped with all my heart that our dark horizons had cleared slightly and surely life would get better as we all moved towards the unknown future.

The publishers hope that this book has given you enjoyable reading. Large Print Books are especially designed to be as easy to see and hold as possible. If you wish a complete list of our books please ask at your local library or write directly to:

Magna Large Print Books
Magna House, Long Preston,
Skipton, North Yorkshire.
BD23 4ND

This Large Print Book for the partially sighted, who cannot read normal print, is published under the auspices of

THE ULVERSCROFT FOUNDATION